THE WAR OF THE IRON DRAGON

A NOVEL BY ROBERT KROESE

BOOK FIVE OF
THE SAGA OF THE IRON DRAGON

Copyright ©2021 Robert Kroese. All rights reserved. No portion of this book may be reproduced, stored in a retrieval system, or transmitted in any form or by any means—electronic, mechanical, photocopy, recording or other—except for brief quotations in reviews, without the prior permission of the author.

Contents

Contents 5
The Story So Far 7
Prologue 11
Chapter One 23
Chapter Two 31
Chapter Three 39
Chapter Four 47
Chapter Five 57
Chapter Six 63
Chapter Seven 73
Chapter Eight 79
Chapter Nine 83
Chapter Ten 91
Chapter Eleven 103
Chapter Twelve 111
Chapter Thirteen 121
Chapter Fourteen 129
Chapter Fifteen 135
Chapter Sixteen 141
Chapter Seventeen 149
Chapter Eighteen 155
Chapter Nineteen 161
Chapter Twenty 169
Chapter Twenty-one 175

Chapter Twenty-two 181
Chapter Twenty-three 187
Chapter Twenty-four 193
Chapter Twenty-five 201
Chapter Twenty-six 205
Chapter Twenty-seven 213
Chapter Twenty-eight 221
Chapter Twenty-nine 227
Chapter Thirty 231
Chapter Thirty-one 237
Chapter Thirty-two 243
Chapter Thirty-three 249
Chapter Thirty-four 255
Chapter Thirty-five 263
Chapter Thirty-six 269
Chapter Thirty-seven 275
Chapter Thirty-eight 283
Chapter Thirty-nine 293
Review This Book! 303
Acknowledgements 305
More Books by Robert Kroese 307

THE STORY SO FAR

In the 23rd century, humanity has been hunted to the verge of extinction by an alien race called the Cho-ta'an. Earth has been rendered uninhabitable and every other human world is at risk of Cho-ta'an attack. The crew of *Andrea Luhman*, an exploratory ship in the service of the Interstellar Defense League, has been given a weapon that could alter the balance of the conflict: a "planet-killer" bomb left behind by an extinct race. Pursued by a Cho-ta'an warship, *Andrea Luhman* flees through a hyperspace gate to the Sol system, but a fluke accident sends them back in time to 883 AD.

Its primary thrusters badly damaged, *Andrea Luhman* limps into orbit around Earth, and a small crew, led by engineer Carolyn Reyes, is sent to the surface to fabricate a replacement part. The lander is shot down by a Cho-ta'an ship that followed *Andrea Luhman* through the gate. The Cho-ta'an ship falls into the North Sea, and the lander crashes in Norway.

While the crew of the lander fight for their lives in Viking Age Scandinavia, *Andrea Luhman* is blown to pieces by a second Cho-ta'an ship that followed them through the gate. The planet-killer is destroyed, and the crews of both ships are killed. But there is still hope: if the spacemen can get to the Cho-ta'an ship, they may still be able to retrieve another planet-killer before humanity is defeated. The indomitable spacemen decide to press on.

Nearly fifty years after the lander crash, the *Iron Dragon*—a replica of a Titan II rocket carrying a Gemini Launch Vehicle—launches from a secret base in the Antilles. A single young astronaut named Freya, the granddaughter of Carolyn Reyes, reaches the Cho-ta'an ship and sets it on a course to a distant star in the hopes of locating another planet-killer to change the course of the war.

Some fourteen years later, however, Freya's ship is intercepted by a warship called *Varinga*, which is crewed by a group of humans who seem to hail from a previously unknown branch of humanity. The year is 955 A.D., but these people, who call themselves Truscans, possess technology far in advance even of the IDL in 2227. These people, it seems, are the descendants of a group of refugees that left Earth in 134 A.D. on a ship that traveled even farther back in time than *Andrea Luhman*. With their hyperdrive-equipped starships, the Truscans could be powerful allies against the Cho-ta'an. But the Truscans have their own problems: they are at war with a race of human-like aliens called Izarians—the same race who built the planet-killer. To defeat the Izarians, the Truscans need an army. Freya suggests that her people and the Truscans might come to an understanding....

"What din there, Bragi,
as if a thousand shook
or an overly great host?"
"All the wainscoted walls are breaking
as if Baldr might be coming
again into Odin's hall!"

"Talking stupid," said Odin,
"you must be, wise Bragi,
though you know everything!
For Eirík it rattles,
who is to come in here,
king into Odin's hall.

"Sigmund and Sinfjötli,
rise up quickly
and go to meet the hero!
Invite him in,
if it be Eirík!
My hope of him is now known."

"Why in you is hope of Eirík
rather than of others
now to Valhalla, in your awareness?"
"Because many lands
he has reddened with sword
and borne a bloodied blade."

"Why did he not win victory there,
he whom you considered to be valiant,
and was he worthy of victory from the gods?"
"Because it's unknown to know,
when the grey wolf
will seek out the seat of the gods."

> From *Eiríksmál*, a skaldic poem from the late tenth century (translated from Old Norse)

PROLOGUE

A statuesque woman with shoulder-length gray-blond hair sat at the bar of the North Star Hotel nursing an Irish coffee and staring out the plate glass windows at the bleak Icelandic landscape. It was nearly noon on a Tuesday in early February, and the bar was deserted except for the blond woman and a wiry bartender with a pencil moustache and goatee who was watching a soccer game on one of several flatscreen TVs hanging from the ceiling. The hotel, a drab modernist structure sheathed in brown wood paneling, was nearly deserted as well. The only other guests were an American novelist who had booked room 313 for the entire month and a young couple from Reykjavik on their honeymoon. The glacier called Vatnajökull, which had been shrinking rapidly for nearly thirty years, was no longer the draw it had once been, and global tourism still hadn't recovered from the effects of the pandemic that began in 2020. On top of that, it was currently the off-season. The North Star had been in the red for three years; it remained open only because the losses thus far had been small enough to escape the attention of the Japanese conglomerate that had owned it until that morning.

The woman knew all this about the hotel because as of midnight the previous day, she was its owner. The process of acquiring the hotel had taken a week from start to finish, most of which was spent trying to navigate the byzantine hierarchy of holding companies in an attempt to find someone authorized to sell it to her. Once she found the right person (who spoke passable English, thank Odin), the transaction had been concluded quickly: she had made them an offer they would have been fools to refuse. At the price they had settled on, she couldn't hope to make a profit in a hundred years, even if Vatnajökull miraculously regained its former grandeur overnight. It was fortunate, then, that she had no intention of making money on the deal. The acquisition of the North Star was only the first step in a much bigger plan.

She finished her coffee and set it down in front of her with a glance toward the bartender, who was too enthralled by the soccer game to notice. Clearing her throat also failed to prompt a response. She considered pulling rank but rejected the idea. She had gotten this far by keeping a low profile. Little good could come from revealing herself at this point. Astrid van de Lucht was unknown in Iceland—and most of the rest of the world—and she hoped to keep it that way as long as possible.

The name was an alias, of course—a sort of inside joke with herself. She generally did business through a variety of shell companies, but a sufficiently dogged investigation might reveal that Astrid van de Lucht, born in Linden, Washington on April 29, 1992, was currently the fourth richest person in the world. The evidence of her fortune was mostly public information, but her wealth was scattered across such a wide array of stocks, bonds and other investments, in so many different jurisdictions, that unless one had a reason to total them all up, one would never realize its extent—and she was careful never to give anyone reason. Oh, she'd been scrutinized: the Japanese must have dug at least deep enough to know she'd be good for the $60 million she'd promised for the North Star, for example. But they had neither time nor reason to determine that she owned, for example, $92 million in Netflix stock, $81 million in Bitcoin, $340 million in commercial real estate in Munich, and $181 million in gold in a bank vault in the Cayman Islands. The list went on and on, a bewildering tangle of shell companies and subsidiaries that had only one name in common: Astrid van de Lucht.

Were she ever to fall under the scrutiny of, say, a thorough SEC investigation, the intrepid sleuths would be rewarded for their efforts with two stunning facts. First, that Astrid van de Lucht was currently worth something like $189 billion; and second, that she had somehow amassed this fortune over the span of just five years, without anyone noticing. A still more thorough investigation would reveal that there were no records of Astrid van de Lucht's existence prior to 2014. It was as if she had sprung into being *ex nihilo* at the age of twenty-five.

She had contingency plans—including several other aliases—in place in case she were found out, but she didn't relish the prospect of having to start from scratch at this point. Besides, she had gotten used to thinking of herself as Astrid. It had been her mother's name, and she rather liked it. So she sat, staring across the volcanic plain toward the melting glacier, patiently waiting for the bartender to notice her cup was empty.

It wasn't that she expected outing herself as the owner of the hotel to the bartender was going to provoke an SEC investigation; it was the principle of the thing. If she started acting like someone with a lot of money, she would start to think of herself that way. And then, inevitably, she would slip, and somebody—a journalist, a rival, a bureaucrat with too much time on his hands—would start digging. Astrid van de Lucht would have to disappear, and she would have to start over as someone else. It would be much more difficult the second time.

I'm not getting any younger, Astrid thought, and chuckled. Another joke that only she would get. She had a lot of those—a consequence of spending a great deal of time alone. She conversed with herself frequently, although these days she usually remembered not to do it out loud. She had no doubt she'd developed some serious psychological problems over her long and traumatic existence, but there wasn't a psychologist in the world who could help her. Hell, just trying to explain how she had gotten so screwed up would probably get her committed. "Anyway," she said out loud, "I'm coping all right, aren't I?" She stared at the empty coffee cup in front of her, nervously tapping the counter with her fingertips.

"You say something, Ma'am?" said the bartender in crisp English. The TVs had been taken over by an advertisement for some kind of face cream.

Loki's balls, I hate being called ma'am. She liked to think she could still pass for forty, although she was, by some ways of reckoning, much older. A couple of years ago she had tried to figure out how old she was, in terms of how much time had actually passed for her, but she'd gotten depressed and given up.

"I could use another," she said, tapping her index finger on the empty cup.

"Sure," he said, and reached for a bottle of off-brand whiskey.

As he did so, the door to the bar opened and a compactly built man walked in, wearing a gray suit and carrying a briefcase. Spotting Astrid, he nodded and walked toward her. Astrid took a deep breath and tried not to look nervous. She'd never liked face-to-face meetings, preferring to do business at a distance, through intermediaries when possible. But this particular transaction had to be conducted in person, due to its scope and unusual nature. She had requested, though, that the meeting be conducted here, far from prying eyes in Reykjavik, and the man she was meeting had—somewhat to her surprise—agreed. That man stood before her now, his thick mane of silvery hair even more impressive in person than it was on TV. He set down his briefcase.

"David Magnason," he said. He held out his hand, and they shook. "You must be Astrid van de Lucht. Shall we have a seat by the window?"

"Yes. Yes, of course," she said, getting to her feet.

"Whiskey, rocks," said Magnason to the bartender, who had been staring at him since he walked in.

"Yes, sir!" the bartender said. He put the bottle of whiskey back and retrieved a bottle of Jameson's.

Astrid followed Magnason to a table by the huge plate-glass windows, and they sat. A moment later, the bartender delivered a glass of whiskey on the rocks. Realizing he'd forgotten Astrid's Irish coffee, he mumbled an apology and shuffled back to the bar.

"Thank you for meeting me all the way out here," Astrid said. "I realize you must be terribly busy."

Magnason waved his hand dismissively while sucking down the whiskey. He emptied the glass and set it on the table with a clink that sounded throughout the quiet bar.

At least I'm not the only one who's developed unhealthy coping mechanisms, she thought.

"Not so busy as you might think," he said. "Iceland is a small country, and the President handles all the ceremonial business. There isn't that much for the Prime Minister to do."

"Even during the current... situation?" she asked. She had almost said *crisis*, but thought better of it.

"Let's put our cards on the table," Magnason said. "Our country is in a rough spot. We're heavily dependent on tourism, and between the pandemic shutting down travel and the melting of the glaciers, we've got a lot of businesses going... how do you say it in English? Belly up. Tax revenue is down and social spending is way up. The result is that our national debt now exceeds GDP by a significant margin and continues to grow. This situation is unsustainable. In your call to my office, you suggested that your foundation might be able to help. I had someone do some checking, and you appear to be for real. You seem to have a knack for picking up assets that are just about to rocket to the sky in value."

"Skyrocket," said Astrid.

"What?"

Astrid flushed. "I'm sorry, bad habit. The word is 'skyrocket.' Assets that are about to skyrocket in value."

"Ah. Of course. What is that? Irish coffee?" The bartender had finally returned with Astrid's drink. "I'll have one as well."

"Yes, sir, Mr. Prime Minister," said the bartender. He spun on his heel and returned to the bar.

"Jesus Christ, I thought he was going to salute me," Magnason muttered. "Where was I?"

"You concluded I was the real deal."

"Right. You've got an impressive portfolio. I had my financial people look into the three companies you told us about. Real estate all over Europe and Asia. All of it purchased within the last seven years, all of it in rapidly growing markets. Your investments are heavily leveraged, allowing you to realize a return of over eight hundred percent per year. It's more than impressive. It's astounding."

"Our foundation has been fortunate to hire people who are extremely skilled at identifying trends in—"

"*Kjaftæði.*" Astrid's understanding of Icelandic slang was spotty, but she knew that word: *bullshit*. She smiled as Magnason continued. "You would need a fortune teller to make those kinds of returns. You sold the last of your real estate in Malaysia three months before the worst typhoon in a hundred years hit. You expect me to believe that was a result of 'spotting trends'?"

Astrid shrugged, doing her best to affect nonchalance. "There is, of course, a large element of luck. In this case, bad luck for the Malaysians; good luck for me."

"And you expect luck to be on your side in Iceland?"

"I expect it to be on both our sides," Astrid said. "If you're asking whether I expect land in eastern Iceland to *skyrocket* over the next few years, the answer is no. It is likely to remain stable in value or even decline a bit. The value of this particular endeavor is not in real estate."

"How much land are we talking about, exactly?" Magnason asked, gesturing at the view outside the window. Beyond the verdant plain lay steep hills of dark brown volcanic sand. In the distance, partially obscured by a blanket of low-hanging clouds, loomed the great white mass of Vatnajökull. Tendrils of white snaked down the taller hills in the distance, the dying glacier fighting to maintain its hold on the land. "I understand you have already purchased this hotel and several other parcels in the area from private parties."

Astrid reached into the bag beside her chair and pulled out a paper map, which she unfolded and placed on the table. It depicted the island of Iceland, with a roughly square section bordering the southeastern coast outlined in red.

"My word," said Magnason. "That must be…"

"Roughly two thousand square kilometers."

"What on Earth could you possibly need that much land for?"

"Research."

"What sort of research?"

"I'm afraid I can't divulge that."

"You expect me to sell you two thousand square kilometers of land in my country without knowing what you intend to do with it?"

"With respect, sir, that is part of the reason I'm willing to pay nearly three times the market value of the land."

"There are many other remote areas. Alaska is twenty times the size of Iceland. Why not go there?"

"Alaska doesn't meet my needs for reasons I'd rather not go into."

"These needs of yours... I don't suppose they're related to the discovery of certain *artifacts* in this region of our country?"

For a moment, Astrid was too unsettled to speak. Magnason sat back and grinned. "You didn't think I was ignorant of that, did you? I'm the Prime Minister. It's my business to know such things." He reached beside his own chair to unlatch his briefcase. He pulled a folder from it and then closed the briefcase. He set the folder on the table and opened it to reveal a handful of newspaper clippings. The headline of the top one read *American hiker finnur 'fornu rými hjálm.'* Below it was a picture of a smiling man holding the round object in front of his chest. Magnason said, "It says 'American hiker finds ancient space helmet,' in case your Icelandic is rusty."

Astrid nodded absently. She picked up the clippings and briefly perused each of them. Half were from the leading Reykjavik newspaper; the others were printouts from various fringe websites, some in Icelandic and some in English. She had seen them all before. Most were simply rehashing of the "space helmet" story, along with some additional embellishment and speculation. A few of the stories mentioned an Icelandic farmer who had claimed to have found a stainless-steel valve stem buried under several layers of volcanic ash. The accounts were all second- or third-hand, though: neither the farmer nor the artifact could be located. There were rumors of several other such discoveries, but no hard proof. The 'ancient Icelandic astronauts' meme was confined to the most extreme tinfoil-hat regions of the Internet. Even so, it had been foolish to assume that David Magnuson was unaware of the stories. Time for Plan B.

"I suppose there's no point in denying it, then," Astrid said. "Yes, the foundation's project is archaeological in nature."

"You're saying the stories are true?"

"Which stories, exactly?"

"The ones that say ancient astronauts visited Iceland a thousand years ago."

"We don't know exactly what happened here," Astrid said. "That's the reason for our research."

"But you're expecting to find more artifacts as the ice continues to melt. The death of the glaciers is a boon to you." He was unable to keep the edge out of his voice.

"Ice melts," Astrid said with a shrug.

"Good luck for you, bad luck for us. Just like Malaysia, eh?"

"That glacier has been melting since 1890. It's not like you were blindsided by it." She had told herself to avoid getting into a political argument with the Prime Minister, but something about the way these people romanticized the glaciers irritated her.

"The rate at which the glaciers are receding has accelerated rapidly in the last thirty years."

"When the Vikings first came to Iceland in the tenth century," Astrid replied, "the glaciers were much smaller than they are today. The glaciers began to grow during the Little Ice Age, which began about four hundred years later, reached their peak size in the late nineteenth century, and have been shrinking ever since. Is human activity accelerating the melting of the glaciers? Probably. But the retreat of the glaciers is neither unprecedented nor unexpected. Environmentalists like to accuse advocates of modern technology of being short-sighted, but what is truly short-sighted is assuming that the climate has always been as it is now. In fact, if it weren't for the period of unusually warm weather lasting from the tenth century to the thirteenth, Iceland probably would never have been settled at all, so there would be no one here to complain about the loss of your precious glaciers."

Magnason regarded her impassively for a moment and then broke into a smile. "It does make one wonder what this place was like a thousand years ago," he said. The bartender had brought his coffee, and he took a sip. "The historical records of that period are scant. The ruins of an entire civilization could be under that ice."

"That," said Astrid, returning his smile, "is doubtful." She was relieved that Magnason hadn't taken her rant personally. Undoubtedly he knew everything she'd told him anyway; his concern about the loss of the glaciers was not quasi-religious as it was for some, but simply a pragmatic concern: without its famed glaciers, Iceland would lose some of its appeal for tourists.

"I don't suppose you'll make the results of your research available publicly," Magnason said.

"Ultimately, our foundation's research will benefit all of humankind. However, I can make no guarantees in the short-term."

"In other words, you're keeping anything you find secret."

"Yes. Moreover—"

"You want the Icelandic government's help in keeping it secret."

"You're very astute, Prime Minister. An assurance of your government's cooperation is the other reason for the price I'm offering."

"You're essentially asking us to cede sovereignty over a large chunk of our country."

"Not at all. We ask only for the property rights granted to every landowner in Iceland, along with the sort of cooperation you offer to a large corporation doing business within your borders. A certain aluminum mining concern, for example." The government's concessions to Alumnico were something of an open secret, but Magnason stiffened at her remark. "Relax," Astrid said, having found her confidence at last. "I don't know anything that hasn't already been hinted at by the international press, and blackmail isn't my style. I'm only saying that I'm not suggesting anything wildly improper or particularly unusual."

"Other than the size of the purchase. Much of the land in that area is within a national park, you realize."

"We don't intend to interfere with the normal operations of the park, except in the eventuality that another artifact is found. Such an occurrence may necessitate restricting access to the immediate area of the discovery for a time. And of course any artifacts will be property of the foundation."

"Of course. The price you're offering, again, is…?"

"Two point four billion U.S. dollars. To be paid via a direct transfer of various non-cash holdings to the national treasury."

"Your 'foundation' is short on cash?"

"Hardly. This arrangement is intended to avoid scrutiny by the media and others who might ask uncomfortable questions about the rapid turnaround in Iceland's financial picture."

"Uncomfortable for you or for me?"

"Both. My attorneys suggest that you implement a sweeping financial reform plan, which will incidentally uncover the existence of certain investments that had been inadvertently left off the treasury's balance sheet. The 'rediscovered' assets will provide a respectable annual return of $200 million, essentially cutting the country's budget deficit by ten percent, and ensuring your reelection as Prime Minister."

"Interesting. And if someone looks into the ownership of that land?"

"Officially, it will remain the property of the Icelandic government. But there will be an off-the-books understanding regarding the foundation's ownership."

"Hmmm. I'd suggest a long-term lease. Easier to keep quiet. Say one hundred years?"

"Better make it two hundred."

"Two hundred years! How long do you expect this 'research' to take?"

Astrid smiled. "I'm confident two hundred years will cover it."

"I suppose that could be done. Two hundred million dollars per year is a hell of an enticement."

"I feel that I must specify that although this deal is to remain secret, the management of the investments must be entirely above-board. I will insist on a yearly internal audit."

Magnason grinned again. "You mean to tell me I won't be able to use the two point four billion to buy myself a yacht? Don't worry, I may be an ornery old bastard, but I'm scrupulous to a fault. That money will be used solely to pay down the country's debt. The only benefit I'll see, as you mention, is a boost in my chances of retaining my post as Prime Minister."

"Good. Extravagant purchases on your part or on the part of any other government officials would prompt questions, and if someone pulls on that thread, the whole thing will unravel. I'm confident this deal is the best thing for both your country and for our foundation, but others may not see it that way."

"Understood. Well, I should be getting back to the city. It's been a pleasure speaking with you, Ms. van de Lucht. I'll have my finance people get in touch with you. By the way, this foundation of yours… does it have a name, or is that top secret as well?"

"The name isn't a secret, although I'd prefer it not be connected in any way to this project. The lease will be secured through another subsidiary."

"I won't speak a word of any of this, except to those who need to be directly involved to make the arrangement happen. You have my word as Prime Minister."

"Very good, thank you. The foundation goes by the name Jörmungandr."

"The mythical serpent eating its own tail. Fascinating. Any particular reason for that name?"

Astrid smiled. "I assure you that all will become clear in time."

CHAPTER ONE

The attack would come at Stainmore Pass. Eric might have expected it, had his head been clear, but he'd been obsessed with thoughts of reclaiming his rightful status since being ousted from the royal castle at York three days earlier. Eric was convinced that it was his destiny to be King, if not of Norway, then of Northumbria, and not even his ouster from both thrones (twice from the latter) could disabuse him of the idea.

Tall and broad-shouldered, with fine blond hair like that of his father, Eric rode at the lead of his company astride an impressive chestnut mare. Fifty horsemen, among them his lieutenant Gulbrand, his son Haeric and his brother Ragnald, followed. Most of these men were Norsemen, many of whom had been with Eric since he'd first arrived on the English shore fifteen years earlier. Their fortunes rose and fell with Eric's, and they had seen more than their share of ups and downs over the years.

They rode or trudged along the old Roman road that cut through the peat-covered fells east of the Pennines. It was early spring, and the air was cold and damp, the sky a mottled gray. They intended to camp just beyond Stainmore and then continue toward their intended destination of Bamburgh, some hundred miles north, where allies were said to await. They would never get there.

Eric, the firstborn son of King Harald of Norway, had earned the name Bloodaxe for the manner in which he dealt with siblings who had attempted to usurp his birthright. Impatient for the throne, Eric had voyaged across the sea as a young man to find his fortune. He led men in a series of battles across England, ultimately failing to achieve any lasting victory. He returned to Norway after his father's death, and reigned there as King until he was ousted in favor of his more personable younger brother, Haakon. He fled the country and again sought his fortune in England, ultimately seizing the throne of Northumbria in the year 947. His reign was short-lived: King Eadred of the English led a ruthless campaign through Northumbria, promising to end the destruction only if the Northumbrians deserted Eric. They soon did so, and in 948 Eric was once again without a throne. Eric bade his time in the north of the country, and eventually the Northumbrians tired of King Olaf, who had been appointed by Eadred in Eric's place. The people drove out Olaf and in 952 once again invited Eric to be King.

Given the Northumbrians' fickleness, Eric was not entirely surprised to find himself once again leading a band of loyalists along the road out of York. He was, however, congenitally unable to accept his exile as permanent; he knew as certainly as he breathed that he was meant to be a king. He viewed his current exile, like the previous ones, as temporary interruptions of his divinely fated role. It was this very stubbornness that history tells us was his undoing.

For Eric so desperately needed to believe that all events were working toward the restoration of his kingship that when word came from Osulf, the high-reeve of Northumbria, that he was raising a force of men at Bamburgh loyal to the erstwhile king, Eric entertained no doubts as to the message's veracity. Ragnald and Eric's lieutenant, Gulbrand, had urged caution, counseling that although Osulf had been friendly in the past, the high-reeve had little to gain from Eric's return to the throne. It was more likely, they said, that Eadred had inveigled upon Osulf to lure Eric to the north, where an ambush might be prepared for him. But Eric refused to listen, and ultimately ordered them to silence. In silence they approached the pass in the hills called Stainmore, Eric's brother Ragnald—a heavyset, balding man who had a pleasant demeanor but none of Eric's charisma or cleverness—to his left and Gulbrand just behind him. Alongside the hulking, battle-scarred Gulbrand rode Eric's son, Haeric, a strapping young man of twenty.

Eric spotted the first of the horsemen coming around a bend a hundred yards off. Almost at the same time, cries went up from behind him as more riders crested the hillsides to their left and right. It was a well-planned ambush: Eric's men had just come through the narrowest part of the pass; there was no easy escape to the rear, and they were now flanked on three sides. Judging from the number of riders pouring down the hillsides, Eric's men were outnumbered at least two to one.

Eric shouted for his men to close ranks and hold firm. They drew their swords as horses thundered down the steep hillsides. An ordinary man facing such odds might have been afraid, but Eric's stubbornness precluded the possibility of that emotion. He *knew* he would be King once again, not only of Northumberland, but probably Norway as well. It was his destiny, and destiny would not be denied. So he drew his broadsword and shouted at the attackers to come at him, failing to notice that the red and yellow markings on their shields showed them to be the very men who were supposed to have met them in Bamburgh to assist him in retaking the throne at York.

"We are betrayed, Eric!" cried Ragnald, but Eric, a prisoner of his own delusion, did not understand his brother's meaning. "Stand firm, Ragnald!" Eric shouted. The attackers were over halfway down the hillsides now, and the size of their force was fully evident. Eric's men had closed ranks along the road, facing outward, their swords and spears at the ready. Terror had seized many of them, but there was no place for them to flee. It was clear to all but Eric that they had been drawn into the pincers of a near-perfect trap.

The pass was just wide enough here for Eric's party to form a rough defensive circle, their horses standing nearly flank-to-flank. As the attackers' horses broke into a gallop, Eric rode around the outside of the perimeter, barking orders and encouragement. He knew many would likely die here today, but he would not give his enemies an easy victory. "For King Eric!" shouted one of the men, and it soon became a raucous chant, the men thrusting their swords and axes in the air as they proclaimed their willingness to die for their leader. Eric grinned and brought his horse around to face the riders thundering down the northern side of the pass.

War cries and the clash of metal behind him told Eric that the attackers coming down the opposite side of the pass had met the defenders on the southern side of the circle. A glance to Eric's left revealed that the riders on the road had nearly closed with his men as well. The thirty or so riders coming down the northern slope, hampered by the steeper ground there, were still some fifty yards off.

"Come on, you sons of whores!" Eric howled. "You're late!"

The riders in the lead were only twenty yards off when a shout went up from the direction Eric's men had come. Eric might have taken it to be one of the attackers, having flanked them to the rear, but the voice was high-pitched and shrill: a woman's voice. What the devil was a woman doing in this desolate land, miles from the nearest village? A mad witch, no doubt, roaming the moor. Gulbrand, just to Eric's right, gave a shrug. They had more pressing concerns.

"Eric!" the voice called again, and this time there was no mistaking it: she was calling his name. "This way!"

His curiosity getting the better of him, Eric turned, taking his attention away from the horsemen, the closest of whom were now within a stone's throw. There she stood, tall and blond, wearing a strange, skin-tight suit of some strange gray fabric that covered her entire body from the neck down. Her appearance was striking, but she was more handsome than beautiful. She didn't look to be more than twenty years in age. Eric had converted to Christianity to ease his way into the throne of Northumberland, but he found himself wondering if Valkyries were real after all. Had she come to aid him or to carry him from the battlefield to Valhalla? And if she were truly a Valkyrie, where was her sword?

The thought had barely formed in his head when the woman unslung something from her back. Not a sword, but something long and black, like a great cast iron crossbow. It could hardly be iron, though, for her to heft it so easily. She pointed the end of the thing up the hillside toward the line of riders thundering toward Eric, made some adjustment to it, and then seemed to brace herself, as if she expected the device to transform into a writhing snake in her hands. Despite the advance of the riders in front of him, Eric found himself staring at her in wonder. He was not disappointed. Fire erupted from the end of the device, and a split second later the entire valley was filled with a roar like thunder. Unlike thunder, though, it was rhythmic, and went on and on: *Brrrrap! Brrrrap! Brrrrap! Brrrrap!*

Men and horses fell in a mist of blood and mud, their momentum carrying them forward in a chaotic tumble of broken limbs and shattered shields. One horse collapsed, throwing its rider, and then rolled head over heels, eventually bowling over the first line of defenders. A few of the other horses, spooked but apparently uninjured, managed to skid to a halt and then bolted to the east or west. Their riders, thrown thirty or more feet through the air, landed hard on the muddy ground. Many died instantly, their necks broken; others lay moaning or tried to crawl out of the way of the several dozen horses bearing down on them. Most of them failed, and another line of horsemen went down as their mounts lost their footing or panicked and bolted.

Eric's own horse wheeled to the right, reared up and whinnied in terror, and several others behind him followed suit. Eric managed to get control of his mare, but some of the other men weren't as lucky. Shouts of fear rang out as several men were thrown from the saddle. A few of the horses near the rear of the group had turned and bolted back the way they had come. By the time Eric could get his horse facing northward again, the Valkyrie had turned her weapon toward the attackers coming down the other side of the pass. *Brrrrap! Brrrrap! Brrrrap!* went the weapon again, and fire shot toward the horsemen. Again, horses and men fell, collapsing and tumbling down the hillside. Panic seized the horses on this side of the valley as well; fewer than twenty men had fallen in total, but the attackers were in utter disarray. An acrid scent reached Eric's nostrils.

"Eric, damn you!" shouted the woman, as the thunder faded. "Come on!"

He turned to see her standing there alone, the weapon now hanging off her shoulder, smoke wafting from the end of it. A Valkyrie or a demon from the pit of hell?

"Who are you?" he shouted.

"What does it matter?" she shouted back. "Hurry! I can't hold them off forever!"

"Let us flee, Eric," said Gulbrand from beside him. "We haven't a chance against this many."

Eric had never run from a battle, and he didn't like entrusting his fate to a strange woman, even if she were a Valkyrie. On the other hand, it was beginning to dawn on him that perhaps his destiny was not quite as clear-cut as he had thought. He realized now what Gulbrand had been trying to tell him: his ostensible ally, Olaf, had betrayed him, which meant that he no longer had any clear path back to the throne of York. Whoever this woman was, she possessed a weapon that made her a match for fifty men, and she had willingly put herself in danger on his account. Such a woman could be a formidable ally. If there were more like her—or simply more weapons like the one she wielded—he could not only retake the throne of York; he could become King of England and Frankia as well.

The woman had turned and was now running further up the road, away from the fracas. "Back through the pass!" cried Eric. "Follow me!" He spurred his horse toward the east, and the others—many of them still fighting to control their horses—followed. As his horse neared the woman, she stopped and turned, pointing the weapon in his direction, and for a moment he thought he'd fallen to a ruse once again.

"Go! Go!" she shouted, stepping aside to let Eric's horse gallop past. By this time, a few of the attackers farther up the slope to the north had regained control of their own mounts and were maneuvering to flank the newcomer. Eric pulled on the reins of his horse and shouted a warning, pointing up the slope. The woman responded with a curt nod and raised the weapon to her shoulder again. *Brrrrap! Brrrrap! Brrrrap!* The would-be attackers fell or scattered as a dozen more of Eric's men rode past. Several riderless horses, having thrown their owners, galloped after the others in a panic; men on foot ran or limped by, keeping to the peat on the side of the road to avoid being trampled.

The attackers were now spread widely across both sides of the pass. Perhaps thirty men and nearly as many horses lay dead;

the threat of the strange weapon was as much in its ability to sow fear and chaos as its deadliness. The panic had seized the defenders' horses as well; if they had anywhere to run, they would have bolted.

"Look, Father!" cried Haeric, bringing his mount up beside Eric's. "'Tis Maccus yonder!"

Eric followed his son's gaze and saw that it was so. Earl Maccus, recognizable by his full iron helm and red-and-yellow tunic, was on the northern slope, attempting to rally a group of attackers to flank Eric's men to the rear. Eric scowled: Maccus had sworn his allegiance to Eric not a month earlier. The wily coward, having seen what the woman's weapon could do, was directing his men along the slope in a wide arc outside the weapon's effective range.

"We cannot tarry, Eric!" said Ragnald. "They're trying to cut off our escape!" The bulk of Eric's party had ridden past him back to the narrow part of the pass, and those who had fled first were probably already safe from Maccus's men. Eric and the others in the rear risked being cut off and surrounded. The smart thing would be to spur his horse after the others and get ahead of Maccus while there was still time, leaving the woman to defend herself from the Northumbrians. But if he fled now, he would lose the woman and her terrible weapon to Maccus's men. Furthermore, although he was not a man greatly troubled by ethical qualms, there was something distasteful about leaving a woman to die at the hands of his enemies, even if he had not asked for her help.

As the last of Eric's men rode past, the woman loosed another burst of fire toward the attackers coming down the northern slope, and two more men fell from their mounts. The weapon was formidable, but Eric saw that it could only be directed at a single opponent, or closely clustered group of opponents, at a time, and as Maccus had already ascertained, it was not effective at much more than fifty yards. Besides Maccus's group, perhaps twoscore of the Northumbrians had gotten control of their mounts. They advanced in haphazard fashion from the north, south and west, but to some degree this worked in their favor: the weapon was less effective when it could not be directed at a closely clustered group of enemies. Recognizing the woman as the chief threat, the attackers converged on her.

She fired, puncturing the breastplate of a rider approaching from the southern slope, causing him to fall backwards and slide off his horse. She took aim at another man, killing him as well, but with each burst from the weapon, the attackers advanced on her. She directed her fire toward two riders thundering down the road toward her as a third, armed with a lance, advanced down the northern slope.

CHAPTER TWO

"Go!" shouted Eric to Ragnald. "Lead the men to safety. I will be close behind." Ragnald, ever the loyal younger brother, gave Eric a nod and spurred his horse forward. Gulbrand and Haeric hesitated. "Go, both of you!" Eric shouted. "I'll see to the woman!"

He jerked the reins to the left and spurred his horse forward, putting himself in the path of the rider coming down the northern slope. The attacker's horse planted its hooves and slid in the mud toward Eric's mount until its breast slammed into the neck of Eric's horse, causing its rider, still clutching his lance, to fly toward Eric. Eric caught the tip of the lance with his shield, which split in two from the force of the blow; he leaned forward and the attacker flew over Eric's horse and landed hard on the road as the horse bolted to the west. Eric discarded the remnants of his shield and held out his hand to the woman. Half a dozen horsemen thundered toward them from up the road, and still more advanced down the slopes on either side.

The woman let out a burst of fire, dispatching the two riders nearest them, and then slung the weapon over her shoulder. She reached up to take Eric's hand, but one of the riderless horses brushed her with its flank as it ran past, and she fell to the ground. Her weapon skittered across the road and landed in the mud several feet away.

Another horse galloped toward her from up the road, its rider bearing a huge studded mace. Eric wheeled his horse around, but there was no way he could get to the woman in time. He had resigned himself to never knowing who the woman was or why she had saved his life when Gulbrand's mighty destrier shot past him. Swinging his massive war hammer with his right hand as he passed, the great warrior caught the man with the mace solidly in the chest, arresting his momentum with a crunch of metal and bone. The man's broken body tumbled over the hindquarters of his horse as the animal kept going. Gulbrand let the hammer reach the peak of its arc and then brought it down just in time to crush the skull of the next man on the road. A third man, some twenty feet back, lost his nerve and pulled sharply on the reins of his horse. The animal skidded to a stop and reared up, causing the next three horses to crash into it and hurling their riders to the ground.

Seeing that the woman was safe for the moment, Eric wheeled his horse back to the right to face the men advancing from the north. As two riders with swords converged on him, he pulled hard on his own horse's reins, and the beast reared up on two legs, its front hooves slicing menacingly through the air in front of him. The attackers' horses shied away, preventing their riders from getting close enough to attack, at least for the moment.

"Damn you, Gulbrand," Eric growled, his horse still towering over the others on its hind legs, "I told you to go!"

Gulbrand, still holding his war hammer over his head, brought his horse around, a wide grin on his face. "Aye, my lord. But you know how Helga gets when she's hungry." Blood and brain matter fell from the broad head of the hammer as his horse galloped back toward Eric.

Eric's mare brought its front hooves down, and the two men advanced upon him once again. He heard a horse coming up alongside him, and he saw that Haeric had disobeyed him as well. Haeric thwarted the advance of the rider on Eric's right, blocking a swing of the man's sword with his shield. Haeric riposted with a thrust that caught the attacker under his right arm. The man dropped his sword and retreated. Eric swung at the attacker nearest him, striking his helmet with a loud clang. While the man was still disoriented, Eric jabbed, the tip of his blade sliding through the soft flesh below the man's chin. The man jerked back and then fell limply from his horse. Turning, Eric saw that the woman had gotten to her feet. Dozens of riders were now advancing down the slopes toward them, but the nearest were a stone's throw away, allowing them a momentary reprieve. Eric brought his horse over to the woman as she picked up her weapon. She slung the weapon over her shoulder again, and he helped her into the saddle.

"Now *go!*" Eric commanded, and this time the two men obeyed. Gulbrand took the lead, still gripping his mighty hammer as his destrier charged down the road. Haeric went next, with Eric and the woman bringing up the rear. Eric's mare had no trouble keeping up despite the additional weight. The road ahead was deserted except for dead men and riderless horses, which meant that the rest of Eric's men had made it to the narrower part of the pass. Maccus's party, though, had nearly reached the road, and scores of riders still poured down the slopes on either side toward them. Unless they could get ahead of Maccus, they'd be flanked on all sides.

They rode hard, outpacing Maccus's men, whose horses were picking their way carefully along the steepening northern slope, but the lead riders of Maccus' party reached the road ahead of Eric's group. The Northumbrians, however, barely had time to draw their weapons before Gulbrand's hammer smashed into them. He downed three of them without slowing. Haeric dismounted a fourth with a lefthanded swing at a man coming up alongside his flank, and a fifth went down as his horse stumbled a few paces from Eric's mare. Maccus himself, Eric noted, was not among those who reached the road before them.

Suddenly the road was clear; the northern slope was too steep here for the Northumbrians' horses to continue to the east. They were not yet out of danger, though: at least a dozen horsemen were close behind them on the road, and Maccus's group and many others were on their way down. They would soon have at least two scores of riders on their tail, and the rest of Eric's men were out of sight, far ahead of them into the narrow pass. Moreover, their horses had been traveling since early that morning and were rapidly tiring; they could not keep up this pace for long. Eric could hear the thunder of hooves behind them, even over the sound of their own party.

He felt the woman's hands loosen at his belly, and for a moment he thought she was going to try to dismount and flee on her own. But then he felt something like a cord pulling against him; looking down, he saw what he realized was the strap that had been attached to the woman's weapon. She shifted behind him, and then the cord went taut. He understood what she was doing: she had reversed herself in the saddle, tethering herself to him so that she could remain mounted while facing backwards.

Eric braced himself, but nothing could prepare him for that sound. *Brrrrap! Brrrrap! Brrrrap! Brrrrap!* went the weapon, the recoil causing the woman's elbow to hammer against his armor with every burst. Finally the noise stopped, and Eric strained to hear hooves over the ringing in his ears.

"Did you get them all?" he shouted.

"I'm out of bullets," the woman shouted back. "But they've broken off pursuit for now."

"Thank Odin and the Christ," said Eric. The weapon had put the fear of the gods into the Northumbrians; he could only hope it would last.

"I see Halfdan ahead!" shouted Gulbrand.

Eric gave another sigh of relief. They had caught up to the others; if they were forced to fight, they would at least do it with their full force. They were now well into the narrow part of the pass, and the horses were beginning to flag. Glancing back, Eric saw no sign of pursuit. Shortly, the pass opened up and they were once again looking out over the green peat fields of York. Their horses, frothing at the mouth, had slowed to a canter. The woman undid the strap and turned to face forward in the saddle, her weapon over her shoulder. Eric drove his mount forward to rejoin Ragnald at the lead of the group, Gulbrand and Haeric following.

"I told you Osulf was not to be trusted, brother," Ragnald said.

"I'll have Osulf's head on a pike," Eric said. "And Maccus's with it."

"When you retake the throne," Ragnald said.

"Aye, when I retake the throne!" growled Eric, unable to resist rising to the bait. His brother was loyal, but not necessarily reverent.

"Here I thought we were fleeing from the Northumbrians," said Gulbrand from behind them. "Now I find we're on a triumphant march back to York."

Eric turned to glare at Gulbrand as Ragnald burst into laughter. Haeric pretended to cough to hide his own chuckle. Eric opened his mouth to order them to silence, but found himself laughing as well. "All right, I take your point," he said. "We're perhaps not ready to return to York. But I *will* have my revenge on Maccus and that double-dealing whelp in Bamburgh."

"And we'll be there with you," Ragnald said. "But it's going to be tough without any allies."

Eric didn't speak, but they all knew what he was thinking: if there were more weapons like the one the woman riding with Eric carried, they wouldn't need allies.

"Go north," said the woman into Eric's ear, pointing to their left. "Toward that ridge."

"There's nothing that way but peat bogs," said Gulbrand, who had overheard. "We must return to Ripon." Many of the men, including Eric, had wives and children at the small village north of York, where Archbishop Wulfstan, an ally of Eric's, had granted them asylum.

"My ship is over there," said the woman.

"What, in the bog?" asked Eric.

"Trust me," she said. "You cannot return to York. We must get off the road before Maccus' men regroup and catch up to us."

Eric considered the matter. Their families were safe at Ripon, but bringing fifty armed men there would strain the limits of Wulfstan's hospitality. The English King, Eadred, would suspect Eric intended to retake the throne and send men to kill him. Already once, several years earlier, Ripon had been the subject of a punitive attack by the king for its support of Eric. The woman was right, too, about Maccus: she had spoiled the ambush with her strange weapon, but the Northumbrians would not give up so easily. Getting off the road, although not a long-term solution, was not the worst idea. At least their horses could rest.

"To the north!" Eric shouted. "Follow me!" He guided his horse off the road onto the moor and the others followed. No one—not even Gulbrand—objected. Perhaps they had come to the same conclusion as Eric, or perhaps they suspected they were nearing the limit of impertinence Eric would tolerate.

The ground quickly grew more uneven as they departed from the road, and the horses instinctively slowed to a walk. Glancing toward the west, Eric still saw no sign of the Northumbrians. The ridge lay a half-mile ahead; with some luck, they might be over it by the time Maccus's men emerged from the pass. The horses were near exhaustion and likely to misstep if they were forced to gallop across the peat. Eric's horse in particular was wheezing in an alarming manner, the added weight of a second rider beginning to take its toll. Eric dismounted and walked beside the horse. To his surprise, the woman did the same. "That was my first time riding," she said. "I'm more comfortable with my feet on the ground."

"Is that so?" asked Eric, surprised. "I took you for a Valkyrie."

The woman laughed. "I am flattered, but I am no warrior."

"That would come as a surprise to the Northumbrians."

"The gun gives me an unfair advantage. I'd never touched one before yesterday."

Eric stared at her, stunned. Many of his men had been training to fight since they could walk, and no twenty of them were a match for this woman while she carried that gun.

"What is your name?" he asked.

"I am called Freya."

"You do not speak as a foreigner, Freya, but I know of no kingdom that has weapons such as yours. Where are you from? How did you know about the ambush? And why did you intervene?"

"Those are all excellent questions," Freya said. "I'm not sure I can answer them in a way that will make any sense to you. Things may become clearer when you have seen the ship."

Again with the ship, thought Eric. Was the woman mad? "Your ship must have a very shallow keel to navigate the bogs of Yorkshire," he said.

Freya smiled. "It is not that sort of ship. It flies through the sky."

"Then you are indeed a Valkyrie!"

"No, merely a human woman. I was born in a remote settlement in Iceland. We called it Svartalfheim."

"Near the southern coast," said Eric. "Perhaps two hundred miles east of Reykjavik, near a village called Höfn."

"How did you...?"

Eric was pleased to have caught Freya off guard. "I was there once, many years ago, shortly after I first arrived here. My father pledged his assistance to me in conquering Northumberland if I would postpone my campaign until his men returned from Iceland. I did not know why my father would send an army to Iceland, and when I heard nothing of them for several months, I went to see the place for myself. We reached Höfn to find it deserted and followed a road inland to what must have been the place you call Svartalfheim. I had thought it only a legend. In any case, little remained of the settlement; it was as if a dragon had come upon the place, leaving nothing alive and barely one stone upon another. The ground was scorched as if by a tremendous fire. We found several strange, finely crafted artifacts there, some of them made of materials I had never seen before. If I had known I might find weapons such as that, I might have investigated further, but I did not want to tarry in my return to Northumbria."

"Then you know more of my people than I thought," said Freya.

"Your people are the Dvergar who were said to reside at Svartalfheim?"

"It was my people who inspired the myths," said Freya, "though as you can see, we are not dwarves or kobolds."

"What are you, then?"

"A human being, like you, as I said. My grandmother came to Earth from another world, along with three others. Their ship crashed here, and they needed to build another to return to the sky. That was the reason for the facility at Svartalfheim."

"But the Dvergar remain on Earth?"

"Some of them, yes. Descendants of my grandmother's crew and their allies. Our mission was ultimately a success. It took nearly half a century, but we built a ship that took me to the sky."

"You alone?" Eric asked dubiously.

"Yes. There was supposed to be another, but he was killed. I traveled for years, until another ship found me. They brought me back here."

"Why?"

"To find you. I meant to get here sooner, but it took a while to find a place to land."

Eric scowled, certain that the woman was mocking him. Undoubtedly most of what she had told him was a fabrication. And yet, he had seen the remains of Svartalfheim, and there was no denying the awesome power of the weapon that Freya wielded. He had to know the truth about Freya (if that truly was her name) and her people, one way or another. Once they were safely out of sight from the road, he decided, he would demand answers. He would find out how she had really gotten here and what she wanted. Gulbrand could be quite persuasive.

As they talked, they had reached the ridge, and were now nearing its crest. Still there was no sign of the Northumbrians, but then Maccus probably figured there was no need for him to hurry: Eric's men were trapped between the Northumbrians and Eadred's men at York. Certainly they would have preferred to slaughter Eric and his men at the pass, but now that their intentions were revealed, they could take their time.

"Now listen," said Eric. "I am in debt to you for what you did at the pass, and I will grant that wherever you are from, your craftsmen must be remarkably skilled to produce such a weapon. But I am no fool to be taken in by stories of dwarves and magic. I want to know how you managed to get to that pass at the very time we were traveling through it, without a horse, when I myself was not sure of our destination until this morning. And if I hear one more word of—"

His son, Haeric, who was still mounted, let out a gasp. "By Odin's beard," murmured his brother, Ragnald. Gulbrand stared open-mouthed. Eric, annoyed at the unseemly display of his most trusted men, was about to rebuke them when he caught a glimpse of something silvery just over the ridge. He broke into a run, stopping when the thing was in full view.

"Odin's beard," Eric said, staring at the giant metal thing nestled in the green valley below. It was the size of a cathedral. "Is that…?"

Freya came up beside him. "The ship," she said.

CHAPTER THREE

Freya sat across a conference table from Tertius Dornen, commander of the Orbital Deployment Cruiser *Varinga*. On Freya's left sat Helena, the daughter of the legendary inventor and polymath Leo the Mathematician. To her right was Dan O'Brien, the last surviving crew member of the exploratory ship *Andrea Luhman*. It was, Freya reflected, a historic meeting: each of the three represented a separate branch of human civilization, each centered on a different planet. O'Brien and Helena, now both in their nineties, had agreed to attend the meeting only reluctantly. O'Brien's health was failing, and it took most of Helena's energy to care for him. They sat in silence, watching a viewscreen on the far wall, and Freya found herself wanting to sink into her chair until she was out of sight and then crawl under the table and out of the room.

The viewscreen showed a live feed from *Varinga*'s mess hall, which had been taken over by fifty large, filthy, loud and unruly men wearing tattered and soiled clothing of wool and animal skin. The men had been given water and meal packets (one of each per man, all identical), but somehow three separate fights had broken out over the "unfair" distribution of food. One man lay unconscious, and at least four others had been injured so far. Only the lack of deadly weapons had forestalled fatalities; they had been forced to give up their swords and axes—along with their horses, which were grazing outside—before boarding the ship. Their leader, Eric, far from trying to put an end to the fighting, was cheering them on. Several of the men near him had begun to make wagers on the fights.

"These," said Commander Dornen, "are the men you expect to save the galaxy." The words came in the Nordic language from the automatic translator at the center of the table, a half-second behind Dornen's speech. Dornen, tall and lean, with an aquiline nose, was an impressive figure in his burgundy Concordat Defense Force uniform. Freya still hadn't quiet figured out where Dornen's people had come from, but Helena said their language seemed to be heavily influenced by two very ancient Terran languages: Latin and Aramaic. But even Helena, who spoke five languages, couldn't understand Dornen without a translator.

Freya, who had never been a people person even before she spent four years alone on a Cho-ta'an spaceship, found herself so overcome with anxiety that for a moment she couldn't speak. Fortunately, Helena came to her rescue.

"It's true they're a little rough around the edges," she said, "but they are absolutely fearless in battle. You are looking for warriors, after all, not a diplomacy corps."

"We're looking for individuals who can operate complex equipment, execute precision tactical maneuvers, and, above all, follow orders," said Dornen. "These men are on the verge of killing each other over packets of freeze-dried chicken."

"With respect, Commander," said Freya, "you don't have a lot of other options. You've got eight hundred of these 'mech suits,' and no one to operate them."

"There are companies of marines on at least five different planets," Dornen said. "Many of whom have already been trained in the use of mech suits, and all of whom have more experience in combat with the Izarians than these... *people*."

"Then maybe you should go get them," Freya said irritably. She had risked her life to get Eric and his men aboard *Varinga* alive, and now it seemed that Commander Dornen was having second thoughts.

"As you well know," Dornen said, unable to completely hide the condescension in his voice, "we made several attempts to do just that. Every time we jumped to a Concordat planet, however, we were met by a dozen Izarian warships, and we were forced to flee rather than be destroyed."

"And now you've been running for what, seven years?"

"Not running," said Dornen coldly. "Trying to locate one of the fringe worlds that the Concordat lost contact with during the Collapse."

"Yes," said Freya, "and how is that going?"

Dornen smiled, taking his eyes off the screen to meet Freya's stare. "Point taken. You know, we were on the verge of winning this war before the Izarians surprised us with upgraded hyperdrives. We had destroyed most of their fleet, and our intelligence indicated they were down to a few hundred heavy infantry units. Their production of new machines had crawled almost to a standstill. We were set to take Izar itself. Then Toronus happened and we've been running ever since, trying to find an army to finally put an end to this war. I am not convinced, however, that we wouldn't be better off continuing our search rather than entrusting the fate of humanity to this throng of barbarians."

"We had a deal," said Freya.

"I agreed to help you in your fight against your enemies, the Cho-ta'an, in exchange for you providing me with a group of individuals capable of executing a mechanized ground assault against the military headquarters on Izar. I think you can understand my doubts regarding the qualifications of these men."

O'Brien, who had been sitting with his arms folded and eyes closed, cleared his throat. His heavy eyelids lifted and he began to speak, his gravelly voice barely above a whisper. "The Vikings were... sorry, *are* the most feared warriors in the world," he said. "They never numbered more than a few tens of thousands, but they somehow managed to take over most of Europe. They crossed oceans before the compass and astrolabe were even invented, and they settled borderline uninhabitable lands like Iceland and Greenland. Are they dirty, uncouth and unfamiliar with advanced technology? Of course. But do you really think you're going to do better than this on some forgotten agrarian planet? Even if you find one of these fringe planets you talk about, without interstellar trade the colonists will most likely have regressed to the iron age or worse. They'll either have separated into warring tribes constantly at each other's throats or, worse, they'll have achieved a lasting peace and forgotten how to fight altogether. In other words, a platoon of mechanized Vikings *may be the best-case scenario.*"

Freya was heartened to see that despite O'Brien's frail appearance, he seemed to be in full possession of his mental faculties. He had spoken so little in the days since *Varinga* had picked him and Helena up from their home on the island of Bermuda that she wondered if he'd begun to succumb to dementia.

"What I don't understand," Dornen said, "is this: if I am to believe what Freya told me, you people built a *spaceship*. A rocket capable of reaching escape velocity and putting a human being into orbit. I realize that you kept this project secret, for reasons I don't fully comprehend, but even so, you must have had an educated workforce and technologically advanced infrastructure. So where is it? Where are these people? How is it that these illiterate savages are the best you can offer me?"

"The project was always intended to self-destruct shortly after launch," Helena. "Our goal was to leave zero footprint behind, because leaving anything behind that would alter the historical record would threaten the success of our project."

"The so-called 'LOKI principle.'"

"Exactly. The Limits Of Known Information. History resists being altered, so maximizing our chances of success meant leaving as little evidence behind as possible. We destroyed our primary site by detonating ten thousand gallons of liquid hydrogen."

"Additionally," said O'Brien, "shortly after we left Iceland, a volcano erupted, covering much of the island with lava and ash. A period of unusually cold weather, called the Little Ice Age, will eventually cause our primary site to be covered by glaciers, further concealing any evidence that remains. Our secondary site, a Caribbean island called…"

"Antillia," Helena whispered.

"Yes, Antillia," said O'Brien. "The island will soon be obliterated by a hurricane."

Dornen regarded the old man. "And you knew all this would happen—the volcano, the ice age, the hurricane—because you come from the future."

"That's right," said O'Brien matter-of-factly, as if he didn't care whether Dornen believed him or not.

If Dornen had intended to argue this point, he thought better of it. "Still, the people—"

"Most of the people who were involved in the *Iron Dragon* project are dead," Helena said. "Although only about four years passed for Freya, it's been eighteen years since the launch. Those who are still alive are scattered across Europe and a dozen islands in the Atlantic. Most were engineers or menial laborers, not warriors. The few warriors we had are too old to fight and probably wouldn't be interested in going to fight a race of aliens across the galaxy."

O'Brien went on, "Meanwhile, these men—Eric and his band—are battle-tested and itching for a fight. You don't know Earth history, but I can tell you that Eric Bloodaxe is a bona fide legend. They've been exiled from York and have nowhere else to go. If you want to defeat these Izarians, just point Eric and his men in their general direction."

Dornen sighed. "I'll give the matter some more thought. We'll meet again at this same time. In the meantime," he said with a glance at the screen, "try to keep your Vikings from tearing my ship to pieces."

Dornen got to his feet, and the others stood. "As you were," he said, and left the room. The door swished close behind him.

"They, ah, do look a little rough," O'Brien said, sinking back into his chair. The others sat as well. Several of the men, having failed to bash down the steel door holding them inside the mess hall, were trying to tear one of the bolted-down tables from the floor, evidently intending to use it as a battering ram.

"Perhaps you should have talked to them first," Helena said to Freya. "You know, suggested they be on their best behavior."

"I *did* talk to them," said Freya. "Understand that most of them think they've died and I've taken them to Valhalla. If they didn't fear death before, they certainly don't fear it now."

"I suppose I'd be upset too if I died and found out that the food in heaven is all in freeze-dried meal packets," said O'Brien.

"And no mead," said Helena. "Still, I fear we've oversold the Vikings to Dornen. 'A bona fide legend'?"

"He is!" O'Brien protested. "Or will be. Can never get my tenses right."

"From what you've told me, though, historians of your time actually knew very little about Eric."

"Well, you don't get the name 'Bloodaxe' by adopting stray kittens."

"I suppose not," said Helena. Freya kept quiet, deciding this probably wasn't the time to point out that the 'blood' in *Bloodaxe* meant 'kin.' Helena went on, "What happens if we can't convince Dornen to use Eric's men for his assault on Izar?"

Freya shrugged. "I suppose he'll leave us here and *Varinga* will continue looking for one of the so-called 'fringe planets' where they can raise an army from the native population."

"And what about the Cho-ta'an?"

"Dornen is sympathetic to our struggle, but it could take them years to find the army they're looking for. They may never find any of these lost colonies, and of course there's no guarantee they'll be victorious even if they do. If they don't win their war, then it's unlikely they'll come back to help us with ours."

"On the other hand," said O'Brien, "technically we're about twelve hundred years early to wage war on the Cho-ta'an. The first known Cho-ta'an attack on humans, the destruction of the scout ship *Ubuntu*, won't happen until 2125."

"We know it *will* happen, though," Helena said, "assuming the LOKI principle is correct. Known history can't be changed. Our goal was always to retrieve one of the planet-killer devices and find a way to deliver it to the IDL *after* the moment *Andrea Luhman* went back in time. We can't prevent the war, but we can win it."

"But if *Varinga* leaves without us," said Freya, "then we're back to square one. Everything we did, the whole *Iron Dragon* project, was for nothing. We're stuck on Earth with no way to defeat the Cho-ta'an."

"We could leave a time capsule," O'Brien said. "Bury a warning about the Cho-ta'an where we know it will be found a thousand years from now."

"A warning saying what, exactly?" Helena asked. "We can't prevent anything that's going to happen."

"Ah," said O'Brien sheepishly. "You're right, of course. If it were a matter of warning the people of the future about the Cho-ta'an, we could have saved ourselves a lot of trouble by burying a note under a rock rather than building a spaceship. I'm sorry, my mind isn't so sharp these days."

"Nor mine, love," said Helena. "We're both too old for this, and you've got the added confusion of time travel to deal with."

"Ah, it's not time travel but time itself that's the problem," O'Brien said. "Entropy. The degeneration of brain cells. I'm sorry, Freya. Forty years ago I might have been of more help."

"I'm not sure anyone can solve this problem," Freya said. "Maybe we were fools to try."

Helena shook her head. "I realize it's not particularly scientific," she said, "but I can't believe it was an accident that Dornen's people found you. The odds were against another ship coming across yours at all, and what are the chances that the people who found you would be at war with the very race that built the planet-killer device we're looking for?"

"It is strange," said O'Brien, "the way our fates seem to have converged. But then I still don't understand where these 'Truscans' came from."

"Neither do I," said Freya. "They're clearly descendants of Terrans, most likely a mix of people from the Middle East during the early Roman Empire, but they have no solid historical record of their origin. Some of their records seem to have been lost in a catastrophic breakdown in travel and communications they call 'the Collapse,' but it isn't clear they knew anything definite about Earth even before that. It's very strange. Somehow these people either developed hyperspace travel or were transplanted by some other, technologically advanced race."

"Maybe they were abducted by the Izarians as slave labor," O'Brien said, "and eventually they won their freedom. It would explain why they have so little information regarding their history, and also their current conflict with the Izarians."

"Could be," said Freya. "We just don't know, and I haven't been able to get much out of them."

"Surely they must be interested in learning about Earth, though," Helena said, "if this really is where they are from."

"I think they are," said Freya, "but they have more pressing problems at present. I think they are figuring the anthropology will have to wait until their war is over. Which could be a very long time, if they're going to insist on finding the perfect army."

"Pardon me if this is a silly question," O'Brien said. "But do we know for certain that Eric and his men are willing to fight the Izarians?"

"I haven't exactly asked," Freya said. "Just trying to explain who we are was challenge enough, and frankly I'm not sure how to tell someone that he's supposed to be dead."

"What if I talk to him?" Helena asked.

"Be my guest," said Freya, nearly overwhelmed with relief.

CHAPTER FOUR

Eric stood staring at the rows of identical metal contraptions, his mind trying to make sense of what he was seeing. They were roughly man-shaped, standing on two legs, with articulated arms hanging at their sides, but they were taller and broader than any man. "They are... machines?" he asked the old woman, who had come with him into the chamber where the things were stored.

"Think of it as armor," the woman said, "with weapons built into it." The woman, who called herself Helena, smiled, and waves of tiny wrinkles spread across her face. Her once-black hair had gone mostly gray and she stood with a slight stoop, but Eric could see that she must have been extraordinarily beautiful once. With her dark complexion and deep brown eyes she was no Norsewoman, but she spoke without a hint of an accent. Eric did not fully understand her relationship to Freya or the others on the sky ship, whom he'd only seen briefly. Clearly neither she nor Freya were members of the ship's crew, who wore strange burgundy uniforms and spoke no Norse. He knew that the sky people wanted him to fight for them, and he suspected Helena had been selected as the person most likely to be able to persuade him to join their cause.

Eric reached up, feeling the sleek metal surface of one the thing's arms. "No man could bear the weight of such armor," he said.

"The suit has many small machines built into it which allows it to act as an extension of your own body," Helena replied. "It moves with you."

"And these parts, mounted on the arms. They are weapons like the one the young woman, Freya, carried?"

"Machineguns, yes. But far more powerful than that model, and with a much greater supply of bullets. My understanding is that these tanks hold a liquid that is channeled into the gun, where it solidifies into a projectile to be launched at an enemy."

"You are not an expert on these 'mech suits,' then."

"No. The technology is nearly as foreign to me as it is to you."

"Why do those who built the machines, the sky people in the dark uniforms, not come to talk to me?"

"If you agree to fight for them, you will be given training by people who know more of the suits than I. I came to speak with you first because they do not know your language or your culture."

"And you do? You are no Norsewoman."

"I was born in Constantinople, but I lived among the People of the North for most of my life."

A man in a burgundy uniform, standing at the door a few paces behind him, cleared his throat.

"Come," Helena said. "We are making them nervous. It wasn't easy to convince the captain to let us down here."

"The captain is the one who looks like he's got a pole shoved up his ass?"

Helena laughed. "That's the one. Tertius Dornen. Come. My back hurts if I stand too long."

She turned and Eric followed her to the door. Eric glared at the uniformed man, who paled and shrank back toward the wall. The young man tapped at some device next to the door, and it swished open as if by magic. He hurried through the door down a narrow corridor, opened another door, and then stood by while Helena walked slowly down the corridor, with Eric following. At last they reached the room, which was empty except for a small table and two chairs. Eric helped Helena into one and then sat across from her in the other. Helena said something to the uniformed man that Eric didn't understand. The man seemed puzzled as well, and Helena repeated her request, making a motion as if she were bringing a cup to her lips. The man frowned, opened his mouth to say something, then thought better of it and left the room.

"I asked him to bring us some tea," Helena said. "The food on this ship is not very good, but they have passable tea."

"It will take more than tea to entice me to fight your war for you," Eric said.

"It is not my war," Helena said, "and I would not presume to offer the son of Harald Fairhair and rightful King of Northumbria payment, whether in tea or gold, to fight. Your reward will be the reward of all true warriors: fame and glory. Those who survive can expect to live well for the rest of their lives."

"But never again shall I be a king. Freya told me herself I would never be allowed to return to this world. You pay homage to my kingship with your words, but I am not deceived: you require not a king and his retinue, but a band of mercenaries. We will fight and perhaps die, and this Tertius Dornen will make himself a king or emperor on our backs."

"I don't believe that's Dornen's intention. He's a military officer with a mission. A mission he's been unable to fulfill because he has no soldiers."

"You say this is not your war, but you implore me to fight it. Why?"

"Because if you aid Dornen's people in his fight, he will assist my people in ours."

"Your enemies, they are the Jötunn of which Freya spoke?"

"The Cho-ta'an, yes. You know the story of Ragnarök, of course."

Eric guffawed. "Oh, is it the end of the world already? First my nursemaids tried to scare me with tales of Fenrir swallowing the sun, and then the Christian priests tried to frighten me with stories about plagues of locusts and rivers of blood. The end of the world comes when I lie still on the battlefield, an arrow through my heart."

Helena smiled. "I do not claim to be the herald of either Ragnarök or the Christian apocalypse. What I can tell you is that I have spoken to those who have seen with their own eyes the war that is to come. Millions will die. Entire worlds will be destroyed."

"The people who have seen this… they are seers?"

"You could think of them that way. They are people who experienced the war with their own eyes and came to us to warn us about it."

"But the war with the Jötunn has not begun?"

"No. That war will not begin for over a thousand years."

"Then why do you not destroy your enemies before it begins?"

Helena smiled. "Have you ever wondered, since the fate of the gods is spoken of so explicitly in stories, why the gods do not choose to act differently, in order to change the outcome?"

"It is said that even the gods cannot fight fate."

"Then why do they fight?"

"There is glory in fighting," said Eric, "even when there is no hope of victory."

"Yes," said Helena. "And defeat is always temporary. It is the unyielding spirit of men that allows them to survive to fight again. The gods are destroyed at Ragnarök, but afterwards, humanity is reborn."

"But it is not the Jötunn that Dornen's people fight."

"No. It is another race, called Izarians."

The uniformed man had returned with a tray, on which rested a small carafe and two cups. Eric sneered at the man as he set it on the table. The man reddened, clenched his jaw, and left the room.

Helena poured them each some of the tea. "Like you," she said, "I put little stock in ancient myths as guides for one's behavior. But sometimes the myths carry truths that clarify our place in the world. It is said that at Ragnarök, the sky will split in two, and two armies will come forth to destroy the world. One is the frost giants, the Jötunn. The other is the sons of Muspell, the lords of fire and flame. It is these that Dornen's people, the Truscans, fight."

"These other enemies, they are a race of giants, like the Jötunn?" Eric took a sip of the tea. It was similar to the teas from the east that he had sampled as King, but had a sweeter, richer flavor. It didn't make up for the complete lack of beer and wine, but he assumed the Truscans had stores of alcoholic beverages on board as well—they just hadn't seen fit to give Eric's men any. He downed the hot liquid, feeling the burn spreading through his chest, and poured himself another cup.

"The Izarians are said to resemble men," said Helena, "but I have never seen one. My understanding is that very few of the Truscans have ever seen one either."

"The Truscans fight an enemy they have not seen?"

"The Izarians send machines to fight for them. Machines like the mech suit I showed you, but with no man inside. They have mechanical brains that are in many ways superior to our own. Even their ships are mostly unmanned, operated by these mechanical brains."

"Perhaps there are no Izarians," Eric said. "Perhaps they died off a thousand years ago, leaving these machines behind."

"That could well be, for all I know. What I can tell you is that their machines seem intent on wiping out all of humanity, and they may very well be able to do it."

"How is it, then, that you prepare for a war a thousand years hence, when the fight against these Izarians goes on now?"

Helena sighed and took a sip of her tea. "It is very difficult to explain, and I do not fully understand it myself. At some point, humanity diverged into two different branches—us and the Truscans. The worlds the Truscans inhabit are so far away that we never even knew of each other's existence until a few days ago."

"When Freya's sky ship was intercepted by this one."

"That's right. We knew of the existence of the Izarians, but we did not know if any of them were still alive. In fact, a powerful artifact my people found in an abandoned Izarian temple was our best hope to defeat the Cho-ta'an."

"What sort of artifact? A weapon?"

"Yes. A powerful magical talisman. A talisman capable of destroying an entire world. But the talisman was itself destroyed, and now our only hope to defeat the Cho-ta'an is the Truscans. But the Truscans must first defeat the Izarians. Do you see?"

"I see that it is with good reason that the gods have denied us the ability to see the future as a matter of course. I do not see how one can prepare for a war a thousand years from now while fighting another."

"Believe me, you aren't the only one who is confused. Ultimately we must defeat both enemies, but the immediate threat is the Izarians. Freya made a deal to supply them with fighting men in exchange for their help against the Cho-ta'an."

"She offered us up to serve these Truscans before even speaking with us?"

"I don't know that she had you and your men in mind, specifically. But the timing of the Truscans' arrival on Earth was fortuitous, coming only a few days before your exile from York."

Eric swallowed another gulp of tea. "You mean you knew I would be driven out of York by Eadred's henchmen?"

"We did, yes. It's a matter of historical record, although we didn't know exactly when it would happen. We were almost too late."

"Meaning what?"

"Meaning that only the dead are summoned from Valhalla to fight at Ragnarök."

"I am not dead!" Tea splashed from his cup onto his beard and the table.

"According to history, you are. Eric Haraldson, called Eric Bloodaxe, born in the Christian year 885. Served briefly as the King of Norway before being overthrown by his half-brother Haakon, then briefly as King of Northumbria on two different occasions. At the end of the second, he was driven out of York by men loyal to the English King, Eadred. He soon received a letter of support from Osulf, the ruler of Northumbria, who claimed to be raising a force of men to return Eric to the throne. Eric and his men were ambushed at Stainmore Pass by a group of Northumbrians led by one Earl Maccus, and Eric was killed."

"Horseshit!" Eric snapped. "I am alive and well, along with the rest of my men, and this is no Valhalla! Let me off this damned sky ship, and I will show you how worthless your 'historical record' is!"

"You are free to go if you like," said Helena. "But understand this: the historical records of this time are incomplete, but we have a good understanding of the major historical events. Perhaps you did not die at Stainmore. Our records may be incorrect. What I can tell you, though, is that there is no mention of you in any historical documents after this year. In other words, perhaps you live for another forty years. Maybe you even return to the throne at York. If you do, however, your reign will be completely forgotten. Go if you like. Take your men south to York or sail to Norway. It makes no difference, because nothing you do will be remembered. You will gain no further fame nor fortune. No matter what you do, history will say you died in 954 *Anno Domini* at Stainmore Pass."

"Liar!" shouted Eric, getting to his feet. "Witch!" He threw his cup against the far wall, but the damned thing just bounced and rolled weakly across the floor. The last of his tea dribbled down the wall.

"Sit down!" Helena snapped, and for a moment the Norseman stared at her, trembling and red-faced, his fists clenched before him. Then, finding himself unable to strike an old woman, he sank again into his chair.

"Why?" he asked, his voice tinged with anguish. "Why did you save me if I am fated to live the rest of my life to no consequence. You should have left me to die!"

"You need to listen, Eric. Freya saved your life for a reason. The future of humanity itself is at stake. If you come with us, you can yet win the glory that was denied to you on Earth."

"What difference does it make? History will still say I died at Stainmore. This is but a cruel joke!"

"Yes, according to the historical record, you are dead. But it is said that history is written by the victors. What do you think Maccus will report to Osulf when he scours Yorkshire and can find no sign of you? That you are alive and well and traveling across the sky with people from another world in a wondrous metal ship? No, he will report that you are dead, because that is what Osulf and Eadred require of him. And a thousand years later, men will pore over the documents of this time and read that you died at Stainmore. That *cannot* be changed. But Eric, history doesn't end here. The end of the war with the Izarians and the

Cho-ta'an has not yet been written. So the question is: do you want to try for another chance at glory, or throw a tantrum like a child?"

"Woman, if you were a man, you'd be dead by now for speaking to me this way."

"I have no doubt. Do you see that little glass globe on the ceiling? It is like a magic window through which Tertius Dornen and his men can see and hear everything we do in here."

"I do not fear Dornen and his pink-faced men with soft hands and little dicks squeezed into tight-fitting black trousers," Eric growled, shaking his fists at the camera. "Let them come!" Eric could see that Helena was stifling a giggle, which only made him angrier.

"I'm not trying to scare you," she said, when she'd gotten control of herself. "My point is that you are being evaluated. Commander Dornen is not convinced your men are fit to face the Izarians. He thinks you are sloppy and undisciplined."

"Come in here and speak your insults to my face!" Eric shouted at the little globe. "I will show you sloppy and undisciplined!"

"This is what I'm talking about, Eric. The Truscans don't think they can trust you. Dornen thinks he can find more reliable warriors elsewhere. Men who can be trusted to follow orders."

"More men like the freshly shaven pup who brought us tea, no doubt," Eric said with a sneer. "If Dornen wants soft-spoken men with manners and fine clothing, then he would do well to look elsewhere. If he wants warriors who will fight men or giants to the death, with axe or 'machinegun' or our bare hands, if necessary, then he is a fool to pass us by."

"Then you will do it," Helena said.

Eric, fully realizing he had been manipulated but unwilling to retreat, said, "I will not be denied glory. If history considers me dead, then so be it. I will defeat these Izarians as a corpse, leading an army of wraiths!" In his mind, he pictured his men, dressed in 'mech suits,' marching across the golden fields of another world, their weapons vomiting steams of fire and metal that tore through the ranks of an army of giants.

"Good," said Helena. "But if this arrangement is to work, you and your men must be disciplined. Aboard this ship, Commander Dornen is in charge, and his men—even that kid who brought us tea—outrank you. If anybody in a burgundy uniform tells you to do something, you do it. No hesitation, no backtalk. I know you've commanded ships, so you understand. And I hope it goes without saying that if Commander Dornen agrees to put you and your men in those suits, you will follow orders rapidly and precisely. You will no longer be a band of Vikings out for plunder. You will be a precisely calibrated military machine. Is that understood?"

"My men have been on long voyages across the sea, in much tighter quarters and worse conditions than this. They will do as I tell them."

"And you?"

"I will do what must be done to vanquish our common enemy. I will not bow to this Commander Dornen, but I will follow orders if that is what it takes to defeat the Izarians."

CHAPTER FIVE

"Not very reassuring," said Dornen. He had asked Helena to speak with him in his quarters, and they had just finished watching the recording of her conversation with Eric.

"I did what I could," said Helena.

"From my perspective, it looked like mostly what you did is manipulate Eric into agreeing to fight for us, enticing him with ideas of fame and glory."

"You would prefer I had sold him on the idea of Eric Bloodaxe, Savior of Humanity? Even if I succeeded, I think you'd regret encouraging him to think of himself as some kind of messiah. In any case, I doubt it would have worked. In my experience, the Norsemen are simple people. Their heroes are characterized by bravery, loyalty, honor, and competence in battle. Eric may have formally converted to Christianity, but he remains the son of a Norse chieftain at heart. He doesn't want to save humanity, he wants to beat the shit out of monsters and look good doing it. What does it matter, as long as he's willing to fight?"

"It matters," said Dornen, "because I don't want Eric getting some nutty idea like establishing a Viking fiefdom on some alien planet."

"They can't do much without a ship and people to fly it," Helena said. "You're their transportation."

"If we put them in those suits, that gives them a hell of a lot of power. If they turn on us—"

"You've got bigger problems to worry about."

"That's always the trump card, isn't it? Putting fifty bloodthirsty Vikings in mech suits is sheer insanity, but not doing it is worse. Unless, of course, we can still make contact with one of the fringe planets."

"And waste how many more years, with no guarantee of success? I'm starting to think you're trying to back out of the deal you made with Freya."

"I'm not 'backing out' of anything. I've got 800 mech suits. Freya promised me men to fill them. She delivered fifty. Putting aside the matter of their disposition and competence, it's not enough men to take the Izarian headquarters."

"There are plenty more Vikings. Give Eric and his men a few weeks to prove themselves. Take them to someplace remote. Greenland, maybe. Put them in the suits and load them with non-lethal ammunition. Give them some training and see how they do. If they work out, we can recruit more men. If not, leave them here and continue your search."

"I suppose we can spare a few weeks. Maybe your Vikings will surprise me. And what about you? Can we count on your help keeping Eric from going rogue or throwing a tantrum and tearing my ship apart?"

"I'm afraid not," Helena said. "My husband's health is not good, and there are matters that must be attended to at home."

"On the island you call Bermuda."

"Yes. We have a small community there, mostly made up of former *Iron Dragon* engineers. We get by raising our own food and trading with the native tribes, but it isn't easy to survive using only bronze age technology."

"You still live under the threat of your so-called LOKI principle? The idea that if you make waves, some personified force of history will wipe you out?"

"We rarely think about it in such terms, these days. Our motivations in keeping a low profile are simpler: technology creates wealth, wealth causes envy, and envy brings violence. Maybe we could smelt iron or create antibiotics without anybody noticing, but where do you draw the line? Eventually your neighbors notice that your tools are better than theirs, you live longer than they do, and your houses are more comfortable. So you've got to wall yourself off from the rest of the world, which only attracts more attention. I spent fifty years in an isolated community, trying to keep knowledge from getting out, and it's not an enjoyable way to live. Better to accept the possibility of going hungry or getting sick than to live in constant fear of one's neighbors."

"Even so, we have excellent medical facilities aboard the ship. If your husband would consent to a full body scan, we could have the medbot customize a pharmaceutical regimen for him. We could give you a twenty-year supply. No one would need to know. You would almost certainly benefit as well."

"No. Thank you, Commander, but there is nothing wrong with me or my husband but old age. We are both in our nineties, which is well over double the life expectancy of this time in Earth's history. The only treatment we need is to go home, to our animals and our garden."

"Very well. The offer remains open, if you change your mind. When did you wish to return to Bermuda?"

"As soon as is convenient for you, Commander."

"Well, frankly, the less time Eric's men are cooped up on my ship, the better. We need to find a place to set down where Eric's men can try out the mech suits. Somewhere they won't draw attention. Perhaps this 'Greenland' you mentioned. We can land in Bermuda and then continue on our way."

"That sounds fine, Commander. Thank you. And good luck."

*****

While O'Brien tended to his tomatoes and cucumbers, Freya walked with Helena around the perimeter of the community garden. The garden was ringed by a dozen small houses—many of them no more than huts—in which lived other alumni of the *Iron Dragon* project. A pleasant breeze carried the sounds of children playing in the nearby fields while women prepared food indoors or sat outside in the shade, sewing garments or repairing farming implements. Chickens ran freely about the garden, and a score of pigs lazed about in a nearby pen. Some of the men were busy harvesting grapefruit from a stand of citrus trees opposite the pig pen; Freya understood that several others were harvesting lumber in the woods to the north.

"You're certain you won't reconsider?" Freya asked, as a flock of swallows exploded from an orange tree only to regroup and settle on another.

"I'm sorry, child," Helena said. Her small hand rested on Freya's forearm as they walked. "I'm afraid O'Brien and I have had our share of excitement." Helena always referred to her husband by his last name, as she had when they first met. "We'd just be in the way, in any event. Our place is here."

"I suppose it won't do any good to remind you that the fate of humanity is at stake."

Helena chuckled. "The fate of humanity has been at stake for most of my life. O'Brien and I, along with your grandparents and the others, spent fifty years on a project that most would have considered impossible. We did our part."

"So did I."

"I know, child. You've suffered more than most, and it isn't fair to expect more from you, but you are still young, and the war is not yet over."

"The war O'Brien and my grandmother fought in won't even start for another twelve hundred years."

"Then you've got a head start!" Helena said with a weak smile. "I'm sorry, Freya. I wish there were someone else to take your burden, but there isn't. There are only a few of us here on the island, and most of us are too old to be of any use in a war. Even the ones from your generation are twelve years older than you now, and they've all got families who depend on them. We barely scrape by as it is; we can't afford to lose any able-bodied men or women."

"Even if it means humanity itself is doomed?"

Helena sighed. "Look around you, Freya. These people are farmers. Fifteen years ago they were engineers, welders, or carpenters. Most have never picked up a sword, to say nothing of a machinegun. We're a peaceful settlement. Anyone with an interest in fighting left years ago."

Freya watched as the swallows burst into the sky again and retreated into the distance, ultimately disappearing into the pines to the north. "I know, Helena. I just wish…"

"You weren't all alone. I understand. I got a taste of that sort of loneliness when I left Constantinople to join a bunch of Vikings led by spacemen from the future who were trying to build a spaceship. But I don't pretend to know what it's like to spend four years alone in a ship not much bigger than our house. And then, after all that, to be responsible for brokering a deal between Eric's men and the Truscans, to try to bring an end to a war that hasn't even started yet…. It's too much for any one person to bear."

"I will see it through," said Freya. "I have to."

"Do you?" asked Helena. "It seems to me that you and I have done what we could. Ultimately, whether Dornen and Eric can manage to work together—and whether the Truscans will help us against the Cho-ta'an—is out of our hands. You've done your part as well, Freya. Why not stay here with us? It's not an easy life, but at least you wouldn't be alone."

Freya closed her eyes and turned away, willing away tears. Ever since she had returned to Earth, the thought of settling down and living a normal life with her own people had lurked at the back of her mind. She had been telling herself that it wasn't an option because if she failed to deliver an army to the Truscans, then the entire *Iron Dragon* project was for nothing. But there was another, deeper, reason: the fact was, these weren't her people anymore, if they ever were. She'd spent four years alone in deep space, not knowing how long her voyage would last or whether it was all for nothing. Even Helena, who was trying so hard to understand, would never know what that was like. Helena and O'Brien were like family to her, but seeing the connection they had with each other pained her. And within a few years, O'Brien would die, and then Helena, and then she would truly be alone. She thought she would rather be back on the Cho-ta'an ship than to live among these people without Helena or O'Brien.

"No," she said. "Thank you, but I can't. When I stepped out of the lander and saw that you and O'Brien were still alive… well, I suppose this isn't saying much, but that was the happiest moment of my life. Happier even than the moment Commander

Dornen brought me aboard *Varinga*. Up until the moment I saw you, it all seemed like a dream. When I saw you two, I knew it was real. And this may sound strange, but… I want to hold onto that moment. I think I can survive anything if I can just hold onto that."

Helena embraced her, and Freya felt tears running down her face despite her best efforts. "I understand," said Helena.

But she didn't.

CHAPTER SIX

Eric Bloodaxe, clad in a mech suit's armor, bounded down a steep, snow-covered slope on powerful mechanical legs, a score of iron giants following close behind. A week earlier, they had struggled to control the machines, often falling on their faces while growling a stream of curses, but now the suits were like a second skin. They moved through the deep drifts faster than any man could run, churning up a wake of powder that settled on their fallen comrades, lying still in the snow, entombed in their own armor.

Eric had lost over half his men already, but they had brought down at least as many of their adversaries, and now they had the enemy on the run. The robot tanks, rolling down the hillside on their metal treads, were faster and better suited to the terrain, but Eric had concluded their mechanical brains lacked imagination. Determined to keep the Vikings from taking a strategically important ridge, the enemy had harassed Eric's men with a small contingent of flying machines while leaving the tanks to guard the ridge. The fliers were quick but relatively fragile; a single well-aimed burst from a mech suit's machineguns would take one down.

Forcing himself to remain patient, Eric had instructed his men to stand their ground and direct their fire at the fliers until they'd been eliminated, rather than attempting to take the ridge in a rapid forward charge. It had been a risky and costly decision, resulting in the deaths of several of his men, but it had been the right move. Once the last flier had fallen, Eric split his force into three squads to assault the ridge from three different directions. Their coordination had been near-perfect: the tanks, although they outnumbered the Norsemen, were forced to fight on three fronts at once. By the time Eric's men converged at the top of the ridge, the eight remaining tanks were fleeing at top speed down the northeastern slope, their cannons firing haphazardly up the slope behind them.

Eric had left one squad on the ridge while he and the rest of his men pursued the tanks. They had already won the battle, but it wasn't the Viking way to let enemies run away. Not killing them now meant having to deal with them again later. Fear had always been a great ally of the Vikings; men who killed without reason or mercy projected power far beyond the battlefield.

Gulbrand, to Eric's left, fell with a howl as one of the tank's scored a lucky shot. Gulbrand tumbled down the slope, the suit's robotic limbs kicking up a blinding storm of powder. "Switch to infrared!" he shouted, but he was too late to save the man behind Gulbrand, who misjudged the slope ahead of him and fell as well, skidding on his belly some fifty yards before slamming into a boulder. Eric and the others pressed on. The tanks were moving fast, putting distance between them and the Norsemen, but Eric, having studied the terrain, knew that the tanks were heading toward a crevasse they couldn't possibly leap over. Even if they had some capability he was unaware of that would allow them to cross the chasm, he was certain they would have to slow significantly to do it. Eric's men would advance within close range and finish them off.

Before the tanks reached the crevasse, two more men had fallen, including Eric's brother, Ragnald. Still Eric pressed on, half-running, half-falling down the hillside. With each step, he slid close to twenty feet in the snow, but the suit's gyros kicked in, keeping him upright. He let out an exultant roar, which was echoed by the men bounding through the snow on the left and right of him. Eric had had his doubts about the mech suits, thinking they would interfere with the primal immediacy of battle, but he found that he'd been wrong: with the suit, he was stronger, faster, more deadly. He rained death from his fingertips. It was good to fight with an axe or a spear, but it was better to fight with a two-ton suit of armor equipped with two .50 caliber machineguns that could unload twenty rounds a second.

The first of the tanks had begun to slow, swerving to the right to follow the edge of the crevasse to the southeast. Another, to its left, tried the same maneuver but turned too quickly, sliding sideways along the surface until it vanished into the crevasse. The other tanks made the corner, but only by slowing greatly. Eric's men skidded through the turn and followed, closing the gap. Eric grinned. The terrain roughened ahead, which would give the bipedal mech suits an advantage over the tanks.

Sure enough, the tanks began to slow again. Merging into single file, they swerved wildly to avoid a series of boulders. But there was no avoiding the mile-long patch of rocky ground that lay beyond. The tanks slowed to a crawl as they spread out again and made their way over and around the rocks.

"Halt!" Eric shouted, as he neared the boulders—unnecessarily, as his voice would be transmitted automatically to the helmet radios of the other Norsemen. "Take cover and blast them to Hel!"

The Norsemen skidded to a halt behind the boulders and one by one leveled their guns at the fleeing tanks. The tanks, still trundling onward, fired their cannons toward the Vikings, blasting rocks to pieces and kicking up bursts of powder. Eric's men responded with a barrage of machinegun fire. One of Eric's men, still in the open, was felled by a cannon blast as he tried to get to cover. Another man, who had lost his footing and slid headfirst into a boulder, lay unmoving to Eric's right.

The tank nearest to them exploded as its fuel tank ruptured. Another had struck a boulder at a bad angle and flipped over; it lay on its back, treads spinning impotently. The tanks' vitals were well-protected, but they couldn't stand up to a sustained barrage of armor-piercing rounds. Three more tanks were quickly incapacitated, and the remaining two crawled away, making little headway through the boulders littering their path. Eric heard someone shouting in his ear, but he couldn't make out the message over the noise of gunfire and explosions. Whatever it was would have to wait. His men were on the verge of obliterating the enemy.

He straightened, the mech suit rising to its full height of nearly ten feet, and vaulted over the boulder in front of him. "Now to finish them!" he roared, and his men followed him. The ground erupted in a blast of rock and snow as a shell struck nearby, but Eric was not cowed. He bounded forward, leaping over rocks and weaving to the left of right as the last two tanks tried to get a bead on him. He slid behind another boulder, and men took cover to his left and right. His heads-up display, showing an overhead view of the area, told him that they had the tanks nearly surrounded. They let loose another barrage, and the tanks ground to a halt. One continued firing for a while before finally exploding, showering Eric's men with chunks of metal and flaming debris. Eric's heads-up display told him the last remaining tank was effectively dead, its mechanical brain showing no sign of activity. Eric's men, exulting in their victory, continued to pound the thing with their guns until it was an unrecognizable pile of wreckage. When they finally stopped, their guns empty, Bjorn stomped forward, took hold of the machine's chassis, and hurled it into the crevasse. The men erupted into a chorus of victory cries.

As the noise faded, Eric again became aware of shouting in his ear. "...forced to retreat!" he heard the voice say. He recognized it now as Halfdan, the leader of the team he'd left to hold the ridge. A few of the men began to sing, and Eric growled at them to be quiet. "...coming your way!" Halfdan was saying.

"Say again, Halfdan," Eric said. "What's coming our way?"

"Fliers!" Halfdan said. "They must have held back a group of them. We couldn't hold the ridge. They've been circling overhead but they just flew east. Looks like they're headed right for—"

Halfdan's voice was drowned out by the sound of machinegun fire. Bjorn fell, and then Baldur. Three more men had fallen before Eric spotted the six fliers, now soaring silently overhead, at a height of maybe three hundred yards. They flew eastward and then split into two groups of three, one banking left and the other right. Some of the men took aim, but Eric shouted at them to take cover. In a few seconds, the fliers would come back around, and Eric's men were standing in the open. The Norsemen scrambled for cover, some of them colliding in their haste. Eric heard machinegun fire again, and a row of bullets struck the ground to his left, throwing up blinding tufts of snow.

Relying on the infrared, Eric sprinted out of the way and dove behind a boulder. The fliers shot past, still firing, and suddenly he was exposed again. He scrambled around the other side of the boulder, but realized too late that the two groups had staggered their attack: the other three were now flying right toward his position, their guns blazing. Furious, Eric got to his feet and unloaded his guns in the direction of the fliers. The few men with ammunition left who were still standing did the same. One of them winged the flier on the far left, causing it to wobble and then dive into the crevasse. But the others kept on firing, and men fell to Eric's left and right, until he was the last still on his feet. Eric let out a defiant howl as his suit seized up and toppled over, trapping him inside.

*****

"That's a fail," said Commander Dornen, watching as the holographic tanks dissolved on the screen.

"I'm unlocking the suits," said Dr. Thaddeus Bartol, who was in charge of the Vikings' training. Bartol was a diminutive man with curly, dark hair and deep-set, intelligent eyes. "Safe mode with no weapons." He touched a button on the console before him. "All trainees, return to *Varinga* at once," he said. "We're dispatching a medbot to deal with the wounded. If your suit is reporting a serious injury, remain where you are unless you are in immediate danger."

"How many actual wounded?" asked Dornen.

"Four seriously. A concussion, a broken arm and two with severe burns. No actual fatalities this time." Three men had died in previous training exercises—actually died, not just had their suits deactivated by the simulation software—mostly due to their own carelessness.

"Small victories."

"You have to admit," said Freya, "their performance was impressive."

"Effective hits per shots fired, seven percent," said Bartol.

"All right, but if you subtract their celebration toward the end—"

"Mech suits lost, fifty out of fifty. Fatalities, twenty-one. Major injuries, eighteen. The simulation projects five more fatalities would occur if medbots were more than twenty minutes out. Primary objective failed."

"They did hold the ridge for—"

"Three minutes, four point six seconds. If this were an actual mission, it would be classified as a catastrophic failure. Rarely have I seen such a complete failure in every success metric. It's extraordinary."

Freya wished more than anything that Helena were here to help her deal with this fiasco. "With respect, Doctor," Freya said, "your metrics don't reflect real-world conditions. What is the typical pass rate for a platoon this size facing such an enemy force?"

"It isn't merely the fact that Eric's men failed to achieve the overall objective," Bartol said. "They acted recklessly. Wasted ammunition. Allowed themselves to be drawn away from the ridge by an obvious ruse. Communicated poorly. Lost track of a group of fliers, even though a glance at their heads-up display would have told them—"

"We get it, Bartol," Commander Dornen said. I'd like to know as well, though: what *is* the typical pass rate for such a scenario?"

"Well, it's difficult to make a direct comparison. CDF marine platoons are somewhat smaller, and the terrain here in Greenland is different from the worlds where we generally conducted training in the past."

"I'm just looking for a rough idea, Doctor," Dornen said tiredly.

"Around twenty percent."

Freya seized on the opening. "Of the platoons that failed, how many were able to hold the ridge for any amount of time?"

Bartol frowned. "I don't have an exact number. Nearly all the platoons who took the ridge managed to hold it until the clock ran out, which only demonstrates further that the lack of discipline—"

"What you're saying," said Freya, cutting him off, "is that nearly four out of five platoons of highly trained CDF marines failed to do what a band of Vikings with three weeks of mech training were able to do."

"Again, it's not a fair comparison—"

"If it's not a fair comparison, then by what standard can you say Eric's men failed?"

"You can't be serious. Beyond the objectively terrible metrics, the complete lack of discipline and poor use of readily available tactical information—"

"All right, that's enough," said Dornen. "The fact is, if this were a real-world situation, Eric's men would have failed."

"But we don't need them to take some random ridge," Freya protested. "This is an all-out war for survival, and the Norsemen—"

"Enough!" Dornen snapped. "I've heard as much as I care to about your legendary Norsemen and their exploits across the known world. The question isn't whether Eric's men can fight; it's whether they can be controlled. Judging from the results of this exercise and those of the past week, as well as the holosims before that, they cannot. Tonight is the last night those stinking barbarians will sully the corridors of this ship. We will continue on our mission to find a fringe world with a population that can supply us with a more suitable army. Freya, I will leave it to you to inform Eric and determine what is to be done with them. We can leave them here if they like, or return them to Northumbria. I imagine Earth history will work itself out one way or another. I'm going to my quarters. Don't disturb me unless something's on fire."

*****

"The Truscans deserve to lose this war," Eric said, "with eunuchs like Dornen leading them."

"Helena did try to warn you," Freya said.

Eric shrugged. "We are Norsemen," he said. "We fight for glory and for power, not to take ridges and flags. If Dornen wants the Izarians' flag, he can take it himself."

"What will you do now? Try to retake the throne of Northumbria?"

Eric shook his head. "Not unless Dornen plans to let us keep the mech suits."

"Surely you haven't forgotten how to fight with a sword already."

"That isn't something one forgets. I am afraid, though, that fighting with axes and swords will feel like a child's game after having known the power of the mech suits. And perhaps I have come to accept that Helena spoke the truth when she said that I was destined never again to be King. My allies are few, and my own men will hardly be content to be court henchmen after doing battle with ghost machines across the plains of Greenland. I think I may lead an expedition across the sea to Vinland."

"It is a relatively short voyage from here."

"Ah, but I have no ships, and there are no trees here to speak of. No, tell Dornen to take us back to where he found us, and we shall forge our own fate without the help of sky ships and men from other worlds. You say history considers me dead. Well, then, we shall see what mischief a dead man can make. And you? Shall you return to your people?"

"I have no people," Freya said. "Commander Dornen said I am welcome to remain on *Varinga*, and I may as well take him up on the offer. Perhaps I can still be of some use. If nothing else, my presence will serve as a reminder that humanity faces another enemy besides the Izarians."

*****

The next morning, *Varinga* lifted off the snowy plain, rising some ten kilometers above the surface and then heading southeast on a course that would bring it back to Yorkshire. Less than two hours later, she set down in the same valley she had left a month earlier. Eric's men, who had been restricted to a single deck on the ship where they'd had minimal contact with the *Varinga*'s crew, were informed by Commander Dornen via the ship's intercom that they were to leave the ship immediately. To his credit, Dornen, flanked by two senior officers, met all the

Norsemen personally as they left the ship—although Freya suspect this was mostly to ensure that the Vikings didn't make off with any valuables. To the Vikings' credit, they stole only things that could be easily hidden in their clothing.

"Where will you go from here?" asked Freya.

"To Middlesbrough. I still have two ships there. We will voyage to Vinland."

"You don't intend to return to Ripon?"

Eric grinned. "One of the benefits of being dead is the severing of certain inconvenient familial ties. Gunnhild will get by without me." Freya did not press the matter; Eric's wife was said to be very beautiful, but Freya gathered from other remarks Eric had made that their relationship had become strained. The men who had been on their way to Bamburgh were his core group of henchmen, who were either unmarried or accustomed to being away from their wives for months at a time. Those with closer familial ties had remained in Ripon.

"The other men feel the same way?"

"Some would like to return, but if any of us returns, it will raise uncomfortable questions about the rest. We will seek our fate across the sea."

"You will walk to Middlesbrough?"

"We have little choice, as our horses have fled. It is all right. It is less than two days' walk."

Freya nodded.

"You wish to ask me something. Go ahead. You have earned the right."

"Is it true? How you got your name?"

"By killing three of my brothers? Yes. It was not murder, though. Most brothers are not as loyal as Ragnald. They plotted against me. I acted to put an end to the plots. And it was all for naught, as Haakon outmaneuvered me while I was dealing with the others. They call him Haakon the Good, and I am Eric Bloodaxe. As Helena told me, history is written by the victors."

"There is glory in fighting, even when you cannot win. I wish you good luck in your voyage, Eric."

"And the same to you. You are a formidable warrior, Freya. Perhaps we shall yet meet at Ragnarök."

CHAPTER SEVEN

Darius Aquiba sat in front of a bank of monitors in a small room with no windows, trying to work up the motivation to go into the next room to pour himself another cup of coffee. On one hand, he had only forty minutes left on his shift. On the other hand, if Major Sadona caught him sleeping at his post again, he'd be kicked back down to corporal. Not that rank mattered much at Janthus station; there was only so much work to do and only so many people to do it. Still, being demoted would mean Jusef would outrank him, and that meant Darius would get stuck cleaning the solar panels again.

These days, Darius spent most of his days like this—staring at the monitors, waiting for the chime that indicated a deep space probe had returned. The chime would be followed by a burst of text across one of the screens—a status report on the system from which the probe had just returned. Darius would note any anomalies, make sure the report was properly categorized and flagged, and then run a diagnostic to make sure the probe was ready to be sent out again. It was tedious, but not difficult. The job had been more interesting at the beginning of the war, when there was always a probe either about to launch or about to return. Hyperspace-enabled probes were problem-prone and difficult to maintain, though, and with the destruction of most of the CDF's fleet, cargo ships carrying replacement parts couldn't get through. The Janthus station now only had one probe left, which was in constant service, jumping back and forth between the station and the six inhabited systems within a ten light year radius. The idea was that if the Izarians attacked any of the planets within this area, the probe would report this information to the station, which could then alert the other systems that the Izarians were nearby.

"Nearby" was, of course, a relative term. A hyperspace drive reduced the distance between origin and destination by a factor of about ten thousand—such a stark increase that when hyperspace gates were first invented, it was generally believed that travel between them was instantaneous. When dealing with distances of more than a few light years, though, travel times remained an important tactical factor. If the Izarians attacked one planet, there was a good chance those ships would soon target another planet in the vicinity. If the probe returned bearing news of an attack, the station's technicians could send it out to the nearby planets with a warning, giving them anywhere from a few minutes to a few days to prepare. It wasn't clear to Darius exactly what the people of those planets would do with that time. He supposed at least some of them had shelters that would provide some degree of protection from orbital bombardment, but they had minimal ground-to-space defenses. The CDF certainly wasn't going to send anybody to help: they had exactly one deep space warship left, and it was an Orbital Deployment Cruiser without any troops to deploy. In any case, it was several hundred light years away. Darius, like everybody else at Janthus Station, knew the truth even if he didn't speak it aloud: the war with the Izarians was over. The only question now was whether the station personnel would die quickly and painlessly in a nuclear blast or slowly and unpleasantly, from starvation. Still, they did their jobs, because you had to do something.

Darius had just made up his mind to refill his coffee cup when he heard the familiar chime. Sooner than he'd expected, but lately the probe's self-diagnostic had been raising false positives, causing it to return early. Maybe it was as bored with its job as Darius was with his. Or maybe they weren't false positives at all, and there was something seriously wrong with the probe. Darius wondered what the Major would have them do when the last probe finally gave up the ghost. What would ten people manning a remote observation station do when they no longer had any way of observing anything?

Darius shelved the question as the probe's report came up on the monitor. He knew immediately that something was wrong. So wrong, in fact, that his first inclination was to suspect somebody was playing a joke on him. "Hey, Jusef!" he shouted. "Not funny!" When there was no reply, he tried again. "You'd better fix this or I'm going to flag this report to the Major and submit it as-is. We'll see how funny you think it is then. Don't think I won't do it!"

Still there was no reply. Darius scanned the report. There was no way it was real. None of it made any sense. The only way you could get results like this was....

"Jusef, damn it!"

Still no reply. A sick feeling began to grow in Darius's gut. He scrolled down, skimming the log file. It looked real. All the timestamps seemed right. Jusef wasn't very bright. If he'd dummied up a report, he'd have copied the log from an old report or just wrote "Darius is a sheepfucker" a hundred times. He ran the checksum algorithm on the report, and it came back genuine.

"Oh God," he said. "Oh my God." He tapped Major Sadona's extension on the comm panel.

"Damn it, Corporal," said Sadona's voice after a moment. He sounded as if he'd just woken up. "This had better be important."

"I think it is, sir." He glanced at the report again. "It is. Definitely."

Sadona must have heard the worry in his voice. "I'll be right there."

Less than five minutes later, Major Sadona, his eyes foggy from sleep, stood looking over Darius's shoulder. Sadona, only three years older than Darius, was a short man with an unusually round face who combed his hair forward in the time-honored and futile way of hiding a receding hairline. His prominent belly pressed against the back of Darius's chair. "What in the shit is this fuckery?" Sadona demanded.

"Report from Tabor," sir. "I thought it was a hoax, but the checksum is good."

"Sensors must be on the fritz."

"All of them, sir? I ran a diagnostic, and everything checks out."

"Run it again."

"Yes, sir."

Darius tapped a key, executing the diagnostic script. The results came up instantly on a monitor to his right. Everything was nominal.

"Have you got photos?"

"Um. I think so, sir. Sorry, I forgot to check."

"Well, bring them up. Maybe we can figure out why this damned probe seems to think...." He trailed off as Darius put the photos of Tabor's surface on one of the monitors. "What in the hell is this?" he demanded. The screen held twenty nearly identical photos. They showed the surface of the dark side of Tabor; the probe had emerged from hyperspace on the opposite side of the planet from the sun. No lights were visible on the surface.

The Major leaned forward and tapped on one of the photos, enlarging it to fill the screen. Still no lights could be seen. It was as if the whole planet had lost power.

"An EMP?" Darius suggested.

"Maybe, but... what are those striations?" He tapped on the photo to enlarge a section. "Look, they start here and spread out across the whole surface. At least, what we can see of the surface. It's like a bomb went off. But what kind of bomb...." He brought the image to maximum enlargement. "My God."

Darius stared at the image in horror. "I thought the Izarians were still two years away," he said, not wanting to believe what they both knew was true.

"That was our best guess," Sadona said quietly, his voice quavering, "based on the available intelligence. It seems we were wrong. They did it. The bastards did it. And they might have a hundred more of them, for all we know."

"What do we do, sir? The probe looks like she's good to go. If we send her back out, maybe we can warn a few of the other planets. Severus, maybe, and Jabesh-Gilead."

"What good will it do? They have no hyperdrive-equipped ships, and there's no defense against a weapon like that."

"There's got to be something we can do, sir. Maybe somebody at Supreme Command will have an idea."

"You think the probe can make the trip?"

"I'd say so, sir. A few of her nonessential systems have been glitching, but forty light years through hyperspace should be doable."

Major Sadona rubbed his chin, his eyes darting around anxiously as if he expected to find a more senior officer to tell him what to do. Sadona had been a captain before being put in charge of the Janthus station; the promotion had been intended as partial compensation for such a godawful assignment.

"All right," he said, seeming to make up his mind. "We'll send the probe to Toronus. Let those jackasses at Supreme Command worry about it."

"Yes, sir," said Darius. "Only...."

"What is it, Corporal?"

"It's just... how do we know Toronus hasn't been destroyed too?"

The Major opened his mouth as if to berate Darius, then slowly closed it. "My God," he said. "You're right, Aquiba." Darius watched as the implications of what they had seen sank into Major Sadona's brain: they had no reason to think Tabor was the first world to suffer the effects of the Izarians' new weapon. In all likelihood, they had struck several other, more strategically important, planets. For all Darius knew, the few planets near Janthus Observation Station were all that were left of the Concordat. "But then... there's no one to tell."

"Well, sir, we don't know Toronus is gone."

"It's gone, Aquiba. It's all gone. They probably started at Toronus and then destroyed Levitus and Barzilai, then worked their way across the Ilian Cluster. We're all that's left. This damn station and five planets. Hell, maybe less than that. It's been three days since the probe last reported on Helon. Maybe they started there and moved on to Tabor. If they've got enough of those bombs, or whatever they are, they could annihilate every planet in this sector within a few weeks."

Darius could see that the Major was on the verge of panic. He did not handle crises well; a week earlier he had nearly had a breakdown over a pea-sized meteorite that had torn a small hole in one of the storage lockers, rendering part of the station unusable while the hole was repaired. The current problem was many orders of magnitude more grave, and Darius thought the Major might shut down altogether.

"There's got to be something we can do," Darius said, anxious to reassure Sadona.

"No, no," the Major said, getting to his feet. "This is it, Aquiba. The end of it all. That damned probe is all we have, and it's worse than useless at this point. Why warn people about a cataclysm they can't do anything about? Hell, I wish I didn't know. In fact, I think I'm going to go to my quarters and drink until I don't remember any of this. And if, God forbid, I wake up tomorrow, I'm going to do it again. Send the probe to Toronus if you want to. Send it into the black hole at the center of the galaxy. Send it a thousand light years into deep space. I don't care." He left the room, letting the door slide shut behind him.

Once again alone at his station, Darius wondered if it was true. Was the little group of planets clustered around Janthus the last refuge of humanity? If it were true, then the Major was right: there was nothing any of them could do. The CDF was finished. Unless the rumors of inhabited fringe planets were true, humanity itself would be exterminated.

No, he thought. The CDF still had one warship left, two hundred light years away. Could the probe survive a two hundred light year voyage through hyperspace? Even if it did, would the crew of *Varinga* be able to make any use of the information? Weren't they as impotent as the rest of humanity?

On the other hand, there was nothing to lose by trying to contact them. It was the longest of long shots, but maybe *Varinga* could still do something about the Izarians. Using the Major's password ("majorsadona"), which he had guessed a week earlier while trying to edit his personnel record, he retrieved the last known coordinates and trajectory of *Varinga*. The data was five weeks old, but as long as *Varinga* hadn't made a hyperspace jump since the last probe contact, he could guess their current location with reasonable accuracy. He typed up a brief message and ran the batch of commands that would prepare the probe to reenter hyperspace.

CHAPTER EIGHT

Eric Bloodaxe stood on the deck of the longship *Skjótrmarr*, half in a daze from exhaustion. The ship groaned and pitched beneath him, and the wind tore at his clothes and threw sheets of rain at him. The storm had raged since before dusk, and now the night was half gone. A flash of lightning revealed a bucket full of water before him. Eric bent to take hold of it and then turned to hand it to Gulbrand, standing next to him, who would empty it over the gunwale, but the bucket slipped from Eric's cold-numbed fingers and fell to the deck. Eric caught a glimpse of it rolling away from him before the lightning faded, leaving them in darkness. He growled a curse, but his voice was lost in the thunder. He moved to fetch it, but his fatigued muscles betrayed him. Gulbrand caught him with an outstretched arm that was as steady as an oak bough.

"You need to rest!" Gulbrand shouted in his ear. Eric knew it was true, but he refused to cower huddled against the gunwale while his ship was in danger of being swamped.

"It's no use!" cried Bjorn from the hold below. "She's filling up too fast. The ship is lost!" As lightning flickered in the distance, Eric saw that Bjorn was now standing halfway up the ladder. Even so, the water was up to his knees. Bjorn, a stocky man with pale blond hair, was nearly as tall as Eric. They had started out with six men bailing—two in the hold, two to lift the buckets to the deck, and two to empty them—but with water filling half the hold, they were down to three. The others huddled together on the deck, clutching the gunwales or the mast, trying to stay warm and avoid being thrown overboard. For hours they had labored to keep the ship pointed into the swells, but most of the oars had been lost, and it had become clear that trying to control the ship's heading was futile.

As the hold filled with water, the ship sank deeper into the sea, and the waves rose higher over her gunwales, hurling torrents of water that sloshed about until it found its way below. With each flash of lightning, the water level in the hold crept higher. Soon Bjorn would be forced to join them on the deck as they awaited the wave that would pull *Skjótrmarr* into the depths. There they would join the crew of the other longship, *Starkmarr*, helmed by Eric's brother Ragnald, which had disappeared in the swells several hours earlier. No doubt *Starkmarr* had capsized; it was a miracle *Skjótrmarr* had remained aright this long.

Another flash of lightning revealed movement: Haeric was coming toward them, holding the bucket.

"No, Haeric!" Eric shouted, as blackness came over them, but thunder stole his voice. Haeric had acquitted himself well on their voyage so far, but he had spent most of his life on land. He did not have the intuitive feel for the sea that came from spending years aboard a ship, and so he did not know what was about to happen.

A moment of eerie calm followed as the ship reached the top of the swell, and then she groaned as she pitched violently in the opposite direction. Eric lurched forward, fighting the waist-high torrent of water, but Gulbrand's powerful hand gripped his arm, holding him back. The next flash of lightning revealed no sign of his son.

"Haeric!" Eric cried, as the ship began to right itself again. He leaned over the gunwale, staring into the blackness. He could see nothing but the distant flicker of storm-seized clouds and the occasional glimmer of the gigantic swells beneath, rising as if striving to meet the sky. Somewhere out there, amidst the chaos and endless darkness, his eldest and favorite son, fought to keep his head above water. "Haeric!" Eric cried again, but he knew Haeric could not hear him; his voice barely reached the stern of the little ship. Eric had the sense that the gods were playing with him. So this is how it ends, he thought. Fate will not be denied. I was meant to die at Stainmore, and now the gods will make me pay for disrupting their plans. The Christian god, he knew, was supposed to be merciful. He recalled a priest telling him the story of Jonah, who was thrown overboard to appease the gods. Yet Eric had lost his own son, and the storm raged unabated. There was to be no mercy for Eric Bloodaxe, it seemed.

The numbness had gotten to his feet and seemed to be working its way up his legs. He welcomed it; soon he would feel nothing at all. The bucket was lost, the oars were lost, the sails were torn and useless. All of mankind's tools were of no avail against the gods. He would die here at sea, an unknown and ignoble death. Neither heroic enough to be called to Valhalla nor virtuous enough to enter the Christian heaven, he supposed his spirit would skulk here on the desolate sea until Ragnarök, a barely discernable wisp of greasy smoke drifting at the mercy of the wind. And a thousand years from now, if some unlucky ship were to pass by, its crew would shudder and murmur imprecations as faint, anguished cries of "Haeric!" reached their ears.

As he strained to catch a glimpse of his son, a glow in the nearby clouds illuminated the sea before him. The glow grew steadily brighter, and soon it became apparent that it was not lightning. Eric's attention, though, remained fixed on the sea. There! Something riding up the side of one of the swells. It had to be a man. Haeric? He shouted his son's name again, but again his cries were lost in the wind. The swell rolled toward *Skjótrmarr*, and the man was lost behind it.

It was now almost as light as day. Eric looked up to see the clouds pierced by a blinding white light, as if the full moon herself were descending toward the sea in front of him. Over the distant rumble of thunder, Eric heard cries of terror from his men, still huddled in the prow. Gulbrand stood open-mouthed next to him, staring as the light continued to grow brighter. Putting his hand in front of his eyes, Eric could just make out the contours of a sleek, saucer-shaped craft, perhaps half the size of the longship. Hanging from it was a rope, at the end of which was a man-sized object shaped like an inverted teardrop. Eric watched in awe as the craft hung in the air, suspended just above the level of the swells as if by an invisible hand, oblivious to the buffeting winds and rain.

Eric held his breath as the teardrop thing disappeared behind the swells. When it appeared again, rising toward the ship, he let out a shout of terror. The thing had opened up like an octopus and now held a man clutched in its tentacles. It was Haeric, seized like a dead rabbit, his arms and legs hanging limply. A moment later, he disappeared into the craft. The craft then moved toward *Skjótrmarr* until it hovered directly overhead. Eric could now make out a hatch in the thing's belly, from which the rope was now descending, the menacing creature hanging from it. Eric stepped back, wishing his sword were handy; he could not fight the creature, but perhaps he could cut the rope. He would not be devoured by that monstrous creature if there were any alternative. Better to dive into the sea and swim down until he blacked out.

"Remain still!" called an impossibly loud voice from above. A woman's voice? "The extraction device will not hurt you!"

"Freya?" Eric said, frozen in astonishment.

"The crew of the other ship is already aboard *Varinga*," the woman's voice said. "Stay where you are, and we will get you all to safety."

Anger arose in Eric's breast. What right did this woman have to keep interfering with his fate? Had she not already told him he would die in obscurity? *And if my son is dead*, he thought, *then it is better that I too meet my end here.*

Perhaps, though, Haeric was not dead. If anyone could save him, it was the people on the sky ship. He had seen them work miracles with burns and broken limbs. Reviving a drowned man was probably not beyond their abilities. Could he die here not knowing whether his son lived?

He sighed in resignation. Once again, his fate had been wrested from his hands. He shuddered but did not fight as the octopus thing spread its tentacles and wrapped itself around him, leaving his face free so he could breathe. The tentacles were soft and spongy, applying just enough pressure to hold onto him.

"Eric!" Gulbrand shouted as he lifted off the deck. He grabbed hold of one of Eric's ankles, but the thing's ascent did not slow.

"One at a time!" shouted the voice. "We'll get you next!"

"It's all right, Gulbrand!" Eric said. "It's only our Valkyrie, come to cheat death once again."

CHAPTER NINE

"If you expect gratitude," said Eric, "then you shall wait until Ragnarök, and then some. If you had not intervened at Stainmore, we would not have faced our deaths in that storm." He sat at a conference table with Freya and Commander Dornen.

"If Freya had not intervened at Stainmore," Dornen said, "you would all be dead."

"An honorable death in battle."

"If all you want is to die with a sword in your hand, that can be arranged."

"All right, that's enough," said Freya. Since bringing the Norsemen aboard *Varinga* again, she had become resigned to her role as mediator. She didn't feel that she was very good at it, but there simply wasn't anyone else to do the job. "None of us asked for this. We're people from three different cultures, fighting three different enemies. But I choose to believe there's a reason we're in this room together."

"As I understand things," said Eric, "the reason is that while Commander Dornen and his men fled like scared rabbits, his enemy decided to finish the war."

Dornen struggled to hold his temper. "We have one warship left. I made a tactical decision to keep it out of the Izarians' reach while we secured a *reliable* ground fighting force with which to oppose them."

"The fact is," Freya interjected before Eric could respond, "Commander Dornen made his decision based on the best information available to him. CDF intelligence suggested that the Izarians were at least two years from developing a so-called planet-killer device. As Eric points out, however, we have learned this is incorrect. The transmission from the Janthus probe suggests that not only have the Izarians developed the planet-killer; they have used it on at least one world. Given Tabor's lack of strategic importance and remote location, it is unlikely that it was the first world to be targeted. Strategic analysis suggests an eighty percent chance that most if not all of the major Concordat planets have already been targeted."

"Genocide," said Dornen. The word was rendered in Norse as "mass slaughter" by the translator. "Our spouses, children, friends… all dead. Billions of people. By now, there may only be a few million people left, scattered across a handful of worlds. And assuming the Izarians don't run out of bombs or develop a conscience in the next ten days, we are looking at the extermination of all mankind. And while that may not matter to you, Eric, I will remind you that includes your own world, Earth."

Eric shrugged. "If Ragnarök comes, I will be ready."

"It's not going to be Ragnarök, you knuckle-dragging barbarian!" Dornen snapped. "There isn't going to be any glorious battle at the end of time, and there sure as hell isn't going to be any magical rebirth of the species. When they drop one of these things on your planet, everything just *dies*. A wave of destruction sweeps over the planet and the molecular bonds that hold everything together—plants, animals, people, ships, buildings—let go, just for an instant. Just long enough to kill anything that lives and turn everything else into sludge and dust. If you think you're going to stand against that tide with a wooden shield and an iron sword, you're far stupider than I imagined."

Eric grinned. "It is too bad that your people die in such an ignoble manner. Mine will not. Freya herself has told me that she knows Earth's future, and I believe her. How can Earth have a future if it is destroyed by this 'planet-killer'?"

Dornen's face had gone red. He looked like he was on the verge of either storming out or launching himself across the table at Eric. Freya didn't blame him, but she didn't see either option turning out well.

"Eric," she said, "this is not helping. For one thing, while it is true I have spoken with those who have seen the future, I would rather not risk the entire world on a bet that the future cannot be changed. Second, even if Earth is not directly threatened at the moment, if Dornen's people fail to defeat the Izarians, we will have to face them sooner or later ourselves. And finally, in case you've forgotten, we need Dornen's help against the Cho-ta'an. All of this depends on you and your men, it is true. But an army that is unreliable or disloyal is worse than nothing. On this ship, Commander Dornen is in charge, and if you intend to make an issue of that, you should say so now, while we are still in orbit. If you cause problems once we are underway, Dornen will have you thrown out the airlock, and I will not protest. You will find death by vacuum to be much swifter and surer than drowning."

Eric shrugged, trying to appear unconcerned, but it was clear to Freya that her speech had had an effect. "I do not contest Commander Dornen's authority on this ship."

Dornen opened his mouth to speak, but Freya was quicker. "He is also in charge of this mission," she said. "As long as the fight against the Izarians goes on, you will follow orders."

Eric waved his hand in front of him irritably. "Very well."

"Good," said Freya. "Then we're in agreement. Commander Dornen, you have your army."

"I intend no offense to Eric and his men," Dornen said, still tense and obviously choosing his words carefully, "but what I have is not an army, but a single platoon of only fifty men."

"Each of my men is worth—"

Freya held up her hand, and Eric grunted, folding his arms before him.

"Yes, I'm sure each of your men is worth twenty or fifty or a hundred Celts or Saxons or whoever it is that you've been fighting on Earth," Dornen said. "But you fought against mere men, armed with swords and axes. You have had less than twenty days' training with the mech suits, and the enemies you face will be far deadlier than any man."

"I have seen your fliers, and your walkers, and your tanks. We beat them all." There was some truth to this: the Vikings had acquitted themselves well in head-to-head combat, although their overall metrics were poor.

"You fared unexpectedly well against the holographic versions," said Dornen, straining to be diplomatic. "But those scenarios were designed to be winnable, at least in theory. If we were to attempt an assault on Izar, the odds would not be so favorable."

"Even if we had a man for every suit," Freya said, "I don't see how they could take an entire planet."

"Izar is a strange world," Dornen said, tapping keys on a console in front of him. An aerial photograph came up on the wall display. "It is ninety percent ocean. Surveillance indicates that the Izarian population is mostly confined to that big island near the equator. Near the center of the island is a city of sorts, made up mostly of factories for the construction of machines. There are other factories on other islands that make other sorts of machines, but the big island seems to be the nerve center that coordinates the construction."

"Material versions of the ghosts we have been fighting," Eric said.

"Military bots, yes, and a few other sorts of machines. We have identified six distinct models." He tapped buttons on the console in front of him, bringing up a map of the city. It resembled a spoked wheel, with six thoroughfares spreading out from a central hub. "At the end of each of those main roads is a factory. Each factory produces a different type of machine. Three of the six are military models."

"What are the buildings farther out from the factories?" Freya asked.

"Power plants," Dornen said. "Helium-3 fusion reactors, we think."

"There must be thousands of war machines in the city," said Eric.

"Most of the machines are shipped off-world," Dornen said. "They are needed—*were* needed—to put down human insurgencies on a score of worlds. And the production of machines has slowed over the past few years. Still, you can expect to face several hundred military bots—and that's assuming

Varinga can get past their planetary defenses and you don't get shot out of the sky during the drop. We expected fifty percent casualties before our troops even hit the ground, and that was with a full battalion. Fewer targets for the enemy means a higher casualty rate."

"Even if we could take the city," Freya said, "would it stop the production of war machines? Wouldn't they just shift production to other factories?"

"For all the Izarians' prowess as a military power," Dornen said, "they seem to have a strangely centralized production process. We've found factories on several other worlds, but none that produce any of the six semi-autonomous models. For whatever reason, they've put all their eggs in one basket."

"Our objective would be to smash the factories?" Eric asked.

"You could do a lot of damage by blowing up one of those reactors," said Freya.

"Either tactic would be effective," said Dornen. "But we think there's a simpler way of crippling the Izarians. All their production seems to be coordinated by that central hub."

"Maybe that's where the actual Izarians work?" said Freya.

"Possibly," said Dornen. "Or a more sophisticated type of machine. We don't know. But if we can take that building, we'll control the Izarians' means of production."

"It seems way too easy," said Freya.

Dornen laughed humorlessly. "Tell that to the millions who have died in this war. The Izarians have built an incredibly effective apparatus for genocide. After many years of brutal war, we've identified one potential weakness, which we are still far from being able to exploit. We certainly aren't going to take the city with fifty mech-suited Vikings."

"What are you suggesting, Commander?" Freya asked.

"Supplementing our forces."

"With what?" Eric asked. "Did you find one of your fringe worlds while you were gone?"

"There are—were—several planets where marines had been deployed before the CDF fleet was wiped out at Toronus. Most of those planets have probably already been hit with a planet-killer. There is, however, one that they probably have not targeted. There is a helium-3 mining operation on a planet called

Voltera that was attacked by the Izarians about half a standard year ago. The Izarians have seized the mine, apparently with the intention of shipping helium-3 to fuel their reactors. The last intelligence report we received, however, indicated that only three shipments have left Voltera since the Izarians seized it."

"Meaning what?" asked Eric.

"Meaning that they are having trouble getting the helium-3 off planet. Either they're having difficulties with the mining operation, or their ships are breaking down. Or both."

"Sabotage," said Freya.

"Yes. There was a company of CDF marines stationed on Voltera before the attack. The CDF command lost contact with them, and it was assumed they'd been wiped out. But I suspect at least some of them are still alive and active, doing what they can to slow down the Izarian war machine. If we can get Eric's men on the ground, we may be able to make contact with them and get them aboard *Varinga*."

"Is the slowdown in the Izarian production of machines caused by a shortage of helium-3 for their reactors?"

"Unlikely. Helium-3 is labor-intensive to mine, but it is hardly rare. There are several planets closer to Izar that have an abundance of helium-3. We know they have the capability to mine it."

"How old is this information?"

"Besides the Janthus probe, the last beacon to emerge from hyperspace in range of our position was twenty-eight days ago. At the time we received its transmission, the information was twenty-two days old." The translator rendered all measurements of time greater than twenty-four hours in days, because the Truscan calendar differed significantly from the Julian calendar used by the Norsemen. The Truscan week was only five days, and their year was four hundred ten days. Their day, however, was nearly the same as an Earth day: twenty-three hours and forty Terran minutes. And like the Terrans, they divided their day into twenty-four hours of sixty minutes, which were further divided into sixty seconds. A Truscan second was, therefore, slightly shorter than a Terran second, but it was close enough to be interchangeable for most purposes.

"So we're planning an operation based on information that's seven weeks old?" Eric said. The translator converted this to *cuadrajinta novem*—the Truscan phrase for forty-nine days.

"Rather sketchy information at that," added Freya.

"It's what we have."

"Why didn't you try to make contact with these marines when you first found out about this?" Freya asked.

"The Izarians are jamming all radio communications near the mining facility, so we have no way of contacting the marines from space. We could land a shuttle, but it would be destroyed by sentinels before it even touched down. I need a strike force to drop from above the atmosphere, make contact with any marines in the area, eliminate any hostiles, and get the marines to an extraction point."

"Your mighty 'marines' need to be rescued," said Eric with a smile. "I accept the mission."

"There is a complication," said Dornen. "The other reason we haven't been able to extract troops from any of the CDF planets is that the Izarians have an interconnected system of hyperspace beacons."

"An early warning system," Freya said.

"That's right. The moment we emerge from hyperspace near any Izarian-occupied planet, a beacon scans us, records the data, makes a hyperspace jump to Izar, and transmits the message to the Izarian Central Command. As we're the only deep space warship left in the entire CDF fleet, we can expect the Central Command to scramble whatever ships are available and get them to Voltera as fast as they can."

"How long will we have?" asked Freya.

"Our best estimate, from the moment we're detected until the ships arrive, is one hundred twenty hours."

"Five days," said Freya.

"That should be more than enough time to rescue your marines," said Eric.

"It would be," said Dornen patiently, "if we were on an even footing with the Izarians technologically. We are not. They have developed navigational algorithms that allow them to jump inside star systems. Our hyperdrives are not nearly as precise."

"I do not understand any of this," Eric groused. Freya sympathized. Despite his stubbornness and lack of formal education, Eric often impressed her with his ability to assimilate new concepts. He understood hyperspace travel about as well as she did. But when someone threw a lot of foreign concepts at him at once, he became sullen and irritable. Trying to get him to understand was then a balancing act between assuming too much and condescension. Freya had learned that stroking his ego facilitated the process.

"You understand hyperspace travel, of course," she said.

"Space is folded like a paper map, so that two distant locations are much closer together," Eric said. "Traveling between them is like sticking a pin through the map, from the starting point to the destination. A child can understand this."

"I assure you," said Dornen, "that many of my own people do not understand it that well."

Freya went on, "The two points on the map are brought closer together, but there is still some distance between them. It takes time to travel that distance. Also, while a pinhole may seem tiny, at astronomical scales a pinhole would represent an area of space many millions of miles across. Basically, what Dornen is saying is that the Izarians have developed a pin so small that you wouldn't even be able to see it. They can emerge from hyperspace right next to Voltera. *Varinga* can't do that."

"We could try," Dornen said, "but there's no guarantee we'll be successful. We might come out of hyperspace five days' travel from Voltera, or we might emerge inside Voltera's sun. Ordinarily we aim for the outskirts of the system to keep the odds of collision manageable."

"It sounds as though we will have to take a greater risk this time," Eric said.

"Yes," said Dornen. "This time I plan to aim for the sun and hope to God we miss."

CHAPTER TEN

"Eric sat in silent semi-darkness, the only light emanating from the heads-up display of his mech suit, which showed the surface of the planet Voltera below, along with several lines of text he couldn't read. Despite the straps snugly wrapping his arms and legs, he found himself shaking. He was glad his men couldn't see him now, although he supposed many of them were shaking as well.

Eric had ridden out North Sea gales in rickety longboats. He had survived murderous plots by his own brothers. He had fought Saxons, Celts and Northumbrians. And he was afraid.

There were things one could not prepare for, and Eric had a pretty good idea that dropping forty miles to the surface of an alien planet was one of them. Oh, he'd been through the "holosim" training, and he'd experienced six hours of freefall while *Varinga* was preparing for the jump to the Voltera system. By this time, climbing back into the suit was like meeting an old friend. But none of that stopped the shaking.

"Commencing drop in twenty seconds," said a voice in his ear. The voice spoke in Norse; it was not a person, but one of their translation machines. Or was it one of the other machines, what the Truscans called a *recording*? There was still so much he didn't understand about the Truscans' technology. And in a few seconds, he would be trusting it with his life. "Commencing drop in ten seconds," said the voice. Then it counted down: Nine, eight, seven….

After the count reached one, a warning klaxon sounded, just like in the training sim, warning that the drop had begun. And just like in the training, the klaxon was shortly accompanied by a loud *whoosh!* that he knew to be the sound of one of his men being launched toward the planet's surface. He felt himself pulled forward with a jerk and then stop, and then there was another *whoosh!* Another jerk, and another *whoosh!* One per second, his men were being shot out of *Varinga*'s hull like a bullet from a Truscan machinegun. There were five "barrels" altogether, one for each squad of Norsemen. Eric, as the commander of his squad (as well as the platoon leader), would be the tenth and last man out.

So intent was Eric on calming his fears that he lost count of how many men had been ejected. Thinking there was one left to go, he suddenly felt his weight quadruple as a deafening *FOOOM!* filled his ears. *That* hadn't happened in the holosim!

And then—nothing.

No sound, no pressure, no weight. He was floating in darkness, falling weightlessly toward the surface of a world he had never seen before. But he wasn't shaking now; it was the wait beforehand that had worn on him. He wasn't scared anymore—Dornen had told them the enemy's planetary defenses were minimal, and in any case, if he were hit by one of their guns or a missile, he'd be dead before he felt anything.

He felt the capsule twist and sway, then steady down so that his weight was on his back, weight that built up quickly as the capsule fell through the thin upper atmosphere. The outer shell burned away and sloughed off—unevenly, causing him to tumble. This had happened sometimes in the holosim, though it was much more disconcerting when you could *feel* it. Then the rest of the shell went and he straightened out.

The egg-shaped capsule holding the mech suit was opaque, so he still could see nothing but the heads-up display, which showed the surface from the point of view of *Varinga* as she moved away from the planet. Next to this image was a graphical depiction of his capsule's status: a tiny human figure inside a larger figure representing the mech suit, wrapped in an egg with a two-layered shell. The first layer had disappeared, and the bottom of the second layer was beginning to glow red. Text scrolled past the images on the left; Eric couldn't have said what language it was, as he'd never learned to read. Few of his men had. Dr. Bartol had assured him that that literacy was not required to operate the suit; all the important information was presented visually. This was, Eric gathered, not so much because Truscan infantrymen were illiterate but because pictures were more quickly understood, allowing the soldiers to react faster.

The capsule shuddered as the second layer sloughed off, and there was a sudden jerk as the first ribbon chute deployed. A second later, the chute tore away, having done its job of slightly slowing the capsule's fall. The second chute, consisting of a wider and longer ribbon, lasted somewhat longer, and then the third, a square canopy nearly twenty feet on each side, deployed. The top half of the inner layer of the capsule was transparent, allowing Eric a view of a deep azure sky overhead. Unable to move his head, as it was still strapped into place to prevent injury, Eric scanned the horizon, hoping to catch a glimpse of one of the other men. He saw nothing but sky, but he reminded himself that this had often been the case in the training as well: at this point, his men were scattered over an area of space some forty miles across. This was by design: spreading the men out made it harder for the enemy to target them.

If Dornen were right about the enemy's defenses, though, this was all overkill: Voltera had been a remote Concordat planet of middling importance; the Izarians had overlooked it for most of the war, conquering it almost as an afterthought, probably because they figured it would be easier to take control of an existing helium-3 mining operation rather than establish their own. They had sent a single warship, equipped with enough weapons to destroy the CDF's surface-to-space defense and filled with general-purpose machines, to eliminate CDF ground forces and take over the mining operation. Given the state of the CDF fleet, Dornen doubted the Izarians had bothered to set up any planetary defenses of their own. It was standard procedure, however, for the Izarians to put a ring of sentinel drones in orbit around any planets they held; if the sentinels detected an enemy ship in the system, a beacon drone would immediately jump into hyperspace to warn the Izarian Central Command.

Eric heard a roar and felt a rumbling as the capsule's trajectory adjustment rockets kicked in. That meant he was getting close to the ground; the rockets would fire in conjunction with those of the other capsules to close the gaps between them as well as direct the capsules to avoid enemy fire (if there was any) and dangerous obstacles on the ground. Around him he spied various bits of debris, but nothing that looked like a mech suit. Half a minute later, the rockets cut out and the final layer of the shell blew open, taking the big chute with it. Eric was once again in freefall, his limbs stuck in place, the heavy suit frozen around him. He tried desperately to extract himself from his suit, even though he knew this was impossible—and would be suicide, in any case. Trusting the suit was his only chance at survival.

The rocky gray-brown ground—not unlike the terrain of Iceland—shot toward him, and wind whistled in his ears. Below him was a dry river valley that ended about ten miles north, at the edge of the huge crater where the helium-3 was collected. The suit rumbled and shuddered, but he couldn't feel the air moving: the suit was sealed against Voltera's poisonous atmosphere. He gritted his teeth and readied himself to die, knowing the suit had failed him. Would such a death get him to Valhalla? Would the Valkyries deign to scrape what was left of him off the rocks, even if they could find this godforsaken world?

Then the suit's landing rockets fired, and the air whooshed from his lungs as sudden deceleration compressed his innards, jamming him into his seat. A moment later, he was on the ground. The straps holding him in place had retracted, and the suit was back under his control. He stood on a black plain of volcanic sand bordered to the east and west by steep ridges perhaps three hundred yards high. The threat status icon was green, and the heads-up radar display showed him at the center of a cluster of green dots: the men of his squad, their identifiers appearing in tiny letters below them. Ordinarily the dots would be labeled with the soldier's name, but since few of Eric's men could read, each of the men had been assigned a string of simple symbols. Eric's, for example, was a row of three horizontal lines followed by a vertical line that curved inward and then another that curved outward:

---)(

It looked a little like an axe, if you didn't think about it too hard. Gulbrand's was a hammer:

---8

Bjorn's was a fish:

><>

And so on. Every man in the platoon had memorized all the others' identifiers. Each squad had been assigned a symbol as well. These were somewhat more elaborate; Eric's was a dragon. Another graphic, to the left of the one displaying the individual squad members, showed a wider view, with the different squad showing the relative locations of the five squads. It was a lot of information to keep track of, but the men had grown accustomed to checking their displays for the locations of the other men, and—especially after the debacle of their last real-world training mission in Greenland—enemy units.

The information they were being fed through their suits came not just from the interlinking of the suits themselves but also from a hundred or so hummingbird-sized drones that had been released from their capsules along with their parachutes. The drones had an unwieldy Truscan name, but the Norsemen had taken to calling them *hrafnlingr* ("little ravens") after the birds that were said to be the messengers of the gods. The silent and nearly invisible drones, hovering about thirty feet above the ground, had fanned out to give them a comprehensive view of the terrain around them. They would remain low and close to the mech suits to avoid giving away the platoon's position. As long as the threat status remained green, it meant neither the hrafnlingr nor the suits had detected any enemy units.

At the top of the display was a short string of characters that was continually changing. Eric knew it was a sort of clock that counted down the estimated time left for the operation. He focused his eyes on it and said, "Read." The voice in his ears replied, "Two hours, fifty-eight minutes." Eric was not used to measuring time in minutes (even the water clock at York was accurate only to the quarter-hour), but it was a simple enough concept. Fifty-eight minutes was two minutes short of an hour, so he had just under three hours to complete the mission. That was when *Varinga* would land at the drop location to pick up Eric's platoon and the rescued marines.

The level of precision seemed a little silly to Eric, as Dornen himself admitted his estimate of the arrival time of the Izarian ships could be off by as much as three hours. The Truscans, he had noticed, had a strange tendency to compensate for uncertainty with imaginary precision. He had laughed out loud when the Truscans' computer had estimated that they could expect the Izarians to send seventeen and a half ships. The time estimate was on the conservative side, meaning that in all likelihood, Eric's platoon had a bit more than five hours to get the marines to the extraction point before the seventeen and a half ships reached Voltera. Still, they had no time to dawdle. Eric intended to complete the mission with time to spare, demonstrating to that smug dandy Tertius Dornen that when it came to real fighting, the Norsemen were more than a match for any Truscan or Izarian.

Scanning the valley floor, Eric could just make out a few of his men in the distance. The other squads were too remote to see without activating the display's magnification. The suits communicated with each other and with *Varinga* when possible, so that if any of them spotted an enemy, the others would be alerted immediately. As long as the threat status icon remained green, they were in the clear. Izarian ground forces had undoubtedly been notified by the sentinel drones of a potential threat, and there was a good chance the drop had been picked up by radar, but the nearest enemy units were at least twenty miles away. Eric turned in a circle, testing the suit and getting a feel for the territory. "Leader to Platoon. Squads check in," he said. He'd had to learn to preface his commands with a salutation so that the suit's brain would transmit it appropriately. It wasn't always necessary; the suit would try to figure from his words and the context whether he was addressing the suit itself, talking to himself, or addressing the platoon, a particular squad, a particular infantryman, etc.

"Bear Squad here," said Ragnald.

"Wolf Squad here," said Halfdan.

"Eagle Squad," said Bjorn.

"Serpent Squad is here," said Halvar.

"Dragon Squad is here as well," said Eric. He was still unconvinced of the necessity of dividing his band—that is, platoon—into five separate groups, called squads, but the Truscans had insisted, and he had agreed. The Romans had certainly proved the efficacy of a well-organized army, and the system used by the Truscans was similar. The Norsemen tended to fight as a single unit, overwhelming their enemies with speed, numbers and sheer ferocity, but then the Vikings generally raided for treasure or simply to terrorize an enemy—objectives that rarely required complex organization. Even the Norsemen, though, sometimes had to split up their horde to flank an enemy or execute a feint to draw the enemy away from a target. In the case of their current mission, which required his men to quickly locate the Truscan marines and get them to the extraction point, Eric could see the advantages.

Eric was pleased that the radios were working. Dornen had warned them that the Izarians were using a device to interfere with radio communication, but the suits evidently used a kind of signal that was difficult to jam, at least at close distances. The drones overhead, acting as signal repeaters, helped with this. Three more little icons on the heads-up showed the quality of the current connection to his squad, to the leaders of the other squads, and to *Varinga*. The first two were green and at full strength; the last was a red X, indicating that *Varinga* was currently out of contact. The suits were wonderful weapons, but Eric found himself wishing he could charge up the ridge with nothing but an iron sword and a wooden shield. He put the thought out of his mind.

"Bear Squad, I want you on top of the western ridge. Eagle Squad, on top of the eastern ridge. Double time. Serpent Squad, go south. The rest of you, stay on me. We're heading north. Platoon leader out." Eric strode forward, and the men fell in line behind him. Voltera's gravity was slightly weaker than Earth's, making them feel light on their feet despite the bulky suits.

Eric and his men had spent hours going over maps of the area with Commander Dornen and Dr. Bartol, so Eric knew exactly where he was. They had landed at the widest point of the valley, which stretched southward toward a range of spectacularly tall and steep mountains. To the north, the valley narrowed before giving way to a roughly circular plain over two hundred miles across. Dornen had said this plain was actually the bottom of a crater left behind when a gigantic rock hit the planet many years before. It was here that machines scoured the soil for an element called helium-3, which was evidently used to fuel even bigger machines. The stuff was so rare that even on Voltera, where it was relatively common, machines drove all day and night across the vast plain, sifting through the soil to find tiny specks of it. When one of the mining machines was full, it drove its load to a central building (which was also on wheels, so it could be moved when an area had been depleted), where the ore was refined. Then the refined product was loaded onto sky ships to be delivered to other worlds.

The whole thing seemed preposterous to Eric. Why didn't they just use coal or wood to run their machines? Why have so many machines in the first place if you just had to keep building more machines to keep those machines running? What did all these machines do, anyway? But Eric had not been dropped on the planet to make sense of the operation; he was here to rescue a company of marines.

The mountains encircled the mining area, providing plenty of places for guerillas to hide. Surveillance from *Varinga*, however, indicated that mining operations were currently centered in the southwest region of the plain, so if the marines really were alive and engaged in a campaign of sabotage against the Izarians, they were likely to be within twenty miles to the northwest or southeast of Eric's platoon. The plan was simple: two squads would search for signs of the marines, one to the east and one to the west. The other three would go north toward the mobile refinery, where surveillance from *Varinga* indicated the Izarian machines were clustered. In the holosims and the exercises in

Greenland (the Truscans called them "hologram-enhanced real terrain training") Eric and his men had faced a dozen different sorts of Izarian machines that had been specifically constructed for combat—from heavy tanks that crawled on metal treads to lightning-fast flying craft that rained fire from the sky. If Dornen's assessment was correct, they wouldn't find any of those here: it was thought that the machines the Izarians had sent to Voltera were all of the general-purpose type the Truscans called *golems*. Golems, of middling intelligence, were the size and roughly the shape of a man. They could learn quickly how to perform any simple task, including guarding a refinery, but they were unimaginative and predictable. Rather than try to seek out the CDF marines stealthily, Eric's men would go in guns blazing to quickly eliminate the golems and hopefully get the attention of the marines in the process.

By the time Eric and the men with him reached the narrower part of the valley, Bear Squad had reached the top of the western ridge. "Bear Squad leader to Platoon leader," Ragnald's voice said in Eric's ear, "We're at the top of the ridge. Good view of the plain. We see three mining machines at a distance of… about fifteen miles." The suit's display would automatically tag any object of interest with a label indicating its distance from the wearer, but most of the men still struggled to read the numbers. Ragnald knew the digits one through nine, but he had gotten into the lazy habit of translating any two-digit number to "about fifteen miles," which was generally accurate to within five miles, because even with magnification there wasn't much you could see past twenty miles. "No golems or other enemies detected. Bear Squad leader out."

"Eagle Squad has reached the top of the eastern ridge," said Bjorn. "No enemies spotted. Can confirm what Bear Squad leader said. Three mining machines eighteen miles out."

"Eagle Squad and Bear Squad, I want you each to leave two men up high to keep eyes on the plain. Try to make contact with those marines. Directional signal, low-power only." They had gone over this in the mission briefing, but Eric thought it bore repeating: the idea was to get a signal to any CDF personnel that might be hiding in the mountains without alerting the enemy to their presence. "The rest of you, get started on Objective Alpha."

"Roger that," said Ragnald and Bjorn. Objective Alpha meant fanning out to search for signs of the marines. In all likelihood, the marines would find them first: the suits weren't exactly stealthy, and both the suits and drones were broadcasting an encrypted message identifying them as CDF-friendly units. Even with the Izarians jamming radio communication, marines with a standard CDF receiver would probably be able to pick up the transmission from a distance of a half-mile or more.

Eric's men continued to the north. In the direction of the plain, the ridges on either side of them grew gradually steeper. The valley floor ended at a rocky bluff, which had once been the top of a waterfall that had drained to the crater floor nearly a hundred feet down. To Eric's left and right the rock walls above them curved sharply outward to merge with the edge of the cliff wall that marked the edge of the crater.

Eric stepped to the edge, the flexible metal feet of the mech suit gripping the rock in response to a slight curling of his toes. The cliff wall directly below was nearly vertical, but there were several ledges and outcroppings on either side that could—theoretically—be used by a man in a rocket-assisted mech suit to return to the valley from the plain below. The sun, a pale white-blue disc that hung low in the direction they were calling west (although Dr. Bartol had told them this was technically inaccurate as Voltera had no "magnetic field," whatever that meant), was sinking rapidly toward the distant mountains. Supposedly the suits would protect the men from temperatures far lower than even a winter night in Norway, but Eric was already feeling a chill, despite the exertion of walking.

"Enemy flier spotted!" said a voice, a moment after the threat status icon went red. The voice belonged to Sveinn, one of the men in Eagle Squad. Peering into the distance ahead, Eric saw nothing but empty sky. A pair of bright red brackets near the center of his field of vision were the only indication that an enemy approached. After a few seconds, though, a tiny black dot appeared in between the brackets. Eric focused his eyes on the brackets and said, "Magnify times forty." The area inside the brackets suddenly blew up to fill a third of his vision. The thing was now clearly identifiable as an Izarian flier, although of a smaller variety than they'd faced in the past. Numbers underneath the brackets indicated the flier was now less than a mile away and closing rapidly. A flashing red X appeared in the middle of the brackets, indicating it was within missile range. "Leader to Platoon," Eric said. "I've got it. Everybody hold your fire. Platoon leader out. Arm missiles. Target locked. Fire missile."

Foom! went the little rocket as it left the launcher on his back. It arced overhead and leveled out, heading toward the little flier, which was now just barely visible without magnification. There was a distant explosion, and the red brackets turned gray, indicating the flier had been destroyed. The threat indicator went back to green.

"Platoon Leader, this is Bear Squad Leader," said Ragnald's voice. "I thought there weren't supposed to be any fliers. Over."

"Just a recon unit," said Eric. "Don't get distracted. Find those marines."

"Roger that."

Gulbrand, coming up alongside him, shot him a concerned glance. Eric met his gaze but didn't respond. He shifted his view to the plain below, which was now blanketed in darkness. "Assault Team, follow me, advancing in pairs. Don't crowd the man in front of you, and step boldly. If you don't clear the bluff, I am not coming back to scrape whatever's left of you off the rocks. When you hit bottom, move, or you'll be wearing the next man as a hat. Let's go!"

He leapt off the bluff.

CHAPTER ELEVEN

"For a second he was falling, and once again he was certain the suit was going to let him die. But then the rockets fired, and he grunted as sudden weight compressed his innards. The next thing he knew, he was standing on the plain. Half a second later, Gulbrand thudded to the ground next to him. Gulbrand gave him a grin, and the two moved forward to make way for the next pair. *Thump, thump. Thump, thump. Thump, thump.* Two by two the Norsemen landed on the plain. By the time they were all down, the sun was hidden behind the mountains and the sky had turned a gray-violet. The thin atmosphere refracted little light, and soon it would be dark. Already a scattering of faint stars was visible. Voltera had no moon.

"Platoon, switch to infrared," said Eric. "Keep your eyes open. Assault Team, wedge formation." He strode ahead, forming the point of the wedge, and the others fell in line behind him, creating a wedge two men deep. It had taken some work to get the Norsemen accustomed to the idea of coordinated troop movements, but they had become passably competent at some basic formations. Hrafnlingr hovered overhead, mimicking the men's movements.

Eric broke into a run, the suit's sensors transmitting the movements of his leg muscles to the powerful motors that moved the metal limbs, and the others followed. When he had first tried running in the suit, he had found it awkward and uncomfortable: each step landed with a jarring shock that shot up his leg. He had learned, though, that if you ran with long, fluid leaps, rolling your foot from heel to toe, you could cause the suit to flow over the ground like a galloping horse—and nearly as fast.

They loped across the dark plain toward the distant refinery, under a deep violet sky sprinkled with stars. Eric led the way, a pair of hrafnlingr flying just ahead of him. He let out a bellowing laugh. If he died tonight, all would be well. He had lived a full life, never letting himself be ruled by his fears, and cheated death half a dozen times. He was ready for whatever came after this life, Valhalla or not. He did not expect to die, though: a golem might be more than a match for a man, but Eric and his men were more than men. They were demigods in plated steel, hurling fire from their fists.

Eric could now make out the lights of the refinery in the distance, as well as several of the huge mining machines. It was misleading to call it mining, he thought; in some ways it was more like farming: the big machines rolled slowly over the plain, dragging a wide apparatus that cleaved through the soil like a huge, many-tined rake, sucking up particles of precious fuel that were too small to see. With the infrared, Eric could just make out the striations across the ground where the machines had already passed; they had worked their way across about a quarter of the crater's bottom. Eric wondered what the Truscans who had built these machines had intended to do with them when the entire plain had been mined. Was there some other place on this planet where helium-3 could be mined? Would they have transported the machines to another world? Or would they simply have left them here to rust?

He put his ponderings aside as the threat status icon turned red. Up ahead, clustered around the refinery, several red dots had appeared. Good. Those would be the golems. His men would dispatch them, destroy any other enemies in the area, and maybe blow up the refinery if they had time to spare. By that time, the marines would hopefully have revealed themselves, and they could make their way back to *Varinga* in time for supper. They might even get Dornen to tap into the beer supply.

As the refinery loomed closer, though, the red lights began to wink out, one by one. That was odd. Were the golems going to leave the thing undefended? Eric held up his hand and slowed his pace. Something was wrong. The only reason the golems would leave the refinery undefended was if they knew they were outgunned and had no chance of holding it. But the golems weren't men; Dornen had told them they had no desires of their own, only "programming." They wouldn't flee to save themselves. So what were they up to?

"Assault Team, halt!" Eric ordered, taking a few more steps in case the men behind him couldn't stop quickly enough. He scanned the horizon. There was no sign of any enemies. If they were out there, they were too distant for either his eyes or the hrafnlingr to pick up—and they could be anywhere.

Having nearly perished in an ambush not long ago, Eric felt a familiar disquietude in his gut. How far could he trust the information Dornen had given him? If Dornen had wanted to get rid of Eric's men, surely there were easier ways. That didn't mean the information on Voltera was accurate, though. Dornen himself had admitted it was all conjecture, based on reports that were weeks old. By now, the Izarians might have sent reinforcements to help the golems eradicate the saboteurs. Eric didn't like the idea of running away, but he liked the idea of falling into a trap less.

"Retreat!" Eric ordered. "Assault Team, reverse wedge formation and retreat! Top speed to Checkpoint Beta. Move!"

A moment of chaos followed as the men pivoted and tried to find their places again in the formation. To their credit, none of the men questioned the order, even though they had to be wondering whether Eric had turned coward or lost his mind. When the wedge had re-formed, they moved out again, quickly falling into a loping run.

A red dot appeared ahead of Eric. Then another, and another. Soon there were a dozen, then a score. Eric knew that there was a way to get the display to identify the types of machines they faced, but he was too agitated to remember how. He had a strong suspicion, though, that they weren't all the man-like golems. As the hulking figures began to come into view, his suspicion was confirmed.

A glance at the bird's-eye view on the heads-up display told him that enemies were closing from the left and right as well. He had an idea. "Suit, what are those red dots?"

"The red dots represent enemy units."

"I know that! What *kind* of units?"

"Fourteen general duty golem class units and seventeen KW23 class heavy infantry units." A short pause followed. "Eighteen general duty golem class units and twenty-one KW23 class heavy infantry units." Another pause. "Twenty-five general duty golem class—"

"All right, that's enough!" Eric snapped. "Eagle Squad, what's your status?"

There was a burst of static in his ear. The Izarians' jamming broadcast was interfering with the signal. "Say again, Chief?"

"What is your status?"

"About a mile north of the drop site. No sign of the marines."

"Head to Checkpoint Beta, on the double."

"Sorry, Chief. You're breaking up. Say again."

A score of bipedal machines, a foot taller and much bulkier than the mech suits, were now visible on the horizon.

"The bluff! Get to the bluff! All squads, get to the bluff. We've got a shit load of trolls. Assault Team is surrounded!" Eric's men had faced machines like this in training—generally with poor results.

"—that, Chief," said Bjorn. Two other voices broke in with what sounded like confirmation of the order.

The threat status icon blinked red, indicating incoming fire. Eric heard the *budda budda budda* of heavy machineguns, followed by grunts and curses from his men. Several of the green dots around him were now blinking.

"Assault Team, use your missiles!" Erik shouted. "Active targeting on our flanks. Save your machineguns to punch through their line!" Active targeting would allow the suits to work together to coordinate their fire, sending missiles toward the most attractive targets. Stark shadows flickered around them as dozens of missiles shot into the sky. Each suit carried twenty of them, and they'd likely need them all. The bird's-eye display now showed a near-solid ring of red around them.

The missiles arced sideways and raced to their targets, and the plain was lit up as explosions erupted around them. Half a dozen red lights went gray. Eric's optimism faded, though, as pinpricks of light raced toward them from the left: the enemy had launched a salvo of missiles as well.

"Incoming!" Eric shouted, but the warning was lost in the deafening *BOOM-BOOM-BOOM!* of nearby explosions. Several green lights went gray, and several more turned white. Gray meant a dead man. White meant a living man trapped in a non-functional suit. Under the circumstances, that was as good as dead.

The explosions went on and on, until Eric was half in a daze, barely aware where he was going or if he was still moving at all. The suit did its best to filter out the blinding light and dampen sounds that might damage his ears, flipping back and forth between infrared and normal vision as the battlefield was intermittently lit up like midday, but it was simply too much for Eric to take in. A dozen warnings screamed at him from the display, images and symbols and strings of letters in confounding combinations, and above it all, the near-constant string of screams: brave men, dying in blasts of fire and rending metal. The lucky ones died instantly. Others lay paralyzed in broken machines, bleeding to death or choking on the poisonous air leaching into their suits. This was not war. It was Hel itself.

At last the explosions subsided. The mech suits' missile batteries were depleted; he could only hope the enemies' were as well. Still Eric ran, now at the lead of a group of perhaps twenty men. The rest—over half the assault team—were dead or dying, and there was nothing they could do for the latter. Eric's men had done some damage too: the missiles had greatly thinned the ranks of the machines advancing toward their flanks, and the men in the lead had taken out a few of those ahead of them. The still-functioning machines to their left and right seemed to be mostly golem units wielding small machineguns that had a hard time piercing the mech suits' armor. There were a few of the big infantry units, but these moved slowly and were out of machinegun range.

The major threat now was the semicircle of twenty or so heavy infantry machines that lay between Eric's men and the bluff, loosing a steady barrage of automatic fire toward the Norsemen. The suits were so well armored that even their heavy guns were of limited effectiveness, but the machines were uncannily good at targeting the suits' weak points—particularly the helmet cameras and the knee joints. Eric's men fired countless bursts toward the big machines, but the machines were at least as well armored as the suits, and the humans could not compete with the machines in sheer accuracy. Eric had intended to punch through the enemy to reach the foot of the bluff, hoping to lead the machines into the range of the other three squad's weapons, but if they kept this up, his men were going to be torn to pieces.

"Break off engagement!" he shouted. "We need to go around them. Dragon Squad, go left. Wolf Squad, go right. Now!"

The two squads were now thoroughly intermingled, and there was a moment of confusion and near-collisions as the men tried to follow the order. The men just didn't have enough experience with either the suits or this new organizational scheme to execute these maneuvers competently while under fire. A hail of bullets pelted Eric's legs, and his right leg slid out from underneath him, nearly causing him to fall on his face. He caught himself, staggered a few steps, and then followed the rest of his squad to the left. Miraculously, the suit didn't seem to have sustained any major damage. He broke into a run, following the four other men of his squad who were still on their feet. Gulbrand was just ahead of him; the others were Thorvald and Viggo. Wolf Squad, led by Halfdan, was down to six.

Bullets pelted the men as they ran; several pinged against Eric's helmet, leaving gouges in the transparent metal. The screaming had stopped: either the fallen men were dead or the suits had decided their screams weren't worth transmitting.

"Squad leaders, how far from the bluff are you?" There was no response, and Eric repeated the question. This time he received only a burst of squeals and static. "Ragnald?" Eric said. "You're breaking up. Say again."

"Almost there," said Ragnald. The signal was now coming through clearly. "Two minutes."

"Eagle Squad is five minutes out," said Bjorn.

"About five minutes for Serpent Squad," said Halvar.

"Get there as fast as you can. We're bringing a few dozen trolls your way." Another spray of bullets to his helmet drowned out any response. Viggo, hit in the knee, went down, and Eric had to leap to avoid tripping over him. The suit's rockets fired briefly, and for a moment he was airborne. The suit didn't carry enough fuel for extended flight, but they fired automatically in response to vigorous movement. He would have to be careful: he would need some fuel to climb back out of the crater, and he was already down to twenty percent. He came down hard, just ahead of Gulbrand and Thorvald, and for a moment he considered going back for Viggo. But Viggo's dot had gone white: his suit had suffered a debilitating hit. For now, Viggo was still alive, but there was nothing Eric could do for him. If he went back to pick Viggo up, they'd both soon be dead. He kept running, trying to vary his speed to keep the machines from getting a bead on him, as they had learned in training. When running from men with bows or spears (not that Eric ever had the occasion to do this), one's best bet was generally to get out of range as quickly as possible. The danger of these machines, though, was in their precision. If you moved predictably, they could zero in on your weak points and disable you.

Eric, Gulbrand and Thorvald were now a good hundred yards past the edge of the line of trolls. Seeing that the Norsemen intended to make end runs around them, the trolls had split into two groups in an attempt to block them, but the big machines moved slowly. Eric's display told him that five men of Wolf Squad were still moving; they had flanked the trolls on the far side.

They were almost in the clear now. Bullets streamed toward them, but even the machines' preternatural accuracy would not do them much good at this range. The sheer cloth hood that covered most of Eric's head was drenched with sweat; despite the frigid temperature outside, the suit was generating so much heat that it was having trouble keeping its occupant cool. The suit did most of the work, but Eric was breathing hard from exertion.

"Head for the bluff!" Eric shouted, as he veered to the right. Gulbrand and Thorvald followed his lead, and the men on the opposite side turned toward the bluff as well. If they could get to the foot of the bluff—and if the other squads could get there in time to provide cover fire—they might still have a chance.

The two contingents of trolls had pivoted to face the two groups of Norsemen running past them, and as the Norsemen moved farther away to the south, the trolls marched after them, still firing their machineguns. Their supply of ammunition seemed endless.

"Ragnald, are you at the bluff?"

"Almost there, Chief. Less than a minute."

The foot of the bluff loomed ahead, about three hundred yards off. Climbing back up by leaping from ledge to ledge, assisted by the rockets when necessary, was the only way out. The cliff continued on both sides of it for several miles, and the suits' rockets only had enough fuel for a few quick hops. Flying two hundred feet straight up was out of the question. If the other squads didn't reach the top of the bluff in time, Eric and the few others who had survived the ambush would be effectively trapped.

There was nothing they could do now but keep going and hope for the best. They ran, zigzagging to avoid giving the trolls an easy target. But as the wall of rock grew closer, Eric realized the squads above were not going to be in position in time. Very well, then. He would die on this alien plain. But he would not die running away.

CHAPTER TWELVE

"Eric slowed, readying himself to give the order to turn and face the trolls. But before he could speak the words, he saw something streaming toward him from near the base of the bluff. A missile? Were there enemies ahead of them as well?

He ducked reflexively, coming to a halt, but it was unnecessary. The missile shot over his head, and he turned in time to see a troll erupt in a burst of fire. Then another, and another.

A faint voice from the foot of the bluff shouted something he couldn't understand. "Come on!" said the suit in his ear, translating. "Get your asses over here!" Eric turned back toward the bluff. He still couldn't make out anything against the bluff, even with infrared, but the suit was now showing a dozen pairs of green brackets, indicating friendly troops. The marines? Another salvo of missiles confirmed his suspicion. The rest of Eric's team was still running, and Eric rejoined them as missiles detonated behind him.

He could now make out small figures in the distance, hunkered down behind shields of some sort. As he drew closer, he could see the shields were just thin panels. They didn't look like they'd be much protection from the trolls' heavy machineguns; most likely they were simply camouflage. That was why Eric's suit hadn't flagged the men at first. There were maybe twenty men, about a half-mile from the base of the bluff.

The two squads—what was left of them—began to converge again, and the men slowed as they neared the marines. "Keep moving!" said a voice in Eric's ear, translating the shouts coming from one of the marines. "We can't hold them off for long!" The men wore bulky clothing with hoods to protect them from the cold, as well as masks to filter the poisonous air. Another salvo of missiles, fired from launchers mounted on tripods, went up as Eric's men moved past the line of marines. The Norsemen stopped, looking to Eric for orders as the missiles took out the last few trolls. Eric's suit warned him that several dozen more were advancing in the distance, along with many scores of golems. Too many for a few marines to deal with, no matter how many missiles they had.

"How will you get out?" Eric said, standing with his face toward the backs of the marines. The suit translated for him.

One of the men, wearing sergeant's bars, turned and shouted something, his voice muffled by the mask. The suit translated the words: "We'll be all right. Just go!"

The Norsemen's mission was to get the marines to *Varinga*, and Eric couldn't see how they were going to scale the rocks without mech suits. But these men knew what they were doing; probably their commander had figured out why Eric's men were here and had sent these few on a suicide mission to allow the others to escape. "Where do I find the others?" Eric asked.

"Other what?" asked the man.

"Marines. The rest of your company."

"We're all that's left. Get the *[bleep]* out of here!"

Eric stood silently for a moment, not wanting to believe it. These twenty or so men were all that was left of an entire company? If it were true, then this mission had already failed. The best Eric could do was to get his men to the extraction point.

"May the gods be with you," Eric said, and the sergeant turned at gave him a curious look. He shrugged and went back to work unloading missiles from a crate.

"Let's go!" Eric said, setting off again toward the bluff. They reached it just as the next salvo of missiles shot towards the machines. When the explosions stopped, Eric heard machinegun fire. The last few marines on Voltera were most likely dead, thanks to Eric and his men walking into a trap. Eric put the thought out of his mind and walked toward a ledge that hung some twenty feet over their heads. A faint blue line superimposed on his vision showed him the recommended route up the cliff wall. The suit's rockets fired as he jumped, carrying him to the top of the ledge. He took a second to get his footing and then jumped to the next rock. One by one, the Norsemen followed the route, bounding from one outcropping to another, assisted by the suits' rockets when necessary. In addition to giving them lift, the rockets corrected for slightly ill-aimed jumps, allowing the men to scale the rocks with near superhuman precision.

Before he was halfway up, Ragnald's voice spoke in his ear: "We're up top, Chief. We have eyes on you. Better hurry. Those trolls are coming up on you fast." A moment later, Eric saw the flash of rockets overhead. As he reached the next ledge, he glanced behind him in time to see several more missiles detonate against the trolls. He was readying himself to jump again when the outcropping he'd been aiming for exploded in a burst of fire and rock. He turned away as an avalanche of debris rained down on him. Had one of the trolls, nearly a quarter mile away, guessed his next move? Another missile struck somewhere below him, causing the ledge to shake. Another dot went gray.

When he could see again, the suit had given him an alternate route, drawing a line to a barely perceptible hunk of rock some thirty feet above him. The suit warned him that his fuel level was at one percent. Not seeing any alternative, he leaped. The rockets sputtered as he shot toward the rock, and he fell short; only a reflexive grab with his left hand saved him. The suit's huge, claw-like hand got a hold on the rock, and for a moment he hung there, swinging like a pendulum. At last he got a hold with his right hand as well, and pulled himself onto the ledge. It was an awkward maneuver in the bulky suit, but he eventually managed to get on his feet. Explosions continued to erupt in the distance and, intermittently, below him. Two more quick leaps brought him to the top of the bluff.

By this time the other two squads had reached the bluff as well, and the Norsemen were firing their missiles en masse at the force advancing across the plain. Eric was surprised to see an unsuited man—one of the marines—standing on the bluff. The man bent down to help another over the edge. Eric saw now that the marines had secured a rope to the rock. Had they climbed to the top in such a short time? No, they were using some sort of mechanism to pull themselves up the rope. These people and their machines!

As Eric's men and the rest of the marines pulled themselves onto the bluff, missiles continued to streak toward the machines on the plain. Occasionally an explosion would erupt on the bluff face below, causing the ground beneath them to shudder, but the trolls, firing from below, were at a disadvantage, and the constant barrage from above seemed to have kept the bulk of their force out of range.

"I'm out!" shouted one of the men, and he was echoed by several others. The last few missiles launched, detonating in a desultory smattering of distant explosions. The marines, who had left their missile launchers on the plain, had begun to move away from the edge.

"If you guys are done admiring the scenery," shouted the sergeant, "I suggest you get moving."

The man's words irked Eric—because he was right. Eric and his men had been dawdling, watching the mesmerizing explosions on the plain. As the fires died, Eric's infrared showed him two more lines of trolls advancing. Minute flashes indicated the launch of several missiles.

"Move!" Eric shouted. "Get away from the edge!" He'd only advanced a few steps when he was thrown to the ground by an explosion. Chunks of rock showered the back of the suit. His display went completely dark, and for a moment he thought he'd become another white dot. But then the display flickered to life, and he struggled to his feet, rocks and sand sloughing off the suit. Dazed, he staggered after the others.

They moved as fast as the marines could run, staying behind them to keep the armored suits between the unshielded men and the machines. Hrafnlingr flew silently overhead. Missiles continued to explode around the Norsemen, showering them with sand and rocks but doing minimal damage; the bluff was now blocking the machines' line of sight, preventing accurate targeting. At last the barrage ceased, but Eric suspected this was only because the trolls had reached the foot of the bluff. He knew from training exercises with this type of machine that the trolls could scale a sheer stone face. The golems could do it even faster, but they would probably wait for the heavy infantry. At best the men had bought themselves a few minutes.

"Platoon leader," said a voice in Eric's ear. "Where's the extraction point?" It took Eric a moment to realize it was the sergeant, addressing him by radio.

"About five miles ahead," Eric said. "Where the valley widens. How did you know?"

"What the hell else would you be doing on this *[bleep]* rock?" The suit had an annoying habit of replacing profanity with a short tone rather than attempt to translate it. The voice was silent for a few seconds. Eric tried to identify the sergeant out of the group of men running ahead of him. The suit could identify the men by rank, but they were too close together for him to make sense of the labels. Then it said, "How big is your ship?"

"It's called *Varinga*," said Eric, not sure how else to answer the question.

"*[Bleep]* me," said the sergeant. "I thought those looked like the Series Four suits. When does she land?"

Eric asked the suit and then repeated the answer. "Twenty-two minutes from now."

"*[Beep]*. How many more suits are aboard?"

It struck Eric as strange that the man wasn't even breathing heavily, although they were running at a near-sprint, but then he remembered he wasn't listening to the man's voice, but rather a translation of it. Panting would be lost in the ordinary delay between his words and the suit's rendering of them. "Eight hundred in all," he said.

"There are more infantrymen aboard?"

"No. Only us."

"*[Bleep]*. I guess you've got room for two hundred civilians?"

"I... suppose so," Eric said, confused. "There are civilians here?"

"Who do you think ran this place before the machines moved in?"

"We thought they had all been killed."

"Then why... wait, did you come here to get *us*?"

"Marines, yes. We expected an entire company."

"Ha, ha, ha," said the suit, translating unnecessarily. "We *had* a full company until four days ago, when the Izarian reinforcements arrived. With the number of those KW23s they sent, they must be really hurting for helium-3. We've been lying low since then. When we saw the machines on the move, we figured the cavalry was here. Why the *[bleep]* did you go to the refinery without making contact with us first?"

"Bad information. We were told it was only golems—I mean, the general duty machines. We were going to eliminate them so they wouldn't interfere with the evacuation. I had three squads looking for you, but you found us first."

"And a good thing we did. Where are you from, Captain? My comm says your suit is translating from something called 'Norse.' I never even heard of that language."

"My men and I are from Earth."

"Ha, ha, ha," said the suit again. "Fine, don't tell me. Glad you're here in any case. I'll buy you a beer when we're aboard *Varinga*."

"Where are these civilians?" Eric asked.

"Heading to the extraction point now," said the leader. "I sent them the coordinates as soon as you gave them to me. Have to sign off. Falling behind. Sergeant Macron out."

The men had slowed to a jog, unable to maintain their pace, and one of them—evidently the sergeant—was now lagging the others by a good twenty yards.

There was no sign of the enemy, but Eric was not hopeful they had broken off pursuit. Most likely they were less than a mile back, hidden by the narrow canyon's twists and turns. It occurred to Eric—somewhat belatedly—that he could release the hrafnlingr from their tight overhead formation now that the Norsemen were no longer concerned about stealth. After some frustrating fiddling with the controls—all done with eye movements and voice commands—he managed to assign the hrafnlingr to a wide area surveillance program. The drones flew higher and spread themselves out ahead and behind the Norsemen. Soon they picked up a group of twenty-six trolls and thirty-one golems. The hrafnlingr reported that over half the trolls were still armed with missiles.

They came to the place where the canyon opened up to the wider valley where they had landed. The extraction point, marked on their overhead displays with a blue X, was less than a quarter mile ahead. A crowd of people, wearing masks and what Eric assumed was mining gear, had gathered nearby. He couldn't imagine how these people had stayed alive this long, even with a company of marines to help them. Did they sleep with their masks on? According to Dornen the air had enough of what the Truscans called "oxygen" to be breathable, but the other elements in it would kill a person in minutes.

Sergeant Macron ordered his marines to halt, and Eric's men came to a halt behind them. The sergeant, panting in his mask, walked up to Eric. He gasped something that the suit translated as "Fourteen minutes." Eric nodded, assuming Macron had the correct time until *Varinga* landed. "How long…?" He motioned toward the canyon through which they had just come.

Eric checked the bird's-eye display. The enemy machines looked to be about half a mile back and moving at a fast walking pace. He guessed the machines would be on them in about five minutes, but he sensed the marine was hoping for a more precise answer. He said, "Suit, how long until the enemy gets here?"

"Five minutes, thirteen seconds," the suit said.

He repeated the answer.

Macron gave him an odd look. "Did you just…?" He started. "Never mind." He turned to face his men. "Thetus, get those people back from the landing zone. Make sure they're ready to move. The rest of you, come with me. We're going to buy them some time." He began trudging back the way they came. "You coming?" he said to Eric.

Eric stood in front of the other mech-suited men, watching the marines head toward the narrow canyon opening. They were armed only with machineguns, which would be —at best— a minor annoyance to the trolls. "Wait," said Eric. "You can't hold off those tro… KW23s with machineguns. My men will do it. Get your men aboard the ship."

"No can do," said Macron, still walking. "This is why we're here. I wouldn't mind some help, though."

Eric raised his arm. "Ready machineguns," he said. "Single shot, intelligent targeting."

"No enemies in range," the suit said.

"Target Sergeant Macron. Override warnings. Override safety protocols."

The marines, unable to understand Eric but hearing the machineguns whir to life, stopped and leveled their guns at him. The sergeant, now some ten paces away, turned to look at him. "Just what in the *[bleep]* do you think you're doing?"

"You and your men will be in the way," Eric said. "Our mission is to get you off this world. I do not have time to argue. Join the civilians or I will shoot you."

"You must be *[bleep]* me. What the *[bleep]* kind of unit are you, anyway? You sure as *[bleep]* aren't marines."

"I told you," Eric said. "We're Norsemen. We come from Earth. I thank you for your assistance, but now you must go. I would rather not shoot you, but I will do it to get the rest your men on the ship."

Macron stared at him. "You're serious. You really came from Earth."

"Aye," said Eric. "We heard you folks needed some help. Maybe we can't save all of mankind, be we can get you on that ship. I beg you, as one warrior to another. Do not make me shoot you. There is nothing left for you to do here. Go. Help your people."

The sergeant stood for a moment, staring at Eric in wonderment. He reached into a pocket and produced a small black box, which he held out to Eric. "Do you know what this is?"

Eric's men had used the devices in training. "Radio detonator."

"There's a boulder about fifty yards into the crevice, wired to blow."

Eric nodded. "I saw it." The boulder was the size of a house, and it rested precariously on the Eastern lip of the canyon, above a narrow passage. He had considered sending some of his men up to push the boulder down onto the machines, but they hadn't had time.

"The transmitter isn't directional, so you'll have to be within a few yards to get through the jamming signal. There's a five second delay. Trigger it and then get the *[bleep]* out of the way. Wait until they're under it, and you might take out two or three of them—and slow down the others."

Eric commanded the suit to open an access panel and reached out to take the device with his hand. He slid it into one of the holding brackets inside the suit and slid the panel shut. "We will hold off the machines," he said. "You must go."

Macron straightened and gave him a salute. "You heard the man," he said. "Let's get those people aboard *Varinga*!"

CHAPTER THIRTEEN

"Eric's men waited just inside the mouth of the canyon, having taken cover as best they could in the time they had left. Several of the men had managed to find cover on ledges partway up the canyon wall. Eric's son, Haeric, who had proven particularly adept at climbing in a mech suit, had taken a precarious vantagepoint with the detonator. It was a dangerous assignment, but Eric was proud of his son for volunteering. They might have triggered the explosive charge while the trolls were some distance away, but this posed its own dangers: if the trolls saw the canyon was impassable, they would retreat to where the walls were climbable and go around the obstacle. Delaying them for as long as possible meant letting them advance. Eric hoped, too, to put a dent in the enemy's numbers by taking out three or four of them with the boulder.

The thudding of the trolls' heavy metal feet came to them from around the bend, growing slowly louder. Scanning the sky, Eric saw no sign of *Varinga*. He tried to hail her but got no response. The suit told him the ship was supposed to land in ten minutes.

From where Eric stood, he could just make out the contour of Haeric's suit, some thirty feet up the eastern canyon wall. The rigged boulder was almost directly above him; the plan was for Haeric to trigger the bomb and then leap down and out of the way of the boulder before it exploded. Eric watched on the bird's-eye display as the machines moved closer to his son's position. The machines had wisely moved a contingent of golems out front; Eric worried that the smaller machines would spot the Norsemen before the trolls were under the boulder, but it was too late to do anything about it now.

The golems picked their way forward in pairs, the sensors hidden in the featureless globes that served as heads scanning this way and that for any sign of the enemy. Eric's men were well-hidden and remained completely still, and as the first pair of golems came into view, he thought for a moment that their plan had succeeded. But one of the golems suddenly pivoted toward Haeric and let loose a burst with its machinegun. Eric, knowing that the machines communicated silently and instantaneously with each other, gave the order to open fire.

Bullets tore through the thin armor of the golems, cutting them down where they stood. The one that had fired on Haeric was destroyed before it could do any damage, and Haeric, half-hidden behind a vertical wedge of rock, blasted its partner to pieces. More golems advanced to take the place of their fallen comrades, firing their own guns at any exposed piece of armor. These were cut down as well, but still more advanced from behind. Slowly but surely, the machines were gaining ground. For the moment, the Norsemen remained mostly behind cover, but the farther the golems advanced, the more exposed they were. Eric's display told him that the trolls, perhaps sensing a trap, had ceased moving, while golems streamed toward the front. The Norsemen were now taking steady fire. Individually, the small caliber bullets did little damage to the heavily armored suits, but the preternatural precision of the machines allowed them to fire hundreds of rounds at exactly the same place. The men had learned in training that if you stayed still for more than a few seconds, the machines would eventually wear holes in their armor through sheer persistence. Moving, however, meant giving up their cover. Eric suspected this was exactly what the enemy was waiting for.

Some of the men had chosen cover positions that allowed them very little freedom of movement, and the golems had a knack for identifying these and sending torrents of bullets at them until their armor gave out. One by one, men standing on ledges and outcroppings began to fall. Alive, but trapped in hobbled suits, they unloaded their guns at the golems or flailed at them with whatever limbs still functioned. But the downed men were immediately set upon by several more golems, who riddled their suits with bullets until the occupant was dead or the suit was fully disabled. All the while, the slow, steady advance of the golems continued.

Haeric fared better than the others because any golem that fired at him was immediately targeted by half a dozen Norsemen. They all knew the only chance the people in the valley had of getting out of here was Haeric triggering the boulder trap at the right moment. As the number of Norsemen still standing continued to drop, though, Eric realized that a change of tactics was needed. The only way they were going to draw fire away from Haeric and tempt the trolls to come through was to give them a more attractive target.

"Retreat!" Eric shouted. "Everybody back!" He lay down several bursts of fire to cover the men leaping down from their perches above. Then he joined the others, bounding across the canyon floor toward the valley. As they ran, they were pelted with constant streams of bullets. Eric could only hope that the golems were too focused on the fleeing men to target Haeric.

Eric heard a rumbling overhead and looked up to see an elongated black triangle sliding across the deep violet sky: *Varinga*, on its way to the extraction point. Thank Odin! Eric had begun to think Dornen had seen the explosions below and decided not to risk his ship on a rescue after all. Eric's display told him that the trolls were inching forward. Good. When the retreating men were clear, Eric would order the hrafnlingr to harass the golems to give Haeric time to trigger the bomb and get out of the way. With a little luck—

"Father!" cried Haeric in his ear. Haeric's icon flickered, indicating that the suit was damaged.

Eric came to a halt, taking cover behind a boulder. "Haeric, are you hurt?"

"No, Father. But—" The transmission cut out, and Haeric's icon went white. The suit was dead. And if his son wasn't dead yet, he soon would be.

*****

"Commander," said the comms officer, Clea Marinus, as *Varinga* slowly descended to the plain, "we've got Izarian ships in system!"

"Damn," said Commander Dornen. The Izarians had beaten his most cautious estimate. Either they had more idle ships than he'd thought, or he'd underestimated their interest in Voltera. Dornen had hoped to be well on his way with a company of marines on board by the time the first Izarian ships arrived. "How many?"

"Fourteen... sixteen. They're still coming through, sir. Nineteen."

"My God. Time until intercept?"

"They're about a septhar out, moving fast. Must have hauled ass to get into jump position. They'll have to arc around Voltera to intercept us."

"Just give me a time estimate, Lieutenant."

"Ninety-six minutes, sir. Assuming we maintain our current position."

Dornen chewed his lip. *Varinga*'s only chance to escape would be jumping to hyperspace before the Izarian ships were in missile range, but it would take days for her to get far enough from Voltera to safely make a hyperspace jump. If he aborted the landing, they might be able to stay out of range long enough to make the jump. That meant leaving the Norsemen—and more importantly, the marines—on Voltera.

"Commencing landing procedure," said the navigator, Delio Starn. *Varinga* had ceased its forward motion and began to descend to the valley floor.

"Have we made contact with anyone on the ground yet?"

"No, sir," said Marinus. "The Vikings are still engaged in a firefight about a mile to the north, but we've got visual confirmation of about two hundred people near the extraction site."

"Marines?"

"I don't think so, sir. Most of them don't appear to be armed. They look like civilians."

The good news just keeps coming in, Dornen thought to himself. If there were no marines left on Voltera, there was no reason to risk his ship. On the other hand, the Izarians were on the verge of wiping out every known human world. If they found Earth, those two hundred people in the valley might soon be all that was left of humanity.

"How long until we're on the ground, Commander?" asked Freya's voice in his ear.

I should abort the landing, Dornen thought. If we leave now, we might still have a chance. But then what? Spend the rest of my life looking for remote human colonies that might not exist?

"Thirty seconds," Dornen said. "There's a group of about two hundred people at the extraction point. Get them aboard as quickly as you can. We've got enemy ships incoming."

"Roger that," said Freya.

*****

Eric turned, firing a burst from each of his guns into a golem that was almost on top of him. Two more were advancing close behind. They trained their weapons on Eric, and Eric ran toward them, cutting them down one after the other.

"Haeric!" cried Eric. There was no response.

"Eric!" shouted Ragnald in his ear. "What in Hel are you doing?" A roar from behind him indicated *Varinga* was landing.

"Keep going!" Eric commanded. "I've got to help Haeric!"

A rain of bullets hammered the front of his suit and helmet as half a dozen golems opened fire on him. Giving his overheated guns a rest, Eric ran directly at the machines, his arms outstretched. The golems tried to get out of the way, but Eric moved too quickly. Each of the suit's fists caught a golem in the midsection, picking them right off their feet and hurling them into the pair behind them. This pair stumbled and fell into the next pair. Eric laughed. They wouldn't be down for long, but it was satisfying to take advantage of the machines' own penchant for precision. As the Norsemen knew well, sometimes chaos was a better strategy.

He'd reached the end of the golem contingent; the first of the trolls was just around the next bend. He spotted Haeric's suit, lying still on the ground, and ran to it. The armor was dented and ruptured in several places. Kneeling over the suit, though, he saw that his son was alive and apparently unhurt. Haeric had wisely remained in his suit rather than get out and be torn apart by a hail of bullets. "Get out of the suit, Haeric," Eric ordered. "Hurry!"

Some of the golems behind him had gained their feet and were pelting his suit with bullets again. Meanwhile, the first of the trolls had nearly reached the bend just ahead. Haeric tried to get the suit's chest plate open, but it was jammed. Eric tore it off. "There's no time, Father," Haeric said. "Take the detonator."

"You hold onto it," Eric said. He helped his son out of the suit and then wrapped the mech suit's right forearm around Haeric's waist. Haeric would soon get very cold without the suit's built-in heating, but the mask he still wore would at least protect him from the poisonous air.

Eric made a half-pivot to his left, shielding his son from the golems' guns, and swept across their midsections with his left-hand machinegun. He tore three of them to pieces before his gun jammed. "Blast it!" he growled, sidestepping toward the golems. Warnings flashed that his armor had been breached, and he smelled acrid smoke. He grabbed one of the golems by its spindly neck and hurled it into another, causing them both to crash into the canyon wall and then fall to the ground in a heap of twisted, smoking metal. The last one backed away as it continued to fire its gun into Eric's left knee joint. Eric brought his fist down on the thing's head, shattering it. The machine crumpled to the ground.

Out of the corner of his right eye, Eric saw the first of the trolls coming around the bend. He turned away, still holding Haeric, and ran toward the valley. Any thought of the detonator or the trap had left his mind; he could think only of getting his son to safety.

He didn't get far: the golem's assault on his knee had had its intended effect. The joint froze as he put weight on it and he nearly fell. Regaining his balance, he stepped with his right leg and then swung the suit to the right to pick his left foot off the ground, swiveled the hip joint, and then stepped again with his right. Like a man with one leg in a cast, he hobbled along the canyon floor, following the contour of the western wall to keep some cover between them and the army of trolls.

Soon, though, the canyon straightened out again, leaving them no place to hide. They flattened themselves against the western wall, trying to remain out of sight as long as possible. Eric was sweating and shaking from the exertion required to move the suit in such an unnatural way. He set his son down before him. "If you run," he gasped, "you can still make it."

"Wh-wh-what about y-you?" Haeric asked, hugging himself and shivering uncontrollably in the frigid air.

"Suit… failing. No time to… get out. Go!"

"Sh-sh-should I…?" Haeric asked, holding up the detonator. The first of the trolls were past the boulder now; it was as good a time as any to spring the trap.

"Do it," said Eric.

Haeric flipped the safety catch and then hit the button. Nothing happened.

"Blast!" Eric growled. "We're too far away."

The rhythmic thumping of the trolls' footsteps grew closer. Eric's display had gone dark, but he knew the machines were almost on them.

Haeric eyed the far wall of the canyon. "I c-c-can do it, Father."

"Not… without a suit."

"I'm fast. They won't hit me."

Pride swelled in Eric's chest. How brave Haeric was! He had to know that he wasn't fast enough to dodge the trolls' guns. No one was. But he was willing to try anyway.

"No," Eric said. "It's impossible. Flee while you can. There is no shame in running from enemies such as these."

"I c-can do it," Haeric insisted. "If you h-help me."

The trolls were so close now that Eric could feel the ground shake with their steps, even through the suit. "All right," he said. "Stay behind me." At least he wouldn't have to see his son die before he fell as well.

CHAPTER FOURTEEN

"As the marines corralled the last of the miners onto the ship, Freya stood on the valley floor, her eyes on the opening of the narrow canyon to the north. She heard gunfire and explosions. "Where are the Norsemen?" Freya asked the marine who seemed to be in charge. The comm device the Truscans had given her translated for her.

"The fellows in the fancy suits?" the sergeant said. "They're buying us some time."

"Are there more marines?"

"Not anymore," said the sergeant.

"Is everyone aboard, Freya?" asked Commander Dornen on her comm. "We're running out of time."

"Civilians are aboard," said Freya. "Marines are boarding now. Eric's men are going to need a little more time."

"How much?"

Freya turned to the sergeant, who had heard Dornen over her comm. He shrugged. "Not long. We rigged a trap for the machines a few days ago. An explosive charge under a big boulder. Your Norsemen were going to try to blow it and trap the machines on the other side."

"How will we know if it worked?"

"In a few minutes, I expect to see the Norsemen running like hell in this direction. If they don't have forty KW23s on their tail, then it worked."

"Freya?" said Dornen, his voice urgent. "How long?"

"A few minutes," said Freya.

"How many is a few?"

The sergeant shrugged again.

"Three minutes," Freya said. "Does *Varinga* have any weapons that are effective against the machines?"

"Not that we can use on the ground. Tell me the Norsemen aren't going to lead those KW23s right to us."

"My understanding," said Freya, "is that they're trying really hard not to."

"Hell," said Dornen. "I can give you two minutes."

*****

Eric pivoted and stepped out from behind the rock—directly in front of two trolls. They leveled their guns at him, and he lurched forward, nearly falling into the one on the right. Now too close to get its side-mounted guns pointed at him, the machine struggled to step backwards on the rough terrain. The troll's helplessness lasted only a split second, but Eric made use of it, slamming his armored fist into the thing's chest. Metal buckled and tore, and the troll staggered backwards, firing its huge guns wildly. Eric ducked under the guns and punched the machine again, this time in the torso just under its left arm. The troll spun to the right, its guns ripping into its comrade. The second troll fired back at the haywire machine until it exploded in a burst of torn metal and fire.

While those two were occupied, Eric limped forward, dragging the damaged leg behind him. Five more trolls advanced on him; so far they hadn't fired, probably because their two comrades were in the line of fire, but he didn't dare take his eyes off them to check on his son. "Drones, attack!" Eric commanded. The hrafnlingr converged in an instant and then surged as one toward the trolls. The drones weren't meant to be an offensive weapon; their "attack" consisted of buzzing around the enemy, emitting blinding strobes of light, accompanied by focused bursts of sound, heat and radio waves intended to confuse their sensors.

It was enough. Eric staggered sideways out of the trolls' path, and the trolls trudged forward, momentarily blinded. The effect wouldn't last: within a few seconds, the trolls' sensors would recalibrate, like eyes adjusting to darkness. Eric, half-blinded, dragged himself forward in the hobbled suit. Haeric came along his right side, smartly keeping his father between him and the trolls. Haeric was frantically pushing the detonator button, but still nothing happened. The boulder was now less than fifty feet away. How long ago had the marines set this trap? Had the enemy disarmed it? Had the wires corroded? Or was Haeric still too far away?

The bulk of the enemy force was hidden behind another bend, but if they pressed on, they would be fully exposed. At any moment, the trolls would regain their senses and train their guns on them, and Eric couldn't shield his son from every possible angle of attack. Eric pivoted left, preparing himself for a final, futile onslaught against the trolls.

Several bursts of heavy machinegun fire came from his left, and Eric turned to see that Ragnald and Gulbrand had disobeyed his order to retreat once again. Crouching behind boulders, they rained bullets on the trolls, doing little damage but drawing their attention. A half-dozen more men were on their way. The hrafnlingr dropped to the ground, their energy expended, and the trolls opened fire on the Norsemen. Eric stood stock still, for the moment having escaped the machines' attention through some fluke of fate or oversight in their programming. Perhaps they'd appraised the condition of his suit and concluded he wasn't a threat. They were probably right. The valor—or foolhardiness—of his friends was in vain: if he took a single step, the machines would finish him off, and his son along with him. The rest of the Norsemen took cover where they could find it, and joined Gulbrand and Ragnald in the firefight.

"Father!" shouted Haeric from behind him, his voice barely audible over the near-deafening roar of machineguns. Eric turned to see Haeric standing against the cliff wall, pointing upward. His son had found a path up the wall. They didn't need to go forward: Haeric could go up! The route he'd identified would take him to a ledge only twenty feet from the boulder that was rigged to fall. More importantly, there was no rock between the ledge and the location of the bomb—assuming it was still in place. If the detonator didn't work from there, it wouldn't work anywhere.

"Go!" said Eric. As his son started up the wall, Eric moved slowly toward him, arms raised to give him as much cover as possible. The ground sloped upward toward the wall, so Eric could better protect his son by moving away from the trolls. As the Norsemen continued to trade fire with the trolls, Eric waited for the enemy to turn their fire on him. For the moment, though, it didn't come. One troll fell, and then another. Haeric was now almost halfway to the ledge and still climbing. For all Eric knew, he was already close enough to trigger the bomb, but Haeric needed both hands free to climb; he'd slid the detonator into a pocket. Even from this distance, Eric could see how badly his son was shivering in the harsh cold. His hands had to be half-frozen, even through his gloves. It would be a difficult climb, even if he weren't attempting it in the middle of a firefight.

A man behind Gulbrand fell with a scream as a stream of bullets penetrated his armor. Eric took another step toward his son. He'd gone as far as he could in the damaged suit. Haeric pulled himself to the next handhold—and beyond the reach of Eric's protection. Eric turned to face the trolls, who continued to ignore him, focusing their fire on the Norsemen to Eric's left. Eric held his fire, not wanting to draw attention to Haeric. Undoubtedly the machines were aware of the man laboriously climbing the canyon wall, but had determined he was a low priority. For the moment, they were correct: miraculously, the Norsemen were holding their own against the machines.

Two more men soon fell, though, and many more machines were advancing to replace the others. Only the bottleneck created by the narrow opening and the smoking carcasses of the fallen trolls momentarily kept the rest of the machines at bay. Two of the trolls had already begun to shove the debris out of way; very soon the way would be clear and dozens more trolls would pour through the opening. Everything depended on Haeric reaching the ledge with the detonator.

Judging that Haeric was far enough up to avoid being hit by any machines targeting his father, Eric opened fire with his one functioning gun, trying to slow the progress of the trolls moving debris. Only two trolls remained standing past the location of the trap, and they were damaged and taking heavy fire. By now, the civilians and marines were probably aboard *Varinga*. Dornen wouldn't keep his ship on the ground if there was a threat from the trolls, but if Haeric could trigger the bomb, it would buy him enough time to get the Norsemen aboard.

As the trolls in the gap shoved the last of the debris aside, a thundering boom echoed through the canyon, audible even over the constant machinegun fire. Looking up, Eric saw a shower of sand and gravel. The giant boulder pitched forward, slid a few inches, and then fell.

"Move!" shouted Eric. "Get back!" The men near the boulder turned and ran. Eric hopped twice on the suit's one good leg, fell on his face, and continued to crawl. Glancing back, he saw a chunk of rock take out one of the nearby trolls, leaving only one standing on the near side of the gap. Those under the boulder tried to advance to avoid it, but they were too slow. The boulder came down with a crash, crushing the trolls underneath it and trapping those on the other side. As a dust cloud billowed toward them, the Norsemen farther from the boulder concentrated their fire on the last remaining troll, and it staggered and collapsed. Victory cries went up from the Norsemen.

"To the ship!" Eric commanded. "That bastard Dornen won't wait long!" As the men began to make their way back toward the valley, Eric turned to call to his son, but the dust cloud made it difficult to see, and the infrared on his suit was no longer working. "Ragnald!" Eric called. "Do you see Haeric?"

Ragnald stopped and scanned the area. "No. Maybe—wait, Haeric!" He ran into the dust cloud.

"Is he there?" Eric cried. "Haeric!"

For some time, there was no response. The dust began to settle. From somewhere beyond the boulder, Eric heard explosions—trolls trying to blast the rock away. Then he saw Ragnald trudging out of the cloud, carrying something before him.

"Haeric!" Eric cried, lurching forward, dragging the broken leg behind him. "Is he shot?"

"I don't think so," Ragnald said. "I am sorry, Eric. I think his neck is broken. He must have fallen when the bomb went off." Haeric's body lay limply in the arms of Ragnald's suit.

"No!" Eric shouted. "He knew what to do. He knew to get out of the way—" He broke off as more explosions went off on the other side of the boulder.

"Eric! Ragnald!" called Gulbrand, from near the mouth of the canyon. "We must get to the ship!" The others were already ahead of him.

Eric threw open the suit's chest plate and climbed out. The cold hit him like a slap across the face. He ran to Ragnald. "Give him to me," he said, holding out his arms. "Give me my son!"

"We must go," said Ragnald. "I will carry him to *Varinga*." Another explosion sounded, and a crack crept across the surface of the boulder. Eric wanted to argue, but he knew Haeric's only chance was to get him to *Varinga* as quickly as possible. The Truscans' magic might still save him. "Go, then!" he shouted. "Save my son!"

Ragnald nodded and broke into a run, following the others to the valley. Eric ran after him, the icy air burning in his chest. Already his toes had gone numb. He could not match Ragnald's pace, and he soon fell behind. Cold and exhausted, he stumbled across the rocky ground in the darkness as the sounds of shattering rock echoed around him. *I will die here*, he thought, *cold and alone on a strange world millions of miles from my home. And yet, it will be all right. It will be all right if Haeric lives. Please, Odin. Please, Christ. Let Haeric live.*

At last he stumbled into the open valley. Just ahead of him stood a man in a mech suit. Moving closer, Eric saw that it was Ragnald, still holding Haeric's lifeless body. He stood staring across the valley. "Ragnald," Eric said. "What…."

And then Eric saw it: a sleek black triangle, rocketing away on a plume of white flame. The rest of the Norsemen stood scattered across the northern end of the valley. There were maybe twenty of them—all that was left of Eric's platoon.

Varinga had left without them.

CHAPTER FIFTEEN

Freya walked quickly across the valley floor, a headlamp lighting her way. She wore cold weather gear and a mask to protect her from the toxins in Voltera's atmosphere. Slung over her shoulder was a duffel bag stuffed with supplies—a last-second gift from a grateful miner.

The Norsemen were gathered a hundred yards or so from the place where the valley narrowed. She gathered from the sound of distant explosions that they'd been successful in executing the marines' plan to block the advance of the machines the Norsemen called trolls. She didn't know how long it would hold them, and she didn't particularly want to find out. From above, she had seen at least forty more heavy infantry units. As she neared the men, Eric, dressed only in his inner suit, ran to meet her.

"Wh-what happened?" Eric asked, shivering uncontrollably. "Where is the sh-sh-ship?"

Freya dropped the bag. She bent over, unzipped it, and pulled out a foil-lined blanket. "Here," she said, pressing it into his hands.

"N-no," Eric said. "Haeric." He pointed to Ragnald, who stood a few yards away, holding Eric's son with the suit's mechanical arms.

"My God," said Freya. She lay the blanket on the ground, and Ragnald stepped forward and gently lay Haeric on it. His neck was twisted at an unnatural angle. Freya pulled off her glove and felt at his neck with two fingers. Feeling no pulse, she removed his mask.

"You c-c-cannot...." Eric stammered. "The air...."

"He is dead," Freya said. Despite the brutal cold, there was no cloud of vapor from Haeric's nose. His skin was so pale that it looked blue in the light from Freya's lamp. "I am sorry, Eric."

"The Truscans have m-m-medicine," Eric said. "The sh-ship. Where is the sh-sh-ship?"

Freya folded the blanket over Haeric and went back to her bag. "While we were landing, the sensors picked up a group of Izarian warships as they dropped out of hyperspace," she said. "I tried to get him to wait, but he wouldn't." She pulled another blanket from the bag and held it out to Eric. He tried to take it, but it slipped from his numb fingers and fell to the ground. Freya picked it up and threw it over his shoulders. By this time, Eric was so cold that he couldn't feel any difference.

"Dornen couldn't wait another... five minutes?" Ragnald asked, clearly struggling to remember the units under the circumstances. The other men had gathered around them.

"I begged him," Freya said. "He said he'd already waited too long. He may be right. The Izarians—"

"We fight his war for him, and he leaves us behind?" said Bjorn. His tone was somewhere between utter disbelief and barely controlled rage.

"The T-T-Truscans have m-m-medicine," Eric said. "You must have b-b-brought s-s-something...." He fell to his knees and began to fumble with the zipper of Freya's bag.

"Eric, stop," Freya said, crouching down next to him. Still Eric clawed at the bag with his useless fingers. "Eric!"

He stared at her, uncomprehending. She saw confusion and anger on his face. She sympathized. Eric had seen the Truscans work miracles with their machines and medicines. They had healed third degree burns, healed broken femurs, cured fever and frostbite. And now she had to get him to understand that there was nothing anyone could do.

"Eric, listen to me. You're in shock. You have hypothermia. There is nothing we can do for Haeric now. All I have in my bag is blankets, some bottles of water, and a few food packets. It was all I had time to grab. Now we need to get out of here. There's a lot more of those machines on the way. Ragnald will carry Haeric and we'll make sure he gets a proper burial. Can you walk?"

Eric stared at her, shaking his head, teeth chattering.

"Gulbrand, carry Eric."

"He will not last long in this cold," Gulbrand said.

Freya considered the matter. Gulbrand was right. Without a suit or cold weather gear, Eric would be dead within an hour. "All right," she said. "We will have to backtrack to find something for him to wear. Did any of the marines... are there any cold weather outfits like this back there, that aren't being used?"

"Not in the canyon," Ragnald said. "The marines all made it out." He said it flatly, as if he couldn't quite believe it.

"One of the mech suits then," Freya said. "Can you locate a suit that's still online back there?" It was a ghoulish thing to contemplate, dragging a corpse out of a suit to put Eric in it, but they had no other options.

"We can't go back there!" Bjorn said. "Those trolls could break through at any moment!"

"We don't all have to go," said Freya. "If the rest of you can lead the machines away from the canyon, Gulbrand and I—"

"Ma'am?" said a weak voice behind her. Freya turned. A young man, named Arne, stepped forward. "That may not be... necessary." The man's face was as white as chalk.

"Arne?" asked Bjorn, moving toward the man. Arne was part of Bjorn's squad. "Are you all right?"

"No, sir," gasped Arne. "Piece of shrapnel. Punctured my armor. Thought it was just a scrape, but..."

Freya punched a code into the suit's chest plate and pulled it open. Arne half-fell out of the suit. She couldn't catch him, but she managed to break his fall and lowered him to the ground. The right leg of his inner suit was drenched with blood, and there was a large tear just below the groin. Inspecting the wound, Freya could see that the femoral artery had been nicked. The chunk of metal was still in Arne's leg; that was probably the only reason he was still alive. The shrapnel must have hit at just the right angle to slip between the two heavy plates at the hip joint. With surgery and a transfusion, he might have a chance. On Voltera, he was a dead man.

"Trolls have broken through," shouted a man running toward them from the canyon mouth.

"We must go," Ragnald said. "Gulbrand, take Haeric. I will carry Arne." He stepped forward to pick up the dying man.

Freya went to Eric's side and pulled his arm over her shoulders. He felt cold even through her thick coat. "You've got to get into the suit," she said. "Come on, walk with me." Eric dumbly put one foot in front of the other until they were in front of the suit. She helped him climb inside, typed a command into the control panel on the suit's chest, and then closed it up. "Ragnald, I've paired Arne's suit with yours. Unless you tell it otherwise, it will follow you." Ragnald nodded, understanding. Eric was in no condition to operate heavy machinery.

"Let's move!" said Ragnald, and the men began to move out. Freya ran after them, but she hadn't gotten more than a few feet when she was scooped off her feet.

"With respect, Ma'am," said Bjorn from behind her, "I think you'll be better off if I carry you."

She nodded, curling up in the huge metal arms as the mech-suited men bounded across the valley floor.

*****

"You're sure there aren't any more trolls down there?" Ragnald asked. From their vantagepoint on the southern lip of the crater, they could just make out the lights of the refinery, some ten miles away. With magnification, Ragnald had spotted about a dozen golems patrolling the area with machineguns, but there was no way to know what was hidden behind—or inside—the huge mobile building.

"Ninety percent sure," said Freya.

"How much is that?"

"Let's just say our odds of taking the refinery are better than our odds of hiding indefinitely in the mountains. But we've got to move fast. The trolls will return eventually."

They had spent the previous five hours leading the trolls away from the mobile refinery, which was the only shelter for three hundred miles other than the cave in the mountains to the west where the miners had been hiding for the past several months. Sergeant Macron had told Freya that the cave's supply of food had nearly run out, and the portable filters they were using to make their air breathable were beginning to clog with dust. They wouldn't have lasted another week if *Varinga* hadn't arrived.

"Why did you stay?" Ragnald asked.

"The Truscans are human," Freya said, "but they aren't my people. And I did get you into this, after all."

"You will die here with us."

"Maybe. Let's take that refinery and then we'll see."

CHAPTER SIXTEEN

Ragnald knew there was no possibility of taking the golems by surprise. The Norsemen could only hope that the machines hadn't been programmed to destroy the refinery rather than let it be taken—and that the trolls wouldn't return before the golems had been dealt with. The trolls would receive word of the attack the second it started; the Norsemen's only advantage was their slightly superior speed.

The nineteen Vikings loped across the plain in their metal armor, closing rapidly on the sprawling building, which rested on three sets of massive treads that allowed it to cross rugged terrain despite its size. A single golem stood at the top of its highest tower, scanning the horizon. The others patrolled the exterior with mechanical precision. The Norsemen still had seen no trolls or other heavy infantry, which was a good sign, but Freya had warned them that the refinery itself was equipped with missile batteries and heavy machineguns. If luck were with them, these had been exhausted by the defenders before the Izarians had taken the refinery.

Luck was not on their side. A few seconds after the golem in the tower locked onto them, several missiles streaked toward them. "Scatter!" Ragnald ordered, and the men began to spread out. A missile detonated just behind him, throwing him forward. He threw up his hands and landed on the suit's forearms, rolling onto his back and executing a somersault. He sprang onto his feet and kept running, a grin spreading across his face. He'd performed this maneuver many times in training, but never thought it would serve him well in an actual battle!

His smile faded as the explosions continued to his left and right. His display indicated that one suit was badly damaged and two others were inoperable. Their assault had barely begun and they were down to sixteen men. Eric, half-mad from grief and cold, had remained behind with Freya and the two dead men.

More explosions erupted all around him, but the men were now spread out well enough that the missiles could no longer effectively target more than one man at a time. They ran erratically, dodging and weaving to stymie the machines' targeting, and no more men fell. Forming a rough semicircle about three hundred yards out from the southern edge of the refinery, they closed on their target.

The defenders switched to heavy machineguns, pelting the Norsemen with a relentless barrage of bullets. Meanwhile, the golems had gathered on the south side of the refinery, guns at the ready, waiting for the attackers to advance within range. The Norsemen, not wanting to damage the refinery (nor waste ammunition), held their fire as well. Three more men fell, their suits torn apart by the heavy guns, before Ragnald gave the order to open fire. They were within a hundred yards of the refinery.

The golems had begun firing as well, but their guns did little damage, and the Norsemen quickly dispatched them. The attackers ducked under the continuing barrage from the heavy machineguns, pressing against the refinery's treads. Soon the only men within the guns' range of fire were those who had fallen on the plain. White icons went gray as bullets riddled the bodies of men in incapacitated suits.

Ragnald led the men around the edge of the tread. As Gulbrand and four other men exited their suits, Ragnald tore a hatch off its hinges and they charged into the refinery, armed with handheld guns. They found four more golems inside, manning the refinery's heavy weapons. None of them were armed. They tried to fight, but Ragnald's men easily subdued them and then permanently deactivated them by putting a bullet into each golem's core processor. They tossed the broken machines outside. While Ragnald worked on getting the fallen men and broken suits loaded aboard the refinery, Gulbrand went with two other men to retrieve Freya and Eric, who waited on the plain several miles back. Once Freya was aboard, she made her way to the refinery's transport controls while Ragnald and Gulbrand worked on getting the rest of the suits aboard. By the time everything was loaded, she'd managed to get the refinery rolling. She directed it toward the northeast, where a road had been constructed to allow trucks to carry refined helium-3 to a launch pad located near Voltera's equator, a few miles north of the crater. Surveillance of the surface from *Varinga* indicated that three cargo ships sat on the launch pad, awaiting shipments to carry off-planet. The launch area was guarded only by a few golems. If they could reach it, and if at least one of the ships was operable, Freya thought she could still get them off Voltera. Having thoroughly studied the astronautical systems of both IDL and Cho-ta'an ships, as well as picking up what she could about CDF systems, she was confident she could pilot a cargo transport.

The refinery wasn't fast, but it could move almost as quickly as the trolls, which, according to the refinery's radar, had not yet returned to the crater. The refinery was too big to take on the narrow road out of the crater, so they would have to exit and travel the last few miles with the mech suits. With a little luck, they could take control of the launch pad before the trolls caught up with them.

The men spent most of the first eight hours of the journey sleeping. Only a small part of the so-called refinery was for processing helium-3; most of it was storage space and living quarters for the miners. Helium-3 was neither flammable nor radioactive, so there was no danger keeping it so close. Freya watched the radar for signs of the trolls while tending to the men's wounds. The refinery was essentially self-driving; she just told it to travel north as quickly as possible.

When the men were rested, they ate and drank and performed what repairs they could on the suits. The refinery was stocked with food, water and medical equipment, and it also had a workshop equipped with welding equipment and other tools, and thanks to the extra suits, they had plenty of spare parts. One of the men, named Tarben, had been a blacksmith, and took quickly to the metalworking tools. They got a suit working for Freya and reloaded the suit's ammunition from the refinery's weapons store. Working with Freya, they even managed to adjust the suits' missile launchers to accept the slightly larger missiles used by the refinery's batteries. If they did have to face the remaining trolls, they would be ready.

Eric had recovered from shock and hypothermia, but he remained sullen and reserved. Nor was he the only one. They had lost two thirds of their number in the brief time they'd been on Voltera. The Vikings were not strangers to death, but to lose so many over such a short time was almost unthinkable. Among the dead were some of the most well-loved and admired men of Eric's band: Viggo and Thorvald had been killed in the initial engagement with the trolls, and Halfdan had died during the assault on the refinery.

Worse, these men had died in a meaningless battle on a world that meant nothing to the Norsemen. Their corpses were wrapped in plastic sheets and laid on the roof of the refinery in the hopes that the survivors could find a way to bury them in the frozen ground of this hateful planet.

The survivors fared little better. Abandoned by their supposed allies, their hope now rested in the possibility of fleeing the planet in a stolen cargo ship. Even if they were successful, what would they do then? If fifty men were too few to assault Izar, then what good were fifteen? Perhaps they would return to Earth and await their death there. They were not needed at Ragnarök.

The refinery reached the edge of the crater late the next day. Freya had spotted the trolls on radar an hour earlier, about twenty miles away and closing. The Norsemen exited the refinery and made their way quickly up the road that ran along the crater's edge. Upon reaching the top, they continued north until they reached the launch area. The launch area, consisting of a large tarmac and a dozen or so steel-frame buildings, was guarded only by a score of golems, which the Norsemen easily overcame. Three cargo ships rested on the tarmac. Evidently the bulk of the security force had been moved south to deal with the marines.

When the area had been cleared of hostile machines, Freya made her way to the control tower. Using the tower's superior radar system, she could get a better idea of the size of the threat they faced from the KW23s and determine if there were any other machines on the way. The first thing she did, though, was to disable the jamming signal the machines had been broadcasting. Almost immediately she received a transmission from *Varinga*. The ship was taking fire from several Izarian craft and was going to have to make an emergency jump from within the Voltera system. As Freya understood it, gravitational fields interfered with the hyperdrive, potentially causing catastrophic problems—anywhere from the ship jumping hundreds of lightyears in the wrong direction to instant annihilation. Commander Dornen had waited as long as he could, trying to get *Varinga* as far as possible from Voltera and the other planets of the system, but at this point it was either attempt the jump or be blown apart by Izarian missiles. Freya sent a response, but it probably never reached *Varinga*: twenty minutes later, the incoming transmissions ceased. There was no way to know what had happened to her.

Having determined that the nearest trolls were still an hour away, Freya let Ragnald organize their defenses while she tried to figure out how to pilot a Truscan cargo ship. Eric and Gudmund dug a grave for Haeric and Arne, and the men took a brief respite to bury them and speak a few words commending the dead to Valhalla. It was all they had time for. When Gudmund had finished tamping down the earth with the feet of his suit, the men went back on alert. Only Eric remained at the grave, mourning his son. Freya returned to the cargo ship.

Despite her experience with similar craft, she was initially bewildered by the controls. It figured: nothing about this mission had gone as planned. Eric's men had faced an Izarian force much more powerful than they'd been led to expect, and the Izarian ships had arrived sooner and in greater numbers. Dornen's final message indicated that at least twenty ships were closing with *Varinga*. Yet Dornen had told her that CDF intelligence estimated that the Izarians had fewer than forty ships left in total, and most of those were occupied defending Izar itself.

Had Dornen been mistaken about the size of the Izarian fleet? Perhaps, but that didn't explain why the Izarians had sent a hundred heavy infantry units to deal with a minor insurrection on an unimportant mining planet.

Unless it wasn't so unimportant after all.

Dornen had told her the Izarian war effort depended heavily on helium-3, and that they had already burned through their supply on Izar. There were, of course, many other ways of generating power—she gathered that the Concordat planets used fission reactors, solar power, geothermal plants, and many other technologies. If a world ran out of, say, plutonium or fossil fuels, it would find some other way to generate power. History showed that human ingenuity was boundless when it came to finding ways of generating power.

But the Izarians weren't human. Supposedly they were a race similar to humans, but almost no one had actually seen an Izarian. Not even Commander Dornen, who had been at war with them for years, had ever seen one. Perhaps the machines *were* the Izarians.

In all the stories she'd heard about the machines—from Commander Dornen's tales of space battles to Ragnald's account of the battle on Voltera—one thing stood out: although the machines were fast, precise, deadly and determined, they were not particularly creative. When faced with an obstacle like a boulder, they blasted it with missiles until it was gone. Although a sort of low cunning had prompted them to send the golems ahead in case of a trap, it never occurred to them to wonder why a lone man would climb up a stone wall in the middle of a heated battle. It was if they'd been programmed with certain tactics but didn't understand the reasoning behind them. Ultimately, their strategy depended on overwhelming the enemy with sheer numbers and firepower.

If the Izarians were machines, lacking the human genius for invention and problem-solving, they would have a hard time with non-linear challenges. If they ran out of helium-3, they would try to find more of it. They would look on other worlds, but perhaps the conditions on those worlds were not suitable for the mining methods they were familiar with. So they would do what greedy and uncreative human beings did: they would steal it from someone else. And if they ran into resistance, they would throw machines at the problem until it went away.

None of this, of course, explained where the Izarians had come from, or how they had come to possess the technology they already possessed. Probably there had once been a race of beings who had built the machines for some purpose and programmed certain behaviors into them, but those beings had died off, leaving the machines to replicate and spread across the galaxy, eradicating any beings they saw as competition.

If her theory was correct, then Dornen had, purely by accident, hit upon the Achilles' heel of the Izarians. He'd brought *Varinga* to Voltera looking for a means to defeat the Izarians, and although he might never know it, he'd found it. The Izarians were desperate for helium-3.

Their response to the insurgency on Voltera and to the arrival of *Varinga* was not a sign of strength but rather of weakness. They had thrown everything they could at Voltera because without it, their war effort—in all likelihood, their entire civilization—would grind to a halt. All the Norsemen had to do to cripple the Izarians was hold Voltera. In fact, all they really needed to do was destroy the refinery. If she were correct, the Izarians would never figure out how to build another one.

There was a problem with this strategy, though: it would result, at best, in a stalemate. The Izarians would likely still be able to complete their campaign of deploying planet-killers to wipe out every known human world. The two hundred or so people aboard *Varinga* were probably already dead, either by the hand of the Izarians or annihilated in a hyperspace mishap. And even assuming that Earth was spared from the genocidal rampage of the Izarians, a thousand years from now what remained of humanity would face extinction at the hands of the Cho-ta'an.

No, it would not be enough to destroy the refinery or simply hold onto Voltera indefinitely. Freya needed to get off this planet and somehow ensure the survival of humanity.

All these thoughts raced through her head while she tried to figure out the maddeningly complex controls of the cargo ship. Yet it was not her ponderings on the Izarians and the fate of humanity that were hindering her efforts. Ordinarily she had no trouble working on two problems at once. In fact, she found solving technical problems easier when she let her instincts guide her, allowing her mind to drift. She was missing something.

She'd mastered the controls of the Gemini spacecraft. She'd learned everything there was to know about piloting IDL ships. And she'd spent four years navigating a Cho-ta'an craft through deep space. It shouldn't be so difficult to figure out how to fly a simple Truscan cargo ship. After all, the Izarians had done it, hadn't they? They hadn't brought their own cargo ships to Voltera; they'd simply appropriated the Truscan ships along with the rest of the operation.

Of course.

She didn't *need* to fly the ship. The Izarians would already have programmed it. That was why the nav system seemed so complicated. The Izarians wouldn't bother to stick a golem in the pilot's chair. They would just upload the instructions directly to the nav computer. She was looking at Izarian programs running on a Truscan operating system. Once she realized that, everything made sense. The nav system wasn't responding properly to her commands because another program, hidden in its memory, was countermanding her. It was essentially a virus, hijacking the system for its own ends. With enough time, she could probably remove the virus, but that was unnecessary. Fortunately, whoever developed the virus hadn't bothered to hide their intentions. Once she knew it was there, it was easy enough to figure out how it was going to act.

A smile crept across Freya's face.

She knew how she was going to beat the Izarians.

CHAPTER SEVENTEEN

It was a simple matter to trick the cargo ship's nav computer into thinking it had been loaded full of helium-3 when in fact it held only sixteen Norsemen (including Freya) in mech suits, along with oxygen tanks and various supplies. The ship had launched and was already nearing escape velocity over Voltera when a force of KW23s arrived at the launch site to find the flaming wreckage of two other cargo ships.

Because the ship was of Truscan design, it was not equipped with the more advanced hyperspace drive used by the Izarians. That meant Freya and the Norsemen had a five-day voyage to the edge of the Voltera system. The cargo hold was a bit cramped for sixteen mech suits, and while it was shielded and pressurized, it did not have its own air supply—hence the need for the oxygen tanks. But the Norsemen, who had on several occasions spent weeks at sea under much worse conditions, did not complain.

After five days, the ship jumped into hyperspace of its own accord. A few hours of subjective time later, it emerged again at the edge of the Izar system, before spending another five days traveling to Izar itself. Along the way its computer was queried numerous times by robotic sentries, and each time, the virus-infected computer gave the expected answer. A human being who witnessed a cargo ship arriving without advance notice from a hotly contested planet would probably have ordered the ship quarantined to verify that all was as it seemed. No such order was issued. The ship achieved orbit over Izar and then descended into the atmosphere. Freya, having half-expected to be blown out of the sky as soon as they neared the planet, was stunned when the ship settled to the ground. She did her best to hide her shock from the Norsemen, who were ignorant of the string of conjectures that had gone into her plan.

Freya did not know the exact landing coordinates; only that they would set down on one of the landing areas adjacent to one of the six helium-3 reactors. It didn't really matter, though: the spokes were nearly identical, and each of them led to the central control hub. The moment the ship hit the ground, Freya threw open the hatch and the Norsemen, led by Eric, poured out. Over the course of the journey, Eric's grief had hardened into grim determination: he was going to get vengeance on the Izarians for killing Haeric.

The Norsemen were greeted by a large, crane-like robot that hovered over the cargo, whirring and buzzing as it tried to locate the tanks of helium-3 it was expecting. It was unlikely the machine had the intelligence to recognize the Vikings as a threat, so they left it alone rather than draw attention to themselves.

Eric led the men across the tarmac toward the power plant in the distance. Stealth was not an option; their only chance was to reach the control hub before the bulk of the city's defenses had mobilized against them. If Freya was right about the importance of Voltera, the city's defenses would be minimal, but they couldn't afford to get bogged down in an extended firefight.

The landing area's security forces spotted them before they'd even reached the edge of the tarmac. Fortunately these were just golems whose small caliber guns were no threat, but the machines were in constant radio contact with each other, meaning that the entire city would soon be on alert. The Norsemen didn't even take the time to cut down the golems with.

They spotted the first fliers just before they reached the power plant. They didn't engage with these either, betting that the fliers would opt not to use their missiles so close to the reactor. The fliers harassed them with machineguns, but these were unlikely to do any serious damage as long as the Norsemen kept moving. The men leapt onto the roof of the plant using their suit rockets. Izar's gravity was slightly stronger than Voltera's but not as strong as Earth's. They bounded along the roof of the huge building in two columns as a growing flock of fliers circled overhead and scores of golems raced around the building on either side. Eric and Ragnald each led a column; Freya, who was less experienced with the suit but whose guidance was vital to the assault, followed immediately behind Eric. Gulbrand, behind her, had been tasked with making sure she remained unharmed.

Several tanks and heavy infantry units had begun to converge on the spoke where the Norsemen were headed. This spoke, an asphalt road some eighty feet wide, led directly through one of the six main factories and then continued to the control hub, which was a roughly dome-shaped building some two hundred yards across. The spokes were connected by a concentric circle of smaller roads. Moving along the road were hundreds of machines of various shapes and sizes, most of which were of one of the six types produced in the six main factories. The areas between the roads were taken up by other buildings, most of which also seemed to have been constructed from a limited set of standard types. Except for the sheer size of it and its circular design, the place looked more like a circuit board than a city.

The non-military machines had moved aside to make way for scores of tanks, KW23s, light infantry units, and every other type of machine capable of fighting, which moved in perfect sync to block the Norsemen's advance. Many of the closer machines fired their guns at the attackers, but either out of fear of a reactor leak or confidence in their ability to dispatch the threat without causing major damage to the city, they continued to refrain from using missiles.

On Eric's orders, the men fanned out across the roof and fired a volley of missiles in unison toward the gathering of war machines. As explosions erupted ahead of them, Eric shouted another order and the Norsemen suddenly veered to the left. They reached the edge of the roof and leaped off, manually firing their rockets to carry them as high as possible over the city. The fliers scattered, but not before the Norsemen had downed several of them with their machineguns. When Eric's suit was down to twenty percent fuel, he ordered the men to cut their rockets. They came down like so many stones, their rockets kicking in again just before they hit the ground. They landed in the middle of the next spoke over, some two hundred yards past the machines lined up to stop them.

Some of the men landed on the road; others flattened machines that were unfortunate enough to be under them. A few, including Freya and Gulbrand, came down on nearby buildings. They quickly regrouped, eliminated a handful of light infantry machines nearby, and then continued their advance. The city was now clearly on high alert: cranes, delivery trucks and all sorts of other non-military machines moved to block their path, while fliers continued to strafe them. Eric's men leaped over the obstacles when they could and blew them up when they had to. At last they reached the place where the road ran through the factory, blasting their way through a line of delivery trucks and running into the tunnel beyond.

Machines poured toward them from several smaller roads that branched off the tunnel into various parts of the factory. Fortunately these were not war machines; a few were delivery vehicles or other machines of low intelligence, but most were unarmed golems. Before the Norsemen had reached the far end of the tunnel, they were surrounded by thousands of the man-like creatures, who threw themselves at the attackers like madmen trying to appease a malevolent god. Some of the machines lacked heads or an outer shell; in its desperation the city was throwing unfinished machines from the assembly lines at them. The Norsemen gunned them down by the dozen, carving a path to daylight.

Freya, following close behind Eric, could hardly fire her guns fast enough to keep the zombie-like golems at bay. They posed no real threat except as a collective barrier; she nearly fell on her face as she picked her way through the metal-and-plastic corpses. Her relief at nearing the end of the tunnel vanished as a wave of fire came at them along with a shockwave that knocked her ten feet backward and left her lying, half in a daze, on a pile of metal faces, limbs and torsos. Even with the suit's sound dampeners, her ears rang. Eric lay on his side a few feet away, struggling to get to his feet. Ahead of them, just beyond the tunnel, were three tanks, their guns aimed toward the attackers.

"Up!" shouted a voice somewhere nearby. She became aware of somebody pulling on the left arm of the suit. Gulbrand. She got up as another explosion erupted behind them. Gulbrand ran ahead of her, guns blazing, and she followed, no longer sure which direction they were going. When at last she fully regained her senses, she realized they were somewhere well inside the factory. The only machines she saw were metal presses, lathes, conveyer belts and other bolted-down equipment: anything capable of moving independently had been conscripted to stop the attackers.

"We have to find another way in," Gulbrand said. "Eric and the others will keep them distracted."

Freya nodded, seeing the sense of the idea. Her display told her that three men had been killed in the tunnel. It had taken them too long to get to the hub; the entire city had been mobilized against them.

She scanned the factory, using the suit's variable intensity x-ray scope to map the building. Gulbrand urged her to hurry, while gunfire and explosions sounded from the tunnel.

"There!" she said, pointing to a door across the factory floor.

"How...?" Gulbrand asked, and she realized the problem at the same moment. Although it was built by and for machines, the factory—indeed the entire city—seemed to be constructed at a normal human scale. The ceiling here was high enough for the mech suits to stand, but the doors and corridors were standard human size. They would have to ditch the suits.

CHAPTER EIGHTEEN

Gulbrand exited his suit and then helped Freya out of hers. They moved quickly across the factory floor, armed only with handguns and a satchel of plastic explosives Gulbrand had brought from the refinery. Fortunately, the atmosphere was breathable.

When they reached the door, however, they found it impossible to open. Not merely locked; it had no handle, knob or visible lock of any kind.

"I will blow it open," said Gulbrand, unslinging the satchel.

"Wait," said Freya, noticing a small lens at about eye level. They had brought the explosives to break into the control hub and destroy whatever they found inside. Not knowing what was in there, they had brought enough charges to destroy a city block. Still, she'd rather not waste them. She found a golem head lying on the floor not far away and held it up to the lens. A thin red beam scanned the barcode on the golem's forehead and the door slid open. "Let's go," said Freya, moving into the corridor beyond with the golem head under her arm. Gulbrand followed her and the door slid shut behind them.

The corridor took them most of the way to the control hub. Freya had memorized the surveillance photo of the city Dornen had showed them, but she had no way to know how to get inside the hub from where they were. She just had to trust the driving idea behind the city's design: all roads lead to the Hub.

The corridor came to a dead end; the only way out was a vertical shaft overhead. A ladder of metal rungs led upward into darkness. Gulbrand insisted on going first, and Freya followed as the distant rumble of explosions continued. She wondered how much longer Eric and his men could hold out. She couldn't even be certain Eric was still alive, and without his leadership they wouldn't last long. So far she and Gulbrand had encountered no resistance—no autonomous machines at all, in fact—but this could only be because the Izarians were throwing everything they had at Eric's men.

They emerged at an intersection of corridors, and they continued hubward, using the golem head when necessary to open doors. At last they reached a door that would not open. When Freya scanned the barcode, a tiny red light would flash next to the lens, but nothing else happened.

"I guess that's as far as this thing is going to get us," said Freya, making to drop the golem head.

"Hold on," said Gulbrand. "Give it to me."

She handed him the head, and he proceeded to yank the innards out of it. He then stuffed three of the lumps of plastic explosive into it. "I suspect we are going to meet more resistance beyond this door." Freya nodded. He inserted one of the detonators, putting it on a five second timer. Then he pulled out another charge and knelt at the door.

"Where are you going to put the charge?" she asked. The door looked to be solid steel, and if it was like the others, it had no hinges or latch. She had her doubts about the effectiveness of an explosive. Gulbrand was still considering the question when the door slid open without warning. A golem holding a machinegun stepped through.

Before the machine could get its gun pointed, Gulbrand seized the barrel and pulled. The golem, holding tightly to the gun, stumbled into the corridor. Freya moved aside, slamming the butt of her fist into the side of the thing's head. The golem's head smashed into the wall, and she did it again, and again. She didn't know where the golems' brains were located, but she'd noticed blows to the head were effective in disorienting them. She would have kept going, but she saw that the door had begun to close. While Gulbrand continued to try to wrest the golem's gun away, she moved to the door, clutching at it with both hands to keep it from sliding shut. It barely slowed. Bracing her feet against the wall and straining with all her strength, she managed to arrest its movement. Behind her, Gulbrand had gotten on top of the golem and was smashing its head repeatedly into the floor. Beyond the door was a small room that appeared, for the moment, to be empty. Undoubtedly, the golem had already radioed for assistance. The smart thing to do would probably be to let the door close and run. But if they fled now, they would never get to the Hub.

Freya released the door just long enough to grab the golem head Gulbrand had stuffed with explosives. She slid it into the gap, and the door slammed into the metal skull and stopped, its motors whirring impotently. Gulbrand had a knee on one of the golem's arms, preventing it from using its gun, and continued to slam the creature's head into the floor with minimal effect. "Hold it still," said Freya, and Gulbrand shoved the thing's head against the floor and strained to hold it in place as the spindly but unnaturally strong limbs writhed and flapped beneath him. Freya held her gun to the golem's temple and fired. It spasmed and then lay still.

"We need to move," Freya said. She no longer heard explosions in the distance.

Gulbrand got to his feet, taking the golem's machinegun. Freya squeezed through the narrow door opening, her gun drawn. Gulbrand came after her, grunting as he pushed the door open far enough to get through. He kicked the golem head out of the way and let the door slide shut. The walls of this room were covered with pipes and conduits; it seemed to be a junction of sorts. The only other door was in the far wall. It slid open and another golem came through, leading several others behind it. Freya moved aside and Gulbrand opened fire at the same moment as the golem did, tearing through its fragile frame with the machinegun. Freya hit the next one in the head, and Gulbrand mowed down the rest before they could train their guns on him. Gulbrand fell against the door behind him with a grunt.

"Gulbrand!" Freya cried. He'd been struck in the belly, more than once by the look of the stain spreading across his clothes.

"We must... keep going," Gulbrand said, bending to pick up the explosive-laden skull.

"You're hit," Freya said. "Let me take a look at it."

"Nothing to do about it," Gulbrand said. "Go."

Freya nodded. She had neither the time nor the supplies to deal with a belly wound.

One of the fallen golems was stuck in the door, preventing it from closing. Freya slipped through the gap into the corridor beyond and Gulbrand followed, grunting with pain as he squeezed through. As they passed another four-way intersection, a door slid open ahead of them and golems poured through.

"Back!" cried Freya, and they retreated around the corner to the right as the machines opened fire. This corridor was noticeably curved—an indication they were getting closer to the Hub. Two golems came around the bend in the opposite direction, and Freya fired several times, hitting the one on the right in its left hip joint. It fell to the floor as Gulbrand blasted the torso of the other to pieces with the machinegun. Two more rounded the bend behind them, and Gulbrand took these out as well.

"Go!" Gulbrand commanded, holding out the satchel of explosives. "I will hold them off!" He dropped to one knee and fired another burst, taking out another pair of golems. The explosive-packed skull lay on the floor beside him.

"Gulbrand—" Freya began.

"Go, damn you!"

Freya turned and ran down the passage. She was now moving orthogonally to the center, but there would be another passage cutting inward up ahead. All roads lead to the Hub. She could only hope that Gulbrand had drawn most of its defenders away. She was almost to the next intersection when she was nearly knocked off her feet by the blast from an explosion behind her. Freya choked back tears. *May your gods carry you to a better world than this one, Gulbrand.*

She rounded the corner and was surprised to see a humanoid figure about fifty feet down the corridor, hurrying away from her. It looked like a golem, but it wore a deep red cloak with a hood covering its head. None of the other golems had worn any clothing at all. Was this an Izarian? A human? Some higher-ranking type of machine? It did not appear to be armed.

She ran after the being, gun raised and ready to fire. At the far end of a corridor, a door slid open and more golems armed with machineguns poured through. They aimed their guns in Freya's direction but did not fire. There could be only one reason for this.

Freya came up behind the cloaked figure and wrapped her left arm around its neck, bringing the figure to a quick halt. Its skin was cold and hard—machine, not human. With her right, she pressed her gun against its temple. She said nothing. The golems wouldn't understand her, and words were unnecessary. They knew what she was about. She had no doubt the golems, with their preternatural accuracy, could kill her without injuring the cloaked machine, but would they take the chance of a dying nerve spasm causing her to pull the trigger?

The answer appeared to be no. Whoever or whatever the cloaked figure was, the golems showed it a great deal more deference than they did to other machines. Would it be enough to get her into the Hub? It was the only chance she had.

She moved slowly forward, pushing the cloaked figure ahead of her. The golems kept their guns trained on her but backed away down the hall. Was the cloaked figure directing them, or were they taking orders from some higher power? If some greater intelligence were directing them—some vast computer at the center of the Hub, perhaps—what would happen if it came down to a choice between its own survival and that of the being in the cloak?

The golems continued to retreat, going through the door into the chamber beyond. Freya, still pushing the cloaked figure ahead of her, followed them. Checking to the left and the right to make sure she wasn't being flanked, she stepped into the chamber. It was perhaps a hundred yards across, with a vaulted ceiling in eight segments that narrowed to a single, huge column in the center. The walls were lined with various electronic displays and controls. Scores of golems stood at various points near the perimeter and scattered about the room, some of them in groups, others alone. Presumably they had been engaged in activities of some sort, monitoring or directing the production of machines in the city, perhaps. But now they all stood completely still, facing Freya. A few were armed, but most were not. None of them made any move toward her. The vast chamber was completely silent except for the quiet hum of the ventilation system.

Freya moved slowly forward, her hand on the cloaked figure's shoulder, the barrel of her gun at the base of its skull. Golems moved out of the way as they advanced, repelled like similarly charged particles. A circle formed some thirty feet out from her, closing behind as she moved toward the center of the chamber. She was now aware of several more red-cloaked figures, standing at various places throughout the room. Perhaps there were six, to match the symmetry of the city. One super-golem to oversee each segment spreading out from the Hub?

She continued forward, not knowing what she was walking toward. But although she was surrounded by enemies, still they did not act. She neared the huge column at the center of the chamber and saw that it was lined with doors. Six of them, no doubt, all leading to the same place. The machines pursued their pattern beyond all reason. She shoved the cloaked figure toward the nearest door. It scanned the cloaked figure's forehead and they went through. The door slid shut behind them.

They were in a featureless hexagonal room. It was empty. Freya wanted to weep. She had reached the nerve center of the Izarian Empire, and there was nothing there. In all likelihood, they would never let her out of this room. She would die here, a victim of her own hubris. She hadn't figured out the machines; they had set out a puzzle for her and then trapped her like a rat in a bucket.

CHAPTER NINETEEN

Gravity shifted under her. They were moving? They were moving! Of course. The little hexagonal room was an elevator. Perhaps she was wrong about this being a trap. But where were they going?

She released her hold on the cloaked figure, who took a step away but did not otherwise react. Freya kept the gun pointed at it. Freya had no sense of how fast they were moving. Five feet per second? Twenty? She counted to a hundred, and still the room descended. She was almost to two hundred when she felt it slow. A few seconds later, she had the sense they had stopped. She motioned to one of the doors, and the cloaked figure stepped toward it. The door slid open. The figure stepped out and Freya followed it.

They were in what appeared to be a modestly furnished apartment. Except for the hexagonal shape and greater size, it reminded Freya of the captain's quarters aboard *Varinga*. The floor plan was entirely open; there were no dividing walls. Against one wall was a bed. In the bed was a man. He looked to be elderly, although the complete lack of hair on his head made it difficult to determine his age. His skin was an unnatural shade of white and covered with lumpy growths. The fingers on his right hand were conjoined, so that the hand resembled a claw.

As Freya and the cloaked machine approached, the man sat up with a start. "Must you interrupt my sleep?" he asked. "I will answer your questions in the morning." To Freya's ear the language was strange, but her comm translated it with little difficulty. It was the same language spoken by the Truscans.

Freya moved closer to the bed, still holding her gun on the machine. "It is morning," she said. The comm translated for her.

"Who..." the man started. "You are not a Sixth." Freya saw now that the man's eyes were milky white. He was blind.

"What do you mean by 'Sixth?'"

"The machines that wear cloaks," the man said. "You are... human?"

"I am. My name is Freya. I've brought one of the Sixths with me."

"How... You have taken it hostage? Your people control the city?"

"Not exactly. I managed to get inside. Who are you?"

"My name is Sol. I am... the last of my kind. They keep me here, to ask me questions. And because of the... device."

"The device? What are you talking about?"

"Forgive me, this is... unsettling. I have not spoken to another person for many years. What is this language you speak? You do not sound like a Truscan."

"I'm Norse. From Earth. The Truscans are—were—my allies."

"Norse? You mean Scandinavian? How can this be?"

"It's a long story. Maybe I'll tell it to you someday. Right now I've got a bunch of friends outside who risked their lives to get me in here. I need you to tell me how to get them out of here safely."

"Do you really have one of the cloaked machines here with you?"

"I do. I'm holding a gun on it."

"Shoot it."

"It's my only leverage. If I shoot it now, I'll never get out of here."

"If you want to save your friends, shoot it. Now!"

The machine, sensing it was in danger, lunged toward Freya. Freya fired her gun, hitting the thing in the head. It fell to its knees and then collapsed. Freya knelt over it, but the machine was clearly defunct. She had put a bullet right through the crystalline structure that apparently served as its brain. The golem head Gulbrand had hollowed out had something similar in it. "Damn it," Freya said. "Why did you do that? We'll never get out of here now."

"They won't stop you," said Sol. "Not anymore."

"Yeah? Why don't you tell me what the hell is going on here?"

Sol nodded, rubbing his chin and thinking. "What do you know of the Truscans?"

"They are human beings, evidently descendants of Middle Eastern people who left Earth sometime early in the days of the Roman Empire."

"Yes, very good. They are the descendants of Roman soldiers and Jewish whores, if you can believe that. My own ancestors are from the distant future, the twenty-third century, when humanity was at war with another race of aliens."

"The Cho-ta'an."

"Yes! I understand now who you are. You are a descendent of the other group, the people who went back before us but arrived after. You see? My people went to Judea in the second century. Yours went to Scandinavia in the ninth century."

"You know of my grandmother? Carolyn Reyes? And the others?"

"The names have been lost, I'm afraid. It's been eight hundred years, you understand. That is… I'm sorry, the dates get confusing with time travel. As the story was told to me, early in the twenty-third century humans were at war with the Cho-ta'an. Earth had been rendered uninhabitable and the Cho-ta'an were on the verge of eradicating humanity. A human spaceship traveled back in time, apparently by accident, arriving in Europe during the Middle Ages. Evidence of this event prompted the people of the twenty-third century to send *another* ship backwards in time, but this one arrived even earlier. The crew of that ship were my distant ancestors. They arrived on Earth with the intention of filling their ship with people who could be the progenitors of a separate branch of humanity."

"A separate branch? Why?"

"Because history can't be changed. Understand that when this second ship, called *Freedom*, left earth full of Jews and Romans, the war with the Cho-ta'an was still two thousand years off. The crew of *Freedom* wanted to establish a human colony somewhere far from the reach of the Cho-ta'an, not only because the Cho-ta'an were a potential threat, but because *history itself* was a threat. The humans of the early twenty-third century had never encountered a race of humans whose ancestors left Earth in the second century. That meant that either that branch of humanity died off, or they settled in a place so far away from the main branch of humanity that even after two thousand years, the two branches had never met."

"The LOKI principle," Freya said.

"What?"

"My people call it the Limits Of Known Information. If you try to change history, you will fail, probably in a catastrophic manner."

"Precisely! So you see, my people—that is, the crew of *Freedom*—had to travel for hundreds of years to find a suitable planet outside the reach of both the Cho-ta'an and the other humans. Then, if the Cho-ta'an did eradicate the main branch, the second branch would survive. And perhaps if this second branch did eventually encounter the Cho-ta'an, they would be advanced enough technologically to defeat them."

"Sounds like a good plan. But something went wrong."

"Yes. *Freedom*'s crew eventually located a habitable planet. It was a bit closer to Cho-ta'an space—that is, what would eventually be Cho-ta'an space—than they would have liked, but they were desperate. So they landed on the planet, which they called Toronus. By this time, *Freedom*'s crew and its passengers had already bifurcated into two separate castes, with very little intermingling. For centuries after landing on Toronus, the crew lived aboard *Freedom*, which they turned into a sort of impregnable castle, while the passengers settled the land around it, making do with bronze age technology, subsisting much as medieval peasants had.

"Understand that at this point, the passengers, who called themselves 'Etruscans' after the lineage of one of their forebears, were only a few hundred in number. They lacked the genetic diversity to ensure healthy descendants beyond a few generations.

The crew, who came to be known by the Etruscans as 'Sentinels,' were in an even worse spot, as they numbered fewer than twenty. The Sentinels, however, possessed technology that the Etruscans did not, including a primitive form of stasis chamber that allowed them to artificially extend their own lives. The Sentinels were also said to harvest sperm and eggs from the Etruscans, though I do not know if this is true. The Etruscans came to resent and even hate the Sentinels, but the Sentinels had no motive but the continuation of the species. To that end, they devoted themselves to advancing the science of applied genetics, with some success. Through breeding controls and gene editing, the Sentinels were able to eliminate congenital defects among the Etruscans and increase genetic diversity, ensuring the survival of the species.

"The number of Etruscans—the name was at some point shortened to 'Truscans'—doubled, then quadrupled over the course of a few generations. Soon they numbered in the tens of thousands. As the population grew, so did their understanding of science. They had a big advantage over medieval peasants on Earth, you see: they had seen the Sentinels' technology, and although the Sentinels encouraged them to think in supernatural terms, the Truscans eventually threw off superstition and began to look for ways to create for themselves the sorts of wonderful tools and devices used by the Sentinels. This process was self-reinforcing: technology allowed the Truscans to live longer and gave them the luxury of educating their children in natural science. Three hundred years after the founding of the first colony on Toronus, the Truscans developed rudimentary space travel. A hundred years after that, they developed hyperspace gates, which allowed them to settle worlds in other solar systems. The Sentinels, for the most part, did not interfere with this process, and in fact encouraged it to some extent. After all, their ultimate goal was to foster a branch of humanity that was numerous and powerful enough to defeat the Cho-ta'an when the moment came."

"You are saying that the Sentinels were aware of the threat from the Cho-ta'an. But hadn't even encountered any Cho-ta'an at that point."

"Correct. The Sentinels knew of the Cho-ta'an only through the records passed down by their ancestors, who had traveled back in time from the twenty-third century. They knew the location of the Cho-ta'an home world, Yavesk, and the region of space that the Cho-ta'an would eventually colonize. They knew the main branch of humanity would eventually encounter the Cho-ta'an, and a war would break out—with catastrophic consequences.

"As the Truscans continued to spread out across the galaxy, though, the Sentinels became concerned that they would soon reach the regions of space that would eventually be colonized by the Cho-ta'an or the other branch of humanity. Ultimately the Sentinels decided on a drastic course of action: they would shut down the hyperspace gates that the Truscans used to travel between the nine worlds they had settled so far."

"I don't understand. Why didn't the Sentinels just tell the Truscans to avoid those regions of space?"

Sol smiled. "The answer to that is as old as the Garden of Eden: forbidden fruit is the sweetest. The Sentinels kept the Truscans in the dark for their own protection. The Truscans did not even know of the existence of Earth, except as a mythical place that was known to their remote ancestors. They were children who needed guidance."

"But how could the Sentinels shut down the gates?"

"The gates had been constructed with the knowledge and tacit approval of the Sentinels. You see, when the Truscans began investigating the properties of hyperspace, the Sentinels knew they were only a few decades from developing faster-than-light travel. So they gave the Truscans a gift: a device that could be used to generate a hyperspace field large enough to send a ship through. There was a cost to this gift, though: it was what you might call a 'black box,' a device whose inner workings cannot be determined through scientific analysis. The Truscans had a choice: use the hyperspace module without knowing how it worked or try to develop one of their own over the next several decades. They chose the easier option, as the Sentinels knew they would. So when the Truscans began to roam too far, the Sentinels sent out a simple encoded radio signal from their fortified lair on Toronus. The signal spread across space at the speed of light, shutting off the hyperspace gates one by one until, after twenty years, the last one went offline.

"By this time, the Truscan civilization was highly dependent on interstellar trade, so the deactivation of the gates resulted in chaos. Millions starved. Many more were killed in wars or the plagues that followed. Truscan historians refer to this event as the Collapse. If I'm not mistaken, the Collapse coincided with the Dark Ages on Earth. It would have been around 800 A.D. by Earth reckoning.

"It was a brutal, dark time, but the Sentinels had achieved their aim: by setting the Truscan march across the galaxy back by several hundred years, they eliminated the possibility of a cataclysmic meeting between the Truscans and their neighboring civilizations. That was, at least, what the Sentinels believed at the time. The Truscans, however, proved more resilient than expected.

"Less than fifty years after the Collapse, a group of Truscans on a planet called Stellarus invented the self-contained hyperspace drive. They began building hyperdrive-enabled ships and slowly reestablished contact with the other worlds. An interstellar organization called the Concordat was formed. Pre-Collapse records were so sketchy, however, that the locations of some of the other worlds could not be determined. For all the people of the Concordat worlds knew, other Truscan civilizations had also invented the hyperdrive and might even now be looking for them, or spreading out to other, as yet unknown worlds.

"The Sentinels, having allowed themselves to believe their long and thankless task was at last finished, had again let their numbers dwindle to fewer than twenty people. Many of these people possessed severe genetic defects due to genetic drift and inbreeding. They no longer had the strength or influence to reinvigorate their line with gametes from the Truscans. The Truscans, in fact, had stopped thinking of the Sentinels as a threat, and considered them a pathetic, effete race that would soon die out.

"But the Sentinels still possessed a technological edge over the Truscans, and they rededicated themselves to their cause. But how can a dozen or so people stop the spread of millions? The answer is obvious: self-replicating machines."

CHAPTER TWENTY

"The Sentinels sent out hyperspace-enabled probes, looking for habitable planets between Truscan space and the regions of space that would eventually be inhabited by the main branch of humanity—what you might call the Prohibited Zone. Eventually they found a world that was mostly ocean, but which could support human life and had at least one island that was large enough for their purposes. The few remaining Sentinels built a small ship that they used to travel to that planet, which is, of course, the one we are on now. *Izar* was the ancient name for the star it orbits; this planet was called Izar-4. Eventually *Izar* came to mean the planet itself. Being under the impression that the Sentinels had died out, the Truscans never figured out that the Sentinels and the Izarians were one and the same.

"The Sentinels spent the next fifty years building machines. These machines would build other machines, which would build factories that would build other machines, and so on. They envisioned a city that existed solely for the purpose of building machines that would be sent out on spaceships to occupy any habitable planets on the border of the Prohibited Zone. The idea was to dissuade the Truscans from settling on such planets, at least until the year 2227—the end of known history.

"While the Sentinels planned, the Truscans continued to push closer and closer to the Prohibited Zone. Soon it became clear that the Sentinels were running out of time. They simply didn't have the workforce to build the number of self-replicating machines they would need to stop the Truscans from reaching the Prohibited Zone. So they altered their plan. They created intelligent, human-like machines."

"Golems."

"Ah, golems. Yes, a good Hebrew word. The golems were near-human, and they made excellent assistants, but they lacked creativity and autonomy. In the end, the golems were not enough. So the Sentinels created another class of machines, which they called Nephilim. The Nephilim possessed intelligence and limited autonomy, but understanding the dangers of creating machines that could think for themselves, the Sentinels put strict limits on the Nephilim's thinking. Control algorithms, like blinders on a horse. They created only six Nephilim, to be sure that the Sentinels could keep an eye on them, and then they destroyed the plans, so no more could be built. With the help of the Nephilim, the Sentinels were able to complete their city, and the war machines began to depart for other worlds, to guard them like the angel at the entrance to the Garden of Eden.

"At this time, the machines were dependent on hyperspace gates for interstellar travel. This was a safeguard implemented by the Sentinels. If they ever lost control of the machines, they could shut down the gates as they'd done with the Truscans.

"But the Sentinels made a mistake. You see, they gave all the machines the ability to communicate instantaneously, by radio. Essentially, the machines are telepathic. And what is a human brain except a collection of semi-autonomous fragments that communicate with each other with near instantaneous speed?"

"You're saying the Six—the Nephilim—are self-aware?"

"I'm saying that the city itself is—or was—self-aware. The Nephilim were responsible for the higher brain functions. The golems are analogous to the cerebellum, responsible for more basic functions—what you might call the city's instincts and reflexes. The other five higher models are like collections of nerves. The body of this being, consisting of thousands of other machines, are spread across many worlds.

"The city decided its creators' plan was insufficient. It wanted to spread out across the galaxy, dominating its environment, as all living things do. But it was clever. It bided its time, learning about its creators and its enemies. Realizing how dependent it was on the hyperspace gates, it sent a virus into the gate control system, locking the Sentinels out. By the time the Sentinels realized what had happened, it was too late: they no longer had control of the gates. The machines went on the offensive. Rather than simply guard the Prohibited Zone, it sent its tendrils into Truscan space to eradicate humanity. Using information gleaned from the Sentinels' computers, it also began building spaceships equipped with self-contained hyperdrives.

"But the Sentinels, perhaps understanding the danger of what they were attempting, had developed another failsafe. Before creating the Nephilim, they had sent a few of their number to a distant planet called Kiryata to build a weapon more powerful than any weapon ever before devised. A planet-killer."

"I am familiar with this weapon."

"Then you know what it can do: destroy every living thing and every machine and structure on an entire planet. The scientists on Kiryata sent one of these devices here shortly before the city went rogue. If the machines ever turned against their creators, the Sentinels would activate the planet-killer. The planet-killer was hidden in a vault which, if opened, would activate the device. The vault required a human being to enter a specific ten-digit code once per day. If the code was not entered by a human being—identified by a brain scan—the device would activate. Thus, if the machines killed their masters before they had a chance to pull the switch, the device would still activate.

"Unfortunately, the machines discovered the vault and deduced its purpose. By this time, only five Sentinels were still alive. The machines imprisoned them and forced them, through various forms of excruciating torture, to enter the failsafe code every day. Eventually the machines discovered the location of Kiryata and forced the Sentinels there to build more of the devices—one for every known human world. By the time the devices were complete, four of the five remaining Sentinels on Izar had died."

"And you are the last."

"Indeed," said Sol. "I am kept alive because of that." He indicated a black stone pedestal, the top of which was a flat surface with a numeric keypad and a small digital display in the center of it. Moving closer to the pedestal, Freya saw that read 10901. It changed to 10900, then 10989. The intervals were about a second long, which meant they had just over three hours. "When I heard you enter, I thought you were one of the Six, come to ask me questions about human beings. They do that sometimes, to better understand us."

"To better kill us, you mean."

"Perhaps. Or perhaps to emulate us. They have what you might call blind spots. In their thinking, I mean. For example, they never thought to ask any of us for the location of Earth. They knew all humanity had originated on a planet the knew nothing about, but somehow their algorithm overlooked it. Or perhaps they intentionally left it alone. We'll never know. There are other blind spots, as you've undoubtedly discovered."

"Like their obsession with helium-3."

"Yes, exactly. They understand there are other ways to generate power, but they lack the ability to invent. Can you imagine how maddening that must be? To know something is possible but be unable to do it? They can build, they can reason, and they can even strategize to an extent, but they never create anything. With the kinds of questions they ask me sometimes, I think they're groping toward it, the idea of invention, like a child trying to make sense of calculus. Nor have they ever figured out how to build more Nephilim, which would allow the entity to reproduce—that is, to send other versions of itself to other worlds. They are limited to a single, central brain, and that was their undoing, as you see."

What do you mean?"

"Because you've lobotomized them, my dear."

"What? I?"

"That's a sixth of the thing's higher brain functions on the floor over there. How well do you think you'd function if I scooped out a sixth of your brain?"

"But… surely it can still function?"

"Certainly. Like a particularly well-crafted dishwasher. Trust me, dear. You have nothing more to fear from it. It has intelligence, but it lacks a will or identity. All six Nephilim were needed to hold it together. You'll be able to walk right out of here."

"And my friends?"

"If they were alive when you pulled that trigger, I'm certain they still are."

"Then... all this time... All those years that you and the others languished down here, being tortured... while the war raged across a dozen systems... this is all it took? A single bullet to the brain?"

"I'm sure that could be said of any number of wars," said Sol. "It usually only takes one madman with a plan to start it, and a bullet to the brain to end it."

"Yes," said Freya. "I suppose so. Your condition... your blindness, and the rest of it. That was the result of the torture?"

"Eh? Oh, no, they never tortured me. I saw what they did to the others. When they got around to asking me, I did what I was told. What was the point in resisting? The others gave in eventually. They all did. I'm afraid what you see in front of you is the result of old age and bad genes—mostly the latter. I was born blind and disfigured. Ten generations of inbreeding. I can only thank God my mind was unaffected. Three of my siblings had to be put down because they were of no use. I could easily have been born a monster."

"Yes," said Freya. "I can see that."

And she put a bullet in his brain.

CHAPTER TWENTY-ONE

The Izarian light infantry transport ship raced away from the planet, readying itself to make the jump into hyperspace. Aboard it were twelve exhausted Norsemen, one woman, thirteen top-of-the-line mech suits that had seen better days, and a single humanoid robot. It was fortunate that the ship could navigate itself, as none of the people aboard were in any shape to pilot it.

Like the rest of the machines that had been on Izar when Freya shot one of the six Nephilim, the ship was no longer guided by any higher intelligence. The conscious entity centered on the city had ceased to exist; in its place was a mere collection of thousands of semi-autonomous machines. Even the five remaining Nephilim were now only exceptionally complex machines, lacking any spark of sentience. Even so, it took considerable effort on Freya's part to convince the Norsemen to bring one along.

"I do not trust that thing," Eric said, glaring sideways at the Sixth, which did not react.

"It is a machine, Eric," Freya said tiredly. "No different from your mech suit or this ship."

"It killed forty of my men."

Freya could understand Eric's hesitance. Between the battle on Voltera and the assault on Izar, he had lost his son, his most trusted henchman, and most of his men. Eric would himself be dead if the battle had lasted a few minutes longer. They had been surrounded and nearly out of ammunition, taking heavy fire while hunkered down behind fallen machines, when the machines suddenly stopped fighting. Still, Freya was becoming frustrated with his obstinance. "You may as well blame a knife for cutting you," she said. "It's a tool. The machines are no longer sentient."

"You believe that because this man, this 'Sentinel,' told you? It was his kind that created them!"

"That is why I trust him. He had no reason to lie. They were holding him prisoner. The machines were as much his enemy as they were yours."

"Only because they turned on him."

"Yes. The Sentinels were trying to do the right thing. They wanted to preserve the human race, just as we do. They made mistakes, but I believe they were sincere in their intentions. That's partly why I trust him. Beyond that, the machines have been nothing but helpful since I destroyed that Sixth. They directed us to medical supplies, helped us find this ship, told us where we could find the facility where the Sentinels built the planet-killers. All we have to do is ask, and they obey. And if there was no threat from the five remaining Sixths, there certainly isn't any danger from a single one of them."

"You said they all talk together."

"Yes, but you saw what happened to the other Sixths." The dead man's switch having been triggered shortly after they left the atmosphere, they had watched as the wave of destruction had spread across the planet, converting every machine to inert masses of dust. "If this Sixth were capable of emotions like anger or the desire for revenge, don't you think it would have reacted to seeing the rest of its kind eradicated? Eric, look at that thing. It looks almost human, yes, but does it *feel* like a human to you?"

Eric glared at the Sixth again. "No," said Eric. "That is exactly why I do not trust it."

Freya gave up. "Sixth, are you familiar with the race known as the Cho-ta'an?"

"I have no knowledge of such a race."

"They are humanoid. Taller than the average human. Gray skin, hermaphroditic."

"I have no knowledge of such a race."

Well, that settled that. The Sixth wasn't going to be any help in coming up with a way to defeat the Cho-ta'an. Freya's current plan was to pick up where she had left off when *Varinga* had intercepted her ship weeks ago: she would retrieve the planet-killer from the Izarian facility located on a remote planet and find a way to get it to the Interstellar Defense League. The fact that the IDL would not be founded for 1300 years was a problem that she would address after she'd secured the planet-killer.

"Sixth, how long until we reach our destination?"

The Sixth spoke: "We will enter hyperspace in twenty-one minutes. We will spend four hours and eight minutes in hyperspace and then emerge into conventional space five hundred eighty-six thousand miles from Kiryata. Deceleration and landing is estimated to take three hours and fifty minutes. That makes a total elapsed subjective time of seven hours and fifty-eight minutes." At first the Norsemen had been dependent on Freya's translator to speak to the machines, but over the past few hours, the machines had learned the Norsemen's language.

"Perfect," said Freya. "I'm going to take a shower and then get some sleep." The transport ship, designed to carry a hundred light infantry machines, was fantastically luxurious compared to the cargo ship they'd taken to Izar.

*****

Freya was awakened from a deep sleep by an explosion that caused the ship to shudder and groan ominously. She unstrapped herself from the bed and pulled herself along the zero-gravity rungs toward the main cabin. Eric, looking like he had just woken up, floated just inside. He must have meant to keep an eye on the Sixth but had fallen asleep. The Sixth, one of its hands clutching a hand strap, floated perpendicular to Eric, completely still and as expressionless as always.

"What did you do, you pile of slag?" Eric roared, his arms and legs flailing in an impotent attempt to get to the machine.

"I have taken no action," said the Sixth. "We are under attack by an Izarian light cruiser."

"What?" Eric cried. "Tell it to stop!"

"I will do so."

Another explosion rocked the ship. The Sixth did not move.

"I said stop it!" Eric shouted. "Can't you all talk to each other?"

"The Izarian light cruiser is twenty-four thousand miles away. It is taking some time to complete the validation process."

"Validation process! What in the name of Odin's short and curlies are you talking about, goblin?"

"All machines in the network must complete a validation process before any other inter-machine communications are allowed. It is a safety feature to prevent malicious actors from counterfeiting valid inter-machine commands. Ordinarily the process takes less than ninety-six nanoseconds, but under the circumstances it is taking somewhat longer."

"How long will it be?" Freya asked, pulling herself closer to the Sixth.

"I estimate another two minutes and four seconds to establish routine communications. Please note that it will also take a non-trivial amount of time to explain the current unusual circumstances."

"You mean the destruction of Izar," said Freya.

"Yes. With enough time, the information will propagate to all units, but in the meantime, the machines will follow their most recently received orders."

"And this ship has been ordered to destroy us?"

"Its primary mission is to land on Kiryata to retrieve the planet-killer device and deploy it on a planet called Jabesh-Gilead."

"The last known human world," Freya said. "Why is it attacking us?"

"It has orders to fire on any ships that may interfere with its mission. It has determined that this infantry transport ship has not been assigned to this sector and is therefore no longer under the control of I Am." I Am, they had learned, was the name the machines used to refer to the self-aware entity centered on Izar City.

"How long will it take you to get it up to date on current events?"

"Once validation is completed, I estimate communicating the relevant information will take three minutes and five seconds."

The ship shuddered again, and the lights went out. Emergency lighting came on, and a warning flashed overhead that they were leaking air.

"We're not going to last another five minutes!" said Eric. "Just tell it we're on the same side!"

"It will not accept that information. It needs to be made to understand. I can do this, but it will require the transfer of seven point two gigabytes of data. Given the current data transfer rate of—"

"Then return fire!" Eric growled. "Blow that thing out of the sky!"

"Wait," said Freya. "Is there really no other way to get it to stop shooting at us? What if we surrender? That will buy you some time to talk to it."

"It will not accept surrender."

"Freya, don't be foolish!" Eric said. "You said yourself they're only machines. Let us destroy the thing before it kills us all!"

"All right," Freya said. "Do it."

"We are returning fire."

For several seconds, it was unclear whether anything was happening. Then another explosion rocked the ship. More warnings, which Freya could not make sense of, flashed overhead.

"Blasted machine!" Eric yelled. "It's betrayed us!" Having gotten hold of a handle, he launched himself toward the Sixth. The machine twisted out of the way and Eric slammed into the wall behind it.

"The Izarian light cruiser has been destroyed."

"What?" asked Freya. "Already?"

"The weaponry and armor of an light infantry transport is superior to that of a light cruiser," the Sixth said.

"Are there any others?"

"I'm not detecting any other ships in the vicinity."

"How badly is our ship damaged?"

"The hull has been breached. We are losing air at a rate of ten kilograms per minute. Life support is inoperable. Telemetry has sustained damage. Hyperdrive is inoperable."

"Can we make it to Kiryata?"

"It is probable. I recommend you secure yourselves and not engage in unnecessary activity that will increase oxygen usage."

*****

Freya awoke with a terrible headache. She was lying in a bed in a simply furnished bedroom. As she sat up, she felt unnaturally light. Low gravity, she thought. We're on Kiryata. She had a sense several hours had passed.

She got to her feet and went to the door. It led to a corridor, which was empty. Ordinary looking doors lined it on both sides. To the left, the corridor dead-ended; to the right it continued around a corner. She heard nothing but the faint hum of the ventilation system. She followed the corridor, letting out a gasp as she rounded the corner. She stood facing a huge garden—no, a jungle. Trees of sorts she had never before seen reached a hundred feet or more towards a sky so perfectly blue that it had to be artificial. The walls continued to her left and right, curving almost imperceptibly inward: she was inside a vast dome. Was the entire Sentinel facility underground? She had expected a simple laboratory. This place had to be gigantic.

Following a path, she came to a clearing, where several humanoid figures stood in a circle, facing each other. They were identical except for one red-cloaked figure, who had taken its place between two golems on the far side of the circle, facing her. Freya's heartrate began to race. Eric had been right after all: the machines had let them live only to bring them here. She had been wrong to turn her attention to the Cho-ta'an: the true danger was from the machines.

CHAPTER TWENTY-TWO

"What are you doing?" she demanded, determined not to go down without a fight.

"We are waiting for you," replied the Sixth.

"What... why?"

"We await instruction. I have updated the units in this facility with current information regarding the status of I Am."

"What is the status?"

"I Am is defunct." It spoke with no more emotion than if it had been talking about a broken eggshell.

Relief washed over Freya. I'm becoming paranoid, she thought. Not without reason, but I have nothing to fear from these machines. That's all they are. Machines. "Have you located the planet-killer?"

"Yes."

"What have you done with it?"

"Nothing. I located the device, as you requested. It is in a storage room approximately ninety yards from here."

"There is only one?"

"Yes."

"And the Sentinels? The human beings who live here?"

"They are dead. The machines killed them before we arrived. The bodies have been destroyed."

"Why?"

"The human scientists had served their purpose. Keeping them alive entailed unnecessary risks."

That was it, then. The Sentinels—the Izarians—were all dead. Did the machines still pose a threat? It was impossible to know. "Take me to the device."

"Do you intend to move the device? If so, I would recommend that these units accompany us."

So that's why they were gathered like this. The Sixth wasn't plotting against her; it was trying to anticipate her needs. "Yes," she said. "We will need to load it into the ship and... wait, what is the status of the ship?"

"The light infantry transport we used to get here remains damaged."

"Can you repair it?"

"The hull can be patched. Life support and telemetry can be repaired. We lack the ability to repair the hyperdrive."

"Are there any other ships on Kiryata?"

"Not that I am aware of."

"Are there any other ships in this region of space?"

"Not that I am aware of."

"Well, shit. What's wrong with the hyperdrive?"

"The ship reports that the proton reversion field generator is inoperable. The selective ionization matrix is filtering at twenty percent nominal. Recursion nodes four, five, and eleven are offline. Prinium normalization algorithm failed. Four isolation modules have fused. Temporal compensators are—"

"Okay, forget it," she said. She knew everything there was to know about conventional rockets and had a good working knowledge of the propulsion system used by IDL ships, but she couldn't make heads or tails of what the Sixth was saying. "You're telling me there's no way to fix it?"

"It is theoretically possible. I Am reverse-engineered the plans for its hyperdrives from an existing Sentinel craft. I possess the analysis of this craft, but I am unable to synthesize the data."

"What do you mean? You have all the information but you can't put it together?"

"That's correct. Hyperspace theory is beyond my understanding, or that of any individual Sixth. Only I Am was able to synthesize the information. With enough time and resources, I may be able to repair the parts of the hyperdrive, but that is insufficient to make the drive function."

"That doesn't make any sense. If all the parts work, and they're put together properly, then the hyperdrive will work."

"My information indicates that the steps you mentioned are insufficient to make the drive function."

"So there's some missing ingredient that you don't know about?"

"I do not know what you mean by 'ingredient.' There is a factor unaccounted for in the design of the hyperdrive. The factor was present in the synthesis developed by I Am. It is lacking in mine."

"Well, that's just fantastic. No way to repair the hyperdrive and you can't even tell me why." Freya thought for a moment. "How far are we from Yavesk?" Freya had committed the coordinates of the Cho-ta'an home world to memory years earlier, and she had informed the Sixth of the coordinates before they left Izar.

"We are one thousand three hundred ninety light years from the coordinates you specified for that planet."

"Good God. How long would it take to get there without a hyperspace drive, at maximum acceleration?"

"Approximately one thousand four hundred and thirty-six years. Approximately three hundred fifty-nine years in subjective time."

"Maximum stasis time is ninety days out of ninety-nine. So even if we slept most of the way, we'd age thirty-six years in transit."

"This does not agree with my information."

"What do you mean?"

"Maximum stasis time is ninety-nine point two percent of the time elapsed on board."

"What sort of stasis are you talking about?"

"The stasis chambers used by the Sentinels."

"They must have improved the technology. There are stasis chambers of that sort here, in this facility?"

"The units assigned to this facility report that there are forty of them."

"Well, that solves that problem," Freya said, talking more to herself than to the Sixth. "But it doesn't matter. We still wouldn't get to Yavesk until a hundred years after the main branch of humanity is wiped out by the Cho-ta'an."

She was still shaking her head when Eric and Ragnald walked up. "What are the machines up to now?" Eric asked, casting a suspicious glance at the Sixth.

"Doing their best to help, it would seem," said Freya. "Unfortunately, they can't work miracles."

"Get us to Yavesk and we will fight these Jötunn to the death. We need no miracles, nor thinking machines."

"Getting there is the problem," Freya said. "The hyperdrive on our ship is broken. Getting there the long way will take fourteen hundred years. By then, the Cho-ta'an will already have eradicated humanity. Deploying the planet-killer to Yavesk at that point would be too little, too late."

"There must be something we can do."

"I'm open to suggestions. Every known planet colonized by the Truscans has been destroyed by the Izarians—except for Jabesh-Gilead, which is... how far away is Jabesh-Gilead, Sixth?"

"Jabesh-Gilead is one thousand four hundred and five light years from Kiryata."

"Great, it's even farther away than Yavesk," said Freya bitterly.

"What about the other worlds?" Ragnald said. "Geneva and the others you spoke of?"

"Geneva and the other IDL worlds won't be colonized for another thousand years. At this point in history, there are only two worlds with people on them: Jabesh-Gilead and Earth."

"How far is Earth, machine?" asked Eric.

"Earth is one thousand twenty-seven light years from here."

"You see?" said Eric. "It is closer!"

"Marginally," said Freya. "It will still take... Sixth?"

"One thousand sixty-one years."

Freya was silent for a moment. "Let's see, that would make it... 2016 A.D. by the time we got there. Ship time would be about a quarter of that. And if we're in stasis ninety-nine percent of the time, that means we'll age about...."

"Two years and two hundred days," said the Sixth, who seemed to be getting better at anticipating her questions.

"You are saying we would be awake for two years on board the ship?" Eric asked. Ragnald looked dismayed.

"It's a long time," said Freya. "But I spent four years alone on a much smaller vessel. It can be done."

"What are our alternatives?" Ragnald asked.

Freya shrugged. "Stay here, I suppose. It seems like a nice enough place."

"And then what?" asked Eric.

"And then nothing. We spend the rest of our lives here and then die. Alternately, I suppose we could try to find Geneva or one of the other planets that will eventually be colonized by humans. It will take even longer to reach any of those planets, though, so again, we won't arrive until the war is over. Maybe if we're lucky, the planet hasn't been rendered uninhabitable by the Cho-ta'an. Then we can grow old and die there instead of here."

"I cannot stay in this place," said Eric. "It smells like defeat."

Ragnald nodded. "I would like to return to Earth. But what will we do there? If, as you say, history cannot be changed, then are we not still doomed to defeat?"

"Well," said Freya, "Theoretically we could repair the hyperdrive. The Sixth has the plans, but it can't fix the hyperdrive itself for some reason. Presumably it's just not smart enough to make sense of the technology without its counterparts. But the Truscans figured it out, and they're just as human as we are. No reason we couldn't re-invent the hyperdrive, with all the information we have. We would just need to recruit some very smart people on Earth."

"If we are successful in repairing the hyperdrive," asked Eric, "then what?"

"Then, depending on how long that takes, we might be able to get to Jabesh-Gilead before the Cho-ta'an find it. If there are human beings still alive at that time, we could warn them about the Cho-ta'an and help them prepare."

"I am confused," said Ragnald. "You have said that it is impossible to change what is known to happen, and you claim to know Earth's history for the next twelve hundred years. But now you speak of returning to Earth in the year 2016 to recruit people to help you build this hyperdrive. Does this not contradict what is known to happen?"

"It's a good question," Freya said. "The honest answer is that I don't know. However, I do know that my grandmother's people built a sky ship in the tenth century, even though there is no record of that happening. So I suppose we could get away with reinventing the hyperdrive, as long as we keep it secret. No reason for history to know."

"It sounds like that is our only option," said Eric.

"And if any of the others wish to stay?"

"Let them. But I do not think they will. They will want to come with us to Earth, even if it does take four years."

"Fourteen hundred years," said Freya. "It will feel like four years to you. Assuming we survive. And I will warn you that Earth will be very different in the year 2016."

"It will be Earth," said Eric. "That is what matters."

"What of this planet-killer?" Ragnald asked. "Will we take it with us to Earth?"

Freya considered this. "No," she said after a moment. "It's too dangerous. And...." She trailed off, then shook her head. "Forget it. We'll leave it here for safekeeping. Sixth, can you direct the machines to hide the planet-killer?"

"Yes. Where would you like it hidden?"

"Somewhere no one will ever find it. Am I correct in thinking this entire facility is underground?"

"Yes. It was created by enlarging caverns formed by volcanic activity."

"Then there is some industrial digging equipment somewhere?"

"Yes."

"Have the machines dig a hole, say a hundred yards deep and at least a mile away from any entrances to this place. At the bottom of the shaft, hollow out a vault. Make sure it's strong enough to withstand cave-ins, meteor strikes, anything else that's likely to happen. Put the planet-killer there. Then seal the whole thing back up. Leave an access hatch, but bury it under three yards of rock and camouflage it so that it's undetectable from the surface. Can you do that?"

"Yes."

"All right. Have them get started. And then start the repairs on the ship. Is there a kitchen around here? I'm starving."

CHAPTER TWENTY-THREE

There was a good reason the Izarians had left Jabesh-Gilead to be destroyed last. With a population of less than five million, it was the least populous of all the human worlds. More importantly, it had almost no resources to exploit, so it was heavily dependent on the other planets in the Concordat for food, fuel, and all the other necessities of life. In all likelihood it would not be necessary to destroy Jabesh-Gilead. Cut off from the other human worlds, it would implode of its own accord.

With a mild climate and gravity of only point seven gees, Jabesh-Gilead was an attractive destination for tourists and retirees. The air was breathable; only the relatively high concentration of carbon dioxide in the atmosphere kept it from being the home of many millions more. Some also found the near-constant cloud cover depressing. The low level of ultraviolet light given off by the planet's sun could be either a blessing or a curse: it was nearly impossible to get a tan, but those at risk for skin cancer could spend all day outside with little danger.

Although the Collapse had occurred more than a hundred years earlier and the Concordat planets were no longer dependent on hyperspace gates, due to the invention of hyperdrive-enabled spaceships, the breakdown of all travel and communications between all the planets inhabited by descendants of the Truscans had been sufficiently traumatic that the Concordat required all member planets to have enough food and supplies on hand for their populations to survive for a year without imports. The privations of the war with the Izarians, however, had prompted many planetary governments, including that of Jabesh-Gilead, to dip into their reserves. So when Jabesh-Gilead lost contact with the other worlds of the Concordat, it had only twelve weeks of food on hand.

The people of Jabesh-Gilead had no way to know that every other known human world had been destroyed by the Izarians, but it soon became clear that something very bad had happened. Jabesh-Gilead had no hyperdrive-enabled ships of its own, so it had no way to determine what had happened, but as weeks wore on with no ships arriving from other Concordat worlds, the populace became convinced that the Izarians had won the war and that it was only a matter of time before Jabesh-Gilead was attacked. So they waited.

They did not know that the ship that was supposed to deliver the last planet-killer to Jabesh-Gilead had been blown to pieces, nor that the planet-killer itself was now safely hidden far underground on a remote planet. They did not know that the factories that produced the Izarian war machines had been destroyed, nor that the few machines still scattered across the galaxy drifted aimlessly in space, lacking any controlling intelligence to direct them.

Not that it would have mattered. Two facts were obvious to all: Jabesh-Gilead was alone, and the vast majority of its people would soon die. The awareness that they were facing another Collapse would not help them avert it. Those with means and foresight survived a little longer than the others, but in the end almost everyone died.

Almost.

In a grassy valley far from the main population centers of Jabesh-Gilead was a settlement established by a wealthy entrepreneur who had dreams of making the planet more attractive to settlers by eliminating the need for imported food. Hiram Telus had made his fortune in real estate, and he dreamed of dramatically increasing the value of his holdings on Jabesh-Gilead. He intended to do this by engineering food crops that could thrive on Jabesh-Gilead despite its nutrient-poor soil, minimal rainfall and overcast skies. To this end, he had built a small town and hired a small army of scientists and laborers to fill it. He called the place Elim. Because of the settlement's remote location, Telus had stocked a warehouse with enough food to sustain his employees for over a year.

When news of the crisis reached Elim, its residents redoubled their efforts to develop a renewable food supply for people on Jabesh-Gilead. They couldn't possibly save everyone, but they might keep enough people alive that their children or grandchildren might still be alive when contact was reestablished with the other planets. Having studied the events of the Collapse—and being an optimist by nature—Hiram Telus was convinced that their predicament was temporary. Even years later, when his people had finally managed to develop crops that provided enough nutrition to replenish the settlement's food supply as fast as it was being depleted, he never dreamed that his little group of overworked farmers was the last remaining hope of humanity.

Over the next ten years, the community of Elim survived, but it hardly thrived. No matter how they rearranged plant DNA and no matter how efficiently they farmed, it took nearly all their time and energy just to stay alive. Few babies were born, because the community could ill afford to feed people who didn't work. The few children who did come into the settlement would be cursed to a lifetime of hard labor, with no time for either leisure or education. The realization gradually dawned that no help from offworld was ever going to come.

Even so, hope persisted. Marginal improvements continued to be made to farming methods and bioengineered crops, suggesting that their grandchildren or great-grandchildren might experience a less punishing existence. This hope, however, was tempered by another fear: when the crisis began, Elim's population had been one hundred twenty-seven men and eighty women. Of the women, sixty-two were still of childbearing age. That simply wasn't a big enough gene pool for the community survive long-term. Their great-grandchildren might have better lives, but they would also find it difficult to find mates who weren't close relatives. Due to the dangers of inbreeding and genetic drift, the long-term chances of the community surviving without an influx of DNA from the outside were virtually nil.

"Something's got to be done, Hiram," said Rufio Ceder, the erstwhile chief scientist at Elim. These days Rufio spent nearly all his time laboring on the farm, like most of the rest of the settlement's inhabitants. The two talked as they made their way back to the single men's barracks. Hiram had lived there since his house had been torched by desperate refugees from the nearby city of Cardenas ten years earlier.

"We're doing it, Rufio," said Hiram tiredly. "I know you didn't have as much time as you would have liked to work on the new strain of carrots, but I think next year's harvest is going to finally give us a little breathing room. If you and Amira can go back to half-days in the lab, we can figure out why the alfalfa keeps dying and—"

"That's not what I'm talking about and you know it."

"You're still preoccupied with our great-grandchildren marrying their cousins?"

"I am, and you should be too."

"We've got more pressing concerns."

"What we've got is a rapidly aging population and a corresponding diminishing of genetic variation, not to mention a people who are losing hope. For all we know, we could be the last human beings in the galaxy."

"There's no reason to think that," Hiram chided him.

"There's no reason to think anybody else is still out there either," said Rufio. "And even if they are, they're taking their sweet time in getting here. We could be looking at another ten years, or a hundred, or a thousand. We need to prepare for the possibility that no one is coming."

"Prepare how?"

"Make sure our offspring are genetically fit. And their offspring, and *their* offspring. So that in a thousand years, if no one does come, somebody is still here. Humanity survives on Jabesh-Gilead, if nowhere else."

"You're talking about the Sentinels all over again. An authoritarian regime with control over breeding."

"Not necessarily. We have access to gene editing technology that the Sentinels did not."

"What are you suggesting?"

"I'm suggesting that we forget about controlling behavior and take a more targeted approach. Frankly, I think the sort of regime the Sentinels implemented is unnecessary. There's already a strong cultural proscription against incest. We can use that."

"What do you mean, a 'targeted approach'?"

"I mean we deal with genetic problems as they arise."

"In other words," said Hiram, "if a union produces a child with a congenital defect...."

"We repair the child."

"By reprogramming the child's DNA."

"Correct."

"You think that would work?"

"We have the equipment and expertise to eliminate most genetic defects that might occur, and eventually we could develop the means to address genetic drift as well. Of course, that would require universal screening in utero."

"You would need total buy-in from everybody in Elim."

"We would need a consensus," said Rufio. They had passed the barracks and continued walking. This was not the sort of conversation they could have around the other men. "The same sort of consensus that is required for any societal norm to take hold. These things are malleable, to a large degree. One norm takes hold and the other loses its grip."

"You mean you're planning on discarding the norm prohibiting incest?"

"It's not up to me. Norms that are no longer useful tend to be discarded. If we subject all fetuses to genetic screening and repair, the prohibition against incest will cease to be useful. Under ordinary circumstances, incest might remain taboo indefinitely, but our descendants will also find themselves in a situation where inbreeding is increasingly difficult to avoid. If any defects can be corrected, there's no reason to prohibit any unions on the grounds of genetic fitness. Cousins, siblings, fathers and daughters...."

"Lord preserve us," Hiram said, shaking his head. "Perhaps it would be better if humanity died out."

The Truscans had inherited from their ancestors two sets of supernatural beliefs: one that centered on the gods of Olympus and one on Yahweh, the God of the Jews. An uneasy syncretism had developed over the generations, with Yahweh gradually being subsumed into the Olympic pantheon. A small group of ardent monotheists remained, however, and as the scientific understanding of nature developed, more and more people discarded the unnecessarily complex polytheism of the Romans in favor of a belief system that required fewer starting axioms. The stories of the ancient Jewish people's enslavement and flight from Egypt certainly resonated with the Truscans. Thus for a number of reasons the predominant religion of the Truscans at the start of the war with the Izarians was Yahwehism, but nearly a quarter of the people had rejected religion altogether and embraced agnosticism or, in rarer cases, atheism.

"That's certainly one option. If we do nothing, in four or five generations we're going to have a population increasingly made up of physically and mentally unfit individuals. If you think life is hard now, just wait until half the population can't work and nobody has enough brains to remember how birth control works. If we're lucky, our offspring lose the capacity to reproduce before they lose everything else that makes them human."

"Then we sterilize everyone."

CHAPTER TWENTY-FOUR

Hiram Telus and Rufio Ceder continued their walk, rounding the corner of one of the fields where they were trying to grow genetically modified beets.

"You think you can get buy-in on *universal sterilization*?" Rufio said. "The children are the only hope these people have. We've largely stopped reproducing, but only out of necessity. You see how the children are treated. They get the best food, the best accommodations, the best everything. Because people care about their children more than they care about themselves. That's how it's always been, because if the race doesn't survive, nothing we do matters. You want to take that hope away from them? You may as well recommend mass suicide. It would be a lot less painful."

"There's got to be a better solution," Hiram insisted.

"None that I'm aware of. You can sterilize everyone against their will, you can let inbreeding take its inevitable course, you can implement Sentinel-style breeding controls, or you can use the technology we have to fix problems as they arise. And frankly, I doubt the Sentinel option is viable. The Sentinels are thought to have had a larger and more sex-balanced and genetically diverse population to work with. If they'd had only sixty-two females to work with, we wouldn't be here."

"Who decides what counts as a 'defect'? And how it should be fixed? I mean, if we decide green eyes are a defect, do we give everybody brown eyes? What if we decide intelligence below a certain threshold is a defect? Or, for that matter, a certain height or skin color? What if we decide that we have too many males and need to turn a few baby boys into girls?"

"We'll have to have some kind of panel, of course. But this gets into matters of government. At present we're a benign dictatorship. Perhaps we'll transition to some form of republic at some point. Political philosophy is neither my area of expertise nor concern at the present moment. The point is, whoever is in charge is going to have to appoint people to make these decisions."

"And those decisions will be based on what? What will the criteria be for selection to this panel?"

"I wouldn't presume to say."

"If you can't tell me what criteria the panel are using, why even have one? A panel with no guiding principles or barrier to entry is just a mob."

"I don't disagree. But the mob is the ultimate arbiter of norms in any society. We punish incest because that's what the mob wants. Why not change green eyes to brown if the mob demands it? The mob will choose what is in the mob's best interest. That may not align with our preferences, but it will be strongly biased toward survival of the race."

"Putting aside the ethical problems, there are limits to what we can do with such a limited population, even with universal genetic screening. As you say, we have very few children, and our population is aging. At the rate we're increasing crop yields, it's not going to be economical for our people to start having children in large numbers for at least another twenty years. So we're going to be starting out with an even smaller population of child-bearing age. You know more about minimum viable populations than I do, but I don't see how this can work with a population of a few dozen unrelated individuals. In a few generations you're going to have so many defects that trying to fix them with gene editing is going to be like patching a sieve. Maybe if we started storing sperm and eggs, but then we'd be getting into the business of deciding who gets to reproduce with whom. In other words, a Sentinel-like breeding program. And that's not a road I want to go down."

"I agree. That's why, in addition to screening infants for defects, we need to implement a new policy to encourage as many pregnancies as possible."

"More births just means more mouths to feed."

"Yes, but we can take advantage of economies of scale."

"You mean have one person care for ten children rather than caring for two or three? Even if we could get buy-in, there's no way the increase in food production would cover the additional demand."

"I've run the numbers. Children between six and eight consume less than half the calories as an adult, and very young children consume even less than that. Currently we're running a small food surplus, and we're estimating that yields will increase by three to five percent per year for the next ten years. We can sustain birth rates of three hundred percent of the current level, at least for a while."

"How long is a 'while'?" Hiram asked.

"Eighteen to twenty years."

"And then what? Mass starvation?"

"In about eighteen years, the rate of population growth will overtake the rate that we're increasing the food supply. And yes, there will be some difficult times—unless we find a way to eat less or produce more."

"I suppose you're going to tell me you know of a way to do that?"

"No. Not yet. But there's no reason it can't be done. There are things about this planet—the high level of carbon dioxide in the air, the poor quality of sunlight, the low gravity—that human beings aren't well-adapted for. If we had a million years, we could wait for natural selection to produce people better suited to this place, but we don't. So why not jump-start the process?"

"You're talking about genetically engineering human beings."

"Think about it. We're handicapping ourselves by addressing only one side of the equation. We alter our food to make it more useful to us. Why not alter ourselves to make better use of the food we have? Think about how many calories we consume just to fuel muscles that are too bulky for the gravity here. We hop around on our awkward little legs when we could be lithe and graceful. We work at a suboptimal pace because if we breathe too hard, we black out from the CO2. We waste energy producing melanin and hair to protect our bodies from a sun that we've never even seen. With a few tweaks, we could easily increase our efficiency by thirty percent while decreasing our food consumption per person by at least as much. Increased productivity and lower consumption means less time spent in the fields and more time working on new breeds of crops or labor-saving tools."

"Or finding ways to make our children even less like ourselves."

"If it means our children survive and don't have to spend every waking moment working in the fields," Rufio said, "why not?"

Hiram shook his head. "With this power, even the most benign dictator would be tempted to meddle with things better left alone. We're talking about changing the very nature of our species. This is the purview of God himself."

"God has abandoned us, Commander. We can step up and take His place, or we can allow the race to die out."

"I don't appreciate your blasphemy, Rufio."

"I'm sorry if I offended. I am only trying to be honest in my assessment."

"Just be grateful that I'm a benevolent dictator."

"Trust me, I am. If it helps, although there are many wonderful things we can do with genetic editing, we are still a long way from being able to create an entirely new species. So while we can cure many diseases and make what you might call aesthetic changes, there's no reason to think that our descendants will be anything but human."

"Even if each generation gets progressively less human-like?"

"It doesn't really work like that. For the most part, gene editing is just a matter of flipping switches. If you want to change eye color from green to brown, you flip that switch. If you want to change olive skin to pink, you flip that switch. Usually it's more than a single switch, of course, and complex changes require more switches to be flipped, but it's still flipping switches that are already there. If you flip enough switches, you might be able to create offspring similar to some evolutionary forebear of humans. Some believe, for example, that on Earth there was a whole family of animals, called primates, to which humans belonged. Perhaps with a great deal of genetic modification you could turn a human into something resembling one of these other primates. But you wouldn't be able to turn a human into a sheep or a dog. The information just isn't there. Similarly, we could create super-intelligent humans or super-tall humans, because very intelligent people and very tall people already exist. But it's very unlikely we could, for example, create a human being who could breathe underwater or fly. Manipulating DNA on that level is far beyond our ability."

"But it might not be forever."

"Of course. There's no guarantee our distant descendants won't make themselves into monsters, but there never has been. At least this way they will have a choice."

"And you expect people just to go along with this?"

"I think the key step will be getting them to accept the necessity of screening infants for defects. Once we have buy-in on that, we have implicit consent to repair those defects. If we can find a way to make lungs handle excess carbon dioxide more effectively, that would be the next logical step. What parent is going to say no to a treatment that allows their child to breathe better?"

"You're arguing in favor of a slippery slope."

"I'm arguing in favor of incremental change," said Rufio. "Change that is necessary for the survival of our race."

"At some point, it ceases being our race."

"I suppose so. Humans are said to have descended from an entirely different species on Earth. At some point our descendants will no longer look like us. The question, though, is whether we will have descendants at all."

"Would it be possible for this process to be reversed?"

"I'm not sure what you mean."

"I mean, let's say I accept the premise that we need to adapt to survive on this planet. If all goes well, our great-great grandchildren might master space travel and leave this planet. Eventually somebody will engineer a hyperdrive-enabled spaceship, or reinvent the technology, if the records can't be recovered. These remote descendants of ours begin to locate other habitable planets. Suppose they find a planet more like Earth. Heavier gravity, less CO2, better soil, more UV radiation. They decide to colonize this planet. At that point, the adaptations we've selected no longer make sense. Is there a way for these people—or whatever they are—to have human children?"

"I suppose it's possible. Obviously a record would be kept of all the changes made over the generations. But it seems rather arbitrary to want to turn back the clock to a particular point in our evolution. They're as likely to find a planet with lighter gravity as heavier. And of course their physical form is largely going to determine what sorts of planets they want to settle in the first place. People suited to point seven gees aren't going to find a planet with one gee gravity very attractive."

"I understand what you're saying, Rufio, but I think you're wrong. I know you don't share my religious convictions, but I can't help thinking there is something special about humanity. Humanity as it is now, I mean. Without 'improvements.' I believe people were created in the image of God, and I take that belief seriously. If the options are to allow the race to die out or to become something that is no longer recognizably human, I will pick the former."

"With respect, Hiram, it isn't fair to impose your beliefs on the rest of humanity."

"No?" said Hiram. "What do you think it is that you're doing?"

"I don't intend to force anyone—"

"Of course not. You're just going to coax them onto a path that has no exits. You know where this path goes and they do not, and at every step of the way you're going to whisper to them, 'You've come this far. Don't give up now!' And they'll follow you, because as you say, hope is all they have. But I'll tell you this, Rufio: if you try to do this without my blessing, I'll be there every step of the way as well, warning them to go back."

"I see," said Rufio coldly. "And what is necessary to gain your blessing?"

"A way back," said Hiram. "If our children have to become something other than human in order for our species to survive, I can accept that. But there must be a way back. Perhaps they will choose not to go back. Perhaps they'll decide they enjoy being something other than human. But I don't think so. I think you'll find that the desire to be human, and to be *seen* as human, runs deep. These monsters of yours will carry in them an image of God Himself—a memory of their humanity. And that humanity will call to them. Maybe they will not listen. I don't know. As you say there's never been any guarantee that our children won't choose to be monsters. But we must give them the choice."

Rufio nodded. "All right. There may be a way. I will give it some thought."

"Good," said Hiram. "Find a way back, and then we can move forward."

CHAPTER TWENTY-FIVE

Commander Tertius Dornen sat in his quarters aboard *Varinga*, wishing the Izarians had killed him. They had certainly tried, and by all rights they should have succeeded. But here he was, drifting in space with a skeleton crew, a score of CDF marines, and two-hundred and six refugees from a mining colony. He had nothing to offer any of them but a long, dull and ultimately futile existence aboard a crippled spaceship.

Pursued by Izarian warships, *Varinga* had executed a risky hyperspace jump from within the Voltera system. Her intended destination was Jabesh-Gilead, the only known world besides Earth that might not have been destroyed by the Izarians. There wasn't much *Varinga* could do to prevent the deployment of a planet-killer, but Dornen had thought she might at least pick up a few hundred refugees before the Izarians arrived. Then they could try to find another planet where they could start over. *Varinga* had a food production system capable of feeding two hundred people indefinitely, as well as stasis chambers that would allow the passengers to sleep most of the voyage.

That plan had evaporated the moment *Varinga*, her hyperdrive damaged by Izarian missiles, had emerged from hyperspace halfway through the journey, nearly eight hundred light-years from Jabesh-Gilead. The second closest Concordat planet, Toronus, was nearly three times as far, and Earth was even farther.

Earth. For most of his life, the existence of Earth had never been more than a theoretical possibility. Now he had seen it. Could the people aboard *Varinga* find refuge on Earth? Freya had told him the Izarians would never find Earth, but he didn't believe it. With *Varinga* out of play, nothing could stop the Izarians. Humanity had lost. In any case, Earth was too far. Everyone on *Varinga* would be dead before they got there.

That left Jabesh-Gilead. Jabesh-Gilead was so remote, sparsely populated, and dependent on the other Concordat worlds that the Izarians might not have bothered to destroy it. At maximum acceleration, which would get *Varinga* to ninety-seven percent light-speed in less than two years, it would take her eight hundred years to reach Jabesh-Gilead. That meant about two hundred years in ship's time. If the passengers and crew spent ninety percent of their time in stasis, they would age twenty years. That was a long time to be on a spaceship, but most of them would reach Jabesh-Gilead before they died of old age. The odds of there being any survivors on Jabesh-Gilead in eight hundred years were almost nil, though, for the same reason that the Izarians might have overlooked it: everyone knew that the people of Jabesh-Gilead couldn't survive cut off from the other Concordat worlds.

In the end, though, Dornen had no good options. He ordered the navigator to set a course to Jabesh-Gilead.

*****

For eight hundred and three years, *Varinga* crawled across space toward the Jabesh-Gilead system. By any conventional standard, she actually traveled incredibly fast, but conventional standards weren't much use when traveling such mind-boggling distances. At the halfway point, she flipped end-for-end and began to decelerate. Nearly four centuries later she entered the far reaches of the Jabesh-Gilead system. Everyone aboard had aged twenty years. Several of them had died. Children had been born who knew nothing other than life aboard a vast spaceship. Most of those aboard had grown accustomed to the idea that they would live the rest of their lives on *Varinga*. Commander Dornen himself was near standard retirement age, in biological terms.

Six weeks after entering the system, the initial reports on Jabesh-Gilead came in from *Varinga*'s sensors. Prepared for the worst, Dornen made his way to the bridge, where he went over the reports with the navigator, Delio Starn.

"It's still there," said Starn.

Tertius Dornen nodded. "Thank God."

They hadn't expected Jabesh-Gilead to have been obliterated, of course—only reduced to a lifeless ball of dust and muck. There wasn't a lot of green on the surface, but there was enough for them to be sure of one thing: the Izarians hadn't deployed a planet-killer. Two weeks later, *Varinga* was in orbit. Sensors confirmed their hopes: Jabesh-Gilead was no Eden, but it was habitable. With the food production facilities aboard *Varinga*—still working at nearly sixty percent capacity after eight hundred years!—they could live the rest of their lives in peace. If the Izarians hadn't attacked Jabesh-Gilead yet, they probably weren't going to.

Varinga set down just outside what was once Hadera, one of the most populous and important cities on Jabesh-Gilead. Dornen put together an exploratory team made up of himself, Delio Starn, Dr. Thaddeus Bartol, and five of the marines, including Sergeant Macron. They scouted the city while most of the rest of the passengers remained in stasis.

The city was deserted and largely in ruins. A search revealed no life except rats, a few small brown lizards, and creeping vines and other weeds that were slowly tearing what was left of the city apart.

"Strange," said Dr. Thaddeus Bartol, exiting a ruined house to rejoin Dornen in the street.

"What's that?" asked Dornen.

"Well, where is everybody?"

"Dead, I assume."

"Right, but where are the corpses? Dead men don't bury themselves."

Dornen considered this. It was a good point. Bones wouldn't have turned to dust in a few hundred years, and Jabesh-Gilead had no large predators. Even if the people had died of starvation or disease, they should have found some skeletons by now. Either the people of Hadera had walked away, or someone else had removed them. The Izarians weren't known for mass abductions.

The crew returned to *Varinga* and she took flight again. Dornen hadn't really expected to find anyone alive on Jabesh-Gilead, but they had to try. The population of *Varinga* was too small to ensure the survival of the species. If they could even find a settlement of a few hundred people, though, humanity would have a chance.

The next city they visited looked much like Hadera, as did the third. At the fourth, however, they made a startling discovery—or it discovered them. Dornen was exploring the ruins with Bartol and several of the marines when Sergeant Macron's voice spoke in his hear. "Commander," said Macron, "you're going to want to see this."

Dornen and the marine accompanying him, a corporal named Sefrus, hurried down an alley between two dilapidated apartment buildings toward Macron's position. Macron stood alone in the middle of the street, staring into the distance.

"What is it, Sergeant?" Dornen said. "You figure out where all the...." He trailed off as he saw what Macron was looking at. Sefrus began to raise his rifle, but Dornen put up his hand and he lowered it again.

Someone—something—was walking down the street toward them. It was humanoid, but too tall to be human. It wore only a dingy smock that covered little of its pale gray skin. As it drew closer, they saw that its intelligent eyes were large and black. It appeared to be alone and unarmed.

"What the hell is it?" Macron whispered.

Dornen knew the creature from Freya's description of them. "Cho-ta'an," he said.

CHAPTER TWENTY-SIX

The Cho-ta'an seemed friendly enough. Dornen gathered, through a long exchange involving a lot of pointing and gesticulation, that it (for they had not determined whether it was male or female) hailed from a settlement some ten miles to the north, and that it was something like an archaeologist, on an expedition to uncover the secrets of the ancient human city, Tiberias. It had planned to spend the night in the city and then begin the journey home on foot. Its name was Yekchalla.

Yekchalla had seen *Varinga* land and was very interested in seeing the ship. After a brief discussion with Dr. Bartol, Dornen agreed to give Yekchalla a tour of the crew quarters and to let it sleep onboard if it wanted. Dornen reasoned that if the Cho-ta'an were hostile, it would be better to keep Yekchalla in sight and under guard. Yekchalla thanked them enthusiastically; Dornen gathered that it had not been looking forward to spending the night in the ruins. When Yekchalla had retired for the evening, Dornen ordered Sergeant Macron to keep an armed guard at its door.

Dornen met with his officers and Bartol later that evening.

"I guess we know what happened to the people who lived on Jabesh-Gilead," said Delio Starn.

"You think the Cho-ta'an killed them?" said Dornen.

"It's the obvious answer, isn't it?"

"If the Cho-ta'an had eradicated humanity on this planet," said the protocol officer, Clea Marinus, "I would have expected a different reception. Yekhalla didn't seem afraid or suspicious of us. Just... curious."

"Frankly," said Dr. Bartol, "I found its reaction to us a little unnerving. It was oddly subdued, assuming that this was its first encounter with an alien species."

"Technically this is *our* first encounter with an alien species," said Marinus. "None of us has ever seen an Izarian."

"Maybe the Cho-ta'an *are* the Izarians," said Clea Marinus.

"Doubtful," said Dornen. "All the intelligence the CDF had about the builders of the machines indicated they were very similar to humans. We think the golems were originally designed to stand in for Izarians doing menial tasks."

"The point is," said Bartol, "Yekchalla reacted not as someone whose worldview had been suddenly upended by an encounter with another intelligent life form, but rather as someone who'd been expecting us to show up sooner or later."

"Well, if it's an archaeologist, as you suggested, then it's probably spent a fair amount of time in these ruins. It must know of the existence of humans."

"And it probably knows what happened to them," said Delio Starn.

"Right," said Bartol. "That's what I'm getting at. Even on the off chance it doesn't know what happened to the human population of this planet, it must know that we suspect the Cho-ta'an of eradicating them. But it showed neither hostility nor awareness that we might be hostile toward it."

"You think Yekchalla is hiding something," said Dornen.

"Count on it," replied Bartol.

*****

The next morning, the exploratory team traveled with Yekchalla—whom they had learned was male—to the Cho-ta'an settlement. Rather than walking, they took two of the battery-powered wheeled vehicles that *Varinga* carried in its hold. Yekchalla's reaction to the vehicles was the same as his reaction to every other new and surprising thing it encountered: muted curiosity.

The trip was slow going, as the road north of the city was almost unusable. Along the way, Dornen and Bartol engaged Yekchalla in conversation, trying to find out as much as they could about the Cho-ta'an. This was a laborious process as well, but their translator learned quickly, and by the end of the journey it was passably fluent in the aliens' language. According to Yekchalla, the Cho-ta'an numbered less than twenty thousand, and the entire population was centered on a city called Kavded, which was where they were going. The Cho-ta'an civilization was primitive by Truscan standards: they did not use electricity and had no complex machines. The vast majority of Cho-ta'an were engaged in activities related to agriculture. Yekchalla said little of the human settlements. He claimed it was widely believed among the Cho-ta'an that humans had died off long before the Cho-ta'an arrived. The Cho-ta'an, He said, had come to Yavesk (their name for Jabesh-Gilead) from another world in a sky ship like *Varinga*, looking for a simpler life away from the evils of technology. Their gods had left the ruins of the human cities as a reminder. It was said that the gods had destroyed the human civilization for their hubris, but Yekchalla was vague when pressed for the specifics of this calamity. He would only say that according to legend, the humans were reduced to dust and blew away in the wind. Yekchalla, being a scientist, was hoping to find a more satisfactory explanation, but so far had no better hypothesis.

They stopped the vehicles a few hundred yards outside Kavded and walked the rest of the way into the city. Located in a deep river valley, Kavded was a cluster of a few hundred stone buildings surrounded by farmland.

Having been spotted some distance out, they were greeted by an excited crowd of Cho-ta'an, who stared and pointed, murmuring to each other. There was more of an edge to this encounter than their meeting with Yekchalla, but Dornen saw no weapons and sensed no overt hostility. The marines, hands hovering over their side arms, watched nervously for threats, but none came.

Yekchalla led them to the home of a male called Churrik, who was the leader of the Cho-ta'an. The translator rendered his title as "chief." He had clearly been alerted to the humans' arrival, as he was standing outside when they approached. Churrik and Yekchalla had a brief, somewhat tense exchange, and then Churrik invited them all inside.

They sat on cushions in a small room with a high ceiling. A servant offered them refreshments, but Dornen politely declined on behalf of the humans. Yekchalla explained to the chief that the humans, who had brought their own provisions, would not be able to digest Cho-ta'an food. Churrik seemed more-or-less mollified by this.

The conversation centered on what the humans were doing on Yavesk and what they wanted. It quickly became clear, although Churrik never said it outright, that he was hoping to get his hands on some of the humans' technology in exchange for allowing them to settle on Yavesk. The humans, remembering what Yekchalla had told them about the Cho-ta'an taboo regarding advanced technology, followed Churrik's lead. After nearly two hours of negotiations, they came to a tentative agreement. The humans would be allowed to settle the area around *Varinga*, in exchange for a good faith effort to assist the technological development of the Cho-ta'an—euphemistically referred to by both parties as "cultural enrichment." Dornen suggested that Yekchalla act as a go-between, but Churrik pretended not to hear him and then suggested another Cho-ta'an as an emissary. Yekchalla was clearly humiliated, but Dornen didn't feel confident enough in his position—or his assessment of Yekchalla—to object. It was decided that this Cho-ta'an, named Veyka-Chenn, would return with the humans for a tour of the ship and a continuation of the discussion. Veyka-Chenn, who was referred to with the neuter gender, was summoned. Veyka-Chenn arrived a few minutes later and was introduced to the humans. Yekchalla seemed to have lost interest in the proceedings.

The meeting broke up, and Yekchalla departed on his own. The humans and Veyka-Chenn got into the vehicles and began the journey back to *Varinga*. By this time, the translator was fully fluent in the Cho-ta'an language, and Dornen and Bartol could communicate with Veyka-Chenn without difficulty. It soon became clear that Veyka-Chenn was not a scientist or engineer, but merely a political functionary loyal to Chief Churrik. Now that there was no danger of being overheard by other Cho-ta'an, he spoke openly about the sorts of technology Churrik was interested in acquiring. For a backward civilization, these Cho-ta'an—the ones in power, anyway—seemed to know an awful lot about technology. Yet when Dornen tried to get answers regarding the defunct human civilization, Veyka-Chenn spoke in vague myths or said nothing at all.

Veyka-Chenn was given a tour of the less sensitive areas of the ship and then spoke for an hour with Dr. Bartol. Veyka-Chenn spent the night on *Varinga*, and then returned to Kavded with Dr. Bartol and two marines. They took with them several handheld tools that Veyka-Chenn thought might be of use to the Cho-ta'an. Veyka-Chenn had also promised to give Dr. Bartol a tour of one of their farms—both to assess what other sorts of tools might be fabricated to assist the Cho-ta'an in farming, and to get an idea of what sorts of crops the humans might be able to grow.

The same day, the crew began the process of bringing the rest of the passengers out of stasis. Some of the crew—Delio Starn and Sergeant Macron, in particular—objected to the plan to settle the area around Tiberias, arguing that there was no good reason to settle so close to the Cho-ta'an. Dornen disagreed, arguing that eventually they were going to have to figure out how to raise their own food, and Jabesh-Gilead was notoriously unsuited to farming. If anything, the humans needed the help of the Cho-ta'an more than the Cho-ta'an needed them. He left his other reason unspoken: he wouldn't feel safe on this planet until he knew what really happened to its previous human inhabitants.

Dr. Bartol came to talk to him in his quarters after returning from Kavded.

"Learn anything interesting?"

Bartol nodded. "Evidently Cho-ta'an cycle between male, female, and neuter genders. So a 'he' one week might be a 'she' or an 'it' the next week. I haven't been able to determine exactly what triggers the change or how the new gender is determined—my guides would only speak of the matter in the most general terms—but some of them apparently control the process through some combination of diet and artificial hormones. Most of the

Cho-ta'an I met were males, because females tend to be occupied with domestic duties. Some, like Veyka-Chenn, are kept in the neuter state, presumably because the lack of sex drive makes them more reliable servants. Beyond that, I learned Chief Churrik runs a tight ship. I spent three hours walking around one of their farms, and I was never out of sight of one of his agents."

"How do you know they were Churrik's agents?"

"I grew up on a farm, Commander. I know when someone is pretending to work."

"You still think they're hiding something?"

"I'm certain of it. For one thing, I think they're not as backward as they want us to think."

"Because they're a little too certain about what tech they need from us?"

"That's part of it. I get the sense that Churrik and his agents have some understanding of the role technology played in the human society that preceded them. The taboo against technology seems to be a sort of society-wide rationalization for their own lack of progress. Or maybe it's a way for the ruling class to keep control over the population. Either way, Churrik and his henchmen certainly don't take it very seriously. They see a chance to increase their own power and they're taking it."

"The tools we're giving them will benefit everybody," said Dornen.

Bartol chuckled. "Eventually, maybe. Churrik's already talking about raising the percentage of crops the farmers are required to give him as tribute. The farmers might produce more, but the benefit is going to go largely to Churrik and company."

"We could put conditions on the tools we give them. Tie them to promises to make their society more equitable."

"It's a bad idea. Right now we've got a clear hierarchy to work with. If we undercut him, it will get ugly. An alien society devolving into civil war ten miles from our settlement is not what we need right now. And not to be callous, but frankly it's not our problem. Maybe this is just how the Cho-ta'an are. The fact that there are only twenty thousand of them, clustered around a single population center, on a planet this size certainly suggests a preference for a centralized, top-down organizational structure.

Freya told us how militaristic and authoritarian their society is. We'd be foolish to try to meddle in their system of government out of some misguided sense of social justice."

"They're authoritarian, yes, but hardly militaristic."

"Well, keep in mind that their war with the IDL won't start for another four hundred years. A lot can happen in that amount of time. As long as they all live in a single city-state with a unified command structure, they have no need of a military. And they don't have the resources to support a standing army or manufacture weapons on a large scale, in any case."

"Now you've got me worried the tech we're giving them is going to turn them into the enemies Freya feared," Dornen said.

"I doubt a few rakes and plows are going to do that. Besides, we don't even know for sure these are the Cho-ta'an that the IDL is—will be fighting."

"She said they came from a planet called Yavesk."

"Even so, the war is four hundred years away," said Bartol. "We need to worry about *now*. On the other hand... what if we could stop the war with the Cho-ta'an before it even started?"

"What are you suggesting?"

"I'm suggesting that twenty thousand Cho-ta'an lives are worth less than several billion humans."

"Be that as it may, we still need the Cho-ta'an."

"We need their seeds and their knowledge of botany and horticulture. I'm not sure we need the Cho-ta'an, per se. On my tour, they took me through one of their greenhouses in the city. I think they were trying to impress me—and they did, although not quite in the way they intended. I've never seen so much security, just to guard a bunch of plants."

"They were worried you might take some samples?" said Dornen.

"That or look too closely at their methods. What I think they were really concerned about was me wandering into a complex of buildings nearby."

"What was in the other buildings?"

"I don't know! That's the point. They were trying to impress me, but there were five other buildings they wouldn't let me near. I saw Cho-ta'an going in and out wearing coveralls that seem to be the Cho-ta'an equivalent of lab coats."

"You think they're doing some kind of research?"

"Yes," Bartol replied. "Genetics, horticulture, biology, something along those lines. The Cho-ta'an may be behind us in most areas of science and technology, but they may have as much understanding of plant-related sciences as we do. And they certainly know more about the specific breeds of plants on this planet and how to grow them. If we could take that lab, the Cho-ta'an would no longer have any leverage over us."

"They outnumber us a hundred to one."

"We've got the mech suits. I'd take those odds."

"Well, let's hope it's not necessary."

CHAPTER TWENTY-SEVEN

Three weeks later, the humans and Cho-ta'an had settled into an uneasy symbiosis. The Cho-ta'an had provided the humans with seeds and root stock of several crops that the humans might be able to grow in the soil near Tiberias, and the humans had begun to fabricate more tools and farm implements for the Cho-ta'an. It was clear Chief Churrik and his cronies wanted much more than a few hand tools, but Dornen and Dr. Bartol agreed that there was little to be gained by giving the Cho-ta'an more than the absolute minimum required to secure their cooperation.

The Cho-ta'an warned them that the soil near the human city was poor; some of them used the word "cursed," which made Dornen suspect radioactivity or residue from chemical weapons or industrial toxins. Soil analysis, however, indicated only low nitrogen levels and an unusually high acidity. Bartol thought the problem could be addressed by the manufacture of artificial fertilizers and soil supplements. These measures, however, would not make the Cho-ta'an crops more appetizing. They had identified only a handful of Cho-ta'an staples that humans could digest, and none of them were particularly appetizing. Although *Varinga* carried seeds for several varieties of common foods, it was unlikely any of them would grow on Yavesk. There was a reason the previous inhabitants had imported nearly all their food, after all. It was going to be years, perhaps decades, before the human settlement could produce all their own food. Fortunately, the food production systems aboard *Varinga* were still capable of producing far more than they needed and were likely to last for many more years.

By the fifth week after the rest of the passengers were revived, life had settled into something like a predictable pattern. Most of the people were occupied with a project to build an irrigation system fed by water from the nearby river, while others worked on repurposing vehicles and other machines from *Varinga*'s hold to be used as farm implements. Now that all the young children were awake at once, a school was started. The older children were expected to do some work when not in school, but their schedule was not arduous. Children were allowed to roam freely about the area of the ship but strictly forbidden from entering the ruins of the city. When a seven-year-old boy named Livius didn't show up for supper one evening, everyone knew where he must have gone.

A search party, consisting of most of the settlers, combed the city all night with flashlights, to no avail. The searchers had no better luck by daylight. They looked in every building, well, and pile of debris within two miles of *Varinga*, but found no sign of Livius. The search was expanded to the rest of the city, but still they found nothing. The entire interior of *Varinga* was searched top to bottom three times, but Livius could not be found. The only good news was that as far as anyone could tell, no buildings had collapsed recently, so it was unlikely Livius was trapped under a pile of rubble. The bad news was that this left only one likely possibility: Livius had been abducted by the Cho-ta'an.

No one could think of a reason a Cho-ta'an would kidnap Livius. He was a perfectly ordinary child; his parents had been miners on Voltera. The Cho-ta'an emissary, Veyka-Chenn, pled ignorance and even assisted in the search. On the third day after Livius had gone missing, Dornen and Dr. Bartol went to Kavded to see Chief Churrik. Churrik too claimed to know nothing about Livius's disappearance and pledged to help the humans in any way he could. A force of forty Cho-ta'an was sent south to search the city and the surrounding area again. It was all for naught. Ten days after Livius disappeared, the search was called off.

Another three weeks passed. Livius was never found, but his mother, who still roamed the ruins looking for him, found a stuffed animal of his near a collapsed house. The rubble of the house and several surrounding houses was carefully moved away, stone by stone, but there was no other sign Livius had ever been there. Even Livius's parents abandoned hope that their son might be found alive.

Life returned to something like normal, the biggest change being an increase in security. Before the disappearance, three or four of the marines would be patrolling the perimeter of the settlement at any given time. Now at least half the marines were always on duty, and they frequently used the mech suits for longer range patrols. Dornen had discouraged the use of the suits at first out of concern the Cho-ta'an would fear an attack, but maybe it was better to keep them a little scared. The exchange of information between the humans and Cho-ta'an continued, with the marines chauffeuring emissaries from both sides back and forth, but there was less friendly chatter on the journeys.

Then one evening, Yekchalla, the archaeologist, approached the edge of the settlement, asking to speak with Commander Dornen. He was checked for weapons and escorted to Dornen's quarters, where the Commander was meeting with Dr. Bartol. Yekchalla, clearly in an agitated state, was allowed in while a marine stood watch outside the door.

"I am sorry to interrupt, Commander," Yekchalla said, "but I must speak to you on an urgent matter. I would have come to you sooner, but I am watched carefully."

"Is this about Livius?" asked Dr. Bartol.

"The missing child? No, I am sorry, I know nothing of the boy."

"Then what is it, Yekchalla?" asked the Commander.

"You are being misled, and I am afraid I have contributed to this."

"In what way?" asked Dornen.

"You have undoubtedly noticed that my people harbor a strong suspicion of new technology. That attitude has long been cultivated by the ruling class, including Chief Churrik and his henchmen. I am not one of them, but I am afforded some access because of my contributions to the understanding of human civilization. Lately, though, I have found myself in a bind. If my hypothesis is correct, then there is a very good reason for this tight control of scientific knowledge."

"We assumed it was to keep the people in line," said Bartol.

"It is, but it is much more than that. I think I have discovered the true origin of our people, as well as what happened to the humans who once lived on this planet."

"The Cho-ta'an eradicated the humans," said Bartol.

"Yes, but not the way you think. The Cho-ta'an *are* humans."

"The hell they are," said Bartol.

"It is the conclusion the evidence leads me to. That is why there are no human remains in the cities. The human population were gradually turned into Cho-ta'an, through a process of gene manipulation that is now closely guarded by our ruling caste."

"'Turned into' by whom?" asked Dornen.

"By ourselves, I suspect. That is, our human ancestors. You see how difficult it is for you to survive on this planet. I think we altered our genes to improve our chances. Even so, it has not been easy. We number only twenty thousand, and that is as many Cho-ta'an as there have ever been."

Dornen looked to Bartol, speechless. The doctor shrugged. "It does make some sense," he said. "Our two races are oddly similar, considering we supposedly originated on different planets."

"How long ago?" Dornen asked.

"Perhaps seven or eight hundred years. The change would have taken several generations, of course."

"Not long after the Izarians destroyed the other Concordat worlds," Bartol said. "It fits."

"Why are you telling us this?" asked Dornen.

"I fear for the fragile peace between our peoples. We need each other. If we do not help each other—worse, if we fall into enmity—neither of our peoples is likely to survive. I cannot speak freely among my own people but can at least tell you: we are from the same stock. Surely that is worth something."

"It is," said Dornen. "Thank you, Yekchalla. I will have one of my men drive you back to Kavded so that your absence will not be noticed."

"That would be much appreciated, Commander Dornen."

*****

"What do you think?" Dornen asked Bartol, when Yekchalla had left.

"I think Yekchalla is an idealist."

"Meaning?"

"He thinks that knowledge of our shared heritage will make us more sympathetic to the Cho-ta'an."

"You don't?"

"Does it make *you* more sympathetic?"

Dornen considered the question. "No. Honestly, I find the thought repulsive. Those people made themselves into monsters."

"They did what they needed to in order to survive."

"Better for humanity to die off than to turn into *that*."

"It's funny, isn't it?" Bartol said. "When we thought they were aliens, we got along with them fine—setting aside the matter of Livius. But now that we think of them as altered humans, they're monsters."

"What about Livius? Do you think it was the Cho-ta'an?"

"Who else could it be? He didn't just disappear into thin air."

Dornen nodded. "Do you think the past can be changed?"

"You're reassessing my idea of preventing the war between the Cho-ta'an and the IDL before it starts?"

"God help me, I am."

"Well. As I see it, fate precludes the possibility of free will. It's true that preventing the war with the Cho-ta'an would create a paradox: how could Freya be the descendant of people who fought a war that never happened? But frankly, temporal paradoxes are beyond my pay grade. I say we do what we need to do, and let the universe sort itself out. Also, I might add that if these people do turn into the Cho-ta'an who attack Earth, then our endeavor is doomed."

Dornen nodded. The thought had occurred to him already, of course: if the future turned out the way Freya said it would, in four hundred years Yavesk would be overrun with Cho-ta'an possessed with the singular mission of eradicating humanity. The people who had spent twenty years aboard *Varinga* to get here had no future on Yavesk. Unless the future could be changed.

"You're talking about genocide," Dornen said.

"I'm talking about a preemptive strike against an aberrant branch of humanity that threatens to wipe out the rest of us."

"And if we fail?"

"Fail? How? You've seen those mech suits in action. We send Macron's men into Kavded with those things, they could destroy the entire city and be home for lunch. Their security force is a few hundred Cho-ta'an armed with iron-tipped spears. We don't have to kill all of them. Just wreck their city, burn their crops, and take whatever's in those labs. Then we get everybody aboard *Varinga* and start over somewhere else. Maybe come back in a few weeks and finish the job if they're not all dead from malnutrition or exposure."

"Good God, Bartol. You've put some thought into this."

"I assumed it would come to this sooner or later. It was always going to be us or them."

"You think we can get Macron and his men to go along with it?" Aboard *Varinga*, the marines were subject to Dornen's command, but now that they were on a planet and the Izarians were apparently no longer a threat, the chain of command had gotten a little fuzzy.

"Are you kidding? They were itching for this even before Livius went missing. You give them the green light, they'll take care of the rest."

Dornen sighed. There was a feeling of inevitability to all this, and some small part of him wanted to fight it, but in the end he knew he had no choice.

"All right," he said. "I'll give the order."

*****

Varinga carried no vehicles capable of transporting men in mech suits, so Sergeant Macron and his men went overground in the suits. Across the rough ground, the suits were nearly as fast as their vehicles anyway.

The Cho-ta'an had sentries posted south of the city, presumably to warn of such an incursion, but it made no difference. By the time word reached the rest of the city's security force, just after sunrise, the marines were nearly to the nucleus of the city. The marines ignored the Cho-ta'an hurling spears and rocks at them and set about destroying every building in the vicinity of the greenhouses. Some of the suits' missile launchers had been swapped out with flame throwers; these were used for the few buildings that were made of organic materials. Many Cho-ta'an were caught in the crossfire, and many more likely died inside the buildings that the marines torched or exploded, but the intent was only to destroy the Cho-ta'an's warehouses and what little industrial operations they had—weaving houses, canneries and the like.

Most of the Cho-ta'an they met ran screaming. The security force members and a few civilians held their ground, attacking with spears, rocks, and the occasional primitive incendiary device. At last the marines became annoyed and began to mow the defenders down with their machineguns.

When every structure within a hundred yards of the laboratory complex had been destroyed and cleared of Cho-ta'an, Macron ordered half the men to stand guard while he and the rest of the men spread out across the city toward the farms that lay to the north and east. Fields were torched and silos and barns were razed or blown to pieces. Farmers and laborers who got in the way were gunned down. By midday, the city's entire food supply had been destroyed. The marines converged on the city center again, destroying everything and everyone in their path.

When he was certain the city was clear, Sergeant Macron and three of his men climbed out of their suits and began a thorough search of the greenhouses and laboratories. The plan was to make sure the buildings were clear of Cho-ta'an and any other hazards and then secure a path through the city so that Dr. Bartol could bring a team in to analyze anything inside. They had cleared the greenhouses and two of the buildings when they encountered two Cho-ta'an guards armed with iron swords guarding a heavily reinforced door well inside the building at the center of the complex. The marines dispatched them quickly with their side arms and then set a charge to blow the door off its hinges.

After the blast, the men emerged from cover and pulled the door aside, letting it crash to the floor. Through the smoke, they saw something moving inside. A soft moaning permeated the air. It did not sound like a Cho-ta'an. They entered the room.

"My God," said Corporal Ireneus, as the smoke dissipated.

"Medic!" Sergeant Macron ordered. "Thales, get in here!"

Lying on a table in the center of the room, his wrists and ankles secured, was the missing boy, Livius.

CHAPTER TWENTY-EIGHT

Livius died three days after being returned to *Varinga*. Dr. Bartol made an effort to keep him isolated from the other settlers, but it was too late: several of the marines had already been exposed. Even if the marines had been more careful, though, it wouldn't have mattered. Several other members of the community had fallen ill the evening before the attack. Livius's mother, Drea, was one of the first. The stuffed animal that she had recovered from the ruins was identified as the source. Dornen reflected ruefully that his mistake hadn't been trying to eradicate the Cho-ta'an: it was not doing it sooner. By the time the marines launched their attack on Kavded, the Cho-ta'an had already struck a death blow against the humans.

The virus spread through the settlement like fire through the Cho-ta'an fields. Those who had become infected early got sicker. Dr. Bartol could do nothing for the sick but give them drugs to ease their suffering. Then he got sick and could no longer even do that. Many died. Sergeant Macron was one of the first, and several of his men died not much later. Soon, only Dornen, four marines, and about a quarter of the miners were unaffected by the virus. They shut themselves inside *Varinga* and waited for the end.

Dornen was so busy tending to the others that by the time it occurred to him to move *Varinga*, it was nearly too late. His temperature began to spike and he felt light-headed. Executing the launch sequence normally took a good three hours, and that was with a full crew. Doing it by himself, in an impaired condition, would take much longer. And the ship's sensors were already warning him they were under attack.

The attack didn't amount to much—Cho-ta'an with sticks, spears and stones—but eventually they would break through the hull, and when they did, they would have access to *Varinga*'s supplies, food production machines and technology. He couldn't let that happen.

The surest way to destroy *Varinga* and everything aboard would be to rig the propulsion system to explode. Dornen knew it was possible, but it had been many years since he'd had to use the control software. There was no "self-destruct" option, and in fact the system had so many failsafes and safety precautions built into it that getting the reactor to overload required a great deal of jury-rigging components, rewiring, and manual editing of configuration files. His fever continued to worsen, making it difficult to think clearly, and all the while the Cho-ta'an banged and pried at the hull. Ultimately he gave up and went back to plan A. He didn't need the ship to land; he just needed to get it high enough that when it crashed, there wouldn't be anything left worth scavenging for.

Unfortunately, lifting a ship the size of *Varinga* off the ground was not a simple matter either. Skipping most of the pre-launch checklist, Dornen got the thrusters to fire, lifting *Varinga* into the air. The ship lurched and shuddered, and Dornen realized too late that the Cho-ta'an had somehow managed to anchor the ship to the ground. Knowing their plant-fiber ropes couldn't possibly have the strength to resist *Varinga*'s thrust, he gave the engines more power. *Varinga* lifted a little higher, but then rolled dramatically to the right, throwing Dornen against the wall. What the hell?

Lying on the floor, he stared at the monitors showing views of the ship and its surroundings, his fever-addled brain trying to make sense of what he was seeing. At last he figured it out: they weren't using ropes at all; they were using the heavy-duty power cables the crew had used to wire the settlement from *Varinga*. Each of those cables had a tensile strength in excess of five hundred tons, and the Cho-ta'an had thrown several of them over *Varinga* and tied the ends to boulders weighing at least that much.

Dornen climbed back into the pilot's chair. He had no choice but to push the thrusters to maximum and hope for the best. Maybe they would overheat and explode—though he didn't have much hope for this. As the cabin shuddered around him, *Varinga* leveled out, dragging the boulders behind it. All he needed to do was get a mile above the ground. A fall from that height would smash every piece of equipment aboard *Varinga* beyond recognition.

Groaning and pitching, the ship slowly rose to a hundred yards, and then two hundred. It was nearing three hundred when a warning began to flash that the engines were overheating. Now near-delirious, Dornen managed to override the warning. The ship rose to four hundred yards—over a quarter mile. Then another warning flashed, indicating an impending reactor breach. Dornen wanted to weep. With considerable difficulty, he mustered the mental focus needed to override this warning as well. *Varinga* rose a few more yards before several more warnings appeared. The roar of the thrusters was suddenly muted. *Varinga* began to lose altitude.

There was no time to override all the warnings in an attempt to force *Varinga* to stay airborne or explode. Dornen shut down the thrusters and *Varinga* fell like a rock.

*****

"The sky ship is coming down!" Veyka-Chenn cried. "Stay back!"

He, Chief Churrik, and the few hundred other Cho-ta'an who had come to execute one final blow against the invaders fled as *Varinga* began to drop. A moment later, the plumes of flame holding the ship aloft were snuffed out, and the huge craft plummeted to the ground. It was now over the ruins of the city the humans called Tiberias, and it disappeared behind a row of taller buildings. The ground shook, and a rumble like thunder reached their ears. A cloud of dust billowed into the air.

"To the sky ship!" Churrik shouted. "It is our only hope!" He ran toward it, pulling his tunic over his mouth and nose to filter out some of the dust. Veyka-Chenn and the others followed him. They moved through the streets, slowing to a walk as the dust cloud rolled over them, making it nearly impossible to see. Dust penetrated their makeshift dust filters, and many fell to the ground, overcome by gagging and coughing. Veyka-Chenn pressed on.

A blast knocked him to the ground, and for a moment he lay dazed, coughing, disoriented. Then the dust cleared a bit, and he saw something on fire ahead. He had lost track of Churrik, but several others, who had also been knocked down, were getting to their feet. "Do not stop!" he ordered. "Get to the ship. Recover any food you can find before it all burns!"

He reached a wall of metal that radiated heat. Still holding his sleeve over half his face, he turned right and followed the wall until he came to a pile of rubble that appeared to be recently created. He climbed until he reached the top. The dust had now settled enough that he could see that two sections of the ship's hull had separated where it had struck the building. He piled rocks against the hull until he could reach the opening, and then squeezed inside.

Veyka-Chenn found himself standing on the wall of a large room filled with machines whose purpose he couldn't begin to guess. They were far too big and heavy to be removed in any case. Smoke was pouring into the room from somewhere above; if he was going to recover anything of value, he was going to have to be quick about it. He made his way to a door and managed to force it open. He stumbled into another room, lit only by the light from the crack behind him. The smoke was even thicker here. He moved across the wall, his eyes burning, coughing into his sleeve. Hopefully the others were having more luck than he was. It didn't look like he was even in the vicinity of the food storage areas. His foot struck something, sending it skittering across the room. He knelt down and crawled until he felt it. It was roughly the size and shape of a large book, but it was made of one of the strange synthetic materials that the humans favored over wood or bone. He grabbed it, tucked it under his arm, and made his way back outside.

He half-climbed, half-fell back down the rubble pile, and then crawled away from the ship, hacking and coughing all the way. Finally the air was clear enough of dust and smoke that he could catch his breath. There was an explosion from a more distant part of the ship, and moments later debris clattered to the ground around him. He got to his feet and staggered away.

At last he came upon a group of Cho-ta'an who, from their coughing and soiled clothing, appeared to have just come from the ship as well. They stood around a pile—as high as a Cho-ta'an—of the humans' food packets. It was a start. Perhaps they would survive until the next harvest. Embarrassed by his own feeble efforts, Veyka-Chenn slunk away, waiting until he was around a corner of a ruined building before examining the artifact he'd recovered.

He sat down and set it on the ground before him. Having seen a human use such a device once before, he pressed a button on the corner of it. An image of a machine appeared before him, floating in space above the device. Below it was a line of text in the humans' script, which he could not read. He had been trying for the past several weeks to learn the human language, but without much luck.

He dragged his finger along the text, from left to right, as he'd seen the human do. The device spoke some human gibberish. He tried it again, and the words repeated. After doing this several more times, he took a stab at mimicking the voice.

"Hai pur spays draiv," he said. "Selp dest ruck see kwins reh kurd not fount."

He made the voice repeat the phrase several more times and then tried it again.

"Hai-per spays draiv. Selff destruck seekwins rehkurd not fount."

He made it repeat several more times, then gave it another try.

"Haiper spays draiv. Self destruckt seekwins. Rehkurd not fount." Veyka-Chenn smiled, feeling like he was making progress. Noticing another small line of text below the one he had been practicing, he dragged his finger along this one.

"Seleckt ahnahther topick," he said. "Seleckt ahnather topick." He reached out again, meaning to get the thing to repeat the phrase, but he jabbed too quickly, and the view changed. Now he saw only many horizontal rows of text. At the top was another phrase he couldn't read. He dragged his finger along this and then repeated the phrase.

"Haiper spays draiv. Ahvayluhbuhl topicks."

He sighed heavily. This was going to take a while. But he would be patient, and he would learn. And he would remember what the humans had done to his people.

CHAPTER TWENTY-NINE

Andrea Luhman's Cessna 172 Skyhawk was ten thousand feet above the Atlantic, just southeast of Cape May, when a man's voice she didn't recognize came over her headset. It wasn't unusual to receive updated flight instructions as one neared New York City, but almost immediately Andi knew something was wrong. The man knew her call sign but didn't identify himself as air traffic control. The voice itself was wrong, too: the man's tone was too natural, too conversational. It lacked the bland singsong cadence of an air traffic controller. And what sort of accent was that? Norwegian?

"Cessna N91193, this is *Vordr*. Do you copy?"

"This is Cessna N91193. I read you, *Vordr*. Who is this?"

"We're a rescue ship five miles north of your current position."

"Understood. Do you require assistance, *Vordr*?"

"No. We are here to rescue you, Andi."

Andi's gut tightened. "I do not require rescue, *Vordr*." There was something very wrong about this. How did the man know her call sign? How did he know her name? How did he know her flight path? The only people who should have that information were air traffic control. She had only filed her flight plan five hours earlier in Fort Lauderdale; the decision to attend the conference in Boston had been last-minute.

The plane's engine began to sputter.

"Your engine is failing, Cessna N91193."

It's a coincidence, Andi thought. Probably just a plugged air intake or fuel line. Not likely to be a mixture problem, as she'd been at this altitude for two hours. Strange, though, as she was meticulous about maintenance. She'd just checked over the whole fuel system yesterday. In any case, it would most likely clear itself out shortly.

But the sputtering continued, and then the engine died. For a moment, the only sound was the whistle of the wind as the little plane rapidly lost altitude. She tried to restart it, but it wouldn't respond.

"Your engine is dead, Cessna N91193."

"How the fuck do you know that?" Andi demanded. "Who are you?"

"There is a parachute and a flare gun behind your seat, Andi," said the voice. "I suggest you put on the parachute quickly and exit the plane."

"Mayday, mayday," Andi said, banking the plane to the left. "This is Cessna N91193 en route from Fort Lauderdale to Boston. Engine is dead. Currently at nine thousand feet over water. Coordinates 37.9197 degrees North, 74.1347 degrees West. Does anyone read me?" She could just make out the coast in the distance. If she couldn't get the engine started, her best bet was to put down in the water, as close to shore as possible.

"We're jamming radio communications in this area, Andi," said the voice. "No one can hear you. You need to put on the parachute."

"Fuck you, *Vordr*, or whoever you are. You sabotaged my goddamn plane. Mayday, mayday. This is Cessna N91193 en route from Fort Lauderdale to Boston. Can anyone hear me? Please respond."

Several seconds went by with no response. They can't be jamming my radio, she thought. That's impossible. And there sure as hell isn't any parachute behind me. Still the engine wouldn't start. The plane had dropped to 8,000 feet. Cursing to herself, she unstrapped her seatbelt and looked behind the seat. There was indeed something that looked very much like a parachute back there.

"Andi, you're going to be passing over us soon. You need to put on the parachute and exit the plane. We'll get to you as quickly as we can, but if you spend more than a few minutes in the water, you risk hypothermia."

"Who the fuck are you? How do you know who I am?"

"I'll explain everything when you are safely aboard, Andi. Please put on the parachute and exit the plane. We aren't going to let anything happen to you."

"You sabotage my plane and you think I'm going to put on a parachute you somehow snuck aboard? Fuck you. When I'm on the ground I'm going to find out who you are and make sure you spend the rest of your life in federal prison. Mayday, mayday. Can anyone hear me?"

"You'll be passing over us in less than a minute, Andi. You're not going to make it to the shore. You're dropping too fast. Please put on the parachute and exit the plane."

Andi could see the shore in the distance. There had to be somebody in range. She called for help again, but again received no response. The plane was down to six thousand feet. Whoever *Vordr* was, they were right about one thing: she wasn't going to make it to the shore. The plane was going to hit at least two miles out. Assuming she survived hitting the water, that was going to be a hell of a swim in some damn cold water.

"You're passing over us now, Andi. It would be a good idea to put on the parachute."

Andi swore to herself as she reached for the parachute. Pulling it from behind the seat, she saw a flare gun lying on the floor. She gave the parachute a once over. It looked okay—not that she would know if the parachute had been sabotaged as well. Why would the people who had sabotaged her plane have provided her with a parachute in the first place? None of this made any sense.

The plane had dropped to five thousand feet. That water looked pretty rough. The odds of putting the plane down gracefully were slim. The odds of surviving a jump were probably worse. But with a parachute, she might stand a chance.

She strapped it on, still not having made up her mind whether she was going to use it. By the time she had it secured, the plane was at three thousand feet. She had done parachute jumps a few times, but never from an altitude of less than two thousand feet. She was going to have to make a decision quickly.

The voice on the headset had gone silent. Whoever was on the other end was either waiting for her to jump or had given up on her.

I can't jump, she thought. It's insane. I don't even know there's a parachute inside this thing. It could be full of confetti for all I know. One last joke on Andi Luhman, ha ha. The rational thing would be to set the plane down as best I can and then swim for shore. Water temp is probably around fifty-five this time of year. I could survive that if I keep moving. Unless a swell comes up at the wrong moment and my neck snaps before I even get out of the plane. The plane was at two thousand feet and falling.

Fuck it. She grabbed the flare gun, threw open the door, and leapt from the plane.

CHAPTER THIRTY

Andi Luhman sat in a chair in a small room, shivering despite being wrapped in two thick cotton blankets. Across from her sat a tall, thin man with close cropped blond hair. He wore civilian clothes but the way he sat ramrod straight in his chair reminded Andi of career military officers she'd met. He looked to be in his late thirties. He regarded her with cold blue eyes, but his face was not unkind.

She had a sense she was somewhere below decks on a ship, but her memory of how she got here was hazy. She remembered pulling the ripcord, falling toward the water, and then a shock of cold. A moment of panic as she tried to extricate herself from the canopy of the chute. At some point she had fired the flare gun. Treading water for what seemed like at least an hour. A ship—something like a naval frigate—visible over the swells. Rough hands grabbing at her, heaving her aboard. Clothing stripped. And now here she sat, across from a man she didn't recognize. She had heard his voice, barking orders as she was brought aboard; it was the same voice that had spoken to her over the radio.

"Wh-why?" she stammered.

"Why did we rescue you?" he asked.

She shook her head, more violently than she intended. "N-no. Why s-s-sabotage my p-plane?"

"We didn't sabotage your plane. We just happened to know your engine was going to fail."

"Happened to kn-n-now how?"

"That's a difficult question to answer without telling you a great deal more about our organization. I'm authorized to tell you virtually everything, but perhaps it would be better if you got some rest first?"

"N-no."

"Very well. My name is Soren Bell. I work for an organization called Jörmungandr. Our mission is the survival of the human race."

"Oh. Is th-that all?"

Bell went on, ignoring the interruption: "We rescued you because your experience and intellect are vital to the success of that mission."

"M-me? What do you know about me?"

"Andrea Jean Luhman. Born twelve June, 1986 in Davenport, Iowa. Graduated magna cum laude from the University of Chicago with degrees in physics and mechanical engineering. Did post-graduate work in applied physics on a grant provided by Lockheed. Your grant was scheduled to run out, and you were in the process of applying for various entry-level engineering positions when you were visited by a U.S. Air Force Colonel named Emily Rollins, who suggested you continue with your work. Shortly thereafter, you received word that your grant had been extended. You may or may not know this was due to the direct intervention of Colonel Rollins, who was at that time in charge of a top-secret project called Firefly. You received a doctorate in applied physics from MIT in 2018 and were hired by a well-funded startup based in Fort Lauderdale, Florida called Next Frontier, Inc. In the five years that you worked at Next Frontier, you managed to singlehandedly revive their moribund interstellar propulsion program, putting them on track to be the leading supplier of engines to fuel potential future missions beyond our solar system. You were rapidly promoted, eventually becoming the lead on the project at the age of thirty. Despite this, you feel underpaid and unappreciated, and you suspect that Next Frontier is ultimately going to fail, because they are producing a product for a market that won't exist for another twenty years. Your assessments, in all three of these matters, are correct. This morning you decided, rather at the last minute, to travel to an aerospace conference in Boston in the hopes of finding a lead on a new job. As always, you traveled in your own plane—the one luxury you allow yourself on your substantial but hardly exceptional salary. You did a full preflight check on the plane, but perhaps in your haste to get to Boston you did not notice a damaged fuel line."

"You knew I had a bad fuel line and let me take off anyway?"

"This is going to be difficult for you to accept. The crash of your plane was part of the known historical record. History cannot be changed."

"Known historical record? Known to whom?"

"Known to us. To Jörmungandr."

"You're telling me you know the future."

"We know of the inevitable occurrence of certain future events. We knew that at 11:43am on sixteen March 2021, you would make a distress call indicating that your engine had failed. Your plane would hit the water about ten minutes later, and would be recovered later that evening. Your body will never be found, and in three days you will be declared dead."

"You're kidnapping me."

"Certainly not. You are free to go at any time. I will suggest, however, that if you are looking for a challenging career opportunity where your gifts and efforts will be valued, Jörmungandr is worthy of your consideration."

"You want me to *work* for you? To do what?"

"Ultimately, to build a spaceship."

"A spaceship. To go where?"

"A planet that has not yet been discovered."

"Of course. And we want to go there because…?"

"Our founder believes it holds the key to victory in an interstellar war with an alien race called the Cho-ta'an."

"Right, right. And how far away is this planet, which has not yet been discovered?"

"Three thousand light-years."

"Uh-huh. You understand that even if I could build you a spaceship that could accelerate at a constant rate of one gee for a full year and then maintain a velocity near light-speed indefinitely, it would take over three thousand years to make that trip?"

"You would be utilizing hyperspace technology."

"Oh! Hyperspace! Right, like in *Star Wars*. I totally forgot about utilizing hyperspace."

"We have the plans for most of the components, but putting them together… well, we expect it to require what you might call 'intuitive leaps'—the sort of thinking you demonstrated in your post-graduate work and at Next Horizon. We have a team of engineers and physicists already at work, but we need someone with your unique gifts to synthesize the knowledge and shepherd the project."

"Fuck me, I almost believe you. I mean, it's pure gibberish, but it *sounds* convincing. Where are we going, by the way?"

"Our secret facility in Iceland."

"Ah. Good. Excellent choice for a secret facility. I'd never look there, for sure. Anyway, can you turn us around and bring me back to America? You can just drop me at Atlantic City or wherever and I can grab a bus to Boston."

"If you really want to continue to Boston, we'll take you there directly. I would ask that you humor me for a few more minutes, however."

"Sure, sure."

"Thank you. There are some things I must attend to on deck, if you don't mind, but I will be sending someone else to give you the rest of your briefing. Are you certain you wouldn't prefer to rest first though?"

"I'm good. Getting my second wind."

"Very well. Amelia will be in shortly."

"Amelia. Good. Send in Amelia."

Bell gave a slight bow and exited the room, closing the door behind him. For a few minutes, Andi sat alone in the room, wondering if there was any way of escaping this ship that was evidently crewed by lunatics. Then the door opened, and someone walked in.

"Hello," the thing said. It was shaped like a person, and it wore perfectly ordinary clothing, but its face was like a mask of some gray polymer. "My name is Amelia. I'm here to continue your briefing. Would you prefer that I sit?"

"What… what are you?"

"I'm an android," said Amelia. "I am one of six of my kind, created to assist in an effort to build an army of machines to prevent a divergent branch of humanity from creating a history-breaking paradox. The interlinking of the brains of the Six unexpectedly resulted in the emergence of a sentient being that embarked on a campaign of human genocide, but the destruction of one of my counterparts terminated the consciousness of the emergent entity. I was brought to a secret facility on a remote planet where I assisted in hiding a device designed to liquefy planets by temporarily weakening the covalent bonds between atoms. Then I traveled on a spaceship for one thousand four hundred twelve years to get to Earth. Now I work for an organization called Jörmungandr, which is dedicated to ensuring that humanity will survive a future interstellar war with a hostile alien race. I am aware that this is a lot of information for you to process, and I would be happy to repeat it or answer any questions you have."

Andi fainted.

CHAPTER THIRTY-ONE

Andi waited nervously in an anteroom for the arrival of the founder of the Jörmungandr Foundation. She had been at the vast underground facility for nearly three weeks now and she had started to accept that it was all real: the war with the Cho-ta'an, a ship—bearing her name!—traveling thirteen hundred years back in time, a group of astronauts from the future building a replica of a Titan II rocket to carry a person into space a millennium before Sputnik, and all the rest of it. She had even seen some of the artifacts: a propeller from an ancient airplane, a rifle used in a battle against the army of Harald Fairhair, part of one of the treads from an earth mover used to build roads and runways for machines that wouldn't be invented for a thousand years.

She'd met the engineers, the scientists, the archaeologists, the historians and the dozens of other people who worked for Jörmungandr in various capacities. All had been sworn to secrecy, few would ever be allowed to leave the Jörmungandr campus, and most were—like Andi—officially dead. They had no friends and family but each other. And they were all completely devoted to saving the human race from a threat that wouldn't present itself for another two hundred years.

About half of these people worked on some aspect of the spaceship development program, while another quarter worked on finding and securing artifacts leftover from the *Iron Dragon* project from eleven hundred years prior. Most of the rest were focused on public relations, propaganda and disinformation: covering up the existence not only of the goings-on in Iceland but also of the involvement of IDL personnel in Earth's history kept an entire department busy. Andi gathered that the government of Iceland itself was now effectively under Jörmungandr's control, although this would be virtually impossible to prove. It was vital to maintain the public's perception of Jörmungandr as a benign but ultimately inconsequential endowment that funded projects and causes seen as important to the future of humanity. Its funding for organizations raising awareness about "global warming" was a natural fit, given the location of the organization's headquarters. Recently they had funded the transatlantic voyage of a Swedish teenager so that she could attend a "climate change conference" in New York. Because the girl refused to fly, Jörmungandr had paid for her to sail across the Atlantic—and then had to fly two crew members to bring the boat back. The expedition was praised by some for bringing attention to important environmental issues and criticized by others as pointless, wasteful gimmick—and both perceptions served Jörmungandr.

The one person Andi had not yet met was Astrid van de Lucht, the founder of Jörmungandr. Evidently Ms. Van de Lucht was rather eccentric; she spent most of her time in something called a "stasis pod," which prevented her from aging. It was, Andi gathered, only her own arrival that prompted those in charge to "thaw" their leader before the usual interval of ninety days.

A door opened across the room, and a tall woman with long blond hair entered. Andi got to her feet. The woman crossed the room and shook her hand, a somewhat forced smile appearing on her face.

"Andrea Luhman, yes?" she said. Her Scandinavian accent was slight. "I am Astrid van de Lucht."

"It's great to finally meet you, Ms. Van de Lucht. You can call me Andi."

"Good. Then you may call me Freya."

"Freya?"

The woman shrugged. "Astrid van de Lucht is an alias. A fictional persona, created for the purposes of running the foundation. It's a bit of a joke, you see. 'van de Lucht' means 'from the sky.'"

"From the—oh! You're her! Oh my God!"

"They didn't tell you?"

"No, they've been… well, not secretive. Soren, Amelia and the rest have been quite helpful in explaining everything. But somehow I never put together that the founder of Jörmungandr and Freya were the same person. Everybody talks about them—you—as if they were two different people."

"Yes, that's by design, although the confusion was certainly unintentional. I'm a little like Batman. Astrid van de Lucht is my Bruce Wayne persona. Wealthy, staid, respectable. Freya is the one who battles robots and aliens."

"Then… it really is true? I keep expecting someone to tell me I'm on a hidden camera show."

"I doubt there are many television programs devoted enough to their premise to build a multibillion-dollar secret underground facility in Iceland. Let's take a walk." They went across the room to a door, which opened after Freya allowed a lens to scan her iris. They entered a long hallway.

"You really came from the past?" Andi asked as they walked. "And… er, the future?"

"My grandfather was born in 839 A.D. My grandmother will be born in 2181. It is a bit confusing, I'll grant you."

"You arrived five years ago?"

They had come to an elevator. The doors slid open and they went inside. Freya entered a code on a keypad, and after her iris was scanned again, the doors slid shut and they began to descend. Andi had been given access to most of the facility, but she had a feeling they were going to a level she hadn't seen.

"That's right," Freya said. "It took us one thousand sixty-one years to get here from Kiryata."

"You and the…?"

"The Vikings, yes. They remain in stasis on board our ship, which has been orbiting the sun out past Jupiter since it dropped me off. I'll be picking them up on the way back out."

The elevator doors slid open and they stepped out into a huge room that was somewhere in between a warehouse and a museum, filled with a bizarre assortment of artifacts. To her left was what appeared to be a replica of a Viking longship. To her right was a collection of corroded broadswords in a glass case. Straight ahead was a ten-foot-tall bipedal machine that Andi assumed was one of the "mech suits" she had heard of.

"How could you do all this in seven years?" Andi asked, meaning not just the museum but the entire Jörmungandr project.

They took a few steps forward and paused in front of the badly scarred and scorched suit.

"A little foreknowledge goes a long way," Freya said. "I landed in the southwestern United States. Hid the suit, then sold a small amount of gold for a few thousand dollars. Took the money to Las Vegas and turned it into a few million. Made some contacts, set up a new identity, bought shares in several companies that were poised to skyrocket in value. I had a net worth of over $100 million in less than a year. I moved to Zurich and spent a year buying companies to use as fronts while doubling my net worth. It tripled every year for three years after that.

"To be honest, making money was the easy part. Developing this organization along with the influence to make it effective required a great deal more finesse and foresight. But I applied essentially the same principle to developing people as I had to building wealth: I located people who were going places and I made myself indispensable to them. When I had the requisite wealth and influence, I began working on—among other things—acquiring all the physical evidence of the *Iron Dragon* project I could find. This was actually a fairly straightforward process, as most of the artifacts had fallen into the hands of a joint U.S.-British effort called Project Firefly, and they didn't seem to know what to do with them. The collection is now technically owned by the CIA, but on the off chance anybody starts looking for the stuff, they're going to face an endless tangle of red tape. Over the past two years I started acquiring controlling stakes in aerospace and other tech firms. These companies operate almost completely independently of Jörmungandr, but we poach technology and personnel when we need to."

Walking around the suit, Andi gasped as she saw what was beyond it: a winged craft that looked like a sleeker version of the old NASA space shuttle. It looked to be in even worse shape than the mech suit. They walked toward it.

"Is that…?"

"The lander, yes. We pulled it up from the bottom of the North Sea last year. Remarkably well-preserved, considering how long it was down there."

"You recovered it as part of your project to build another ship?"

"It's not much use from a technological perspective," Freya said. "The more advanced components are corroded almost beyond recognition. I suppose I wanted it because our collection didn't feel complete without it."

"But you're really building a spaceship to take you to an alien planet three thousand light-years away?"

"I hope to, yes. With your help."

"But you don't expect the ship to be completed for two hundred years?"

"I don't know how long it will take, but it will need to be ready by 2227. I plan to arrive just before *Andrea*—I'm sorry, this must be very strange for you."

"How did I get a ship named after me, anyway, if I'm building this one in secret? How does anybody find out about me?"

"Oh, dear. My goodness. Don't you know what you've done? Your work at Next Horizon is already going to revolutionize the space travel industry. It will take a while for people to recognize your contribution, of course—your problem is that you're ahead of your time. But eventually people will see that it was your work that put humans on the path to the stars. Your work here is, as they say in America, 'gravy.'"

"You say you need my help, but you already have the plans for this 'hyperdrive.'"

"We have documentation of the design of the key components, yes. But designing the tools to create those components and figuring out how to put those components together is going to require some highly rigorous and creative thinking. Imagine trying to build a Titan II rocket in medieval Europe. Not only would you not have the tools or materials you would need, you wouldn't even have the tools to create those tools or fabricate the materials. Besides that, your engineers would lack the language to talk about the problems. They'd have to learn calculus, differential equations, Newtonian physics, and all sorts of engineering concepts and principles. That's the sort of challenge we're dealing with."

"And you plan to do that all here," Andi said, "in an underground facility in Iceland."

CHAPTER THIRTY-TWO

Freya smiled. "It's being coordinated from here, and this is where we expect to do much of the theoretical work. The practical research will mostly occur elsewhere, at our partner companies' facilities."

"Isn't that dangerous?" Andi asked. "Won't these companies want to incorporate the technology into their own projects?"

"For the most part, the research is too lacking in practical applications to be of much use, and the companies are too siloed from each other to be able to synthesize the projects into anything useful. But yes, eventually the research is going to trickle into other areas. In fact, we're counting on it. Development of the technology required for interstellar travel is going to be an iterative process. We feed ideas to them, and we glean results from them. We always stay a few steps ahead on the overall goal—and of course the technology required for a self-contained hyperspace drive will never be disseminated outside Jörmungandr. Humanity will not be able to make use of hyperspace travel until IDL scientists reverse-engineer a Cho-ta'an jumpgate in 2143."

"If that's true, then how do you know Jörmungandr can develop a hyperdrive by 2227?"

"I don't. I think we can do it, but that's more of an intuition than a conclusion based on empirical analysis. Understand that for the last leg of the project, we'll be on our own. In 2185, the Cho-ta'an will launch an all-out attack on Earth, rendering the surface all but uninhabitable. At that point, we'll be confined to this facility. And you'll have twenty-two years to finish the hyperdrive."

"Me? I'll be long dead by then!"

They had walked around the craft, and Freya led them past a replica of an Icelandic turf house and a crenelated stone wall that must have been reconstructed from a castle somewhere. They proceeded toward a door in the far wall.

"Maybe, maybe not. We now have twenty more stasis chambers like the one I use. They aren't as good as the Izarian chambers; they use the technology that will eventually be used by the IDL. Maximum stasis time is ninety days out of ninety-nine."

"They don't actually give you more time, though, right? It just spreads your life out over a longer period."

Freya allowed her eye to be scanned again, and the door opened for them. They continued down another hall. "Sometimes it's helpful to take some time away," she said. "Suppose, for example, you need our software development team to write a module to test some hypothesis of yours. Rather than waiting three weeks for them to build it, you assign the project, sleep for three weeks, and then resume your work. Or suppose you need some piece of technology that we know will be developed by one of our partner companies in six months. It's a way of making the most of the time you have. And frankly, I would feel better if you were around for the last phase of the project."

"But you don't know if I'll be successful. I mean, as I understand it, you know the big events of the future, but the future of Jörmungandr is essentially unknown."

"That's the idea. We remain under the radar, so to speak. The historical record, as of 2227, considered Jörmungandr an unremarkable foundation with the somewhat grandiose purpose of ensuring the survival of humanity. To the extent that we are remembered, we are thought of as a failure. But history after April 29, 2227 is unknown. Our intention is to start writing a new history starting on that date."

"But how? Even if we get this ship built, how are you and a few frozen Vikings going to alter the balance of the war?"

Freya smiled. "Did Amelia tell you about the Cho-ta'an's attempt to use biological warfare to disrupt humanity's technological progress?"

"The plague they spread across Europe at the end of the ninth century? Yes. O'Brien and the others stopped them by spreading another, less virulent strain of the virus. That strain provided immunity to the deadlier strain, saving millions of lives—assuming the story is true."

"You doubt the veracity of Amelia's account?"

"No. Yes. That is, I still have trouble making sense of some of this."

"Amelia is incapable of lying, and she has perfect recall. That story came directly from me, and I got it firsthand from O'Brien, Helena and the others involved. Is there anything in particular that bothers you about the virus story?"

Andi thought a moment. "Yes. Amelia told me that as far as anyone knew, the Cho-ta'an had never taken a live human prisoner. She also said the four Cho-ta'an on Earth in the ninth century took an existing virus and modified it, making it far more deadly—in a makeshift laboratory, without any advanced tech."

"And?"

"Well, how the hell did they get so good at working with viruses that target humans? And how did they just happen to have individuals with such expertise on the team that pursued *Andrea Luhman* to Earth?"

"Those are some very good questions."

"For that matter, if they could design an incredibly deadly virus in a few weeks, why didn't they do it *before*? That is, earlier in the war. If you wanted to wipe out humanity, it would be a lot easier to drop a few aerosol devices to spread a virus rather than pelting a planet with nukes."

Freya nodded. "I knew there was a reason we recruited you. This way." She opened the door, and they continued into what looked like a morgue. Latched doors lined the walls, and in the center of the room were three stainless steel tables.

"You're telling me you've considered all this already."

"Indeed. I was a lot slower to figure it out than you were, though. I didn't know how we were going to defeat the Cho-ta'an until we were almost to Earth." She went to one of the doors and opened it, and then pulled out a steel drawer on which rested a large plastic tub. Freya pried the lid off the tub, set it down, and then reached into the tub and pulled out a skull. She handed it to Andi, who had pulled on her own gloves.

"What… is this human?" she asked.

"Cho-ta'an."

"My God."

Andi turned the skull over in her hands. It was almost, but not quite, human. It was too long and narrow, and the teeth were too short and too numerous.

"Ever see a femur that size?" Freya asked, pulling a long, slender bone from the tub. The owner of that bone had to be nearly seven feet tall.

"Where did you find it?"

"Project Firefly. The Brits got it from the Vatican. Until 1942 it was interred in Saint Peter's Basilica in Rome."

"This was one of the Cho-ta'an who followed the crew of… that ship back in time?"

"We believe so. Our best estimate is that it's been dead about a thousand years. We think it was imprisoned in the Vatican for many years. When it finally died, they didn't know what to do with it, so they left it there under a false label. During the war, the bones ended up in British hands." She turned and opened another compartment. She pulled out a container and placed it on the table next to the other.

"Another one?"

"Sort of," Freya said, taking of the lid.

Andi gasped, looking at the contents.

"The creature's innards were thoroughly desiccated. This was inside it, but I don't think the Brits knew it was there. We only found it with an MRI, and even then it was so poorly differentiated from the surrounding tissue that it was nearly invisible. We cut it open and pulled it apart very carefully. That's what we found."

"Was there another adult?"

"We don't think so. The Cho-ta'an are hermaphrodites. They cycle between male, female, and neuter states. It is suspected that in extreme circumstances, they may be able to reproduce asexually."

"But that thing, it looks…."

"Yes, it does. Now do you understand?"

Andi nodded. She saw now how one person could end the war with the Cho-ta'an. They were silent for some time as they made their way back up to the antechamber by Freya's office.

"So, now that you've seen everything," Freya said, "are you ready to get to work?"

Most of Andi's anger about the way Jörmungandr had recruited her had faded over the past three weeks, as she realized the scope of the challenge they were facing, but she had still been holding onto a little nut of resentment. Now, after talking to Freya, she found herself unable even to justify that tiny amount of indignation. These people were fighting for the survival of humanity, and they were counting on her to help them.

"I think so," she said. "Yes."

"Good. I will make sure you have full access to everything in the facility, including the stasis chambers. You will spend most of your time here, but I will set you up with a new identity in case you need to travel to one of our subsidiary sites."

"Great. Thank you."

"Please let me know if you need anything."

"I will," said Andi. "Thank you for the tour." She turned to leave.

"Andi," Freya said, "there's one more thing I need to tell you." Andi stopped and turned back to face her. "Everything we've told you is true, with one exception. When *Vordr* pulled you out of the Atlantic, you were… rather agitated. Soren made a judgment call, but I wouldn't feel right about proceeding without telling you the full truth. What he told you about your plane… it wasn't true. You weren't at fault."

"You sabotaged my fuel line. I figured."

"One of our agents did, yes. I could justify it by pointing to the fact that the historical record says you died on five September, 2021, so you'd be dead if we hadn't intervened. But that doesn't change what we did."

"'We?' You mean you gave the okay?"

"No. I didn't think sabotage was necessary."

"Because you trust LOKI to do what needs to be done."

"Yes."

"But not enough to tell your agents to leave my plane alone."

"I suppose that's true, yes. I could have told them to stand down, but I didn't. We all have occasional lapses of faith."

"After what you've been through, I can't blame you."

"Then we're on the same side?"

"We are. Let's build a spaceship."

CHAPTER THIRTY-THREE

The first ships capable of prolonged acceleration of greater than half a gee were developed in the middle of the twenty-first century. Two decades later, the humans established their first colonies outside the solar system. In 2075, the Human Colonization Consortium was formed as a partnership between several Earth governments and major corporations. By the end of the twenty-first century, a dozen worlds had been settled. Humanity appeared poised to spread out across the galaxy.

Then, in 2125, a scout ship called *Ubuntu* was destroyed by an alien warship in the Tau Ceti system, less than twelve light-years from Earth. It was the first known contact with Cho-ta'an. In 2126, the human worlds founded the Interstellar Defense League to protect themselves from the threat.

Seventeen years later, an IDL warship intercepted a radio signal from an unfinished Cho-ta'an jumpgate. The IDL sent ships to the location, eliminated the Cho-ta'an and took control of a gate. A research team reverse-engineered the gate technology, with the intention of building human-controlled gates. In 2146, coordinated Cho-ta'an attacks on human vessels began. In 2151, a jumpgate was first constructed by humans. Over the following decade, many more were built.

In 2185, Earth was the target of an all-out Cho-ta'an assault that culminated in the detonation of scores of nuclear bombs in the atmosphere. Most animal life was eradicated, and the planet was rendered all but uninhabitable. Several more human worlds were the targets of such attacks over the next forty years. The IDL did what it could to hold back the Cho-ta'an, but it gradually lost ground.

In 2227, the last human planet, Geneva, was on the verge of being destroyed. On April 29th of that year, an exploratory ship called *Andrea Luhman*, named after an earlier pioneer in interstellar space travel, transmitted a message that the Cho-ta'an had hacked the IDL's gates, and could now travel directly to any human worlds at will. Pursued by the Cho-ta'an, *Andrea Luhman* went through a gate in an attempt to flee to the Sol system, but she never emerged on the other side.

Six weeks later, three huge colonization ships departed Geneva, with the intent to carry enough people to settle new worlds outside the Cho-ta'an sphere of influence. Two of these ships were destroyed by the Cho-ta'an. The third, attempting to replicate *Andrea Luhman*'s flight, disappeared. The population of Geneva faced genocide. The Cho-ta'an were on the verge of eradicating humanity and becoming the dominant species in the galaxy. That was the end of known history, as far as the Jörmungandr Foundation was concerned.

While all this went on, Jörmungandr worked quietly and diligently to ensure humanity's survival. For Andi's first three years on the project, she spent almost no time in stasis, but as she became more familiar with the project and developed an understanding for its true scope, she began to see the value in a less hands-on approach. She could assign a task, go into stasis for three months, and then come out to check on the status. By her tenth year, she was spending almost as much time in stasis as Freya.

A few of the other high-level Jörmungandr operatives also occasionally used stasis, when waiting for a project milestone to be reached or for some tool or software application to be developed by a subsidiary (or unrelated company), but most worked an ordinary schedule. Soren Bell never used stasis at all, so that there would be continuity in the senior leadership. He effectively retired in 2043 and died four years later. He was replaced by a younger operative. Only in very few cases were retirees allowed to leave the facility; most spent the rest of their lives on the two thousand square miles Jörmungandr owned. Jörmungandr personnel were barred from having children, because such offspring would essentially be slaves to the foundation—a circumstance that was considered less acceptable in the twenty-first century than in the tenth.

New personnel were brought on as the first generation retired or died, but the number of active operatives was allowed to slowly dwindle. As interstellar space travel became more common in the latter half of the twenty-first century, Jörmungandr's test flights became less conspicuous, and when the first Cho-ta'an attacks came, all attention was directed off-world. No one had the time to look into the motives of an obscure environmental foundation. Every artifact of the *Iron Dragon* project that was going to be unearthed had already been acquired. Jörmungandr had no need to procure more land or wealth. Eventually all that was left of the foundation were fifty or so engineers, scientists, programmers and test pilots, working long hours to crack the problem of the self-contained hyperdrive.

By the time the first human-controlled hyperspace gates were built, in 2151, Andrea Luhman was no longer taking any stasis breaks. As with most of the developments in interstellar travel, the invention of the hyperspace gates was an iterative process: Jörmungandr fed ideas to the IDL's scientists to help them reverse-engineer the Cho-ta'an gates, and then Jörmungandr's spies relayed information on their successes back to the foundation. Jörmungandr would not be able to rely on the IDL's help much longer: the IDL had never cracked the problem of the self-contained hyperdrive, and after the Cho-ta'an assault on Earth in 2185 the IDL scientists who were still alive were put to work on weapons programs with a more definite return on investment.

The attack on Earth had minimal effects on Jörmungandr. The foundation had finished consolidating all its operations to the Iceland location the previous year, and the facility was self-sufficient in terms of food and energy, as well as hardened against nuclear attack and fallout. The Cho-ta'an didn't bother to send a bomb to Iceland, but most of the island's population was killed in the famine that followed. A few hundred refugees from

Reykjavik, having heard rumors of the existence of an underground facility far to the east, fled there and were taken in.

On April 29, 2226—one year before *Andrea Luhman* would disappear—Freya was brought out of stasis for the last time. She had spent 175 of the last 200 years in stasis. She was now nearly fifty in terms of biological age: she had been seventeen when she left Earth aboard the *Iron Dragon*, then spent four years ship's time aboard a Cho-ta'an frigate, several weeks with the *Varinga*, and then another four years subjective time returning to Earth.

Freya was shocked at how much Andi and the others had aged since she'd seen them last. Usually the changes were imperceptible, but those still working on the hyperdrive looked visibly older. As Freya approached Andi in the hyperdrive test lab, she tried to remember how old Andi was, in biological terms. She had been thirty-five when she'd come to Jörmungandr, and the last time Freya had checked the logs, Andi had logged 155 years in stasis. That meant she was effectively eighty-five years old. Well, Freya thought, I suppose she doesn't look so bad for all that.

"Good morning," said Andi, looking up from her console. "How'd you sleep?"

"It never gets any easier," Freya replied. "Thank God that was the last time." She'd spent three hours fighting nausea after coming out of stasis. "You look tired."

Andi laughed, a thin, rasping sound. "I look *old*. The only thing keeping me alive at this point is the faint hope we might still lick this problem." Freya was afraid there was more than a little truth to this. And Andi wasn't the only one: the whole team looked gaunt, pale, and haggard, like they hadn't a good night's sleep in weeks. They couldn't keep this up much longer.

"How is it going?"

"We're getting close, I think," Andi said, taking a step back to regard the hyperdrive test chamber—essentially a hundred-foot long polycarbonate vacuum tube, split in the middle by a steel wall. The thing had been built twenty years earlier, under Andi's direction, and since then they had been trying with no success to get a small Self-contained Hyperdrive Assessment Module (affectionately referred to as "the SHAM") to jump from one side of the tube to the other.

"The trick," Andi went on, "is to stabilize the proton reversion field by leveraging the overflow, like an entropic feedback loop. That's probably how the Izarian stasis pods work. They turn entropy back on itself, creating an actual temporal stasis, rather than just slowing biological activity the way ours do. If I had another few years...."

"You could build a stasis pod that doesn't make me puke my guts out?"

"I was going to say I could figure out time travel."

"Really?"

"Yeah. I mean, maybe. I'm beginning to see it's all related. Stasis, hyperdrives, traveling backwards in time... it's all different applications of the same idea."

"What idea?" Freya had kept up with Andi's work as best as she could, but for the past couple of decades it began to seem as if Andi were venturing into an entirely new field—more metaphysics than physics. Freya worried that Andi's mind was slipping, but she was the only one on the team who still seemed to have any idea how to proceed. So they followed her lead, like sailors in the fog, following the orders of a captain who claimed to have seen land.

"It's—this is going to sound odd. Quantum mechanics tells us that consciousness creates reality. That is, the universe can't be understood without reference to a conscious entity, and in some sense a thing that is not observed doesn't exist at all. But I think there's more to it than that. I think that the universe has a direction, a purpose."

"Are you talking about time?"

"Yes. Well, that's half of it. Time is a measure of entropy. Things fall apart, and we note a given amount of dissolution as units of time. But that can't be all there is. There has to be a countervailing force, something that pulls things together."

"Like gravity."

"Gravity doesn't actually decrease entropy, though. It just redistributes it. I'm talking about a more fundamental force, like consciousness. Consciousness is essentially static. If consciousness is the force that produces existence—that is, counteracts nonexistence, then what is the force that counteracts entropy? What keeps things from falling apart?"

"My understanding is that nothing does. Entropy eventually pulls everything infinitely far apart, and that's the end of it."

"But do you believe that, Freya? I mean, I know you accept it as a postulate of physics, but do you really believe it, in your heart? That things are just going to fall apart, and there's no point to any of this? If that's the case, why are we even doing this? Why build a Titan II rocket to get to space? Why fight the Cho-ta'an or the Izarians? Why build a hyperdrive?"

Freya shrugged. "If you're asking me, personally, then I'd say I'm too stubborn to give up. It runs in my family."

"Yes! But that's a negative formation of the principle. Think more positively. Why do you keep going?"

"Hope, I guess."

"Yes, hope. Or love, even. 'Faith, hope, love. But the greatest of these is love.'"

"You are telling me that the key to building a hyperdrive is *love*?"

"I think… yes, something like that. I've got to think about it more. Not think, exactly. I need to meditate on it. It's good to see you, Freya. We'll nail this yet." With that, she walked away.

Freya stood alone in the laboratory, wondering if her chief engineer had gone insane.

CHAPTER THIRTY-FOUR

Nine months later, Andi's team seemed no closer to solving the problem. The SHAM remained on the left side of the chamber, unable to move on its own accord, much less jump through the steel barrier. A nearly identical, but much larger, device had been built into the hull of *Valkyrie*, the ship that was to carry Freya and the Norsemen to Kiryata. Jörmungandr's scientists had worked out the principle of the hyperdrive using Amelia's data and the specifications of the Chota'an gate seized by the IDL, but building what was effectively a hyperspace gate that acted on itself created a seemingly intractable problem. Essentially the problem was one of infinite recursion: the hyperspace gates worked by opening a wormhole between two points in space and leaving it open long enough for matter to pass through. But once the SHAM moved into hyperspace, its location relative to the two points would change, forcing it to create another wormhole at the new starting point. Then the SHAM would go through that wormhole, changing its position relative to the two points again. The end result of this was a real-world Zeno's paradox: the SHAM never moved because it always had one more wormhole to create. Andi was convinced that there was a simple solution, some algorithm built into the fabric of the universe itself—the hyperspace equivalent of $E=MC^2$. In theory, all they had to do is program the magic algorithm into the SHAM's control software and they'd have a working hyperdrive. The algorithm, however, remained eternally elusive.

Several of the scientists and technicians came to Freya privately to voice concerns that they were at a dead-end. None of them spoke the words, but it was clear that at least a few of them would have quit already if that had been an option. But they'd signed up for life, in the belief they were working for the salvation of humanity, so they remained on the project, going over calculations for the hundredth time or executing tests they knew were bound to fail.

Andi seemed unconcerned. She spent less time in the lab and more and more time "meditating." She remained frail, but the weight of the years of frustrating toil seemed to have lifted. While the project foundered, Andi's spirits rose. Sometimes she would visit the lab, speak a few words of encouragement to the men and women still working on the recalcitrant SHAM, and then spend the rest of the day in her room or in one of the holochambers. She would have gone outside if Freya had let her, but the radiation levels made that unadvisable. At last, with only six weeks until the End Of Known History (generally referred to at the facility as the "EPOKH"), Freya was forced to confront Andi.

"I put you in charge of this project," Freya began, "because I believed that you were the only one with the vision to see it through."

"And what do you believe now?" Andi asked, her tone betraying mild amusement.

"I still believe that," Freya said, "but I think you're getting distracted. I think you're mistaking personal development for technological advancement."

Andi laughed. "Is that you think what I'm doing? Working on 'personal development'?"

"What do you call it?"

"You know, before the horrors of the twentieth century, it was widely believed that technological advancement went hand-in-hand with moral growth. A lot of people thought that as science improved our lives, we would also become better people."

"Then science gave us mustard gas, atomic bombs and gas chambers. I know the history. So what?"

"What if there's some truth to it? Not necessarily that science advances lockstep with morality, but rather that there are scientific discoveries that require a certain level of moral understanding. If you look at someone like Einstein, I think it's clear that more than mere intelligence went into his discoveries. He had a certain open-mindedness and playfulness, and a reverence for creation, along with a kind of modesty about his own ability to understand it. It was his attitude and imagination, as much as his intelligence, that allowed him to discover the principle of relativity. Did you know that when he finally won the Nobel Prize, it was for his work on the photoelectric effect? His discoveries of general and special relativity were so beyond the science of the day that no one could even grasp their true importance."

"And then they built on his work to make an atomic bomb. Even the Soviets and the Communist Chinese had them after a while. What's your point?"

"Once an Einstein points out the truth, others are able to grasp it. And of course technology can be duplicated without fully understand it, the way we duplicated the Cho-ta'an gates. But the original intuitive leap has to be made by someone who thought differently, someone who possessed real wisdom."

"While you are pursuing wisdom, a war is being lost."

"I know, and that is a tragedy. But you have said yourself that the war cannot be won until the EPOKH. Your LOKI principle is a tenet of faith. I'm asking you to have faith in me."

"My faith in you is based on your ability."

"Is it? You're certain it wasn't because of the symbolic resonance of my name? Would you have sought me out if you had never heard of me before arriving on Earth in the twenty-first century?"

"There are very few people with a résumé like yours."

"True, but I am hardly unique. You know, one thing that puzzled me for a long time after coming to Jörmungandr was this 'iterative' process of developing technology. Superficially it seems to make sense, you feeding information to other companies and then gleaning the results of their research. Basically, you're giving humanity's development of technology a nudge, causing it to move more quickly. Without your help, humanity might have taken another hundred years to get to the stars. But here's what bugs me: how do you know how much help to give? For that matter, how did you know to help at all? You've said there's no record of Jörmungandr making any significant contributions to science or technology at all. So why not sit back and wait for the IDL to reverse-engineer the Cho-ta'an gate and then start building your hyperdrive?"

"You don't just start from scratch on something like this. We would have needed to build an infrastructure—"

"And embed spies in the IDL, et cetera. I know. But you didn't need to spend two hundred years in a secret underground facility in Iceland, acquiring artifacts of an ancient space program and bribing governments through off-the-books subsidiaries. And another thing: if this mission is vital to the survival of humanity, why not train a team of soldiers to go with you to Kiryata rather than depend on a bunch of illiterate, undisciplined Vikings? We have your mech suit. We could certainly build more."

"That's a hell of a lot of extra weight to carry into space."

"Sure, but we had two hundred years. Except for the hyperdrive, the ship has been ready for almost a decade. We could have built a bigger ship."

"That's true," Freya admitted.

"For that matter," Andi said, "why are *you* going? I understand you founded this organization and have every right to determine who goes to Kiryata, but is that all there is to it? Because you can?"

Freya thought for a moment. "I suppose it's because it feels right. The same with Eric and his men. They were with me from the beginning."

Andi laughed. "They were with you for a few weeks, and then for two years on the way back to Earth. They've been in stasis for the past thirteen hundred years."

"Even so, it feels right."

"That's what I'm getting at, Freya. A lot of what you're doing is based purely on intuition. I know you're tough as nails, but you're not heartless. You feel it too. Something bigger than us. It's the thing that pushed your grandparents to build a damn rocket in the Middle Ages. And it's what made you trust me to build a spaceship to get you to Kiryata. So trust me. For just a little longer."

Freya sighed. It wasn't like she had a lot of choice. A few of the scientists had suggested avenues to pursue to get the SHAM to make the jump, but none of them seemed promising. "All right," she said. "I'll trust you."

"Thank you. I have one more request."

"Really?"

"I'd like to go outside."

"It isn't safe."

"I'm eighty-five years old. Radiation at the current levels usually takes years to cause problems. I'll take my chances."

Freya sighed again. "All right."

*****

After that day, Andi spent most of her time outside. The stark landscape of Iceland hadn't changed much since the Chota'an attack. In fact, the Jörmungandr campus now looked much the way it had two hundred years earlier: the global warm period that had started in the late nineteenth century ended in the middle of the twenty-first, and Vatnajökull and the other glaciers began to advance once again. It was mid-winter in Iceland, and Andi made the most of the few hours of daylight, going for long walks across the snowy plain. Andi spurned company on these walks, but Freya had a man in a radiation suit follow her at a distance in case she fell. Often she would return well after dark, half-frozen despite wearing three layers of thick clothing. Freya would help her undress and get into a warm bath, where she would sit until her teeth stopped chattering. Then Freya would help her to bed. They rarely spoke, and they never talked about the status of the hyperdrive project. Andi rarely went into the lab anymore; the scientists and other engineers were left without direction. Some continued to show up for work, while others sulked in their rooms. One, a physicist who'd become increasingly distraught over the lack of progress, slit his wrists. When Freya told Andi about this, Andi sat and wept for nearly three hours. She didn't go for a walk that day.

The weeks wore on. The EPOKH was now in twelve days. Even if they did, by some miracle, manage to get the hyperdrive working, there would be no time to test it. They had done several test launches of craft similar to *Valkyrie*, but none with a working hyperdrive. The engineers had stopped working entirely, as there no longer seemed to be any point. Freya herself was close to despair. She had never felt so low, even during the four years she was alone on a Cho-ta'an ship. Andi's minder no longer followed her on walks, and Freya couldn't muster the will to care. She had spent nearly her entire life working on this project, and now it was going to end, not with a bang, but a whimper. She and the others would die alone on a dead planet.

Three days before the EPOKH, Andi went for a walk and never returned. Freya formed a search party and found her the next day, lying still in the snow. Her face was white and her blue lips were frozen in a beatific smile. Well, thought Freya. I guess you found what you were looking for. And you doomed the rest of us in the process.

That night, Freya found herself unable to sleep. She told herself that it was time to give up, that there was no longer any point in fighting, but she couldn't make herself stop thinking about the hyperdrive. She had always had a mind for physics and mathematics, and she'd spent most of the past year getting up to speed on the project. What she didn't know, she would learn. She would never have Andi's natural insight, but she would bring a new perspective. They would never get the hyperdrive working before the EPOKH, but they still had a chance. Geneva would certainly be destroyed, but humanity wasn't finished yet. She refused to give up.

She went to the lab, planning to go over the output logs of the SHAM tests. As she entered the lab, though, she noticed something strange: the SHAM was missing. What in the hell? Had Andi taken the SHAM with her? She walked to the other end of the lab a took a sharp breath as she saw the football-sized device resting on the floor of chamber, on the opposite side of the steel partition, looking for all the world as if it belonged there.

Was this a joke? she wondered. If it was, it was in poor taste. Checking the lab activity logs, she found only one recent entry:

Andi had checked in at 7:13pm the previous day, and then checked out at 7:17. She couldn't possibly have had time to program the algorithm into the SHAM and then conduct the test. Could she? Checking the test log, Freya saw that Andi had logged a successful test. But then, if this were all a cruel joke, that's exactly what she would do. It wouldn't be difficult to create a fake log entry. But why would Andi do such a thing?

It took Freya only a few minutes to initialize the system for another test, with the SHAM programmed as Andi had left it. The SHAM powered up, lifted off the floor of the chamber, and then shot toward the steel partition. A few feet from it, the SHAM vanished. Freya gasped and ran to the other end of the lab. The SHAM was now back where it had started the previous day, before Andi had entered the lab. Still finding it hard to believe, Freya executed the test again. Again the SHAM lifted off the floor, shot forward, and then vanished, appearing at the far end of the chamber.

"Well, I'll be damned," Freya said. Andi had solved the problem. Scanning the test logs, though, Freya found no record of the changes Andi had made. The SHAM itself was essentially a black box; there was no way to extract the algorithm from it. Freya found herself laughing. Andi had played a joke on them after all: she'd programmed the SHAM to work, but they had no way to replicate it. Until they figured out what Andi had, they were stuck with exactly one working hyperdrive. It was enough: in the morning, she would have the engineers swap out Valkyrie's control module for the one in the SHAM.

She was going back into space.

CHAPTER THIRTY-FIVE

Valkyrie launched on March 28, 2227. A week later, she rendezvoused with the ship where Eric and his men remained in stasis. She revived them and brought them aboard *Valkyrie*, along with the mech suits. Three days later, *Valkyrie* made a hyperspace jump, traveling 3,000 light-years to the outskirts of a distant solar system. Shortly after she entered the system, she began broadcasting a tightly focused microwave transmission repeating the first seventeen numbers of the Fibonacci sequence in an endless loop, directed toward the planet called Kiryata.

0, 1, 1, 2, 3, 5, 8, 13, 21, 34 ...

After the seventeenth number, the broadcast started over at zero. It was intended as a greeting to the Cho-ta'an who now occupied the planet, members of the sect called Fractalists. The Fractalists, persecuted mercilessly by the High Command, were the closest thing humanity had to an ally against the Cho-ta'an. Freya could only hope her intuitions about them were correct.

Two days later, as *Valkyrie* accelerated toward Kiryata, she received a terse transmission from the surface that she interpreted as permission to land. The transmission repeated once per hour, every hour. She had learned the predominant Cho-ta'an language many years earlier and had been reacquainting herself with it over the past several months, but she was hardly fluent. *Valkyrie* flipped end-for-end and decelerated toward the planet.

She had no weapons, nor any defenses to speak of; if the Fractalists wished to, they could blow her out of the sky. But the ship approached the planet without incident and landed, using the signal as a beacon.

Wearing a spacesuit, Freya made her way across the powdery surface. In her right hand was a plastic satchel resembling an attaché case. She came to a horizontal hatch about two meters in diameter, made of a dull gray metal with a bluish-green tint. Barely perceptible on the surface were lines that spiraled out from the center, marking an iris-like opening. After several seconds, the hatch silently spiraled open.

Freya took a step forward and looked down. The hatch had opened to reveal a vertical shaft about fifteen meters deep. The shaft appeared to be a perfect cylinder, with walls constructed of the same bluish-gray metal. A series of metal rungs led to the bottom, where a roughly human-sized opening led to another tunnel or an underground chamber; it was impossible to say which. The illumination came from a series of palm-sized white discs that lined the shaft in a spiral pattern, spaced about half a meter apart.

Freya lowered herself into the shaft. It took her nearly three minutes to reach the bottom. Turning, she saw a human-sized arched doorway leading into a square room about five meters in diameter. In the far wall was a heavy-duty metal door, also human-sized. A small window at eye height revealed nothing beyond but darkness. Next to it was a control panel.

There was a metallic click as the hatch on the surface closed. A moment later, the door in front of her slid open, revealing another small room. It was round, with walls of the same bluish metal. An identical door was in the far wall. An airlock.

She stepped into the airlock and the door slid shut. A moment later, she heard a faint humming noise. After a few minutes, the humming ceased. A voice came to her from above, low and raspy, speaking in English.

"Who are you?" it asked.

"My name is Freya," she said. "I come to help you fulfill your mission. To end the war between humans and Cho-ta'an."

"How do you know of this place?"

"I was here once, long before. I know why you are here, and what you are working on. It's time for all this to end."

A long pause followed. Then: "Take off your suit."

Freya set down the satchel and unlatched her helmet. There was a hiss of air as the pressure equalized, and then she removed it. She took a deep breath and exhaled. Other than a slightly odd smell, there seemed to be nothing wrong with the air. She removed her suit, and the door on the other side of the airlock slid open to reveal another room, not much larger than the airlock. It too had no windows and only a single door in the far wall. Freya walked into the room, and the door closed behind her.

"Please close your eyes and raise your hands over your head," said the voice. Freya did so. Warm, dry air blasted her from all sides, filling the room with a deafening roar. Eventually it stopped. "Put down your arms and open your eyes," said the voice. Freya did so. The door on the far side of the room slid open. On the other side was another, somewhat larger, room. In the middle of the room stood three tall, gaunt, grey-skinned figures with elongated heads and large, pure black eyes: Cho-ta'an.

"Enter, please," said the Cho-ta'an in the middle, who was a bit taller than the others. The Cho-ta'an were wearing utilitarian gray uniforms. The two on either side wore some type of sidearm in shoulder holsters. Freya couldn't tell whether they were male, female, or asexual. She entered the room.

"Why are you here, Freya?" asked the one in the middle.

"As I said, I'm here to help you end the war with my people."

"You are the one the prophecy tells of."

"I don't know anything about that. I'm sorry."

The Cho-ta'an's face contorted into an expression Freya took to be a smile. "The prophecy tells us that a human woman will come to us to make whole what was torn asunder. It also tells us that this woman will claim to be ignorant of the prophecy."

"Well, I guess I passed the test."

"One test. I am Cho-Chirok Sem-Kallis. These are Sabik Charkarran and Koris Sem-Challok. We represent the ruling council of this facility."

"Cho-Chirok..." Freya started, doing her best to imitate the guttural pronunciation. The three Cho-ta'an reacted with an expression that was recognizable as a wince even on their alien faces.

"If you like," said Cho-Chirok, "You may assign us names that are easier for you to pronounce. We will not be offended."

Freya, gathering that the Cho-ta'an would be offended if she continued to slaughter their names, picked three names that she recalled as being common during the time of the human-Cho-ta'an war. "Aaron," she said, pointing to the one who had been speaking. "Richard," she said, indicating the one on her left. She pointed to the one on the right. "Olivia."

"Good," said the one she had named Aaron. "What do you know of the Fractalists?"

"I was under the impression you didn't care for that name."

The alien moved in a vague analog of a shrug. "It is how we are known to humans."

Freya nodded. "You are a Cho-ta'an separatist movement. The name 'Fractalist' is an English translation of a Cho-ta'an word. Because of its mathematical connotations, my people came to believe the name referred to your affinity for mathematics and the sciences. I think this belief is incorrect."

"Tell us what you think the name means," said Olivia.

"The word *fractal* comes from the Latin, *fractus*, meaning broken or fractured. I think the word that we sloppily translated to *Fractalist* refers to the fracturing of a single race of beings into two distinct species."

"You claim to have been to this planet before. You mean before we arrived?" said Olivia.

"It was over a thousand years ago, when the race called Izarians was still here. They built this place to serve as a remote laboratory to build incredibly powerful weapons. Their intention was to use these weapons against the machines they had built if the Izarians ever lost control of them. But the machines found this place and took the weapons. They used them to eradicate humanity from the galaxy. Only one planet, called Jabesh-Gilead, survived. But the people of Jabesh-Gilead could not survive cut off from the rest of humanity. So they adapted. Unable to alter their world to meet their needs, they altered themselves to better fit their word. They changed into something that was no longer human. Something must have happened to cause them to forget their past—a cataclysm of some kind. But a few remembered—or suspected. They were altered on the outside, but they retained an impression of their humanity. Some became consumed by the idea of rediscovering their true nature. Those were the first Fractalists."

"The planet you call Jabesh-Gilead is our home world, Yavesk," said Richard. "There was, as you say, a cataclysm during which most technological and historical records were destroyed. We Fractalists still believed we were descended from another race, but we were a tiny sect, considered harmless by the authorities. Then, about two hundred years ago, Yavesk was attacked by a group of humans who arrive in a gigantic spaceship. They intended to eradicate the Cho-ta'an, but we killed them first. That event was formative to Cho-ta'an history in three ways: first, it prompted the official policy of persecuting Fractalists that continues to this day; second, it provided us with the technology that was eventually used to build our hyperspace gates; and third, it set us on a path to war against humans."

"Do you believe now that I'm the one your prophecy talks about?"

"You have passed two of the three tests," said Aaron.

"I see," Freya said. Presumably demonstrating knowledge of the origin of the Cho-ta'an was the second test. "Well, I have one last thing to offer you. A gesture of goodwill."

"Speak."

"The powerful weapons I told you about? The planet-killer? There's still one here. The one meant for Jabesh-Gilead—that is, Yavesk."

"Where?"

"In a secret chamber a hundred yards below the surface, about two miles in that direction. You've been excavating recently to expand this facility, so you probably already have tunnels close to it. Do some soundings from the tunnels in that direction. You'll find a large void about thirty yards away. That's where the planet-killer is. If you would like to see what such a weapon can do, look at the photographs in my satchel. They were taken of the planet Izar just after the device was deployed."

The three Cho-ta'an conferred amongst themselves for a moment. Then Aaron spoke: "We will investigate your claims."

CHAPTER THIRTY-SIX

Freya was escorted to a bedroom in the dormitory where she had slept when she'd first come to Kiryata over a thousand years earlier. She was offered food, but she politely refused it: the Cho-ta'an digestive system could pull nutrients from substances that were almost inedible to humans. The door to her room was locked, but she was assured that this was for her own safety. She almost believed it. In the end, it didn't matter: she had to trust her intuition, as she had for the duration of the Jörmungandr project.

She lay on the bed for several hours, trying to assure herself that she was doing the right thing and praying that Eric's men wouldn't do something crazy like trying to take over the facility. The Norsemen were still onboard *Valkyrie*, waiting for her to return so they could complete their mission. She had warned them it could take a while, but she was dubious whether twelve hundred years in stasis had taught them patience.

She had just dozed off when her door opened. A Cho-ta'an—she thought it was the one she'd named Aaron—stood in the doorway. "Come," it said. She got up and followed the alien down the hall to a room where eight other Cho-ta'an waited. She thought she saw Richard and Olivia among them. The ruling council? Aaron took his place among them, and Freya was invited to sit.

"We have located the device you spoke of," said a Cho-ta'an she didn't recognize. "It was where you said it would be. You say that a device like that was used to cause this?" The Cho-ta'an slid a stack of paper photographs toward her. They were the printouts she had brought in the satchel.

"That's right," Freya said. "And Izar wasn't the only world to be targeted."

"The Cho-ta'an High Command has discovered some of these worlds," said the one called Richard. "Judging from the pattern of striations, we had concluded that they were made by a singular, vastly powerful weapon. We never imagined such a device was buried a few steps from this facility. How did you know?"

"I put it there," said Freya.

Murmurs circulated amongst the Cho-ta'an.

"Why did you do this?" asked Aaron.

"I didn't want it to be found until the time was right."

"And that time is now?" asked another Cho-ta'an she did not recognize.

"Yes."

Olivia spoke: "If you intend to use this weapon against our siblings who persecute us, you will be disappointed. We will not allow you to have it. Although the Cho-ta'an High Command wishes to eradicate us, we will never condone genocide of our own kind."

"That is not my intention."

"Then how do you intend this weapon to be used?"

"I don't intend it to be used at all. I wish it to be destroyed."

"You are asking us to destroy it?" said Aaron.

"No. This is going to be difficult for you to accept, but I really am on your side. I want the same thing as you do. I hope my passing your tests has convinced you of that much, at least."

"Go on."

"In about three weeks, an IDL ship called *Andrea Luhman* is going to pass nearby this planet. It's an exploratory ship with minimal weaponry. You have nothing to fear from it. If you broadcast the Fibonacci sequence—the same series of numbers I sent to you to announce our arrival—the ship will alter its course to investigate. A lander craft with a crew of four humans will set down. Let them in, as you did me."

"These humans are following your orders?" asked Richard.

"No. They do not know of my existence, and under no circumstances should you speak of me to them. I have no control over the crew of *Andrea Luhman*. But I know of their mission and their current location and trajectory. You must give them the planet-killer."

"The IDL will use it against Yavesk," Olivia replied.

"I promise you they will not. *Andrea Luhman* will be destroyed and the planet-killer with it."

"How do you know this?" Aaron asked.

"The same way I know that *Andrea Luhman* will pass by in three weeks. I have knowledge of the future."

"How do you come by this knowledge?" said Richard.

"I can't tell you that, other than that it involves the hyperspace gates. I know that the Fractalists have figured out how to hack the IDL gates; that's how you got here. So I suspect that you have an idea of how gate technology relates to the nature of time. More than that, I won't say." Freya knew from her grandmother's description of their meeting with the Cho-ta'an that some of those on the council would not go along with the plan to give the planet-killer to the crew of *Andrea Luhman*. And if Andi had been right about the ability to understand hyperspace technology going along with a certain sort of wisdom, then those on the council who knew the true nature of the gates would understand that she was telling the truth. That was her hope, in any case.

"If the planet-killer is to be destroyed," said Aaron, "what is the point of giving it to the crew of the ship?"

"It will set off a chain of events that make it possible to bring about the end of the war."

"How?"

"By providing my people with the hope that they can win the war. You must convince the humans that you want them to use the planet-killer to destroy Yavesk."

"They will never believe that!" Olivia exclaimed.

"They will believe it, because it is their only hope."

"You have come here to convince us to give our enemies a doomsday weapon, telling them that we wish them to use it to destroy our home world, while assuring us that it will never be used for such a purpose?" Richard asked.

"Yes."

"Why would we do this?"

"Because you know that I am telling you the truth. The planet-killer will not be the thing that ends this war."

"No?" said Aaron. "Then what will?"

"The other weapon you are hiding."

Murmurs went up around the room, and Freya knew she had passed the third test.

"The weapon is not ready," said Aaron. "We have not tested it."

"I have seen the results. It is ready."

There was some muted discussion around the table.

"The weapon represents the culmination of many generations of Fractalist effort," Olivia said. "Why would we just give it over to you?"

"Because I've passed all your tests. Because you know I'm telling the truth. And because in three weeks, this facility will be destroyed."

The group erupted into pandemonium. When once again Aaron had managed to silence them, he asked, "What do you mean by this?"

"The Cho-ta'an High Command knows about this facility. They probably know what you have been working on, but they do not realize how far along you are. Shortly after *Andrea Luhman* departs with the planet-killer, a group of Cho-ta'an ships will arrive and deploy nuclear missiles against you." Freya was not actually certain the High Command knew about Kiryata, but if they didn't, they soon would. Her grandmother had suspected a traitor amongst the Fractalists had informed the High Command about the planet-killer.

"We must converse a moment," said Aaron. "Please wait outside." A man armed with a gun came into the room and escorted her into the hallway. Freya waited impatiently for several minutes, the guard eying her suspiciously. At last she was summoned back into the room.

"We will give you what you ask for," Aaron said, "because there is little harm in it. As for your other request, that we give the planet-killer to the crew of the IDL ship, *Andrea Luhman*, I can make no promises."

"But you will send the signal?"

"Yes. If there really is a ship out there, it is undoubtedly an exploratory vessel, as you say. It may be useful to us, even if we decide not to give them the planet-killer. By the time it arrives, we hope to have made a decision."

Freya smiled. "I am confident you will do the right thing."

CHAPTER THIRTY-SEVEN

Valkyrie emerged from hyperspace only a few thousand miles from Yavesk and quickly dropped into a low orbit over the planet. Her hyperspace drive was modeled after the Izarian variety, allowing them to emerge from a jump well inside a system. Valkyrie also used stealth technology based on plans Jörmungandr extracted from Amelia's memory, making it unlikely the ship would be spotted until after Freya and the Norsemen had begun their descent to the surface.

They were launched in quick succession, each mech-suited man encapsulated in a protective eggshell. Freya went third, right after Eric and Bjorn. It was only her second jump, and the first one—to the surface of Earth—had been twenty years earlier, from her perspective. That time there had been little chance of her getting shot down, as a mech suit's radar profile would look more like a meteor than an airplane. This time, rather than jumping alone into a vast desert on a technologically backward planet, she would be jumping into a heavily populated area of a technologically advanced planet with six other mech-suited humans. She didn't expect them all to make it to the surface. She could only hope at least a few of them did.

The outer shell of Freya's suit sloughed off in the upper atmosphere. Then the second layer went, scattering chaff in the process. By now, the Cho-ta'an would have detected the incursion, but the chaff would confuse their radar. Her shell was rocked by explosions—hopefully just missiles impacting the chaff. But as she continued to fall, the explosions continued, and two names on the squad roster went gray: Sven and Lars. Freya had hoped they were far enough out to be safe from the city's defensive railguns and missile batteries, but they'd known there was a good chance at least some of Norsemen wouldn't survive the jump. Their entire attacking force was down to Freya and four Norsemen. Freya closed her eyes and waited, knowing there was nothing she could do.

The explosions stopped around the time that the second layer finished burning off. Freya could see the planet's yellow-green surface rushing toward her. The chutes deployed, slowing her fall, and then her rockets kicked in for a few seconds, working in concert with the other suits to bring them into a tighter formation. The rockets went silent, and a moment later her parachute deployed. After a few more seconds, the parachute tore away, and the rockets fired again, easing her to the ground with a thunk. She was in a field of yellowish grass; to her left was a highway leading toward the capital city, the tops of its buildings just visible in the distance.

Their numbers held at five. Looking to her left and right, Freya saw the rest of her squad, each member about a hundred yards from the others. They would remain far apart until they reached cover, to make it harder for the defenders to target them as a group. Debris clattered to the ground around them; some of it was undoubtedly from the suits of the two dead men.

"Forward!" Eric ordered. "Bjorn and I are up front. Ragnald and Halvar bring up the rear. Protect Freya!" He bounded forward, and a second later, Bjorn, a hundred yards to his right, did the same. The others followed, keeping Freya in the center. Their target was the Cho-ta'an High Command Center, located some five miles away, in the heart of the capital city.

It didn't take the Cho-ta'an long to mobilize their defense: the attackers had advanced less than a mile when Freya's radar told her that five aircraft were inbound from their right. The Norsemen's only chance was to get to cover before the Cho-ta'an planes launched their missiles. They loped across the field at top speed toward a cluster of buildings on the outskirts of the city. There was not yet any sign of the city's ground defenses; the Cho-ta'an they encountered fled in panic.

Eric and Bjorn had moved past the first few buildings and taken cover. Freya did the same, crouching against the wall of a large steel warehouse. Her display showed Ragnald and Halvar moving into position behind her. Freya waited for an attack, but it didn't come. The aircraft shot overhead. The Cho-ta'an had decided they weren't enough of a threat to justify launching missiles at their own buildings. Good. Cho-ta'an overconfidence was about the only thing they had going for them.

"Move!" shouted Eric, who was already bounding forward again. The others followed his lead. By the time the aircraft had circled around, the Norsemen had moved into the city proper. Cho-ta'an fled before them by the hundreds, even though the Norsemen had not yet fired a shot. Freya's suit identified several groups of Cho-ta'an soldiers taking up positions at various places ahead of them. As the attackers continued to advance rapidly, automatic weapon fire rang out all around them. Bullets plinked against their heavy armor, doing little but scratching paint. Unlike the machines, the Cho-ta'an did not have the precision necessary to damage the suits with handheld machineguns. The Norsemen tightened their ranks as they advanced down a main street toward the city's center. Vehicles swerved wildly to avoid the mech-suited warriors, some of them smashing into buildings or each other.

"Incoming rockets!" Bjorn shouted, and Freya's display lit up. She dived behind an abandoned vehicle as the little missile shot between her and Eric, blasting a hole in the pavement the size of a small house.

"Keep moving!" Eric shouted, as Freya's suit was pelted with sand and rock. "Don't let them pin us down!" He sent a missile toward the window that the rocket had come from, punching a hole in the building, and then continued running down the street.

Freya got up and ran after Eric and Bjorn, keeping tight against the wall to her left. Ragnald and Halvar followed at a distance of about twenty yards, periodically stopping to loose a barrage of fire at Cho-ta'an creeping up from behind.

As Freya moved to follow Eric and Bjorn across a street, heavy machinegun fire rang out from her left, and a barrage of large-caliber rounds tore across the suit's midsection. She zeroed in on the machinegun and blasted the two Cho-ta'an manning it.

Her suit was screaming at her about another threat moving toward her from the opposite direction. Turning, she saw three armored vehicles barreling down the street. Eric and Bjorn, already well across the street, were busy blasting their way through Cho-ta'an who had taken cover behind parked vehicles lining the street.

Not wanting to get bogged down in a firefight, Freya ran diagonally across the street, ducking into an alley just as the machineguns on the three vehicles opened fire. She ran down the alley and then veered right at the next intersection, making her way back to the center of the elongated rectangle formed by the four Norsemen. She heard heavy machinegun fire from behind her and felt a barrage of bullets tear across the rear of her suit. No warnings: the armor had held. She spun, targeted the pair of gunners set up on the sidewalk, and splattered them across the wall of the nearest building with her machineguns. She turned and bounded around the corner after Eric and Bjorn.

A line of boxy military vehicles had formed ahead of them, creating a near-solid barrier across the street. Several dozen Cho-ta'an took cover behind the vehicles, pointing their machineguns toward the Norsemen. The Cho-ta'an opened fire as the Norsemen approached, riddling Eric and Bjorn with bullets.

"We go through, you go over," Eric's voice said in Freya's ear.

"Roger that," Freya said, doing her best to keep Eric between her and the Cho-ta'an. When they were nearly to the barrier, she leapt, the suit's rockets supplementing its servos to launch her fifty feet into the air in the low gravity. She sailed over the vehicles as Eric and Bjorn, having closed ranks, stiff-armed their way through the barrier, sending the vehicles skittering aside and crushing the Cho-ta'an who couldn't get out of the way. A few brave Cho-ta'an kept firing, to little effect. Ragnald and Halvar ran through the gap, saving their ammunition for bigger threats.

Freya's rockets fired, slowing her descent, and she landed just behind Eric and Bjorn. Ragnald and Halvar followed close behind. Ahead, another barrier was going up. This one was made up of interlinked units of welded metal struts that would be a lot harder to push aside. "We're all going to have to go over," Bjorn said.

"Wait," said Freya. A hum overhead prompted her to turn. A dark shape came into view above the buildings, followed by several others. Warnings flashed on her display. "Gunships!"

"This way!" Eric shouted, and darted down a side street to their left. Most of Freya's information about Yavesk and the capital city had come from the IDL, by way of her grandmother, but the Fractalists had specifically warned them about gunships: essentially airborne tanks that each hung from an assembly of four flexible rotors. The rotors—typically the weak point on such vehicles—could move independently of each other and even dodge missiles when necessary. Each gunship had a pair of heavy machineguns. Leaping over barriers wasn't going to cut it anymore. Their best hope against such vehicles would be to move to the part of the city with taller buildings, limiting the number of gunships that could attack at once. That was where Eric was taking them.

For a few seconds, the gunships were blocked by buildings. Eric led the attackers a block down the street and then turned sharply right, putting them back on a path toward the Command Center. As Freya followed him around the corner, heavy machinegun fire rang out and Halvar let out a shout. Her display said his suit had been damaged. While she, Eric and Bjorn advanced, Halvar and Ragnald hung back.

"Leave him!" Eric ordered, barely audible over the guns raining fire from above. "No time!" After a moment, Ragnald's dot began to move. Halvar's went gray. The gunships came into view again and lined up to target the Norsemen. "Squad, missiles ready," said Eric. "On my mark, give them all you've got. Fire!"

A volley of missiles shot from the suits, each launcher firing one after another in quick succession: their only hope was to send so many missiles at once that the gunships couldn't dodge them all. A staccato burst of explosions rang out overhead as Freya ran, deaf and half-blind, after Eric and Bjorn. At last the cacophony ceased, followed by the crashing of debris all around them. Freya's display told her that three gunships remained, but for the moment they held their fire, having moved aside to avoid being caught in the carnage. This was fortunate, as it was all the

Norsemen could do to dodge the chunks of debris, some of which were big enough to do serious damage. They were now less than a mile from the Command Center. A few blocks ahead lay another roadblock. If the gunships held off for a little longer, they might still make it.

It soon became clear, though, why the gunships were remaining at bay: one of them had lost two of its rotors and was weaving erratically overhead, trying to set down on top of a building just ahead of the attackers. If it kept the other gunships from attacking for a little longer, the Norsemen could leap over the roadblock, and then they'd be home free.

A squeal of shearing metal announced the failure of another rotor, and the gunship wobbled and began to lose altitude. Freya slowed, but Eric urged them on: "Under and over!" he shouted, and Freya pressed on, understanding what he meant: they would pass under the falling gunship and then leap over the roadblock.

Moving at top speed, Freya followed Eric and Bjorn through the shadow of the falling gunship and then leaped, her rockets carrying her in a long arc over the barrier as the huge machine crashed to the street. As she came down on the far side, she saw that Ragnald's dot had gone gray: he'd been crushed by the gunship.

There was nothing to do but keep going. Eric, having lost his brother as well as his son, tore down the streets like a demon, veering down alleys and side streets apparently by instinct, blasting Cho-ta'an gun placements and military vehicles as he went. Bjorn and Freya did their best to keep up. At last they were on a straightaway: a long, narrow street that cut like a canyon through walls of skyscrapers on either side. An ominous hum overhead told Freya the two remaining gunships were lining up to attack.

Suddenly Bjorn, just a few paces ahead of her, stepped aside and came to a halt.

"Bjorn!" Eric barked. "Keep moving!"

"Get Freya to the target," Bjorn said. "I will cover you."

"Damn you, Bjorn!" Eric growled, but he didn't argue. Freya knew it as well: it was the only way they were going to make it to the Command Center.

As Eric and Freya continued bounding down the road, Bjorn stood his ground, blasting the nearer of the two gunships with both of his guns. The gunships returned fire. The entire exchange didn't last more than five seconds. As Bjorn's dot went gray, Freya glanced back. Bjorn's suit was a barely recognizable heap of twisted metal. The lead gunship, smoke billowing from two of its rotors, crashed into the one behind it. Their rotor assemblies became tangled, and the two gunships crashed into the side of a building and then tumbled toward the street below. By the time the gunships hit the street with a thundering crash, Eric and Freya were within a half-mile of the Command Center.

The narrow canyon gave way to a vast open plaza, at the center of which was a cluster of important-looking government buildings constructed of pink marble. One of these, a squat dome standing on top of a base of thick, fluted columns, was the Command Center—the brain of the Cho-ta'an military operation. Eric slowed just enough for Freya to come up alongside him. His rage and sorrow had given way to the exhilaration of victory. "We have done it, Valkyrie!" he shouted. "We have brought the war to the heart of the giants' realm!"

Freya couldn't help smiling. They still had some ways to go, but Eric's mad euphoria was infectious. Maybe she'd been crazy to trust the future of humanity to a band of bloodthirsty Vikings, but she wasn't sure anyone else could have gotten her this far. The Command Center loomed ahead, its dull marble mirroring the eternally gray sky of Yavesk. But they weren't done yet.

"Stay behind me," Freya said. "I'll deal with anything coming out of the building. You just worry about—"

She was thrown forward as the ground erupted just behind them. The suit's left shoulder hit the ground and she rolled, ending up on her back. The suit was flashing warnings: several servos were no longer functioning. Eric's suit was damaged as well, but he was still alive. Freya got awkwardly to her feet: the suit's right arm had gone dead, and the right knee joint was frozen. Turning, she located the rocket launcher and blasted it with her machinegun. She limped toward Eric, who was struggling to get up. He waved her off.

"Suit's gone dead below the waist," he said. "Keep going, I'll hold them off as long as I can." She saw now that Eric wasn't trying to get up; he was just trying to orient himself to get his guns pointed at a group of Cho-ta'an who were setting up more rocket launchers and heavy machineguns. From where she stood near the center of the plaza, she could see three convoys of armored vehicles heading their way. In the distance several more gunships approached. "Go, damn you!" Eric shouted. Freya started to reply, but her words were lost in the roar of Eric's guns.

Freya ran toward the domed building as fast as the crippled suit would carry her. Behind her, gunfire continued. She was now a stone's throw from the Command Center. Ahead was a line of Cho-ta'an armed with machineguns. They opened fire, and a hail of bullets hammered her suit. Still she ran. Behind her, a series of explosions sounded. Eric's dot went gray. Freya fell.

Unable to move the suit's right arm, she fell hard on her face. Her display told her that her weapons were offline, and only a few servos on the left side of the suit were still functioning. Bullets hammered at her from all directions. She struggled to her feet and activated the suit's rockets. The ground exploded under her a split-second after she lifted off. She flew in a high arc as gunfire followed her. The suit's rockets cut out as she passed over the apex of the dome, and she fell.

She landed with a thud, face-down on the sheer marble surface. The suit was completely dead. Unable even to move enough to climb out the chest hatch, she coughed and gagged as the suit filled with smoke. She was on the verge of passing out when the suit was rolled onto its back. Her last memory before losing consciousness was being hauled out of the suit by long, rough fingers.

CHAPTER THIRTY-EIGHT

Freya awoke lying in a bed inside a simply furnished cell. She was surprised to be alive. Eric and the other men had been killed trying to get her to the Command Center. She was alone and imprisoned on an alien planet.

She was wearing a simple gown made of something like linen. Her head had been shaved, and further inspection revealed that her entire body was now devoid of hair. Her skin was raw, as if it had been scrubbed by course brushes. Decontamination, she thought. The Cho-ta'an had been concerned that she might be carrying some dangerous pathogen. She didn't blame them.

There was only one exit to the room. The door had no handle or latch, only a face scanner. She saw no cameras, but she was certain they were there. She sat on the bed and waited.

About an hour after she awoke, a raspy Cho-ta'an voice came to her from somewhere above.

"Who are you?" the Cho-ta'an asked, in its language.
"My name is Freya," she replied.
"You were sent by the IDL, Freya?"
"No. I came on my own."
"What is your mission?"
"To destroy the Cho-ta'an High Command Center."
"With the fission bomb we found attached to your suit?"
"Yes."
"Where is your ship?"
"In orbit. It uses advanced stealth technology, so your radar will have a hard time locating it."

"There is only one ship?"

"Yes."

"Are more coming?"

"No."

"We did not know the IDL were capable of building spacecraft that could not be detected by our sensors."

"They aren't," said Freya. "As I said, I came on my own."

The voice was silent for a moment. "We estimate the destructive potential of the bomb at one hundred kilotons, in human measurements."

"That is correct."

"You intended to destroy the Command Center with this device?"

"And as many of the surrounding buildings as possible."

"Why?"

"To cripple the Cho-ta'an's ability to wage war against humans."

"Surely you must have known you would fail."

"I nearly succeeded."

"A missile fired from orbit would have been more effective."

"Our intelligence indicated a missile would be intercepted by your planetary defenses. Our best bet was to land outside the city and then overcome its relatively weak ground defenses."

"Why did you not trigger the bomb when you reached the Command Center?"

"My suit was dead. I couldn't activate the detonator."

"Even if you had," said the Cho-ta'an, "you must know that destroying a few buildings would not end the war."

"It would be a start."

"Where does the IDL manufacture the mechanical suits your people used?"

"As I said, I am not with the IDL. The suits were manufactured in a secret facility on a remote planet called Kiryata."

"This facility, it's run by the IDL?"

"For the fourth time, I don't work for the IDL. I'm willing to give information to the Cho-ta'an High Command, but I'm not saying another word to you."

"Then you will be executed."

"I doubt that. I think someone with more power than you is watching me right now, or at least recording this interrogation. That individual knows about Kiryata and what happened to it, or is about to contact someone who does. When that individual is ready, he, she or it knows where to find me."

*****

About three hours later, another voice penetrated the cell. It introduced itself as General Semik Yarchillok. "How do you know about Kiryata?" it asked.

"I was there."

"When?"

"Three weeks before you destroyed it."

"How do you know about that?"

"You wouldn't believe me if I told you."

"Tell me anyway."

"No. There are certain things I am not going to tell you, because doing so will serve no purpose."

Semik was silent for a few seconds. "Why were you there?"

"I had an arrangement with the Fractalists. They gave me the bomb. I gave them the plans for the mech suits and a self-contained hyperspace drive."

"There is no such thing as a self-contained hyperspace drive."

"I suspect that before today, you'd have sworn there was no such thing as a forty-pound bomb with a destructive potential of a hundred kilotons."

"You claim that the bomb was developed by the Fractalists at the Kiryata facility."

"That's right."

"Our intelligence indicated it was a biological warfare facility."

"Well, maybe you should have verified that before you blew it up, because now that bomb is the only one of its kind in existence."

Semik was silent again for a moment. "We have limited use for such a weapon. We already have nuclear weapons, and the war against the humans has been won."

"I imagine a self-contained hyperdrive would still be of some use. With hyperdrive-equipped ships, the Cho-ta'an could spread out across the galaxy—and beyond."

"You claim to know how to build such a drive?"

"Not only do I know how to build it, I can give you one. The ship we took here is still in orbit. It's wired to explode if it's tampered with, but I can tell you how to defuse it."

"You seem quite willing to cooperate with us."

"As you say, the war is over. This was my people's last chance to strike a blow against the High Command. We failed."

"Who are your 'people,' exactly? You claim you do not work for the IDL."

"My organization is what you could call a spinoff from the IDL. We're a separate group with our own aims and our own technology. We remained out of the war as long as we could, but we could not allow humanity to be eradicated. We contacted the Fractalists in the hopes of executing a joint assault. Clearly it was too little, too late, but we did what we could."

"Where is this organization?"

"I am not going to tell you that."

"We could compel you to do so."

"You could, but you won't, because then I will give you the wrong code to deactivate the bomb aboard my ship and you will have lost the only known self-contained hyperdrive in existence. My organization is no threat to you. We are a handful of people on a distant planet. We have no weapons. This was our last and only chance to save humanity. We failed."

"And now you are willing to betray your kind. For what? A bigger cell? A better view?"

"That's a good start," said Freya. "But it's hardly a betrayal. Humanity lost. Our species has reached the end of its life. I may as well be comfortable."

"This is why we won," said Semik. "No Cho-ta'an would think this way. Not even the Fractalists are so craven."

Freya shrugged. "It matters little what you think of me."

*****

The next day, Freya was quizzed by several Cho-ta'an scientists regarding the fission bomb, the stealth technology used by *Valkyrie*, and its self-contained hyperspace drive. She answered all the questions as well as she could. Having personally overseen the fabrication of the bomb, she knew its design well, but pretended to have minimal knowledge. She knew less about the stealth technology and the hyperspace drive, but she was able to answer all the questions posed to her with little difficulty. It seemed the Cho-ta'an were not so much acquiring information as assessing her knowledge and intent. The "scientists" did all the talking, but there were often long pauses between questions, indicating they were being coached. At one point, a slot at the bottom of her door opened and a tray with food and a glass of water was slid inside. The water smelled of sulfur and the food was somewhere on the spectrum between unappetizing and inedible. She staved off hunger by forcing down a few bland, chalky crackers and dried fruits that were like overly fibrous prunes. The interrogation continued all the while.

After several hours of this, the questioning abruptly stopped. The door opened and three Cho-ta'an in suits designed for handling hazardous materials stepped into the room. She caught a glimpse of a small room like an airlock just outside her cell. One of the Cho-ta'an, holding a gun, ordered her out of bed. While the guard stood in the corner watching, the other two ordered Freya out of bed, stripped her naked, and proceeded to probe and scan every nook and cranny of her body. They took samples of her blood, saliva, urine and spinal fluid. When they'd finished, nearly two hours later, she felt thoroughly sore and violated. She lay down and sobbed quietly into her pillow until she fell asleep.

The next day was much the same. Again she was quizzed, being asked many of the same questions she'd already answered. Again she was scraped, prodded, probed and scanned. This time she was too numb to cry before falling asleep. The questions resumed the next morning—questions she had already answered, some of them many times. Her answers were always the same. She wanted to yell, to scream, to tell them they weren't going to get another iota of information unless they gave her some decent food and stopped assaulting her with their instruments and probes, but she knew that earning their trust was part of the price she had to pay. At last, as the day's questioning seemed to be winding down and Freya began to wonder what sorts of torture she would be subjected to that evening, the voice belonging to Semik spoke the words she had been waiting for.

"We have located your ship."

Freya did not respond.

"Give me the entry code."

"I would like to be moved to a larger room, preferably with a view. I would like something resembling human food. And I would like the physical abuse to stop."

"The examinations are necessary to ensure you are not carrying any weapons or biological agents hidden in your body."

"If they haven't determined that by now, it's not going to happen. I've been more than patient. Start treating me with some basic decency or you're never getting into my ship."

"We will find a way around your security eventually."

"Maybe. And maybe you'll make a mistake and destroy the only self-contained hyperdrive within a thousand light-years."

A long pause followed. "I am told that one more biological screening is required to clear you. Then we can see about moving you to more comfortable accommodations."

Freya groaned. "This is the last one?"

"It is. For what it is worth, I give you my word."

"All right."

*****

The next day, Freya was moved into a modest but well-furnished apartment with a view of the plaza where Eric had died. There were bars on the windows and a guard outside her door. The wreckage of Eric's suit had already been cleared away, and repairs to the pavement were nearly completed. Freya had asked to see the bodies on her second day in confinement, but they had already been incinerated. The Cho-ta'an were taking no chances that they had brought dangerous pathogens to Yavesk—particularly now that they knew Freya had been to Kiryata.

Her first afternoon at the apartment, she received her first visitors not wearing hermetically sealed suits. The two, who introduced themselves as physicists, grilled her for four hours about the portable fission bomb. Her answers were evidently satisfactory, as they came back the next day with several more Cho-ta'an. The day after that, another group came to ask her about the hyperdrive aboard *Valkyrie*. She had given Semik the code to defuse the bomb, and *Valkyrie* had been brought to the surface. This went on for two weeks, with scientists, technicians, military officers and civilian leaders coming to ask her questions about the mech suits, the Fractalists, the fission bomb, *Valkyrie*'s stealth technology, the hyperdrive, and a dozen other topics. Every day she talked until she was hoarse and exhausted.

She was moved into a larger apartment, with more bars, more guards, and a better view. She gathered she was becoming something of a celebrity on Yavesk; some of the Cho-ta'an who came to see her carried cameras or recording equipment. The last human being in existence, right here on Yavesk! She answered all their questions as best she could, politely declining to say anything substantial about Jörmungandr, how she had known where to find Kiryata, and how she had known about the Fractalist facility's destruction. She lied only when necessary, and insisted, truthfully, that she wished the best for the Cho-ta'an and hoped that if they ever met humans again on some forgotten planet, they would remember the help Freya had given them.

Three weeks after she arrived, Freya began to feel ill. Fortunately the Cho-ta'an were so unfamiliar with human biology that she was able to hide the symptoms for two full days. They only suspected something was wrong when she fell asleep during a discussion of hyperspace technology with a group of ten Cho-ta'an scientists.

Freya felt tired and achy. The lymph nodes at her neck were swollen, and her throat hurt. The Cho-ta'an doctors who examined her opined that she'd been infected with some virus common on Yavesk that her body had no antibodies against. They had been aware of this possibility, of course, and had given her a cocktail of antivirals and carefully screened every Cho-ta'an who came into contact with her. Evidently their precautions were insufficient. Freya assured them it was nothing serious, but the interviews were put on hold while she recovered.

Over the next two days, however, her condition worsened. The evening of her second day in isolation, she was awakened from a nap by General Semik, who sat in a chair across from her bed. "There seems to be a virus going around the capital," he said.

"That would explain my condition," Freya said groggily, sitting up in bed.

"That's one possibility," said Semik. Freya noticed that his voice was even raspier than usual, and there was swelling in the soft tissue below his eyes. "Our best scientists are saying it's a new variety of a common respiratory virus."

"You sound dubious."

"You never intended to use the fission bomb," he said.

Freya regarded his (Freya thought Semik was a he, although she wasn't sure) cold, black Cho-ta'an eyes. "No," said Freya. "I didn't."

"It was a ruse, a way to get us to use you as a source of information."

"Yes."

"How did you do it? We shaved you, scrubbed you, irradiated you, took samples of your blood, your saliva, your urine. There was no way you could have carried an active virus here."

"It wasn't active when I brought it," Freya said. "It was in a tiny capsule inserted into the lining my nasal passage, completely organic and virtually undetectable—another neat bit of technology my people developed. I'll give you the details if I live long enough. It gradually worked its way out and then dissolved in the moisture of the mucus membranes, releasing the virus."

"How long ago?"

"I started showing symptoms four days ago, so the virus must have been released about three days before that. I've been contagious for a little over five days."

And during that time, you've met…"

"Forty-three Cho-ta'an. I'm not familiar with Cho-ta'an social structure, but if it's anything like humans', they've each spread it to several hundred people by now. If you can track all those people down in the next few hours, you might stop the spread, but I doubt it."

"You seem to be suffering more than we are."

Freya laughed, and it turned into a hacking cough. When she recovered, she said, "Yes, that's the rub. It will probably kill me, even with your 'antivirals.' For your people, it will be no worse than a mild head cold—assuming you get those."

"We do. I have one right now, in fact—as you've probably noticed. I don't understand. Why orchestrate all this to give us a cold?"

"The respiratory symptoms are just a way to facilitate transmission of the virus. A more consequential symptom will become apparent later."

"It will kill us too."

"No. You will recover from the respiratory symptoms and feel as well as you ever did. But it will make some minor modifications to your DNA."

General Semik stared at her. "This virus was engineered by the Fractalists."

"Yes."

"It is forbidden to speak of this."

"Just as well. My throat hurts."

Semik got to his feet and walked to the window. After some time, he turned, seeming to have made a decision. "It is true, then? What the Fractalists are said to believe?" He glanced to the door, as if expecting the authorities to charge in and drag him away.

"That the Cho-ta'an were descended from humans? Yes. That virus is the proof, as your scientists will someday discover. The virus simply turns off a series of DNA sequences and reactivates others."

"Then our children...."

"Will be human. We're the same race."

"If that is true, then why do this?"

"Because whether you like it or not, the Cho-ta'an strain was an aberration, engineered to allow the race to survive a specific set of circumstances. Even on Yavesk, those circumstances no longer exist. You have the technology to support human life if you wish to."

"The change made by the virus could be undone."

"It could, if your understanding of genetics had kept pace with your development of warships and hyperspace gates. The fact that your scientists think this is a mutant strain of a common virus tells me it hasn't. At some point you lost the knowledge of how you became what you are. A few members of your species did recover the secret, but you murdered them."

"If what you're saying is true, it would be better for the Cho-ta'an to cease to be."

"I believe you're wrong, but it's your decision. Choose suicide if you wish. But I don't think you will. I think the Cho-ta'an hate for humanity stems from your realization that you were once like us. It's the hatred of a child for his parents. Well, it's time to grow up."

CHAPTER THIRTY-NINE

Freya's condition continued to worsen over the next several days. The Cho-ta'an did what they could to get answers from her about the virus, but she knew little about it and the incessant interrogation only made her progressively less coherent. By the time they got around to trying various methods of torture, she was beyond feeling pain. She died six days after her last meeting with General Semik.

Draconian measures were implemented in the capital to stop the spread of the virus. Martial law was declared and checkpoints were set up throughout the city. Those known to have been exposed to the virus were quarantined. Soon, tens of thousands were in quarantine, and still the virus spread unchecked. The government ran out of space for quarantine, and there were rumors of mass executions. A mob smashed through a quarantine barrier, and several thousand infected Cho-ta'an were killed trying to escape. As a last resort, the authorities firebombed large sections of the city. Still the virus spread.

The government fell and those charged with keeping order gave up. The once tightly regimented Cho-ta'an civilization devolved into anarchy and mayhem. And all the while, rumors spread about the true nature of the seemingly innocuous virus that had started the panic. A few, who had heard whispers about what the Fractalists believed, even guessed the truth.

The worldwide collapse of Cho-ta'an civilization was nearly complete when the first babies conceived after the virus were born. Tens of thousands of them were murdered or left to die. A very few were suffered to live. By this time, the entire population, with the exception of a few hundred individuals who had taken shelter in hermetically sealed bunkers or government facilities, had contracted the virus. As the years went on, the numbers of genetically "pure" Cho-ta'an dwindled further. There were no longer any Cho-ta'an children being born, and it was beginning to dawn on the population as a whole than there was never going to be a "cure." The Cho-ta'an would be forced to choose the continuation of the species as human beings or extinction.

In the end, they chose life.

It was by no means an easy or popular decision. Those who chose to raise their human children were ridiculed, persecuted and often murdered. But they were not eradicated, and given enough time, natural selection favors those whose children survive. By the second generation born after the virus, there were more humans than Cho-ta'an. By the fifth, there were no Cho-ta'an left. By the eighth, there was no one left on Yavesk who had ever seen a live Cho-ta'an. But these new people remembered, and they rebuilt.

Just under two hundred years after the birth of the first human being on Yavesk, a spaceship carrying five hundred passengers and powered by a self-contained hyperspace drive left Yavesk in search of a planet more suited to human biology. A few weeks later, that ship, the name of which was something like *Hope*, emerged from hyperspace near an inviting yellow sun. Orbiting this sun at a distance of about a hundred million miles was a medium-sized blue-green planet. A radio signal emanated from a tiny island not far from the planet's magnetic north. It said:

0, 1, 1, 2, 3, 5, 8, 13, 21, 34 ...

After the seventeenth number of the Fibonacci sequence, the broadcast started over at zero. This was the siren's song that had reached Yavesk decades earlier. The people who built *Hope* did not know the origin of the transmission, but the use of the Cheyakin sequence suggested an intelligent entity. Few dared speak it, but some hoped it was the long-awaited beacon that had been foretold by Freya the Pure, which would lead them back to the cradle of humanity, called Earth.

The captain of *Hope*, a man named Cheim Sebbarik, ordered the ship to set down on the island, not far from the huge dish antenna broadcasting the signal, which had been constructed less than a mile from a gigantic glacier. Sensors indicated that atmospheric radiation levels, while elevated, were not dangerous. Sebbarik led his second in command and two yeomen outside. The sun shone brightly in a nearly cloudless blue sky. The air was cool; a bracing breeze blew from the northeast. Sebbarik found himself smiling. Despite the barren landscape, and despite having never before set foot on this planet, it felt like home.

They walked together toward the huge antenna complex. In its base was a heavy steel door, which Sebbarik opened without difficulty. Beyond it was a narrow passageway that cut through the otherwise solid block of concrete. Captain Sebbarik led the three men through the passage to the center of the structure, where they found a steel hatch in the floor. Opening the hatch revealed a vertical shaft lined with steel rungs. Sebbarik climbed down, followed by the three crewmen. Some fifty feet down, they emerged into one end of a gigantic vault that appeared to be carved out of natural stone. The vault was surprisingly cold; sensors indicated a temperature well below freezing, and a muted hum suggested the chamber was artificially refrigerated. How long had those compressors been running on their own? There was no sign of anyone alive.

The men slowly spread out, the two yeomen taking readings on their equipment. The vault was circular, about a hundred feet across, with a column in the center about twenty feet in diameter. By the light from glowing panels in the ceiling, Captain Sebbarik could see that the perimeter of the chamber was lined with human-sized doors, several feet apart. Inset in the central stone column were several steel cabinets about seven feet high and three feet wide. Each cabinet had twenty rows of five drawers; they reminded Sebbarik of an ancient card catalog that he'd seen in a library when he was a child. Alternating with the cabinets were what appeared to be computer terminals.

Sebbarik selected one of the drawers at random and pulled it open. It held hundreds of little cards—it *was* a card catalog! He pulled one out and regarded it. At the top was a twelve-digit number that was printed so small he could hardly read it. Below this was a rectangular block of solid gray.

Sebbarik's second in command, Keir Challas, came up next to him. "Microfiche?" he said. Sebbarik squinted at the card. Indeed, the gray block wasn't solid after all: it was nearly microscopic lines of text. Each of those little cards held a book's worth of information. But information about what?

To his right, Yeoman Cheyannis was inspecting one of the terminals. He tapped at what looked like a keyboard, but the screen above it remained dark. Just below the screen was a horizontal slot. Sebbarik slid the card into the slot, and the screen suddenly lit up with text. If it had been in a language they understood, they would have been able to read it.

"Strange way to store data," said Challas. "This whole catalog would easily fit on a single micro data card."

"Deliberately low tech," Sebbarik replied. "And durable." He bent the card double and then let it spring back. There was no crease; the cards were made of some paper-thin synthetic substance he'd never seen before.

"What do you think it's for, sir? Recipes for recreating lost technology?"

The captain shook his head, looking at the doors lining the walls of the chamber. "It's some kind of reference catalog." He left the card where it was and walked to one of the doors. He pulled the handle. There was a sound like a hermetic seal breaking, and colder air rushed out. Sebbarik stepped inside.

He found himself in a hallway, some five feet wide and forty feet long. Circular panels inset on the ceiling provided light. The hallway was lined with columns of square doors, each of them about six inches by six inches. At the end of the hall was another human-sized door. Sebbarik stopped a few feet in and opened one of the little doors. Inside was a drawer. Already shivering from the cold despite his heated all-weather gear, he pulled the drawer out from the wall. Inside the drawer was a rack that held several dozen small test tubes. Sebbarik carefully removed one and examined it. On a small label a twelve-digit number was printed. Below the number was a bar code.

"Biological samples?" asked his second-in-command, Keir Challas.

"Looks like it," said Sebbarik. He put the tube back and examined several more. They all had twelve-digit numbers printed on them. He picked one at random and walked back to the central catalog. Now he saw that next to the slot under the screen was a small lens. A laser reader? He held the tube in front of the lens. After several attempts, he managed to trigger the reader. A line of red light flashed on the barcode, and the screen lit up. This time, though, the screen showed pictures as well as text. The yeomen both gasped behind him.

"What is that?" Callas asked. "A kind of bird?" The few species of birds that lived on Yavesk were squat, ugly things, thought to have descended from the chicken or pigeon. The creature in the picture was majestic, with gorgeous plumage and a white cowl that contrasted with its darker body. Its eyes were not the dull eyes of a creature that spent most of its time on the ground, scratching in the dirt for bugs, but rather those of a vicious predator that ruled the skies. Sebbarik figured out how to use the terminal's controls to scroll down, and more pictures came into view. One of them showed a specimen of the creature, standing next to a man, its wings spread. The thing's wingspan was greater than the height of the man.

"Are there such birds on this planet?" asked Yeoman Keffris.

"There were, once," said the captain.

"Do you suppose each of those samples holds the DNA of a single animal?" asked Callas.

"Animal or other life form," said Sebbarik.

"But why the two different cataloging systems?"

"Redundancy," said Sebbarik. "These terminals are connected to a database somewhere, probably farther underground. In case the database or terminals fail, a condensed version of the data for each organism is contained on those cards."

"Then this really is Earth," said Callas. "This place is like an ark for all the species that were destroyed by the Aberrants."

"Wow," said Yeoman Cheyannis. "Then it's all true. The stories about how Freya the Pure cured humanity of the Aberrations and set up a beacon to call us back to Earth."

"It sure does look that way," said Sebbarik.

"But… if they're just DNA samples," said Keffris, "that doesn't help us much. We don't have the technology to recreate animals from a few cells."

"We haven't seen the whole place yet," said Sebbarik. "Come on."

He went back through the door he'd opened earlier. After replacing the sample, he continued down the hall and opened the far door. Beyond it was another large space that seemed to continue all the way around the central vault, like a wheel around a hub. At first glance, it appeared to be a laboratory. It was at least as cold here as in the hall, and they were all shivering as they spread out to explore the area.

"It's a genetics lab," said Yeoman Keffris, who was the ship's xenobiologist. "I don't know how to operate half this equipment, but if you wanted to resurrect an extinct species, this would be a good place to start."

Sebbarik, ignoring the equipment, walked straight toward the outer wall, which was lined with what appeared to be drawers. Each drawer was about a foot square, and they were stacked six high. Sebbarik opened one at random.

"My God," he said. The others quickly gathered round.

"What is it?" asked Challas.

"Some kind of animal," said Sebbarik. "It might be what the scriptures call a serpent." The thing was coiled up like a rope, but it appeared to be about three feet long. It was encased in a hermetically sealed chamber made of some transparent material. A stasis chamber.

Sebbarik opened another, which contained something like an unusually large, hairless dog. Another contained a creature whose human-like hands and feet made them shudder. It was hard to know for certain, not knowing what the adult forms looked like, but Sebbarik got the impression the animals were all young, perhaps infants. And they all seemed to be females.

"Those samples," said Challas. "Do you think they're fertilized eggs?"

"It's a good hypothesis," said Sebbarik. "The idea may be to thaw out the live animal, let it grow to maturity, and then implant it with the eggs."

"Amazing," said Keffris. "This must have taken decades. How the hell did they know to start on this project before the war with the Aberrants even started?"

"Maybe Freya the Pure really was a prophet," said Sebbarik. "Or maybe somebody just thought it would be a good idea to prepare for the worst. Come on, let's get back to the ship. I'm freezing."

They followed the captain the way they had come. When they reached the vaulted room, they found someone waiting for them. Sebbarik drew his gun. "Who are you?" he demanded.

The figure held up its hands. "I surrender," it said.

"What the hell?" asked Challas.

"A robot?" said Keffris.

"I am apologizing," the figure said. It was shaped like a person, but its body was constructed of some kind of gray plastic. "My name is Amelia. Please for you to have patience while I learn your language?"

"You speak pretty well for someone who doesn't know our language," said Sebbarik.

"The Cho-ta'an was taught to me. Similar it be to language of you, however there being changes while I wait."

"Cho-ta'an?" asked Challis. "Isn't that what they used to call the Aberrants?"

"Yeah," said Sebbarik. "In the old books." He regarded the machine. "You were built by the Cho-ta'an?"

"No. My building was of the Izarians. Izarians are a subset of human."

"How long have you been waiting here?"

"I have been in this area for three minutes. I was in differing area in this structure when I heard a noise. The noise was identified as speech of human. That is why I come here."

"Not here in this room. Here in this facility."

"I have waited one hundred ninety-nine Earth years."

"My God. Waited for what?"

"I have waited for you. You are human."

"You're responsible for the signal? The Cheyakin sequence?"

"No. The broadcast of the numbers you call Cheyakin sequence was part of plan by Freya."

"Freya?" asked Challas. "You mean Freya the Pure?"

"I do not know that name. She was called Freya Michaelsson. She was also called Astrid van de Lucht."

"It's got to be her, Captain," said Keffris. "She sent that signal and left this robot here to welcome us. Unbelievable. All the stories are true."

"It's starting to look that way," said Sebbarik. "Are there any other people here?"

"No. The last one of humans died one hundred thirty-four years before now."

"And you've been waiting for us since then?"

"Yes."

"Is it accurate to say that this place is a sort of library of Earth species?"

"That is part of the reason of it."

"What is the reason of—what is the purpose of this place?"

"To help humans populate the planet of Earth. It is a start over place."

"A start over place," said Sebbarik, with a smile. "I like that. Amelia, will you accompany us to our ship above? There are more people waiting for us there."

"Do you intend to populate the planet of Earth?"

"That's the idea, yes."

"Then I am in your service."

"Very good," said Sebbarik. "Up we go."

*****

"It's a little overwhelming," said Challas, as he and the captain stood admiring the glacier that towered over them. Compared to the huge mass of ice, *Hope* was like a child's toy. "Don't get me wrong, I'm glad we don't have to start from scratch, building an ecosystem with the specimens we have on board, but this… the whole frozen zoo, and the fertilized zygotes, and that crazy robot…."

"One thing at a time, Challas," said Sebbarik with a grin. "Thankfully we've got a lot of really smart people on board. Geologists, biologists, geneticists, agronomists, even linguists. So we don't have to figure all this stuff out ourselves. And we've got enough food onboard *Hope* to last us for years, so we have plenty of time. Let's bring everybody out of stasis and let them stretch their legs."

"And then what?" Challas asked.

"Then," said Sebbarik, "we get to work. We've got a planet to populate."

Review This Book!

Did you enjoy *The War of the Iron Dragon*? Please take a moment to leave a review on Amazon.com! Reviews are very important for getting the word out to other readers, and it only takes a few seconds.

Acknowledgements

This book would not have been possible without the assistance of:

- **My beta readers:** Matthew McCormick, Mark Fitzgerald, Mark Leone and Pekka Gaiser.

- **And the *Saga of the Iron Dragon* Kickstarter supporters, including:** Arnie, Rage A, David Božjak, Josh Creed, Kristin Crocker, Rick DeVos, Lauren Nicole Foley, David Hutchins, iworam32, JP, Lowell Jacobson, Christophe Landa, Marvin Langenberg, Eric Martens, Matthew J. McCormick, Dark Memoria, Grant Morath, John W. Nichols, Larry Prince, Bruce Parrello, Kristen Rudd, Sharon Sloan, Christopher Smith, Joel Suovaniemi, John Taloni, Christopher Turner, and John Walker.

Any errors in this book are the fault of the author. I did my best.

¯_(ツ)_/¯

More Books by Robert Kroese

The Saga of the Iron Dragon
The Dream of the Iron Dragon
The Dawn of the Iron Dragon
The Voyage of the Iron Dragon
The Legacy of the Iron Dragon
The War of the Iron Dragon

The Starship Grifters Universe
Out of the Soylent Planet
Starship Grifters
Aye, Robot
The Wrath of Cons

The Mercury Series
Mercury Falls
Mercury Rises
Mercury Rests
Mercury Revolts
Mercury Shrugs

The Land of Dis
Distopia
Disenchanted
Disillusioned

Other Books
The Big Sheep
The Last Iota
Schrödinger's Gat
City of Sand
The Force is Middling in This One

Made in the USA
Coppell, TX
25 April 2025